radiate

radiate

by Marley Gibson

Houghton Mifflin Harcourt

Boston New York 2012

All rights reserved. Published in the United States by Graphia,
an imprint of Houghton Mifflin Harcourt Publishing Company.

For information about permission to reproduce selections from this book,
write to Permissions, Houghton Mifflin Harcourt Publishing Company, 215
Park Avenue South, New York, New York 10003.

Graphia and the Graphia logo are trademarks of
Houghton Mifflin Harcourt Publishing Company.

www.hmhbooks.com

The text of this book is set in Garamond Pro.

Library of Congress Cataloging-in-Publication Data
Gibson, Marley.
Radiate / by Marley Gibson.
p. cm.
Summary: Just after making the varsity cheerleading squad the summer
before her senior year of high school in Maxwell, Alabama, Hayley Matthews
learns she has an aggressive form of cancer in her leg, and she turns to her
family, her cheerleading, and her Christian faith to sustain her through her
treatment.
ISBN: 978-0-547-61728-2
[1. Cancer—Fiction. 2. Cheerleading—Fiction. 3. Interpersonal relations—
Fiction. 4. High schools—Fiction. 5. Schools—Fiction. 6. Christian life—
Fiction.] I. Title.
PZ7.G345Ra 2012
[Fic]—dc23
2011020501

Manufactured in the United States of America
DOC 10 9 8 7 6 5 4 3 2
4500363615

To all those who have struggled and overcome.
Never say never.
Never give up.
You, too, can radiate.

PROLOGUE

*If children have the ability to ignore all odds and percentages,
then maybe we can all learn from them. When you think about
it, what other choice is there but to hope? We have two options,
medically and emotionally: give up or Fight Like Hell.*

—LANCE ARMSTRONG

YOU KNOW HOW YOU always think there's something . . . *more?*
Like there's something else you can be doing? A way you can
put yourself out there more. An effort that will plant you in the
spotlight and make people finally recognize that, "Hey, you're
special."

Sure, your parents tell you that all the time. They're supposed
to. It's, like, in the parents' handbook they get when they take you
home from the hospital. Still, it's not the same as acceptance from
the general public, and more specifically, your peers. Not that
I'm narcissistic and need to be told this every hour of the day like
Chloe Bradenton in my class does. But right there, who or what
decided that Chloe Bradenton and others like her get to *be* special
while people like me . . . just exist?

Chloe's a cheerleader; she dated the quarterback off and on;
she's been on the homecoming court all three years of high school
and will probably be voted queen our senior year. Total cliché;

then again clichés are clichés for a reason. She thinks everyone's pea-green with envy of her and her lot in life. I'm not jealous of her—seriously, I'm not. I just want the same opportunities, you know? Is that too much to ask?

For my three years in high school, I've semi-anonymously played my trumpet in the Polk High School marching band. Not even my own trumpet, but one handed down from my big sister, Gretchen, who's ten years older than me. She gave it up way back when she was in tenth grade and lost interest and started hanging with kids Mom called "the rogue element." I wanted to play something delicate and beautiful like the flute. However, my parents said I should take a shot at the trumpet since we already owned one. I made the best of it, took lessons, and excelled with my lipping and fingering. I'm pretty damn good, if I must say so myself. Got the "Best Brass" trophy two years in a row. (Please . . . no comments.) And band's been fun. What can I say? I've got an itch, though. I want to expand my horizons and get the full high school experience however I can. Where's the rule that says I can't take my own stab at something . . . *more?*

Okay, I want to be popular. I'll admit it. What teenager doesn't?

I'm not a social leper at all . . . but again, I just feel like there's something else I can be doing.

I want to be *seen* and not just blend into the other hundred who are dressed in red and blue polyester uniforms. I don't want to be part of one cohesive, marching unit.

I want to march to my own drum.

So, one Saturday afternoon while watching *Bring It On* on DVD for like the kajillionth time, I thought of the craziest thing I could do, the one thing that no one in his or her right mind would expect out of me.

I tried out for varsity cheerleader.

And I made it.

Me. Hayley Matthews. A virtual no one to a well-known someone.

I got my wish.

I got popularity.

And that . . . desired *more.*

In fact, I got a hell of a lot *more* than I ever bargained for—something that stopped me in my tracks.

A diagnosis that would change my present and bring into question my future.

A challenge of epic proportions to overcome.

The need to find hope when everything seemed hopeless.

This is a story of how cheerleading saved my life.

CHAPTER ONE

Everyone has inside him a piece of good news.
The good news is that you don't know how great you can
be! How much you can love! What you
can accomplish! And what your potential is!

—ANNE FRANK

I NAILED IT!

That was the best damn round-off back handspring I've ever done!

Beads of sweat roll down my back as I pump my fists in the air in time with the adrenaline coursing through my limbs. Nothing can stop me. Across the gym, at the long table ahead of me, I can see that the judges are impressed with my efforts, as well. Pencils move furiously over score sheets, and I beam from ear to ear as I quickly move into a perfectly executed herkie. It should be perfect . . . I've been practicing for weeks on end. I stretch my fingers out to meet up with my pointed right toe before landing back on the gym's shiny parquet. My Nikes hit the floor with a firm *thwack*, and I move into my next jump.

With the agility of a jaguar leaping through the jungle, I wind up and hurtle myself into the air, elongating my legs in front of me in the pike position. My arms parallel in the air with my legs until the tips of my fingers again touch my outstretched sneakered toes.

My tryout partner, Shelly Kingsford, slips behind me and plants her Reebok in the middle of my back as she climbs up onto my shoulders. I grip her calves and adjust into a tall, straight position, balancing her hundred and eighteen pounds just so. Looking up, I watch as she pulls her left foot to her right knee to strike the star pose. I don't swerve or teeter as all of her weight goes to my right side. I just smile that eye-squinting grin of mine and yell out along with Shelly, "Go, Polk, Go!"

She jumps forward to dismount and lands flawlessly with me catching her around the waist for stability. Again, the judges nod their approval and continue to make notes on the score sheets.

I stand at attention with my hands fisted on my hips while Shelly does her tumbling run. Cartwheel. Cartwheel. Cartwheel. *Ugh . . . what is she doing?* She was supposed to do a cartwheel into two back handsprings. We'd practiced it for weeks. What is she thinking? You totally have to show the judges more agility than just a cartwheel, which you learn, like, in kindergarten.

Poor Shelly. I hope they won't deduct points because of her lackluster tumbling. She didn't even do them that well, hesitating between each one. Can't think about it, though. I have to finish our routine. I have to make sure *I* do everything right.

The music begins and blares out a Techno beat. We snap into performing the dance we've both spent hours rehearsing. I pop. I snap. I crunk. Moves I've honed in front of my bedroom mirror in the late-evening hours, much to Mom's chagrin—especially when the chandelier in the dining room started shaking. I laugh. I smile. I wink. But most of all, I have fun. The groove of the music pumps through my veins, fueling me on.

After our dance routine, we barely have time to catch our

breath before Shelly and I line up together to execute a formal school cheer. This part is about the precision of our moves, our silent clapping with cupped hands, and the ability to project our voices throughout the gym.

I have no problem with the latter. My dad has always called me "the Mouth of the South." He took me to an Alabama vs. Auburn game once (Roll Tide!), and he said I was the loudest out of more than a hundred thousand people. Today, it's going to play to my favor.

I clap my hands together. "Our team. Ready?"

"Okay," Shelly says with me.

Pop. "Our team . . . is great"—arms tight; fingers straight—"and, we just can't wait"—legs locked—"to show"—left hand fisted on hip; right arm forward, pointing—"you . . . just how"—spin; slap arms to side—"we rate." Knee to chest; arms pumped out front. "We're"—step forward—"Number"—index finger pointed to the sky—"One!"

Another herkie into a spread eagle. And more cheering as I advance on the judges, urging them to root, root, root for the Patriots with me, my voice carrying much farther and louder than Shelly's meeker one. Two of the three judges clap along while the third nods his head and smiles. All three of them are from the squad across town at Maxwell State University. They totally know their stuff. They've finaled in the college nationals the last three years in a row.

Perspiration moistens my skin in an exhilarating sheen of accomplishment. Shelly and I embrace, stoked that we got through the tryout and relieved that it's over. We grab hands and run back to the locker room where the other girls are waiting—those who've gone before us and the two teams still left to go.

Ashlee Grimes hands me an iced bottle of Aquafina from the cooler at the end of the bench. "How'd it go?" she asks.

Gulping the delicious water, I wipe my mouth and say, "That was the hardest thing I've ever done in my life."

Ashlee giggles. We've been good friends since fifth grade. And, even though she was a cheerleader last year and I was in the band, we've managed to stay tight. She's been so helpful since I shocked her with my idea to quit band and do something . . . *more*. She's even been mentoring me through the whole practice sessions leading up to tryouts. "If you make the squad, tryouts will look like a piece of piss compared to actually being a varsity cheerleader," she says with a nod. "How did you like it?"

"I loved it!" I say without hesitation.

It's no lie. It's a high like nothing I've ever felt. Belting out the school fight song on my horn never gave me *this* feeling. This is so much better than cheering up in the stands in my band uniform while the short-skirted girls on the field perform gymnastic stunts, pyramids, and dances that get the whole crowd into the game.

The next team of Melanie Otto and Lora Russell gather their things and head out to face the judges. It seems like a year and a half before they return, exhausted and sweaty. When they collapse on the bench, the last pair to try out vanishes out the door.

A quiet Shelly fingers the label on her water bottle. "I don't think I'm going to make it."

My head snaps. "Why do you say that?"

Her orangy curls are starting to escape her high ponytail. "I think the band is more my speed. I don't know why I let you talk me into this. Marching and formations aren't nearly this exhausting. You know, I quit gymnastics freshman year because of the bruises and muscle aches. I swear, Hayley, I've never been so tired . . . ever. My heart is *still* racing from all that exertion."

I didn't exactly talk her into this. When I told her I was going to try out, she thought it would be "fun." Now I frown at her. "You know cheerleading's hard work. It's one of the toughest sports out there," I say passionately. "It's gymnastics, dance, cheers, pyramids—you have to be in top shape."

"I know," she says with a nod. "I don't think I'm up to spending my entire summer working out and practicing all the time instead of hanging by the pool. Band camp lasts only two weeks. Besides"—she pauses dramatically and drains her water bottle—"I totally botched my tumbling run."

"You did not," I lie.

Her blue eyes lack confidence. "We'll see."

The adrenaline rush from my routine still surges through me, and I can't sit still. I tap my left foot up and down impatiently, waiting for the last team to return to the locker room. The tension is so thick in here, you could butcher it into a dozen prime steaks and serve it at the football banquet. Everyone is a nervous wreck.

Everyone except Chloe Bradenton.

Yeah, her.

She's sitting on the bench by the back wall with her legs stretched out in front of her. She's got her iPhone and is busy texting as if she hasn't a care in the world. Then again, she probably doesn't. Her dad is the president of the bank, and her house on Parrot Peak is the most expensive one in Maxwell, Alabama. I don't hate her or anything—I barely speak to her—but everything just seems to come easily to her. She didn't even break a sweat in her tryouts. Her makeup wouldn't dare run, and her thick black hair wouldn't think of coming out of that slicked-back ponytail.

Suddenly, she lifts her ice green eyes and steadies them on me. For a second, it's as if I'm going to burst into flames from the hatred she's throwing at Shelly and me. I know perfectly well how she thinks us "band types" should "stay in our place." She made that perfectly clear during tryout practice when she was teaching the cheers to everyone. The odds are totally against us in this day and age when newbies rarely make a cheerleading squad. But thanks to graduating seniors, there are spots available. I believe in beating the odds.

Being a good Christian girl, and hearing my mother in my head saying to "love thy enemies," I smile back at Chloe. Not that I'm any threat to her or consider her an enemy. Funny thing is, we used to be friends back in elementary school when we were both in Brownies. And in seventh grade, we spent our spring break together at Dauphin Island at her parents' place, cooking barbecued shrimp and floating in the Gulf of Mexico on noodles. Our grandmothers were best friends growing up—and still are—but Chloe and I just slid into different cliques when we reached high school.

The closest we've been to interacting with each other was last year when I got the chickenpox from her. Her little brother had the chickenpox and then gave them to her. While she was out, I dropped off some homework from our computer class at her house. That had to have been how I got the nasty skin rash. I'd never contracted the childhood disease in, well, childhood, so, at sixteen, I was sick as a dog. The pox were everywhere—in my eyelids, in my nose, in my mouth, in my stomach—everywhere. I couldn't eat or even keep liquids down. It was nasty as all get-out. I missed two weeks of school because of it.

The door opens and Janine Ingram, one of the school's librarians and the cheerleader sponsor, pokes her head in. "They're ready for y'all."

My heart skips like five beats at her announcement. This is it. No matter what, I tried, right? I worked hard and put my best foot forward. But I want this *soooo* badly. I *want* to spend my summer practicing cheers and building pyramids and learning how to split to the left ('cause I can only split to the right). I want to wake up early and go for a jog to stay in shape. I want to work out on the school's weight equipment to bulk up my strength. That way, I can lift my partner, whoever she may turn out to be, like she weighs nothing at all.

I don't want to report to band camp and march in the three-thousand-degree heat, getting a farmer's tan, marking time, and standing at attention while the gnats land on my face. I don't want to memorize formations, commands, and music. I don't want to be hidden under a band hat—not in my senior year.

I want everyone to know who Hayley Matthews is—and that I'm here to make my mark!

Okay, in my head, I talk a good game, but on the outside, my palms are sweating, my hands are shaking, and I feel like I could totally throw up the half a grilled cheese and six Cheetos I managed to nibble down at lunchtime.

My heart is slamming inside my chest, and nausea bubbles in my tummy and up into my throat.

Mrs. Ingram claps her hands. "Come, come, girls! The judges are waiting!"

We all scurry out into the gym and stand in two lines, no order to the mayhem. I wonder if the girls who were cheerleaders last year are as nervous as I am. Does confidence zip through their system or is there worry? If Chloe Bradenton is any indication, they all know it's in the bag. It's very unlikely that a former squad member won't repeat in making the team. That makes the chances of me snagging a spot even smaller.

I stand next to Shelly, taking the end spot of the first row. The three cheerleaders from Maxwell State University hand over a sheet of paper to Mrs. Ingram. It's done. The decision is final. These judges have tallied their scores and made their choices.

Mrs. Ingram steps to the microphone, and I tense up to wait and hear how I'll be spending my senior year.

Will it be back in the marching band?

Or will there be something *more* for me . . . ?

CHAPTER TWO

To accomplish great things, we must not only act, but also dream; not only plan, but also believe.

—ANATOLE FRANCE

THE CREAK OF THE gymnasium door steals my attention from Mrs. Ingram momentarily.

My heart sinks to my feet. *What are they doing here?*

Boys.

They stream in from outside and begin filling the bleachers.

"They aren't supposed to be in here," Shelly hisses.

From the row behind us, I hear Brittney Alexander say, "They do this every time. They want to check out who'll be cheering for them next year."

Good Lord. Not just any boys—it's the football team. Which means . . .

My throat goes dry before I can even think his name, because at that moment, Daniel Delafield saunters into the gym like he owns the place, which he pretty much does. He's not the quarterback on the team, but he's the star receiver who's broken every Polk High School record and who'll probably have every major university in the Southeastern Conference and beyond dangling scholarship offers at him.

I watch as he climbs up two steps, plops down on the steel bench, and leans back with his arms spread next to him, taking up enough room for three people.

Everyone at Polk High School knows Daniel Delafield.

He doesn't know I exist.

Freshman year, the Pep Club had secret pep pals. I, of course, chose Daniel. For the entire football season, I decorated his locker, left him spirit notes, and baked him cookies. When the big reveal came as to who was the secret pep pal, someone had to point me out to Daniel. And we're in the same grade! Hello! He thanked me by tousling my long hair in Algebra II.

Wow. You're welcome.

I must have spent more than two hundred dollars on things for him.

"Pay no attention to those boys," Mrs. Ingram says, bringing me back to the here and now.

Right. Right. Ignore the cute, popular boys. My future hangs in the balance of that score sheet.

Mrs. Ingram leans into the microphone. "You all did a wonderful job. So many talented girls. But, as you know, we have only twelve slots on the team next season. We're looking for girls with a good, strong cheering ability, coupled with fantastic dance moves and a complete knowledge and execution of gymnastics. Well, here we go!"

She crinkles the paper in her hand and my palms get itchy. I don't move a muscle, though. *Please, please, please, please, please, Lord . . .*

"In no particular order," Mrs. Ingram says. "First is Chloe Bradenton."

Of course she's first, I think in a snarky, inside voice.

Chloe squeals like it's some big surprise . . . not. Big surprise? She's been on the squad since freshman year.

"Next is Melanie Otto."

More screeches from behind me. My nerves pick up like a ticking time bomb. Like I said, it's probably a foregone conclusion that all nine of last year's returning cheerleaders will once again be on the team. Three available spots. One *has* to be mine.

Mrs. Ingram continues reading names off: Hannah Vincennes, Lora Russell, Ashlee Grimes, and Ashleigh Bentley. As the girls run out front to hug and huddle, the rest of us stand here anxiously rocking back and forth on the heels of our sneakers . . . waiting.

"Tara Edwards," Mrs. Ingram announces. That's a new name. The tall brunette pulls her hands up to her mouth and screams. Tara's family moved to Maxwell last year from Pensacola, and she's been in tight with Chloe Bradenton. She dates Chloe's twin brother, Phillip, who's the kicker for the football team. It all makes sense.

Of course, that means only two "new" spots.

"Brittney Alexander," is announced, and I clap. Brittney started off in band with Shelly and me in sixth grade, but when she got braces, she had to give up the trombone because her lips kept bleeding. She's an amazing dancer, so she totally deserves another year on the squad.

More names follow. Samantha Fowler, a petite freshman, aka newbie, steps forward to join the winners. Lauren Compton rejoins the squad, as does Madison Hutchinson.

One more spot left. I glance over at Shelly. She shrugs at me. I smile weakly.

I want this spot. I need this spot. I have to be a cheerleader. It's all I can think about. How cliché that it's coming down to the last name and only four girls left standing.

Let it be me, Lord . . . please . . . I've worked so hard for this.

Mrs. Ingram pulls the paper away from in front of her. "And the last slot on the team goes to . . ."

Everything moves in slow motion. The words. The actions. The thoughts. The announcement.

"Hayley Matthews," the sponsor says.

Snap! Zoom! Boom! Then the world is on fast-forward.

Shelly grabs my arm. "You did it, Hayley!"

I did? I did!

She said my name! I made it!

I squeeze Shelly back and then skip over to the group of winners. *I'm* a winner. I'm a varsity cheerleader. I. Made. It.

Random arms embrace me. Congratulations flow as much as the tears of joy. I'm engulfed in the celebration, and I return the hugs of my fellow teammates.

Chloe faces me, and a feigned smile crosses her pretty face. "Well, I suppose I should say congrats, Hayley."

"Thanks, Chloe," I say heartily, ignoring the veiled venomous tone in her voice.

"This isn't going to be like band, you know?" she continues. "You're gonna have to work your ass off. We have a reputation to uphold, and I won't let a lucky newcomer stand in the way of this team's success."

Well, excuse the hell out of me for living, I think, noticing she doesn't move to give the same speech to Tara or Samantha. I smile, though, that exaggerated cheerleader smile that obviously helped land me the role. "You can count on me, Chloe."

Before anything else can be said, Ashlee Grimes launches herself on me. "Dude! You totally did it! I told you that you'd make it!"

We hug like long-lost sisters who've just found each other, and I can't stop the tears from escaping my eyes. Thank heavens my makeup is waterproof.

"Maybe we can be partners since Megan is graduating and I don't have a base anymore," Ashlee says. *Base* is cheerleader talk for the girl who does all the heavy lifting of the flyers, the term for the girls on top.

"That would be cool. When will we know?"

"After we vote on a captain, she'll decide the pairings. But who cares about that now! You're on the squad, and we're going to have an awesome senior year!"

My pulse trills out a rhythm in my ears. I'm picturing everything. Wearing the cool uniforms to school on game day, helping to lead pep rallies, driving to away games, standing in front of the whole school and leading cheers, and, before that, practicing all summer, hanging out with new friends, learning dance routines, and perfecting my tumbling. And actually doing my hair and makeup for games instead of scrunching it up under a band hat. There's homecoming with its parade and bonfire and celebration . . . and maybe a date with a football player this year. Yep, senior year here at PHS is going to totally *rock!*

Lora Russell comes over to hug me. She and I were lab partners in biology last year, but she's another with unattainable status in Maxwell. Her father died when she was little, so she and her mom live with her rich uncle, Ross Scott, president and CEO of Game On, a sports franchise based here. "I'm so proud of you, Hayley!" Lora says with much enthusiasm. She smashes her face against mine, and I feel as though I belong.

"Thanks, Lora. I'm jazzed beyond words."

"We're gonna have a great squad! Welcome to the team."

Before I know it, the football players descend from the bleachers and join in the mayhem. Skipper O'Rourke, one of the defensive backs I know from Spanish class, gives me a fist bump. "All right . . . Matthews."

There's a melee of faces in and out of my vision congratulating me, welcoming me, coming at me so fast that I feel I might faint dead away.

And then, before I know it, *he's* standing right next to me.

Daniel Delafield in his O'Neill Surfboards T-shirt and baggy gym shorts. His thick, wavy brown hair is held back off his face with a pair of sunglasses on the top of his head. He smells sweaty and musky and all boylike from being outside roughing around with the guys. I gasp a deep breath when his blue eyes turn my way.

"Good job, Hayley," he says nonchalantly, as though we've been the best of friends for years.

He knows my name?

"Um . . . thanks, Daniel. I'm totally super-juiced."

Daniel smiles. "There's a party at Anthony Ricketts's house this weekend. You should come."

"I should?" I can barely breathe.

"Of course. All the cheerleaders will be there. You're one of them now." Then he knocks into me with his shoulder, all playful like, and flips the end of my ponytail.

"Oh. Okay. Awesome. Cool. Definitely." *Shut up!*

"See ya . . ." he says, and then he's off.

You're one of them now.

Yes, I am. I'm a cheerleader. And senior year is going to be like none other.

* * *

"I'm so proud of you, Hayley!" my mother, Nan, says when I burst through the back door of the house to report my news. "I knew you could do it!"

She hugs me so tightly that I actually feel the love and pride coming from her. "I guess all of those gymnastics and dance classes with Miss Kathy have finally paid off."

"Totally," I say with a grin.

"Call your grandparents and tell them," Mom says. "Mother will be thrilled."

My gray kitty, Leeny, rubs on my leg and I bend down to hoist her into my arms and give her kisses all over her face. "Oh, I will in a bit. When will Dad be home?"

"He should be here any minute. He closed the store early to-night." She pulls the roast from the oven and starts basting the meat. The aroma of steaming potatoes, carrots, and roast beef fills the air. Yankee pot roast—one of my all time favorite meals. Awww . . . Mom did this in anticipation of my making the team. Knowing her, it would have been termed a pick-me-up had I not succeeded.

I hear Dad's truck pull under the carport and the door slam. Leeny jumps from my arms to run and welcome him home. I gasp when he walks in with my brother, Cliff, who must be home for the long weekend from his job up north in Birmingham, and a bundle of balloons that read "Congrats!" and "You Did It!"

I burst out laughing. "What were you going to do with those if I hadn't made the squad?"

Dad hugs me to him. "Not an option. Fred Grimes stopped in the hardware store. Ashlee called to tell him the news."

I slump. "He told you?"

"He wanted me to be prepared. And aren't you glad," he says with a wink. Dad kisses the top of my head. "Congrats, Little Kid."

"Yeah, Hay. Way to go," Cliff echoes. "Just don't go sleeping with all the football players now. Wouldn't want to have to come back to high school and kick some ass."

I smack him hard on the arm. "Geesh, Cliff. Don't be gross."

Our scrumptious dinner is interrupted by phone calls and texts galore. Grandmother and Granddaddy call from across town to tell me how proud they are of me. Sadly, I don't hear from my older sister, Gretchen. Then again, we never really hear from Gretchen unless it's a major holiday or the obligatory call from Boston when it's someone's birthday. She's the oldest and sort of the black sheep of the family because of *something* that happened when she was in high school that no one will tell me about. Still, after helping load the dishwasher with the dinner dishes, I run upstairs to leave a message on Gretchen's Facebook page to share my news. My Uncle Roger, Mom's brother, calls from San Francisco where he works as a doctor, and Dad's sister, Aunt Eva, calls from New York. You'd have thought I just won the lottery.

Well, I did. I hit the high school equivalent.

And life will never be the same!

CHAPTER THREE

Toughness is in the soul and spirit, not in the muscles.

—Alex Karras

June in south alabama is one thing and one thing only: blue-blazing hot.

But the ultraviolet rays have never felt better on my skin than they do today. I literally skip out of the house in my PHS shorts and Varsity Cheerleader tank top as I toss my purse and my gym bag into the front seat of Dad's truck.

Today marks the beginning of cheerleader practice. And I am champing at the bit to get over to Brittney Alexander's house for the first session. We're voting on captain, and then we'll find out who our partners are. I'm beyond jazzed!

"Hey, Hay," a voice calls out to me, interrupting my thoughts.

I tent my eyes over my sunglasses to block out the glare and get a good look at who called out to me. The voice seems familiar, but it can't be . . .

Or can it?

There's no way the tall, muscular figure approaching me is who I think it is. However, a skitter of surprise bolts me to the ground as recognition takes over and my mouth drops open. "Oh my God. Would you look who's back?" I say with laughter in my voice.

He walks across the driveway, sauntering really. Funny, he never sauntered before. Soft brown eyes light up when he smiles at me. Gabriel Tremblay. Gabe used to live across the street from me before his family moved to Cincinnati, Ohio, after sixth grade. He was a gangly, geeky kid then, but we were tight as two neighbors sharing a mud pie could be.

Now, I take in his appearance from his green Scooby-Doo "What Happens in the Van Stays in the Van" T-shirt to his well-worn Levi's with the cuffs turned up, just like he did when we were younger. Others might barely recognize him, but I'd know that face anywhere, even though his hair is a bit longer, with bangs sweeping down over his forehead. He's seriously a lot taller, and he's been eating his Wheaties or working out like a crazy person as I take in the broad chest and his rippled arms. He's certainly a far cry from the scrawny ninety-pounds-soaking-wet kid that he was back then.

"Awesome to see you, Gabe," I say, and then move forward to give him a neighborly hug. He shyly returns the affection, though his eyes land on my chest to take in the words spread across my shirt.

"Gabriel. I go by Gabriel now." Hmm . . . how grown up. Although, I bet his nana still calls him Gabby.

"I haven't seen you since Vacation Bible School when we were eleven or something."

He nods and grins. "Right. 'Onward Christian Soldiers,' bagged lunches, and macaroni art."

"Something like that," I say softly. "Then y'all just up and moved."

"Yeah, well, you know how things are," he says as he kicks at a rock in my driveway, sending it scooting back into the flower bed.

Gabriel turns to me and I feel somewhat awkward standing here not knowing what to say to him. Which is totally weird, because Gabriel and I used to play together all the time. We each collected Hot Wheels and would make paper towns for them to drive through. He killed a nest of earwigs in my front yard when I was freaking out that they were going to attack me. And he bandaged my knee when I fell off my bike because his dog, Cricket, came out of the yard, barking like all get-out and scaring the crap out of me.

But right before we started seventh grade at Polk Middle School, Gabriel and his family just . . . up and left. He didn't say goodbye, there was no neighborhood sendoff or party, and he and I haven't talked since. Sure, I friended him on Facebook last year, but he hasn't been the kind to obsess with updates.

Gabriel's father frequented Matthews Hardware, my dad's store, but not even gossip from the barbershop next door could produce a reason as to why the Tremblays moved out of Maxwell so suddenly.

"So . . ." I say with a bit of a sigh while shuffling from one foot to the other.

"So," he echoes. "You're a cheerleader now?"

The beaming smile returns. "Yeah! Crazy, isn't it?"

"Things really do change," he says.

"I'm actually on my way to practice."

He balks a bit, as if to leave. "I just wanted to say 'hey.' We're three houses down. Bought the Lucas place."

I turn to glance at the brick Colonial that's had a For Sale sign since January. "Awesome." It's the only thing I can think to say. Then I blurt out, "What are you doing here? I mean, back in Maxwell."

Gabriel chuckles at me. He scratches his chin with his thumb and forefinger. "That's direct."

"I didn't mean—"

He holds up his hand. "No, really, it's okay. People are bound to ask." Then he continues. "See, my grandpa's really sick, and we don't know how much longer he has. Mom and Dad decided to move back to help take care of him."

"Oh, Gabe . . . I mean, Gabriel, I'm so sorry," I say, thinking about his sweet grandpa whom I haven't seen at church in forever. I've been so caught up in cheerleading that I hadn't even noticed.

"It's okay." He shrugs. "It is what it is. So, here I am, back in Maxwell."

I smile sweetly. "It's really great to see you. You'll have to come over some night so we can catch up."

His eyebrow lifts. "I bet your social calendar's a little too full these days for a boring night at home going down memory lane."

There's no bitterness in his voice, but I do sense regret from him. Regret for ever leaving town? Or regret for coming back. Either way, I do my best to welcome him back. "You should come to Skipper O'Rourke's party Friday night. Everyone will be there."

I've been to so many pool parties and backyard barbecues since I won my slot on the squad in mid-May, I can't keep them straight now. "I bet there's still time to try out for the football team, if that interests you," I add. I remember back to elementary school where Gabe, I mean, Gabriel was a pretty promising peewee football player. He could outrun them all.

Gabriel shrugs again, that thing so many boys love to do when faced with something they don't want to answer. "I actually ran into Coach Gaither at Pasquale's Pizza the other night. He was impressed by how I've, um . . . filled out and up. I think he said I was 'buff,'" he says with a laugh.

I laugh heartily at the break in tension and then move to knock him on the upper arm. "Dude, you *are* buff."

"Lots of hours in the gym," he says with a slight smirk.

"Are you going to try out for the team?"

"No . . . I don't really want to do sports anymore. But Coach Gaither asked me to be a trainer for the team. Weightlifting. Drills. Stuff like that. Pretty cool, huh?"

I bob my head up and down. "That's awesome, Gabriel. It's great to have you back in town."

The back door opens, and Mom sticks her head out. "Hayley! Ashlee just called, looking for you. Said you didn't answer your cell."

"I'm leaving!" I yell back. "Just saying hey to Gabriel. You remember him, right?"

Mom steps out and wipes her hands on her tan pants. "Why, Gabriel Tremblay. Look at you all grown up! I'd heard your parents were back."

I watch as Gabriel's tanned face reddens under Mom's scrutiny. "Hey, Mrs. M. Nice to see ya." Then he turns back to me. "I'll catch you another time, Hay. Have fun at cheerleader practice."

"Thanks!" I say, waving to his retreating figure.

As I watch him saunter—and yeah, he does—back to his house, I can't help but note how he's grown up and changed from the kid I knew. Guess we all grow up eventually.

* * *

"AGAIN!" CHLOE BRADENTON SHOUTS out through her blood-red megaphone with "captain" written on it in white lettering. Yeah, like I didn't see *that* one coming.

My new partner, Lora Russell, and I exchange glances, and she rolls her eyes. I give her the "Don't look at me, I didn't vote for her" glare and wipe my sweaty palms down the side of my navy blue athletic shorts as I'm trying to catch my breath from the dance routine we've been practicing for the last two hours.

When we first arrived at Brittney's, there was the whole hugging and laughing and drinking Diet Cokes stage, followed by a secret ballot for captain. I voted for Lora, since I've thought for the past two years she was the best cheerleader PHS had. She actually understands the game of football and knows what cheers to start when. But Chloe took it in a seven to five vote. Think she voted for herself? So, imagine my surprise and delight when newly crowned captain, Chloe, assigned Lora Russell to be my flyer because Chloe wanted Lora's former flyer partner, Melanie Otto, to be her flyer. So, now, Lora's retraining as a flyer from being a base. It's a bit of a mess, all to accommodate Chloe and her desires. Whatever. The terminology and politics. What can I do?

Lora bends over and puts her hands on her knees to catch her breath.

"Is she always this bitchy?" I ask.

Lora rolls her eyes. "Welcome to the squad."

Chloe snaps at everyone, and, I swear, I think Tara Edwards is going to cry. Poor freshman. "We'll stay here all day until we get these moves right, ladies!"

I snicker at the situation. When most kids my age are busy spending their summers traveling with their family to cool places, going to Disney World or visiting relatives, possibly even touring potential college campuses, I'm standing in Brittney Alexander's yard sweating like some sort of farm animal and gyrating to a Techno beat like a spastic reject from the Pussycat Dolls.

But I won't complain. Like the McDonald's slogan, I'm *lovin'* it!

And I think it's awesome that I'm paired up with Lora. We're going to be a great match.

Speaking of loving it, Chloe adores the power she wields over our cheerleading world. The movie *Bring It On* was right in terming it a "cheerocracy." Chloe is the head dictator.

And so it begins.

For the next two weeks of practice, Chloe is the task master, keeping us on point. While she's helpful with the dance routines, jumps, and moves, she tolerates me at best. I'm working hard, sweating as much as the rest of them, and getting stronger. I lift Lora over my head as if we've been doing it for years. Chloe laid out the intense, aggressive summer practice schedule, and she let us pick which PHS uniform to retire and which new one to purchase. (We ditched the ugly midriff-revealing white sweater and split skirt and went for a new crisscross back with a straight front skirt. Totally chic.) At the end of the second week, her mother served the team a mega-welcoming formal tea and made everyone matching hand-painted water bottles decorated with our names, our graduation year, and the Patriots' logo. You'd think Chloe could take a page from her mother's book of hospitality and friendliness.

Thing is, cheerleading is serious business. Chloe is the boss, and we are her minions. And she's still not a hundred percent convinced that the band geek can cut it on the varsity cheerleader squad. Even though I made the team, I still feel as if I have to prove myself over and over and over to the girls who've been around the last couple of years. But I've got the stamina, the fortitude, and the drive to be the best cheerleader I can be. So, I wipe away the perspiration, tighten my ponytail, and get back to the physical grindstone.

Cheerleading is work. But it's well worth the effort. It's what I've always wanted, and I can't wait for the first football game so I can be down on the field, close to the action, and in front of the crowd, showing my school spirit.

I saw this article online from ABC News that said cheerleading is the world's most dangerous sport with the most injuries. Seriously . . . people have been paralyzed doing stunts; some have even died. I totally believe it. Hell, just last week, Samantha Fowler got these nasty-ass grass burns on both elbows from Lauren Compton and Ashlee Grimes not scooping her properly on a cradle out. Good thing Melanie Otto's lawn is so finely manicured and packed with lush, cushy grass. Samantha could have really hurt herself.

Pain is part of the game.

And it's something I have to confess to my partner.

Lora's stringing new laces in her Nikes when I plop down next to her with a half-drunk bottle of Gatorade. "I hate to admit it, but my left leg is really sore."

She peers at me through her blond bangs. "Did you pull a muscle or something?"

I shrug. "Not sure. I started feeling it last night. I'll just slap a little Bengay on it when I get home from practice."

With a small laugh, Lora says, "With the way we practice, everything throbs."

I take a sip and return the cool bottle to my sore left calf muscle. "My eyelashes and hair even hurt."

"Should we tell Chloe?"

I drain the remaining blue liquid and chuck the bottle over toward my gym bag. "Nah. It's nothing. I'm sure it'll go away. I'm certainly not giving Chloe a reason to bag on me."

"Gotcha. Just keep me posted," Lora says sweetly.

See, there's more to cheerleading than the cute uniform and the instant popularity. I love the physical challenge. I've already lost six pounds (mostly water weight from sweating since I'm not fat at all), and my muscles, while cursing at me inwardly, are toned and strengthened and ready for more work.

Two measures in to the Daft Punk mix, Chloe stops the action.

"Hayley," Chloe calls out. "You've got to watch Hannah next to you and not get out in front of her during the routine."

She says it nicely enough, but there's an underlying "you idiot" implied in the undertone.

I catch my breath and nod. "You got it, Chloe."

"Madison, you're a half beat off," she continues.

I push my damp hair out of my face, wishing I'd brought a couple of bobby pins for the loose wispies. Seriously, it's a huge distraction when my hair is sticking to my skin. All us cheerleaders have long hair. It's a good thing, because Chloe literally has a schedule for the fall of how we'll wear our hair for each game: high ponytail, bun, messy bun, French braid, back with barrettes—you name it, she's got it planned out.

I think if anyone got a bob or short do, our captain would kick her off the team.

Chloe claps her hands together. "From the top."

The music cranks back up and I jump to action.

Kick, step, kick, pop.

Swing, lunge, clap, clap.

Stretch, crouch, spread, jump.

Oww . . . left leg hurts . . .

Pump, pump, pump, pump.

Bend, turn, pop, lock.

Crunk, crunk, spin, juke.

Ouch . . . Ouch . . .

"Good! Better!" Chloe hollers over the music. "Y'all got it. Go, go, go!"

To see Chloe Bradenton this happy with the new squad this early on means we're doing something right. It means *I'm* doing something right. When the music stops, we all clap and cheer for ourselves. Chloe walks up and down the line, smiling and nodding with great pleasure.

"Perfect, as always, Brittney," she says. "And Tara, good form. Watch your elbows and keep them closer to your body. You've got the routine down." Madison gets a high-five, Ashleigh and Ashlee get fist bumps, and then the captain stops in front of me.

My chest heaves up and down from the exertion as the adrenaline continues to flow like a raging river through my veins. *Please don't tell me I suck.*

Chloe flattens her lips into an indiscernible expression. Dare I call it a smile? "Yo. Band geek," she snaps.

Great. Will I be stuck with that moniker all year? "Yeah?" I ask with a bit of disgust tinting my tone.

A half grin crooks the corner of her mouth and she nods approvingly. "Strong dancing, good timing, and on top of that, it looks like you're having fun." She pauses dramatically and then says, "Maybe you're not a band geek anymore. Go high on me."

Seriously?

Chloe raises her hand and I do the same. High-five.

Just like that, I feel like I might actually belong.

CHAPTER FOUR

Know, then, whatever cheerful and serene
Supports the mind supports the body too.

—JOHN ARMSTRONG

ARE YOU LIMPING?" MOM asks with concern painted across her forehead when I walk into the house later that afternoon. The smell of her famous forty-cloves-of-garlic roasted chicken fills the very air around me, and I involuntarily drool.

Spent and exhausted, but button-popping proud of myself, I drop my duffle to the kitchen tile and collapse into the nearby wing chair. "Not really. I think I have blisters on my blisters, however."

I carefully kick off my Nikes and white footies and squiggle my feet around to loosen them up. A small fiery pain shoots up my left leg, and I massage my ankle to work loose the apparent charley horse. I hope that's all it is.

Mom chortles at me, but the motherly worry is still there. "You're not overdoing it, are you Hayley?"

"It is what it is, Mom," I say with a smile. As she hands me a cold bottle of water from the fridge, I regale her with deets of the day, including how Melanie's mother had Tastee Town cater our lunch with fried chicken, potato salad, and corn on the cob. "We each host a week of practice," I tell her. "Mine is next week."

She cracks the oven door to peer in at the roasting chicken and then closes it. "Sweetie, I hope you don't expect me to order catering for your friends."

"Of course not," I agree. Then I waggle my tongue at her. "But maybe you can make a batch of your yummy egg salad?"

With a wink, Mom says, "We can work something out."

Dad walks in, seeming tired and exhausted in his own way. He plops a stack of mail on the kitchen table and lets out a long burst of air.

"What's wrong, Jared?" Mom asks.

He rubs his head. "Nothing. Everything. Nothing to worry about, Nan."

"Right, Dad," I say. "And she'll quit breathing, too."

Mom gives him "the look," the one that says he had better tell her what's wrong . . . or else.

Dad nods. "The numbers are low so far this month for the store. Slow economy, you know. People don't need hammers and nails as much. At least, not ours."

"I would think in a slow economy, people would be doing a lot of DIY projects," I chime in.

Mom doesn't give up. "What about bridal registries for the summer wedding season?"

Dad reaches for his reading glasses and begins shuffling through the mail. "They've got Crate and Barrel, Macy's, and everyone else online for that."

"I should come back to the store and work."

"Now, Nan, don't start that again. I'm doing perfectly fine with—"

Pacing the kitchen, Mom says, "I knew it. I knew it. I told you, Jared. Last fall when Homestead Hardware built their super center out on the highway, I knew this would affect our business."

He holds his hands up. "Now don't go jumping to conclusions.

A lot of the businesses in downtown are hurting. We're not out on the highway where you get the college foot traffic and the people on their way to the beach in Florida."

I down the water in about three gulps and then toss the plastic bottle into the blue recycle bin by the back door. This seems like the ideal time to leave the parentals and make myself scarce. Family finances shouldn't be my business. "I'm gonna go take a shower," I announce. "Lora and I are going to the movies tonight after dinner."

"I think it's sweet that you're spending so much time with your new partner. But what about Shelly? Are you not hanging out anymore?"

"She's in Mobile this summer with her dad, and then she's going to summer music camp. It's not a bad thing, Mom. We just have different interests now."

"Leave her be, Nan," Dad says from over the top of his American Express bill that seems as thick as the last young adult novel I read.

"Don't be out late," Mom says quickly, taking her eyes from Dad's for only a second. Then she adds, "And take your cell phone. That thing's been buzzing all afternoon."

Damn! I forgot I'd left it in the charger overnight and didn't take it with me to Melanie's today. I wonder who's been calling.

I hobble over to the phone, and thoughts of Matthews Hardware Store battling a corporate giant fade away. I nearly swoon when I see the name on the caller ID:

Delafield, Daniel S.

"Omigod, omigod, omigod!" I repeat over and over as I stare at the number.

"Is everything okay?"

I can't exactly talk to my mom about boys. I mean, sure, we had the whole "how babies are born" talk over a plate of heart-shaped pancakes when I turned thirteen and everything—which took a bigger toll on her than it did on me—but she's like forty-eight years old and totally ancient. She and Dad have been married forever and have three kids. She's my *mom*. She's not a girlfriend to share secrets with. She's the woman who birthed me, changed my diapers, and now houses and feeds me. I'm not saying that's bad or she's bad or untrustworthy—we're just from different worlds.

"Everything's awesome. Just cheerleading stuff," I say, brushing aside the fact that Daniel Delafield has been calling me. How did he even get my number? "I'll be back down for dinner."

I bolt up the stairs, two at a time, scaring the crap out of my cat Leeny, who was napping in the sunshine at the very top. Once behind the door to my personal sanctuary, I fling myself onto the quilted bed on my stomach and immediately dial my voice mail.

"You have three new messages," the lady with the calming voice says. Does she not understand she needs to be a little more psyched when delivering this news to me?

"Received at 3:43 p.m. — Hey, Hayley . . . This is Danny. Daniel Delafield, you know. Got your number from Lora. There's a pool party tonight over at Justin Agace's house. Thought you might want to come and hang out, you know, whatever. It'd be cool. Call me back or text me."

Danny? And he's inviting me to a party?

"Next message, received at 4:21 p.m. — Hey, Hayley . . . Danny again. I guess you're at cheerleading practice. Phillip and I rode by Melanie's house and saw all the cars. Listen, the party at Justin's starts at seven, so hope to see you there."

Wow. He, like, seriously wants me there. Awesome casserole!

"Next message, received at 4:57 p.m. — Hayley . . . Me again. Don't think I'm stalking you or anything. Will Hopkins has the hots

for your girl, Lora. Bring her along with you tonight. We'll help hook them up, too."

Too? Hook them up . . . *too?* Does that mean Daniel wants to hook up with me?

My heart stops. Well, not really. But hyperventilation is surely on the horizon for me. *Breathe . . . breathe . . . breathe . . .* Who can be calm at a time like this? My high school dreams are about to come true. The hot hottie of all hotties at Polk High School wants to get with me. Me!

I text Lora . . .

FORGET THE MOVIE. WE R PARTYING W/
DANIEL & WILL @AGACE'S!
WHAT?
3 VMS FROM DANIEL. WILL WANTS U
BAD!
SHUT UP! BEEN IN <3 W/HIM SINCE
FRESHMAN YR
2NITE'S THE NITE

I toss my phone down. This calls for some serious preparation.

Thorough shower. Shampoo and deep conditioning. Shaving of the legs and armpits. Break out the new bottle of Clinique Happy. Get the new Aldo shoes out of the box. And maybe even have the guts to wear that new Op bikini that I bought for the family's beach trip we're doing in Destin this August.

My phone rings. It's Lora.

She squeals through the phone. "I'll be by to get you in an hour."

I'd better get a move on. There's a cute boy waiting for me!

31

CHAPTER FIVE

Physical strength is measured by what we can carry; spiritual strength by what we can bear.

—Author Unknown

I DON'T KNOW WHY YOU bothered curling your hair," Lora says with a snicker as we park on Royal Crest Lane outside Justin's house. "It's just gonna get wet."

I glance around at the now-familiar array of vehicles: Ashleigh's Volvo; Madison's Eclipse; Hannah's RAV4; and Daniel's Dodge Ram 4x4 pickup. Just seeing his truck makes my skin tingle. "At least I can start the night out semicute, right?"

Lora laughs and pulls the keys out of the ignition. "So, he really said Will's got the hots for me?"

Shaking my head, I say, "I only played the message for you like six times already."

She giggles. "I know. I just have to keep pinching myself. Let's get in there." She swabs a tube of gloss over her lips for good measure.

We grab our beach towels and trudge through the in-need-of-mowing grass, around the side of the house, and through the black wrought-iron gate. These sandals are killing my feet. I don't know if it's because they're new or because that damn stupid pain in my leg won't go away and only keeps intensifying.

I brush the thought aside and consider going barefoot.

Football players and cheerleaders are everywhere—people I've merely passed in the hallways or sat next to in class the past three years. A few of them haven't given me the time of day since we were in Mrs. Keegan's kindergarten class. Now they wave at me and include me in their fun. It's a veritable potpourri of Pops—what the popular kids at school are called—and I'm now part of the pack.

As we're surveying the scene before committing to a specific position, Ricky Knoxville, the center for the Patriots, chooses *this* particular moment to catapult his two hundred and fifty pounds of offensive lineman girth into a cannonball formation, slushing at least one-third of the pool's contents projectile toward . . .

"Watch out, Hayley!" Tara screams.

Lora dives to the left, but I'm anchored in place in my new shoes.

Keeeeeeeeersplash!

Water cascades over me in a wall of ozonated liquid, drenching me from formerly curly-coifed head to fashionably sandaled toe.

"Holy crap!" Madison calls out, rushing over to me with her towel. Mine is drenched.

I want to be sick. I want to cry. There goes my makeup. There goes my hair. Stupid Ricky. Stupid fat-ass dive bombing the pool and making me look like a drowned rat.

Lora swipes her towel under my eyes. "Your eyeliner's running."

"Great. Just fan-freaking-tastic."

"It's okay," my partner says, trying to soothe me.

"It's so *not* okay."

Daniel chooses that moment to appear by my side. "Damn, Knoxville," he says to his friend. "Way to treat a lady, ass clown?"

Ricky clings to the side of the pool and tries not to laugh. "Sorry about that, Matthews."

I'm not surprised that Ricky knows my name, because his older brother, Eddie, used to date Gretchen before she left Maxwell. So, I try to be a good sport despite the drenching and laugh through my embarrassment. Things could be worse, right? "It's okay, Ricky. It's not a party until someone gets soaked."

"Good attitude," Daniel says while patting me on the back. It's all I can do to keep my knees from nobbling together at his closeness. "Here, come over to the cabana," he says. "I've got an extra towel and a dry shirt you can put on."

The thought of wearing something of Daniel's all night makes me swoon like one of the O'Hara sisters at the Twelve Oaks barbecue.

I follow him over, still wondering how I caught his eye and got him to notice me. Guess I shouldn't look a gift horse in the mouth. I don't even know what that means, but my dad says it all the time.

"Get out of those wet clothes," he instructs.

Trying not to laugh at how suggestive it sounds, I do as I'm told. I wrench off my soaked T-shirt and take the towel Daniel offers me. As I'm standing there in my bikini, I can't help noticing he's checking me out. Wow. Daniel Delafield is giving me the once-over, and it appears he likes what he sees.

Dabbing my face with the towel, I luxuriate in the softness of the fabric, coupled with its Downy freshness. "Thanks," I mutter from behind the cotton. From the way he's smiling at me, I don't care that my hair is wet and stringy and I don't have a stitch of makeup on anymore. He certainly doesn't seem to.

He passes over a long gray T-shirt that reads "Property of Polk Patriots." "This should do if you get cold."

"You're so sweet to me," I say, all Southern belle-y sounding.

"It's easy to be sweet to someone as cute as you."

My breath hitches in my throat as I try to comprehend the words. Did Daniel Delafield just say I'm cute?

"Th-th-thanks, Daniel," I say.

The cabana is angled away from the party and is shadowed by the setting summer sun. Burnt orange, yellow, and a hazy purple dance on the horizon and are reflected in Daniel's twinkling blue eyes. He reaches for another towel and begins to dry my hair in the tenderest way . . . just like my dad used to do when I was little and I'd sit in front of him as he watched the nightly news.

"Your hair is really pretty," he says, stroking it with the towel.

Although it's still quite hot out this evening, I have chills up and down my arm.

"So is yours," I say, not thinking, and then laugh at myself. *What a dork.*

Daniel doesn't seem to think I'm a geek or anything. He slowly moves his left hand into my hair and uses his fingers to comb the wet strands. Almost as if he's worshiping me, he strokes the tresses carefully and then turns me to face him.

"I'm glad you're on the cheerleading squad. It'll be nice to see you standing on the sidelines rooting for me."

My pulse has surely stopped because all I can feel is his finger on my cheek.

My tongue darts out to wet my lips and I say, "Just like when I was your spirit pal in ninth grade."

Daniel seems perplexed as he runs through his memory bank. Then he grins widely. "Oh right! You made me the peanut butter crisscross cookies. Those were awesome."

He remembered.

"Yep, that was me."

His eyebrows dance up. "You were my cheerleader even back then." Then he leans forward.

I hold my breath knowing what will surely come next.

That moment that I've only imagined.

The dream that will soon be a reality.

Right here, in the twilight of a Thursday evening in June, Daniel Delafield pulls me to him and gives me the most amazing kiss that I've ever had—okay, I've only had two previous ones to compare. Strong, firm lips, a warm tongue, and the soft whispers of promises yet to come.

I am literally melting in his arms. Nothing else matters. Not my smeared makeup or messed-up hair or the forceful ache thudding in my left leg.

I open my eyes and see Daniel smiling down at me as he moves to nibble at my ear. Mmm . . . nibbling's good. Me likey.

However, over Daniel's shoulder, I notice Gabriel Tremblay watching us from off in the distance by the water slide. He's glaring, in fact. Disapproval—or perhaps even disappointment—crosses his features.

Flashes of memories photograph me in a blinding light. I remember when we were both just kids in school, not in a clique or part of the Pops scene, but in a simpler time when high school status didn't matter as much as getting dirty and playing until the sun went down. Now, Gabriel is also a Pop by de facto of his team trainer status. I'm one because I'm a cheerleader. Are we posers? Visitors invited into the feast to sample the treats we've only heard about before?

We're both outsiders in a new world, and his eyes tell me we both know it.

Even if I am making out with one of the most popular guys in the whole school.

I slice my eyes away from my neighbor and concentrate on the hunk and a half in front of me. I'm *not* a poser. I earned this spot in the PHS stratosphere. No one's going to make me feel bad about where I am. Not Gabriel. Not anyone.

I glance back at Gabriel and telepath my thoughts to him. After a second, he turns away and climbs up the water slide. So be it.

Returning my full attention to Daniel, I slide my hand up his bare shoulder and coyly ask, "So, where were we?"

And for the next two hours, we make out in the cabana like the high school kids we are.

* * *

JUNE IS AS STEAMY as ever in Maxwell, and I wished like anything that my parents had actually put that ground pool in several years ago when the hardware store was thriving and Dad was looking for a good investment. Instead of the luxury, he put the money into home improvements and bought Mom a new Viking accessorized kitchen and a fifty-six-inch flat-panel television for our den.

Because, if we had the pool, I'd be lying on a blowup float right now relaxing and cooling off from the immense workout we've just had. It might help with the nagging pain in my leg, too.

"Ready to go, Hayley?" Lora asks after toweling off her face.

"Yeah. Gimme a sec."

The cheerleaders are sprawled out all over my backyard as each set of partners practices moves like the scorpion pose and the star. Lora and I have a few moves of our own that we want to try out to impress Chloe.

I dash into the house and into Mom and Dad's bathroom, looking for the Aleve. It seems to be the only pain reliever that's really helping with this annoying pain-in-the-buttocks leg injury. I toss two of the blue pills to the back of my mouth and then cup my hand under the faucet. The water is cool and refreshing as I wash the medication down.

Staring into the mirror, I say, "Work, dammit. I've got too much to do to be injured."

Back out in the yard, Chloe eyeballs me and sneers. "Just because it's your house doesn't mean you can take a break whenever you want."

Not particularly liking her tone of voice, I say, "I had to pee."

She harrumphs and goes back to working with Melanie.

"Let's try that move again," Lora suggests when I return.

I assume "the position," crouching with my legs bent and my arms held over my head, ready to accept my flyer. Lora plants her foot in the small of my back and literally crawls up me to straddle my shoulders with a sneakered foot on each side. I stretch my arms high to grasp her calves as she gets her balance. I steady my weight between my feet and make sure Lora doesn't fall off, even though Ashleigh and Samantha are standing by spotting her.

"Don't lock your knees, Lora," Ashleigh instructs.

I feel my partner relax a bit more. I'm not calm, though. My body sings out its soreness. My leg, in particular, aches like I've just run the Boston Marathon — twice.

Chloe is suddenly up on us and growls my way. "Hayley, stop holding your breath!"

I let out a gust of air, unaware that I had it pent up.

"You can't do that," Chloe tells me, completely in my face as Lora still teeters on my shoulders. "You'll black out, drop your partner, and we'll be down two team members. This is all about perfecting our routines for camp at the beginning of August. Everyone has to be in top form so we can bring home the top trophy for once."

While I'm technically listening to her, I can't help but acknowledge the continuing dull thump in my left calf muscle. The Aleve just ain't cutting it. Tears sting the backs of my eyes as I realize I've got some sort of sports injury. It's quite common for cheerleaders, only I don't want it to stop me.

Great . . . just great.

I'm certainly not going to fess up at this point, especially with Chloe now on the rampage about cheerleader camp.

I call up to Lora, "Ready? Dismount."

Lora steps forward and hops down. I catch her at the waist as her feet touch the ground. Immediately, we position ourselves again for a stunt. I spread my legs shoulder width and bend my knees. Lora places her left foot at the apex of my thigh and torso and then swings her right leg up to do the same. I grab her underneath her armpits and steady for the move.

"On the count of three," I say. "One . . . two . . . three." And down . . . up. In a swift action, I hold Lora in the air as she splits her legs out to the side and holds them up with her arms.

"Whoohoo!" Brittney hollers. "Awesome move."

"Straighten your left leg, Lora," Chloe instructs. "I like this stunt."

Trying not to grunt, I say, "Saw it on ESPN last summer."

"I like that, Matthews," Chloe compliments. "Taking the initiative. Good job."

The adrenaline high of Chloe's praise is enough to divert me from my pain.

"Okay, girls," Chloe says, clapping her hands. "Good work. Time for a break." She twists to face me. "You got any food in this joint?"

I smile back, thinking I just might manage to impress the ice queen after all.

Running inside the house, I snag the cooler with the ice-cold water and Gatorade that I've been chilling since this morning. True to her word, Mom not only made egg salad sandwiches, but she also set out bowls of chips, a platter of fresh strawberries and cantaloupe, tuna to scoop up onto lettuce, and sun-ripened tomatoes from her garden. Since not all the girls are into carbs, this is a good selection all around.

"Need help?" Hannah Vincennes asks, bounding into the kitchen behind me. She's a sweet African American girl who can do an aerial backflip like nobody's business. Her jet-black hair is slicked back into a high ponytail and her dark skin shines with sweat. "I could drink about eighty bottles of water right now."

"I'm with you." I stoop to tug the cooler out, and my left leg hitches a little bit. I wince out in surprised pain. "Son of a . . ."

"Are you all right?" she asks.

"Yeah, I guess . . ."

Glancing down at my sore left leg, I notice a small knot poking out midcalf. I rub my hand down the length of my limb, pressing firmly where a bump now appears to be. "That's strange," I note, nonchalantly. "Must have hit my leg somewhere."

"That's a nasty bump," she points out.

"No worries," I say. "Part of the business, right?"

Hannah scoffs. "Girl, by the time we get to camp in August, we'll all be bruised and battered. Battle scars. Battle. Scars."

I laugh nervously and try not to think about what might be ailing me. There are hot, hungry cheerleaders to feed.

CHAPTER SIX

To fear is one thing. To let fear grab you by the tail and swing you around is another.

—KATHERINE PATERSON

MONDAY MORNING, I WAKE up with one thought: *I'm afraid.*

I'm not talking scared at the annual haunted house scared. I mean, truly afraid. Like heart palpitation-y fearful.

Not only is the pain in my leg not going away, but it's starting to scare me.

What if I've mucked myself up royally?

I pull my bottom lip into my teeth and methodically take the steps down one at a time, wondering how to approach this with my mom. I suppose the direct, truthful explanation is the best way around this. I can't let fear of the unknown win out.

No big deal . . . I'll just go see the doctor, get a prescription, and I'll be good as new.

As I reach the bottom of the staircase, I listen to the echoes of the silent house.

"Mom," I call out in a small voice I don't recognize as my own. "Are you here?"

"In the kitchen, Hayley."

A long sigh escapes my chest. I glance over at a framed cross-stitch on the wall that someone my grandmother knows did. Pink, yellow, and red floss spell out the comforting phrase, *Fear not, for thou art with me.* Suddenly my courage blossoms.

"Mom, I think I need to go see Dr. Colley."

As I limp down the hallway and enter the kitchen, I can't help favoring my right leg. Mom stops scrambling the eggs on the stove and stares over at me. "What have you done to yourself, Hayley?"

I shrug because I honestly don't remember hurting myself at practice. "I can't really say." Sure, my muscles are sore from all of the exertion and hauling Lora up over my head, but that's normal. This . . . isn't.

Dad rounds the corner from the breakfast nook, his newspaper folded up underneath his arm. Slowly, he sets his coffee cup down on the counter. Before I know it, he's kneeling in front of me inspecting the limpy leg in question. "Tell me where it hurts."

He presses firmly midcalf and I squeal. "Right there. Feel that bumpy thing?"

His eyes lift up to my mother. Worry covers both of them in a tattered blanket.

"Hayley, what have you done? Did you bang your leg somewhere? Trip and fall?"

"No, sir," I respond. "Nothing at all."

"We need to get you to the doctor."

Mom's eyes fill with tears. "Jared, don't you think I know that?"

"Y'all, could we—"

"I was worried about all this practice being too strenuous on you," Dad continues. "Cheerleading is one of the most dangerous sports around. I saw this piece on *Nightline.*"

I whistle long and high and plop down into the kitchen chair. "Yo! Stop it! I haven't injured myself at practice. This has nothing to do with cheerleading." At least I don't think it does. "This isn't like my other aching muscles. This is a knot under the surface. It's got, like, mass to it." My voice quivers on the last sentence.

Rushing to me, Mom rests my head on her stomach and hugs me to her as if I'm still a little baby that needs comforting. "It's okay, Hayley." She kisses the top of my head, and I feel safe and secure in her motherly embrace.

Dad stands and pulls his cell phone from his jeans and immediately dials a number. "Hey, Emma-Jean. This is Jared Matthews. My little girl's got a lump on her leg that I'd like Dr. Colley to take a look at ASAP. Can he fit her in today?" He pauses and listens. "Really? That's great. Thanks so much. We appreciate it. You know these cheerleaders. Have to keep them in shape."

He snaps the phone off and looks back at me. "When did you first notice this?"

I bite my lip and try to remember. Things are literally a blur for me since making the squad, going to practice every day, fitting in with the Pops, and most important, hanging out—and making out—with Daniel. All I think about twenty-four/seven is cheering. I do the routines in my sleep. I practice the chants in my head. Every step I take reflects on how I'll represent the school come the last week of August. Every image I have of myself includes a uniform, pompoms, and the school-colored Nikes.

"Not long," I admit. "Like I said, practice has been so physical, I would know if I hurt myself."

Mom shifts her eyes to Dad's. "Maybe it's a massive pimple under the skin that needs to be lanced."

"Eww . . ." I try not to gag. "That is, like, totally gross, Mom." Just the phrase "needs to be lanced" makes me cringe.

Dad comes over and kisses me on the forehead, as well. "Emma-Jean said Dr. Colley can see you first off, so go get dressed and let's head over to his office."

I screw up my face into a grimace.

"What?" Mom asks.

"Cheerleader practice is at Chloe's this week, and it starts promptly at nine."

Hands firmly on her hips, Mom states, "Do I look like I care what Chloe Bradenton thinks?"

I laugh in spite of the sitch. Chloe's so not going to be psyched that I'll be late, but shit happens.

I text my captain.

> GONNA B L8 2 PRACTICE. CHECK UP @
> DR 'RENTS SKEDULD

Two minutes later.

> NOT COOL. GET HERE AS FAST AS U CAN
> WILL DO. THX!

I'll just pop over to Dr. Colley's, he'll tell me it's nothing, give me a prescription for a pain killer or muscle relaxer, and I'll be at Chloe's in two shakes of a lamb's tail, as my minister's wife, Miss Agnes, says.

Yep. It'll be that easy.

* * *

"THERE'S MISS HAYLEY," DR. Colley says as he enters the antiseptic, cold examining room. I swear you could hang meat in this room. "I haven't seen you since that nasty bout with the chicken-pox. Never seen a sixteen-year-old get them so badly."

I smile weakly and try not to think of the deep scars on my hairline, the left side of my nose, and weirdly enough, each one of my boobs. "No, sir. That was pretty gnarly."

Dr. Colley, in his late sixties, reaches out and ruffles my long hair. Then, he stretches his hand out to shake my dad's. "Jared, good to see you, as always."

Once we've dispensed of the howdy-dos, I tell Dr. Colley what's troubling me.

"Put your leg up on the table there, Hayley, and let me take a look."

I push off my tennis shoe and sock and extend my left leg on the examination table. Dr. Colley peers over his glasses and pokes and prods my entire leg. He presses the length of it from ankle to knee and notes how I squirm and grimace when he hits the sore spot.

"Well, you've definitely got a mass of some sort there."

My eyes pop wide, tamping down the fear that's threatening to strangle me. "It's not going to keep me from cheerleading, will it?"

His smile broadens. "Are you a cheerleader over at Polk now? I thought you played the trumpet."

"Used to." I return his grin. "I'm on the varsity squad. I don't want anything to slow me down."

He pats my knee in a grandfatherly way. "My Stella was a cheerleader when she was your age. Just loved it. You will, too." He pulls my chart, makes some notes, and then hands a piece of paper to my dad. "Jared, take her down the hall to X-ray. I want to get a better look at this. Might not be anything more than a calcium deposit, but let's just be sure."

"You got it, Doc," Dad says.

An hour later—ugh, Chloe's going to be pissed at me—we're back in Dr. Colley's office sitting in front of the large, wide computer monitor that shows a digital image of my left leg. And . . . eww . . . *What is that?*

Echoing my thought, Dad points to the globby mess that resembles white foam, and is attached to the small bone in my leg. "What *is* that, Doctor?"

Because it's an X-ray, it's black and white and a little gray. There appear to be air bubbles within the mass of goo that looks like the shaving cream I use to mow down my leg hairs. That can't possibly be inside me, can it?

Dr. Colley lifts his glasses for closer inspection. "I'm not a radiologist, but to me, it looks like a calcium deposit. I've seen them before in our community's athletes. It seems to be focused right here" — he points to the middle of the image that reflects my midcalf area — "around the left fibula."

Right . . . The fibula is the small bone in the leg. Fibula, tibia, the big one, femur, the thigh bone, and patella, the kneecap. Look at me remembering tenth grade physiology. A calcium deposit. That doesn't sound bad. After all, we need calcium in our bodies to build strong bones. Maybe I just got a little too much.

"What do I do about it?" I ask my doctor. I'm not terribly worried. As long as it's not broken or fractured, I can keep cheering. If it's something I can wrap in an Ace bandage or down a few Tylenol for, no big whoop.

"Jamal Ridgewood over at Polk Community College had one on his elbow last year. Didn't slow him down any. He's starting at running back for Maxwell State this fall."

Selfishly, I don't give a rat's ass about Jamal Ridgewood. I want to know the prognosis for me. The scowl that's surely on my face causes my doctor to move closer and set his hand on my shoulder.

"Hayley, just to be safe, I'd like to send you and your folks down to Dothan to see an orthopedic specialist," he explains. "It's the same one I sent Jamal to. He's going to know a lot more about this than an old country doctor like me."

"Just to be safe?" I question. Seriously, I can't have conflicts in my cheering schedule like this. "Is it something I can do on the

weekend so my captain won't get annoyed at me? If I miss practice and stuff, I get demerits."

Dad clears his throat forcefully. "Hayley, your health is the
most important thing. Dr. Colley's right, Little Kid. A second
opinion is always a good thing."

"Especially when it's a possible athletic injury," the doctor says.

"But this isn't from cheerleading," I state. "In fact, had I not
been practicing so hard, I don't know if I'd ever found this. It
only pops out when Lora and I do our partner stunts."

"Then it's a good thing you made the team, isn't it," Dr. Colley
says with a hearty laugh. "You'll be back at practice in no time."

I hope Chloe's going to be cool with this.

The doctor writes down the name and number of the referral
in Dothan—about an hour south of Maxwell—and hands it
over to me. "Dr. Alfred Maddox. I don't know him personally,
but he retired not long ago from the army in Fort Rucker and set
up a private practice. He'll fix you up right."

I stare at Dr. Colley's messy handwriting, but all I can think
about it that I'll miss more cheerleader practice.

Dad must read my mind. "It has to be done, Hayley."

"Okay, but nothing's going to keep me from going to cheerleader camp."

* * *

LATE WEDNESDAY AFTERNOON, MOM pulls our Toyota Sienna
into the medical park off Ross Clark Circle in Dothan. Chloe
and the rest of the team weren't put off by this appointment today
since we practiced from nine a.m. until two p.m. A quick forty
minutes down to the Circle City and we're just in time to make
Dr. Maddox's last appointment of the day. I played the whole appointment low key with the cheerleaders and told only Lora what

was going on. She was afraid she'd hurt me somehow, but I insisted that wasn't the case. But what do I know? I'm not a doctor.

And I need to get back to Maxwell ASAP because Daniel and William are taking Lora and me to see a movie. Which one, I don't know. Nor do I care as long as I get to spend time with the hottest guy in school.

"You're okay, right Hayley?" Mom asks sweetly.

"Sure. No big." And it really isn't. These appointments are more of a hassle than anything. I need to get over to Gill's Uniform Company and get fitted for the new outfit the school is footing the bill for. They're going to be the cutest! Blue and white double-colored straps that will "X" us across the back, white fabric with a flare in the front that shows the same blue and a red PA across the front. As we sit in the waiting room of Dr. Maddox's practice, all I can do is picture myself in the new outfit, hanging out in the hallways of PHS with my friends, and maybe even getting to wear Daniel's letterman jacket with it.

"Hayley Matthews," the nurse announces from the doorway leading to the examining rooms.

Mom and I gather our things and follow the woman back to the starch white room. There's a computer monitor set up, much like the one Dr. Colley had in his office, and a table with that crinkly white paper covering the leather padding.

"Why do they do this? I mean, you just rip and wrinkle it when you crawl up here."

Mom stifles a laugh and then returns to serious mode.

Over the next forty minutes, I flip through two *Woman's Day*, one *Oprah*, and a *Good Housekeeping* that are all at least four years old. Mom sighs heavily every five minutes but doesn't say anything.

Finally, I hear shuffling and muffled voices outside the room.

"Tell Dr. Covington that I can tee off with him Friday morning at ten a.m. sharp."

I roll my eyes, hoping a frickin' golf date hasn't kept me waiting like this.

The door opens, and in walks a petulant, short, bald man in a crisp white coat and black reading glasses hanging from a silver chain that circles his neck. *Alfred S. Maddox III, M.D.* is embroidered on the left breast pocket, and I see what appears to be a very expensive fountain pen clipped to the inside of it.

Without even making eye contact with me, Dr. Alfred S. Maddox III flips through my chart and reads aloud. "'Hayley Matthews, age seventeen, complaining of severe pain in the left calf area. Preliminary X-rays show mass on left fibula. Possible athletic injury or calcium deposit.'"

He glances up at my mom. "Are you Hayley?"

I harrumph. As if.

Mom actually blushes for a moment and then indicates to me, the one who's, like, sitting *on* the doctor's table. Geesh, what's this guy's glitch.

"I'm Nan Matthews. This is my daughter, Hayley. Dr. Colley said you were—"

The man turns black eyes onto me and interrupts. "You're Hayley, huh? Did you have new film taken yet?"

"No, sir," I say, almost afraid of this guy. I have to remember, he was in the military and probably isn't used to dealing with teenage girls. "We've been waiting for an hour to see you."

"That's how it is in the medical profession," he says flatly. He snatches the phone off the wall and presses an extension. "Christine, do we have the pictures on this patient?"

He slams the phone back down and then returns to me. I don't know whether to choose fight or flight. He stretches his hands out and feels the glands in my neck. Then, he places a stethoscope to my chest.

"Breathe in and out slowly," he orders.

I do as I'm told, although I don't know what the hell my breathing has to do with a ridiculous, inconvenient lump in my leg.

"How long have you had pain?"

"Since the second week in June," I say.

The doctor tugs on my leg and does the same poking, pressing, and squeezing that Dr. Colley did. Only, he's not so gentle and friendly about it. I yelp when he mashes the sensitive area too hard. "Ouch!"

He screws up his mouth into a combination of a contortion and a glower, and then he moves to his desk. A password is input and my name pops up on the screen. He clicks on it. Several images of my leg appear on the monitor. Side views, front views; the original picture Dr. Colley took two days ago.

"What do you think it is, Doctor?" Mom asks hesitantly.

He adjusts his glasses on the tip of his nose and drags his finger across the milky white area on the X-ray. His tongue clicks as he stares at the screen. "This doesn't look good. Not good at all."

The thudding of my heart actually deafens me. His harsh words reverb against my eardrum, obliterating inane thoughts of what to wear tonight on my date. This is real. This is now. This is happening.

Not good at all?

"How so?" Mom asks as she reaches for my hand.

I don't remember how our fingers got tangled, only that I'm clutching hers as though my life depends on it.

"Well, I can tell you it is definitely *not* a calcium deposit." Dr. Maddox sighs and squints at the image. He toggles between the pictures and leans in to get a better view. His finger taps the screen over and over, pointing at the mass that's gathered around my bone.

Slowly, he turns to face us. Mom's standing next to me; her grip on my hand tightens. I think it's more for her benefit than mine. This guy's just a jerk and doesn't know how to deal with civilians. I'm not worried. It's no big deal. Right? I've been perfectly healthy my whole life aside from a cold here and there and the occasional flu that got past my yearly vaccination. Of course, there was the horrendous, god-awful bout with chickenpox last year, but everyone gets those at some point.

This is just par for the course for a cheerleader who's tumbling, running, and dancing all the time.

Mom gulps hard, though, and I begin to share her trepidation.

My eyes implore hers to not let this be bad. It can't be. I won't let it be.

"Mrs. Matthews . . . Hayley . . ." the doctor starts. "Bedside manners are not my forte, as you can imagine coming from thirty years in the army. I'm going to be very honest with you and not sugarcoat things."

Now I gulp.

He stares directly at me. "Hayley, I'm afraid you have malignant cancer."

"Cancer?" Mom shrieks, clutching my hand so tightly that it hurts.

"C-c-cancer?" I manage to say.

"Yes," the doctor affirms. "The only way to save you is to amputate the leg."

My ears ring.

Tears sting the back of my eyes.

My world goes dark.

CHAPTER SEVEN

In time of test, family is best.

—BURMESE PROVERB

CANCER!
Cancer?
Cancer.
C-a-n-c-e-r.
Can. Cer.
I roll the word around inside my brain to try and wrap some
sort of meaning around it. Especially in conjunction with me.
Me. Cancer. Leg. Tumor. Cancer. Bump. Malignant.
Amputation?
Surely I didn't hear *that* word. That was merely my imagina-
tion running away from me while sitting bored to death in that
rude doctor's office. All I can remember is staring at the poster
of undersea life, noting the angel fish, sharks, dolphins, pelicans,
starfish, eels, barracuda and all the other species I couldn't iden-
tify on the vibrant blue image. All of the sea creatures living in
harmony and peace . . . at least for one moment as the artist cap-
tured their images. No larger prey consuming the smaller ones.
No overaggressive amoeba overtaking some plant life or fish that
couldn't fight it off.

That's what cancer is, though. An intruder in your body that seeks to conquer all. A disease of epic proportions that can alter your life—or even frickin' end it.

I stare out the windshield. Unblinking.

The asphalt passes by in waves, the fingers of white lines twisting and swaying, doing their best to confuse my already muddled mind.

Mom clears her throat, a near-deafening cannon in the silence of my anguish. "So, what do you say we stop at El Palacio's and pick up a whole mess of chicken enchiladas? You know how much your dad loves their food."

I slice my eyes over at her hands death gripping the steering wheel to the point that her nail beds look the color of Valentine's Day red hots.

Cancer.

Malignant.

"Um . . . sure, I guess," I say, still stunned. I don't even remember leaving the doctor's office. All I recall is Mom turning beet red and grabbing the impolite doctor by the sleeve of his coat and hauling him out of the examining room. From the small window in the door, I could see Mom reading him the Riot Act, her eyes beady with anger.

"We should get some sopapillas, too," Mom adds as she switches lanes.

A dull headache begins to tippy-tap over my left eye. My eye twitches in response. "Sure. We can do that."

Don't you want to talk about what just happened? What did happen?

I muster up the courage. "Mom, what did—"

She stops me with her hand. "Come to think of it, we'll have your grandparents over tonight, too. Daddy loves their queso and chips. You know they make all their own? Absolutely delicious."

Sure, have Grandmother and Granddaddy over so we can shock them with the news over beans and rice. "Mom . . ."

I see a glisten in the corner of her eyes. The tension in her face, obvious by the vein in her neck, makes me want to reach over and hug her. But I'm belted in. And she's driving.

I try again. "Mom . . . can we talk about what happened back there?"

The car swerves a little too much to the left, and a passing car lays on his horn. The driver mouths something at Mom while flipping her his middle finger. Lovely.

"Oh dear," she mutters, and rights the vehicle, slowing down a bit.

Funny thing is, I'm not upset. And I'm not freaking out all that much. I just want to understand what the hell is going on. I need to know what's next. What will tomorrow be like? Can I go to cheerleader practice? Can I just check into the hospital and let them cut this thing out?

As if reading my mind, Mom wets her lips with her tongue and says, "That appointment never happened."

"What?"

She nods. "That was only a formality. He's just one doctor." Then she sneers. "Besides, what does he know? I've never met such an arrogant, disgusting person in all my life."

"He was a dick," I mutter.

Mom snickers, knowing she can't correct me when I speak the truth. Still, she gives me "the look."

"So, what do we do, Mom?" I pull my foot up onto the seat and wrap my arms around my leg, resting my chin on my knee. "I've got this . . . this . . . *thing* . . . growing inside me."

"I know exactly what we'll do," she says with a confidence returning to her eyes. She fumbles next to her and nabs her cell phone. I'd rather she not drive and dial—like the rest of the free world—but right now, I'm not going to speak up. It's a speed dial number, and she sets the phone on speaker.

On the third ring, I hear, "*You've reached Dr. Roger Swonsky. If this is a medical emergency, please press zero to be transferred to my answering service. Otherwise, please leave your name, number, and a message and I'll return your call as soon as I can.*"

Beeeeeeeeep.

Mom clears her throat again. "Roger, this is your sister. I need to talk to you as soon as possible. I know you're two time zones behind me, but I don't care how late it is. This is a family emergency." Her voice catches momentarily and then softens into that of a small child. "Please call me."

She clicks End and tosses the cell phone down next to her. "I don't know why I didn't think of that before." A confident nod follows as she pulls into the upcoming turn lane to take us into El Palacio's.

I let out a long sigh. Not in frustration, but in relief.

Uncle Roger is Mom's little brother. I say "little" in that he's five years younger. Uncle Roger is also a doctor. Not just any random, run-of-the-mill doctor—he's a radiologist. The dudes that stare at black and white images and come up with all sorts of discoveries and finds. According to the accolades I hear from Grandmother and Mom all the time, his specialty is detecting breast cancer in time to treat it. He's like . . . renowned in his field.

Throughout my life, Mom has called him for every sniffle, scratch, or wheeze. When Dad had that bout with bursitis, Uncle Roger got the call. When Cliff broke his collarbone skateboarding, Uncle Roger got the call. When Granddaddy had gall bladder stones removed, Uncle Roger got the call. I guess I shouldn't be surprised that's who Mom called for reinforcement.

I relax a little into the seat.

Mom smiles. "Yes . . . Mexican food will hit the spot, right?"

"Yes, ma'am," I say, and breathe normally for the first time since we left the medical plaza.

Dr. Alfred S. Maddox the Third, be damned.

Mom just brought in the heavy hitter.

* * *

AGAINST MY PARENTS' WISHES, I go to practice the next two days and pretend nothing's wrong. The pain in my leg is wicked, but I grin and bear it. I work hard on the new pyramid we invented, and I help spot the other girls doing their tumbling runs. Chloe doesn't give me too much of a hard time when I don't do the same. Instead, I practice my splits, which are essential for any cheerleader.

When I get home late Friday afternoon, all icky and sweaty, I strip out of my clothes and wrap up in a soft, fluffy towel, ready for a cold shower and then a long, hot soak in the tub.

First, a quick look at Facebook.

I log on and read a status update from Shelly:

THE STEP SUX. WON'T LET ME DO ANY-
THING!!!!!!!! FML

Fuck my life. A fave saying of my generation.

Poor Shelly. I know it's hard for her with her parents calling it quits earlier this year and her father moving away to Mobile. Now she has to do split time between here and there. At least she's close to Gulf Shores and the beach, although it doesn't sound like her tether reaches that far. The whole Splitsville sitch was made worse when Shelly's dad remarried about two seconds after the divorce was final. "The Step," as Shelly refers to her, is only twenty-four years old and is fresh out of the ΠΦΨ sorority house at Maxwell State where her father used to teach. Now he teaches at the University of South Alabama and "the Step" does all she can to spend his salary and make Shelly's life miserable. Imagine having a stepmom who's only six years older! I understand why she says "FML."

But as I scroll through the status messages of friends and acquaintances and see their complaints of the day, I'm struck with a realization of how easy it would be for *me* to post an "FML." Not just an "FML," but a full-blown pity party diatribe all about me and my woes. Everyone would comment and "like" and tell me to hang in there, that they're praying and rooting for me. I don't need the sympathy, though. I can get through this.

I mean, if *anyone* can say "FML," I think it's certainly me. It's not necessary at this point. It's cancer . . . so what? Big whoop. They cut it out and I'm back at practice in no time. Right? People get cancer every day. It's on the news, all over the Internet; there are charities and fundraisers for this, that, or the other form of cancer. I won't let it be an "FML."

Instead, I type in my update:

44 DAYS UNTIL CHEERLEADER CAMP—PHS
PATRIOTS ARE GONNA RAWK!

Not a minute later, five of the twelve girls on the squad have either "liked" or commented on my status. I lean back and smile when I see "Chloe Bradenton likes your comment."

"Whattaya know?" I say to no one. Okay, Leeny's asleep on my bed, so technically, she can join me in basking in a small victory. Then I see the chat window pop up. It's Daniel!

DANIEL DELAFIELD: HEY WHAT UP?

HAYLEY MATTHEWS: HEY U!

DANIEL DELAFIELD: HOW WUZ PRACTICE

HAYLEY MATTHEWS: KILLER AS USUAL

DANIEL DELAFIELD: CAN'T WAIT TO C U
IN UNIFORM

HAYLEY MATTHEWS: <BLUSH>

DANIEL DELAFIELD: PLANS 4 2NITE?

HAYLEY MATTHEWS: NOT REALLY. HANGIN
W/LORA AND ASHLEE

DANIEL DELAFIELD: COME HANG W/ME

HAYLEY MATTHEWS: SURE WHERE?

DANIEL DELAFIELD: CHEEZBURGER PAL-
ACE @8

HAYLEY MATTHEWS: U GOT IT!

DANIEL DELAFIELD: C U THEN

HAYLEY MATTHEWS: AWESOME TTYS! =)

I click off the chat window and bounce up in my chair. Another night hanging with Daniel. Is there anything better? Nope. Not really.

FML? Seriously?

No way.

Not when a cute guy is waiting for me.

Cancer, bump, tumor thingy . . . whatever. I'll deal.

* * *

THE SMELL OF SIZZLING bacon and sweet pancakes tickles my nose early Saturday morning. Mom knows it's one of my favorite meals of all time. I love the way the salty bacon mixes with the sugary syrup. An involuntary drool bolts me out of my warm, dreamy bed-cocoon, where I've been reliving last night's make out session with Daniel. I walk zombielike down the stairs and into the kitchen to load up on the yummy goodness.

"Well, good morning, Hayley."

I stop in my tracks when I see none other than Uncle Roger sitting at the table with a steaming mug of coffee in front of him and his laptop computer.

"Hey, Uncle Roger," I say, smiling. After a cheek kiss and a hug, I pause. "Oh my God, it must be really bad."

He peers over his glasses. "What is?"

"My prognosis." I nearly choke on the words. "Mom called you, and now you're here. It's got to be the worst."

Mom walks into the kitchen with a huge basket of laundry under her arm. "Roger, Jared's at the store until five, but maybe after then we can—Hayley! You're up. Look who's here."

"I know. I can see," I say with a bit too much 'tude. Spinning back to my mom's brother, I ask, "What made you come all the way from San Francisco on a Saturday to be in Maxwell, Alabama?"

Uncle Roger peels off his glasses and rubs his eyes with his thumb and forefinger. "Truth be known, Hayley, *you* did."

My shoulders slump in anticipation of more talk of surgery, treatment, and missing cheerleader practice, school, and football games. I won't have any of it.

I stab my fisted hands onto my hips, not in ready-to-cheer mode, but defiant as I've ever been in my life to adults. "Uncle Roger, if you're here to tell me to quit the cheerleading squad, it's not going to happen."

He slides a chair out for me. "Of course, that's not why I'm here. I'm here for you, Hayley."

I bite my bottom lip in angsted shame and let out a sigh of relief.

Placing the clothes basket into the laundry room, Mom then moves over to the counter to serve me up a plate of bacon and pancakes. It's all hot and steamy, just the way I like it, and the flaps have butter swimming on top and over the sides. I focus my attention on the breakfast treats and take the offered chair next to my uncle.

"Eat, sweetie," Mom says.

I plunge my fork into the food and scoop it into my mouth as if I've never eaten before. Nothing soothes worries like Mom's homemade pancakes.

Sitting next to me, Mom reaches for a Sweet'N Low packet to pour into her coffee. She stirs the liquid slowly, methodically, as if hypnotized by the black swirl. "I called Roger because cancer is his specialty. And, because we need a second opinion we can *trust*."

I nod in understanding.

Uncle Roger slides his laptop to the middle of the table, up onto the lazy Susan so Mom and I can get a better look. "I got your X-rays from Dr. Colley and from Dr. Maddox so I could study them more and be sure of what we're dealing with."

Seeing that gross, foamy-looking . . . *thing* that's growing inside me makes the yummy pancakes turn to paste inside my stomach. I set my fork down and push the plate away.

Mom's concern is apparent. "Roger, we should have waited until she finished eating."

"It's okay, Mom," I assure her. "Let's get this over with."

Uncle Roger pulls a laser pointer from his pocket and then enlarges the X-ray of my leg so that it's full screen. I swallow hard as I listen to him describe what's going on in my body.

"I've been studying this nonstop since it was e-mailed to me. Right here"—he points to the middle of my fibula where the growth is—"appears to be a juxtacortical or surface tumor.

They're defined as those kinds of lesions that arise adjacent to the outer surface of the cortical bone. These surface tumors have the tendency to arise from any of the mesenchymal elements present along the bone surface or from the pluripotent cells found within the periosteum."

Uncle Roger has always been one to use big words that no one else understands. These apply to me, though, and the nausea begins to bubble up into my throat. He lost me after "appears to be . . ."

But he continues. "In most cases, it's hard to determine whether the sarcoma arose from within the periosteum or from other juxtacortical connective tissues. As you can see, there seems to be a variety of histological tissue types within here. Possibly caused by a viral infection or something of that effect. It's hard to tell at this juncture whether it's benign or malignant, so that's why we need to approach this in a conservative, slow manner instead of resorting to intrusive surgical evacuation."

"What do *you* think, Roger?" my mom pleads.

"This is merely a plain radiograph, so the lesion demonstrates heterogeneous ossification. To understand its makings more, you would need to conduct bone density tests, an MRI, more in-depth radiology. From a purely observational standpoint, I would say that it has the potential to be a high-grade osteosarcoma. Hayley's demonstrated an enlarged, painful mass and swelling that is symptomatic of a high-grade osteosarcoma. The duration of the symptoms prior to diagnosis is relatively short because of the pain. Most patients catch it in one to six months of the lesion development."

My eyelid twitches from the stress, and my heartbeat accelerates. His words are a cacophony of confusion to my eardrums. It's like being battered with wave after wave of unwanted information. I have to stop him. "Uncle Roger, I don't really get anything that you're saying to me. I mean, I'm not stupid or anything. I get it. There's a big, honking lesion-thingy in my leg, and it's so not a good thing. What do we have to do to get rid of it?"

Mom takes my hand and squeezes it as we both focus on my uncle's suggestion.

"I've made several calls, and you have options. These types of tumors should be approached aggressively, with wide surgical resection. You could come to San Francisco and I could refer you to a colleague of mine who specializes in orthopedic cancers. Or, you could go to the Mayo Clinic, which is world-renowned for its cancer treatment."

San Francisco? No way. That's on the other side of the country! "Where's the Mayo place?" I ask.

"It's in Rochester, Minnesota."

My eyes roll from the information. "California? Minnesota? I can't be that far away. I have practice, and camp, and—"

"Hayley!" Mom snaps at me. "This is your life."

I cower in the chair, still not believing the severity of this . . . this . . . cancer that's attached to me. I won't let it get the best of me. I mean, medical technology is at its best these days. I'll go to the hospital, they'll do a few tests, cut it out, and I'll be back to cheerleading in no time.

"Any place closer to home?" I ask Uncle Roger calmly.

"The Mayo Clinic has a location in Jacksonville, Florida, which is closer."

"That's about six hours from here," Mom says.

I continue to gnaw on my bottom lip as all of this unfolds around me. "That's so far."

Uncle Roger lays his hand on my arm reassuringly. "There's one more option, Hayley. I've got it on good authority that there's a doctor that specializes in not only orthopedic cancers, but juvenile cases. His name is Dr. Tanner Dykema, and he's been written up in *Cancer* magazine for his accomplishments. He approaches each case methodically and slowly, being conservative about surgical options and postoperative treatment."

Slowly? No, I need a doctor that'll do this quickly. "Where is he?" I ask.

"The University of Alabama in Birmingham. UAB, my alma mater," my uncle says with a broad smile. "It's only three hours, and your brother is in the area. Your parents will have a place to stay while you're in the hospital, and your dad can drive back and forth to Maxwell."

"Your dad wanted to be here for this, but he had to be at the store. He and I agree this is the best option for you. We don't want any rash decisions. We need to find out exactly what this is and how to treat it," Mom says.

"I know it's hard to look at this in any kind of positive light, Hayley," Uncle Roger starts, "but you're very lucky. I believe you caught this in time, and your parents are getting you medical treatment right away. Back in the eighties, these types of cancers were rarer and the options were fewer. However, progress and technology are on our side, and Dr. Dykema and his team will get you fixed up in no time."

I certainly hope so!

I hang my head, thinking of the lost time with my cheerleader practice. It's a necessary thing, though. We're talking *cancer* here. Not a cold or the flu or a pulled muscle or a sprain.

This is my time . . . my time in the spotlight . . . my time to shine. Nothing's going to slow me down for long.

Lifting my chin, I turn to Mom. "I trust y'all. And I know I've got to get this done. Just promise me that I'll be back in time for cheerleader camp."

"That's not up to me," Mom says. "It's up to you, Hay."

"When do we leave for Birmingham?"

"Monday morning," Uncle Roger says. "I'll make all the arrangements."

"The sooner the better," I say.

Suddenly my spirits perk up, and I sense the adrenaline zooming through me, perhaps rushing toward the unwanted guest in my leg, ready to do battle.

And fight like hell, I will!

CHAPTER EIGHT

The human spirit is stronger than anything that can happen to it.

—C. C. Scott

CHLOE IS PISSED AT me.

Like I *chose* to have cancer and go to the hospital.

"Am I supposed to hold your spot for you?" she asks me in the snarkiest way imaginable Sunday afternoon at Madison's house. Mrs. Ingram and my mom called a special meeting so I could inform the team of what's going on with me.

"Um . . . yeah," I say, dumbfounded.

I don't know what I expected from Chloe. Perhaps that she be *human,* if that's possible? I certainly didn't expect tears from her like I got from Ashlee, Ashleigh, and Tara. The other girls surrounded me and hugged me, saying they'd pray for me and that I can beat this. Cancer's not an everyday word at PHS, so to hear a cheerleader has it really rocks the house.

Lora's right there, too, holding my hand like the dedicated partner she is. "I'll work with other bases while Hayley's away. It's no big deal."

"It *is* a big deal!" Chloe screams out. "We've got six weeks until camp, and we still have a lot of work to do on our routine, our pyramids, our stunts, you name it. And now we're down a person?"

"It's not like she planned it," Lora snaps.

"This was supposed to be *our* year," Chloe says. "First place at camp."

I'm paralyzed in place by Chloe's insensitivity. What a royal bitch. I understand that camp is important . . . but this is, like, my life!

Before I can get my incensed thoughts to spill from my lips, Mrs. Ingram finally speaks up. "Now, Chloe, I appreciate your passion for the squad, but Hayley's one of ours, and we have to support her." She turns to me. "Besides, it's only for a few weeks, and then Hayley will be back. We can just work around the hole in the routine and cheers. We'll make it work."

It's definitely my goal to return. Nothing's keeping me from camp. "Yes, ma'am. I promise to practice the cheers and dance moves in my head until I'm back on my feet."

Chloe harrumphs and mutters, under her breath but loud enough to hear. "You should have stayed in the band where you belonged."

Mrs. Ingram snaps. "Chloe! How rude. You are her captain, and you will support her. All of us will."

She relents. "Yes, Mrs. Ingram. Sorry, Hayley . . . I'm just thinking about what's best for the team. We're all concerned about your health and getting better." The words are coming out of her mouth, yet the candy coating around them is just that. Sweet and fake.

Still, I smile. "Thanks, Chloe. You can count on me."

Lora hugs me. "Of course we can!"

Everyone hugs me one last time, and I feel the support surrounding me.

"I'll come up to Birmingham and see you," Lora promises. "Text me and call me. Anything you need from me, you've got it."

A thin mist covers my eyes as my heart feels like it'll pound out of my body. "Thanks Lora. You're the best."

"No, you are." Lora says. "Give 'em hell, Hayley."

* * *

I TOSS MY STUFF into the back seat of the truck and look at my cell phone for the fifth time in the last ten minutes. I texted Daniel, but I haven't heard back yet.

From behind me, I hear, "I heard the news."

Gabriel's there, inching toward me cautiously. He's wearing beige cargo shorts, a baggy I've Got Soul T-shirt with a picture of the Grim Reaper, and he's carrying a plastic bag.

"Hey," I say, and smile. It's weird to have him back . . . weird in a good way. He was such a good friend. Maybe when I get back from Birmingham, we can resume the good old days. Minus the earwigs. "Yeah . . . the big *C* word, huh?" I say jokingly, still not exactly grasping what I'm about to face.

He grins back halfheartedly. "My aunt had breast cancer last year. She had surgery and treatment and is doing great. Doctors do wonders, Hayley."

"I know," I say. "I'm not worried." See, when I think of cancer, I think of it happening to older people, like Gabriel's aunt. Not to teenagers like me.

"Good," Gabriel says. "You have to have a positive attitude. Don't let this shit get you down."

"That's what I'm trying to do."

"Oh, I've got something for you." He reaches into the plastic bag and withdraws a white box. "Here . . ."

I stretch my hands out and accept the nice gesture from him. I pull open the tabs to the box and see what appears to be a book. Then I look closer and see that it's an e-book reader. "Cool! Thanks, Gabriel!"

He moves toward me. "Yeah, and I downloaded a bunch of free books for you. Classic stuff like Dickens, Shakespeare, Jane Austen, the Brontës, and such, and then a bunch of romance books." He tosses his hair out of his eyes and squints at me. "That's what girls read, right?"

A giggle explodes out of my chest. "Girls do read romance. This will be awesome."

"There's sudoku, too," he adds.

I stretch my arms out and hug him tightly. I begin to tremble a bit and hold on to him for a bit too long. His arms are strong and sturdy, and I feel safe, just like I did six years ago when he protected me from the nest of earwigs.

Gabriel rubs me on the top of the head and whispers, "You'll kick cancer's ass."

"Thanks," I mumble back.

Mom and Dad walk out of the house just then, and Gabriel and I pull apart.

"Ready to go, Little Kid?"

I lift my eyes to Gabriel's and smile brightly. "As ready as I'll ever be."

*   *   *

DAD TURNS THE TRUCK onto I-65 north just outside Mont-gomery, and I finally tug the earbuds off and take a break from the Electronica I've been blaring into my skull the last hour. I'm in the back seat with my small suitcase packed with my new e-reader, my toiletries, a few changes of clothes and underwear, my favorite black Reef flip-flops, my netbook, my Bama teddy bear, cell phone, and a deck of cards that Mom threw in. You'd think I was going off to camp instead of to the hospital.

"How much farther?" I ask like a little kid going to Grandma's house for Thanksgiving. Too bad there's hospital food at the end of the ride instead of a succulent turkey and all the fixings.

"Two hours, if we don't hit Birmingham traffic," Dad reports.

"That was nice of Gabriel to come over and see you off," Mom says from the passenger seat. "He's grown into such a nice-looking young man."

"I guess." Never really thought of him that way.

"Did you reach that other boy you were trying to get?" Mom asks.

"Daniel. His name is Daniel," I note. "I texted him."

"Daniel. That's a nice name," she says in such a motherly way. I giggle in spite of her.

"That's Franklin and Dora Delafield's boy, right?" Dad asks.

"Yep. That's him."

"He's the team quarterback?"

"Wide receiver. Set the PHS record for receptions last year."

Dad smiles at me in the rearview mirror. He knows I'm a football fanatic. Especially when it comes to the PHS Patriots.

"So, what did Daniel say?" Mom asks, nosily.

I shrug. "He said he was sad we won't get to hang out, but he'll text me."

Actually, it was more like this:

```
CAN'T GO 2 SKIPPER'S W/U ON FRIDAY
Y????
GOING 2 B'HAM
PARTY IN IRON CITY?
NO . . . HOSPITAL
```

```
?????
LUMP IN LEG NEEDS SURGERY
WHAT? THAT SUX
YEAH, IT DOES
HOW LONG U B GONE?
NOT SURE COULD B COUPLE OF WKS
SUX ASS WILL U STILL CHEER
YES!!!!!!
GOOD
WILL HAVE 2 FONE CALL ME
ILL MISS U
MISS U 2
PHILLIPS HERE, GOTTA GO WILL TXT U!
```

I lay my phone in my lap and stare out the window as the farmland and roadside billboards whiz by.

Mom clicks her tongue. "I don't think they let you have cell phones in the hospital."

"That's such a 1990s rule, Mom."

"Well, what do I know?"

We laugh together, but I'm anything but jovial. Back in Maxwell, the squad is at Madison Hutchinson's house, practicing jumps and dance moves and formations. Daniel's doing guy stuff with Phillip Bradenton, and everyone else is moving on with the rest of their summer.

And me? I'm stuck in a truck that's driving me to the hospital.

Up until now, I've been pretty nonchalant about this whole thing, thinking it's no biggy. But it is. A big, freaking, inconvenient biggy. Is the universe against me? Did some evil person wish this for me? What did I do to deserve this?

Anger now roiling through my veins, I jam my earbuds back in and crank up the Ultra Dance CD as loud as it will go. I close my eyes and visualize the dance moves and motions that we've choreographed to go with this number. *Punch, kick, groove, clap, wave hands, crunk, crunk, bop, snap . . .*

As Dad hits a big bump in the road, I hold on to the sissy bar.

Yep. That's all this cancer is . . . just a big old bump in my road.

CHAPTER NINE

How many desolate creatures on the earth have learnt the simple dues of fellowship and social comfort, in a hospital.

—ELIZABETH BARRETT BROWNING

THE NEXT SEVERAL DAYS are a gigamonic blur.

Dad dropped us off at Cliff's apartment where Mom and I are sharing the fold-out couch. We've barely been here as we've been a fixture at UAB Hospital where I've been poked, prodded, and questioned.

I've had vials of blood taken, I've peed (and pooped . . . eww) in cups, I've had about three dozen X-rays taken of my leg, and I've sat in more waiting rooms watching more daytime talk shows than I care to think about.

Who are these awful people who go on these shows to find out the paternity of the baby?

I digress.

Finally, on Thursday, Dr. Dykema admits me to the hospital.

He's a cocky sort of guy. Tall. Bald. Jet-black goatee. White coat with expensive pens in the pocket and his name stitched in cursive embroidery. I could totally see him in a tan robe playing the part of Jesus in an Easter pageant or something, which is ironic, because the man has a big God complex. I suppose that is a good quality for a doctor to have when he's about to slice my leg open and see what's growing inside it.

Fortunately, I'm in a private hospital room with my own TV, phone, bathroom, and shower. The nurses even brought in a cot and a recliner for Mom, who insists she's not driving the eight miles to Cliff's apartment every day only to leave her baby (that would be me) here all alone. Poor thing. I'm in this flexy-bendy-posable bed with the awesome bed pad, and she's sleeping on a crappy cot.

"I'm not leaving you, Hayley. I will be with you through all of this."

A weak smile crosses my face, then hers. "Thanks, Mom."

"I love you."

"Love you, too. And I'm sorry about this. I know hospitals aren't cheap, and if your insurance covers—"

Mom places her finger on my lips. "Shhh . . . don't even worry about things like that. Your father and I are making sure you have the best possible care. All you need to do is focus on getting better."

"Yes, ma'am."

Just then, a tall redheaded nurse walks in. "Hey there, I'm Ginger. You'll be seeing a lot of me," she says.

Mom stands and introduces herself. "I'm Nan Matthews, and this is my daughter, Hayley. Thank you for taking care of her."

"Whatever you need, honey," the nice nurse says. "I'm here during the week, Rochelle does the night shift usually, and Wanda and Beverly work the weekends. You'll get tired of seeing us," she says with a laugh.

"I'm sure we won't," Mom says.

Ginger hands her a menu and a pencil. "Circle here what Hay-

73

ley wants to eat, and we'll get it into the kitchen. Doctor says she can be on solids until the surgery, and then we'll reassess her diet."

I stretch my hand up to reach for the paper. "Let me choose, Mom."

She relents, but then Ginger steps in. "Let your mom do that. We need to get an IV into you, hon."

"Why?"

"To get you ready for your biopsy on Saturday."

I sit tall in the bed. "So soon? Awesome!"

Ginger cocks her head, a bit perplexed. "I ain't never seen anyone so excited to have surgery before," she notes as she adjusts a blood pressure cuff to my upper left arm.

"Chicken noodle or pea soup?" Mom asks.

I make a horrid face over the green choice. "Gross! Chicken noodle, please." Turning my attention back to Ginger, I say, "It's not that I'm excited. I'm just ready to get all of this over and done with so I can get home."

She pumps up the cuff until it squeezes tightly around my skin. "Cute boy waiting there?"

Oh yeah . . . well, him too . . .

Mom asks, "Chicken Caesar salad or roast beef with potatoes and green beans?"

"The second thing, please." To Ginger, I say, "Yeah, but mostly it's because I'm a cheerleader and I don't want to miss too much practice."

"A cheerleader, huh? That's cool. I was one way back in the Stone Age."

I laugh at her. She can't be much more than Mom's age.

"Pudding or Jell-O?"

"Pudding."

The nurse places the stethoscope in her ears and slides the end into the crook of my elbow. After a moment, she removes the device from my arm and says, "One-seventeen over seventy-six. Very good. You must not have 'white coat syndrome.'"

"What's that?"

"Nerves from being around doctors and nurses and hospitals. Makes people's blood pressure shoot through the roof." She pats my arm. "You're just fine."

"I sure hope so."

At the same time Ginger walks out, a herd of people in white coats enters. My heartbeat jumps a few notches when I see the young, eager faces. This must be the *white coat syndrome* Ginger was talking about.

A young woman with a high brunette ponytail steps forward. "Hi there, Hayley. I'm Dr. Stanislovitis. I'm one of Dr. Dykema's residents. These are my interns who will be working along on your case. We just want to ask you some questions."

"Okay. This is my mom, Nan."

Mom nods and sits down as the six interns gather around my bed. Dr. Stanislovitis picks up my chart and starts talking about me like I'm not here. "We have a seventeen-year-old Caucasian female with intense pain in her left leg. Initial X-rays show a lesion attached to the left fibula, toward the surface, however, could be growing toward the tibia. Suggested course of action?"

The short Asian guy with glasses speaks out first. "Pre- and postoperative chemotherapy."

"A bit aggressive to start, Dr. Ling, but a possibility."

The young girl in the back nods her head. "Aggressive radiographs to determine depth of tumor. Possible biopic evacuation of sample tissue to test degree of malignancy. Definitely start with an MRI and other bone density tests."

Dr. Stanislovitis smiles. "Very good, Dr. Perkins. The patient is scheduled for a biopsy on Saturday to remove a portion of the tumor and send it to pathology for review of cell materials."

The medical chatter bounces around me like a Ping-Pong ball out of control. Mom sits quietly, listening to their every word so she can report it back to Uncle Roger, more than likely. He had to return to San Francisco to care for his own patients, but he told Mom to keep him posted. Again, I just want it all over and done with. This waiting is slowly driving me insane.

The one called Dr. Perkins addresses me directly. "How did you discover this?"

"I'm a cheerleader," I say proudly. "The pain just got to be too much."

The new doctor moves her head in approval. "You're lucky to have caught this when you did."

"I know."

Once the cavalcade of interns evacuates my space, I relax into the bed and let out a pent-up sigh. There's peace in the room for about ten seconds, and then an orderly enters.

"Miss Hayley Matthews?" the gangly guy in green scrubs asks.

"C'est moi."

He's pushing a wheelchair and invites me to step into it. "I have to take you down for your MRI."

Mom stands, wringing her hands. "May I come with her?"

"No, ma'am. That's not allowed. But she'll be just fine."

"Don't worry, Mom. I'll just lie there like a good girl while they're zapping my insides." I laugh for good measure, but the humor is lost on her. "Seriously. It's fine."

Famous last words. I sit in a hallway for almost an hour waiting for my test. I look around at other people being wheeled up and down the hallways, nurses and technicians running this way and that and I'm just sitting here.

I glance over at my IV drip of glucose and notice there's a blood trail leading from the spot where it's connected to my hand to about halfway up the tube. "Oh my God! What's happening?"

A guy in blue scrubs is walking by and stops to check on me. "What's going on here?" he asks, as if I know or something.

"There's, like, freaking blood in this tube. That can't be right," I say as calmly as I can.

"So there is," he says, and then kneels next to me. His soft brown eyes venture up and down the tube, and he examines the connection into my hand. "Hmm . . . seems like this is a little loose. Let me fix this for you."

"Um . . . okay."

He fiddles with the tape that's holding the IV needle in my skin and adjusts the angle of the puncture. He disappears and returns with a syringe in his hand. "I'm going to put some saline in to flush this out."

"You are a doctor, right?"

"No," he says with a crooked grin. "I'm a phlebotomist."

I snicker. "Is that legal in this country?"

"Blood specialist. I work in the lab down the hall. Lucky for you I was going for some coffee."

The tube is now clear and free of my blood that was apparently backing up. "Thanks for taking care of that. I was beginning to think I was transparent."

"Where are you supposed to be?" he asks.

I lift my arms in an overexaggerated hand and shoulder shrug. "Something about an MRI?"

"I'll be right back."

A moment later, a chubby, older nurse comes out with her hands on her hips. "Are you Hayley Matthews?"

"The one and only," I quip.

"They were supposed to bring you to radiology an hour ago for your test," she says, as if it's my fault.

"I've been sitting here that long."

"I sawanee," she says, throwing her hands up. She rounds the back of me and steers my wheelchair down the hall. Calling back, she says, "Thanks, Brett!"

"Yeah, thanks, Brett," I call out.

* * *

I GET BACK TO my room to find a party going on.

There's a balloon bouquet, several get-well cards taped to the end of my bed, and a flower arrangement on the side table. In the middle of the bed is a huge box full of muffins, pastries, and cookies. I can smell the cinnamon from here in the doorway.

"There she is!" a bubbly woman calls out. "You must be Hayley!"

"I am," I say, looking around. "Who are you?"

"I'm Lily. Lily Danbury. I'm your brother's girlfriend."

Lily's what I'd call a wannabe hippie. She's dressed in a long, flowing flowery skirt that falls loosely around her round hips and long legs. Birkenstocks adorn her feet, and her hair is long, straight, and parted in the middle. If I didn't know any better, I'd think that I just time traveled to a pre-Woodstock soiree.

"Did you do all of this?" I ask, nearly gasping at the festiveness of the drab hospital room.

"I did! I have a bakery in Mountain Brook called Lily of the Valley, so I brought you some of my more popular tasty treats. I hope you enjoy them. They're all organic and made from natural ingredients."

"Oh my God—how can I not? The smell is amazing!"

The orderly lets me out of the wheelchair, and I walk over to the bed. Crawling back into the covers, I reach for a thick-topped chocolate muffin and immediately dig in. Sooooo sweet, soft, moist, and delicious. I'm about to wolf the rest of it down, but I can't eat all of this, or else I'll never fit into my cheerleader uniforms. "Do you mind if I share these with my nurses?"

Lily waves her hand in the air. "I don't mind at all."

The door to the room opens, and in walk my mother and brother.

"There they are!" Lily exclaims.

Cliff sidles up and puts his arm around Lily. They're cute together, but a totally odd match. Cliff is twenty-six, works for the United States Post Office, and is all Mr. Clean-Cut Conservative. Seems weird for him to be with Miss Free-Flowing Hippie Chick. I'm cool with it, though. Whatever works for them. I mean, look at Daniel and me. Not exactly from the same social stratus, but now that I'm considered a Pop due to my cheerleading status, I fit into his crowd.

I wish he'd call.

"This is simply lovely, Lily," Mom says. "Thank you so much."

"No problem, Mrs. M. I'm happy to do it. When Cliff told me what his little sister was going through, I just wanted to make her feel at home."

"It's really sweet," I say with a weak smile.

Home. Maxwell. Daniel. Cheerleading. Routines. Dancing. Lifting Lora over my head. Strengthening my muscles. Hanging out with my new friends. Getting ready for the best senior year ever.

Or not.

Lily's face reflects my pout. "See, Mrs. M. I was right. The little darling is depressed."

I snap out of it. "I'm not depressed. Really, I'm not. I'm just . . . melancholy."

"Same difference," Cliff says.

"I just wish I weren't stuck here in this room. I'm a cheerleader! I need to, like, be doing cheerleading things."

Lily and Cliff share a look.

"Yes, you do," Lily says. "And I've got the perfect distraction for you."

Intrigued, I lift a brow at her. "Yes?"

"Tomorrow, dear one. Wait until tomorrow. I've arranged everything."

Lily's a little nuts, but I think I like her very much.

CHAPTER TEN

At times our own light goes out and is rekindled by a spark from another person. Each of us has cause to think with deep gratitude of those who have lighted the flame within us.

—ALBERT SCHWEITZER

HAYLEY, YOU HAVE SOME very special visitors," my nurse Ginger announces to me Friday afternoon.

I click off the television that I've been channel surfing for the last hour and sit up in the bed, smoothing out the sheets. Has Daniel driven all the way here to Birmingham just to see me? Man, I have no makeup on, my hair is a mess, and . . . holy crap . . . did I brush my teeth today?

It's not Daniel, though.

Remarkably, I'm not terribly disappointed when the visitors begin filing in.

There's clapping. Lots of it.

People I've never seen before in my life.

People who make me smile like a Cheshire cat.

Girls in red, white, and blue uniforms. White skirts with red in the pleats and a summer sweater of white with blue and red "BHS" emblazoned across the front. Fourteen of them. All thin, fit, and smiling at me.

They gather around my bed and begin cheering.

"P-P-P-a-t-r-i-i-i-o-t-s . . . P-a-t-r-i-o-t-s . . . Patriots the *very* best!"

Mom sits up from her crossword puzzle and claps along. I beam at her and say, "They're Patriots, just like me."

"I see that!"

The cheer shifts into another.

"Hey, Patriots! We're back to fight with pride, so step aside, yell 'Go, Fight, Win.' Hey, Raiders! We're back to attack. We'll show no slack. Hey, Hayley! You're here to fight with all your might. Yell 'Red, Blue, and White!' Go Patriots!"

The girls jump in place and cheer as if it's a state championship game. Yet, they're cheering for me. Egging me on and rooting for me to defeat my enemy—this stupid-ass cancer.

"When you're up, you're up; when you're down, you're down. When you're up against the Patriots, you're upside down!"

Oh! I know this one. "Hey, hey, mighty Patriots," I cheer back at them.

"Hey, hey, mighty Patriots," they chant in unison.

I join their voices. "Hey, hey, mighty Patriots. Let's have a victory tonight . . . woot!"

Mom applauds wildly, and I sit up on my knees in bed. I can't believe what's going on! Where did these chicks come from? Who sent them?

A tall girl with crystal blue eyes steps forward. "Hey, Hayley! I'm Emma Beauregard, captain of the varsity squad from Birmingham High School. We were sent here by Lily Danbury to cheer you up. And we brought you a cheer basket!"

Mom puts her hand to her chest. "That Lily. She's a keeper."

"That's amazingly sweet of her, and y'all," I say, excitement lacing my voice.

An older woman with salt-and-pepper-colored hair steps into the room carrying a ginormous basket that is literally overflowing with goodies. It's a cheer basket. How cool! There's a ton of stuff and red, white, and blue balloons to boot.

"I'm Lynda Loges, the girls' sponsor at BHS. Lily was one of my students when she was in high school, and she called me to tell me what you were going through and how you were away from your own cheerleading squad. We thought you could use a pick-me-up."

"Could I!" I say. "This is fan-freaking-tastic."

Mom just shakes her head at me.

"Well here, dear," Ms. Loges says to me. "This basket is for you."

I rummage through the contents. "It's all stuff I love," I tell my mom. Diet Coke, candy bars, Cheetos, a Kaskade CD, a Bama Roll Tide T-shirt, young adult books, a hairbrush, toothpaste, shampoo, conditioner, body wash, a toothbrush, slippers with the BHS logo, more playing cards, a gift card to download iTunes, and other fun items piled in.

"This is amazing! Thanks, Ms. Loges, Emma . . . thanks, all of y'all."

The girls all take turns to hug me and introduce themselves. I completely feel a part of their team since mine is miles and miles away.

"So, when's your surgery?" Emma asks.

"Tomorrow," I tell her.

"Are you going to be on crutches?"

"I hadn't really thought of it," I admit. "I guess so."

Emma chuckles. "I was on them two years ago. Broke my foot on a long tumbling run. Ran right into a wall."

"Snap!" I say, wincing a little bit.

Emma pats me on the leg. "You'll be fine. We've been to visit other teens here. You're in the right place."

My eyebrows rise. "Y'all do this regularly? The whole cheer basket thing?"

"Yeah, sure," she says. "Being a cheerleader isn't just pep rallies and football games. It's about representing. About helping others. And if we can bring some joy . . . and cheer to people who are away from home or in a weird place, then we've done a good thing."

"You certainly have," Mom chimes in. "This means the world to Hayley and me."

Ms. Loges claps her hands together. "Lovely. Lovely. Well, Hayley, you have an open invitation to come to one of our practices at Birmingham High School. I'll leave all the information with your mom, and maybe she can bust you out of the hospital next week for a small road trip." She winks at Mom.

I can't contain my enthusiasm. "That would be *wicked* awesome!"

"Then it's a date," Emma says. "You can learn some of our Patriot cheers to take back to your school, and maybe you'll share one or two of yours with us, huh?"

"Absolutely!"

The girls all wave and cheer more as they exit my hospital room.

I'm blown away that complete strangers just totally made my day.

* * *

SATURDAY AFTERNOON, I GROGGILY wake up from the quick biopsy surgery performed by a resident on Dr. Dykema's team.

I remember getting on the gurney, being wheeled down the corridors, and taken to the cold surgical room. Everything after that is a complete and total blur—not even a dream, because I usually remember those. This is more like . . . a ripple in time. I was in one place at one moment, and now I'm back here, in my hospital room.

I muster all the strength I can and try my best to lift my eyelashes up so I can see what's going on. However, I'm weak as a newborn kitten and don't have the power to even squint. As I vacillate between consciousness and a dead sleep, I vaguely see Dad's face hovering over me, making sure I'm okay. I think I smile at him. Cliff and Lily are there, as well. I hear my brother's voice and I smell his girlfriend's jasmine perfume. Mom, ever the worrywart, is over in the corner.

In the fog of my brain, I hear Cliff talking to Mom, their whispered voices cutting through the density of my wooziness.

"You need to call her and let her know what's going on."

"Your sister knows our numbers," Mom says in a low hiss.

Gretchen? They haven't told my sister, Gretchen?

"She deserves to know, Mom," Cliff snaps. "If you won't do it, then I will."

"Clifford, don't back talk me."

"Mom, I'm an adult. I'll do what I want. Gretchen adores Hayley. She needs to know."

Dad's voice chimes in. "Cliff, your mother and I will call Gretchen tonight. Let's drop it, okay? We need to concentrate on Hayley. She's all that matters right now."

Awww . . .

"Hay's phone keeps bleeping," Cliff notes.

"Probably that boy from back home," Mom says. She must look at the phone because she gasps. "Oh my . . . so many messages. From her partner, Lora, other cheerleaders, that Daniel boy, and oh, look at this, from Gabriel Tremblay, too. So many people wishing her well. Pastor Tewes at the church said he's going to visit next weekend."

There's a loud thud of something hitting the table. I attempt to lift my lids to see what it is, but I'm just too drowsy from the anesthesia. "What's that, Jared?" Mom asks.

"Cards," Dad explains. "A ton of get-well cards people sent to the house. People really are pulling for Hayley."

"Boy, word got around fast," Cliff says.

"Maxwell is a close-knit community," Mom says. "It was bound to get out that she has . . ." Mom stops and I hear a hitch in her voice.

"You can say it, Mom. Cancer. It's not a curse word," my brother says.

Mom sniffs. "I just can't believe . . ."

Dad intervenes. "This is all still very hard for your mother and me, Cliff."

I sense Mom walk over toward my bed, and then I feel her hand in mine. I squeeze her fingers just to let her know I'm aware she's nearby. She sniffs again. "You won't understand until you have children of your own, Cliff. When your kid is hurting, you hurt for them. I would do anything in my power to swap places with her so she doesn't have to go through this."

"Now, Nan, everything happens for a reason," Dad says in a consoling voice.

"I don't understand why this happened to her," she says with a sniff.

Neither do I . . .

"Let's just hope and pray they can fix up our baby and get her well," Dad says.

Amen to that . . .

Mom leans over and kisses my forehead. "We're here, baby. I'm not going anywhere."

I know, Mommy . . .

With that, I fall back into a deep, relaxing sleep, knowing I'm protected and loved.

CHAPTER ELEVEN

When you come to the end of your rope, tie a knot and hang on.

—FRANKLIN D. ROOSEVELT

ANOTHER SURGERY?" I INCREDULOUSLY ask Dr. Stanislovitis and the team of interns. My fists dig into the fresh sheets on my bed, and I crinkle the cotton fabric tightly.

The young doctor speaks up. "It's what Dr. Dykema requires. We only went into your lesion about a quarter of an inch. Pathology tests indicate that the portion we resected was benign. Due to the size of the tumor in your leg, we feel it's best to do another biopsy, this time testing deeper into the tissue."

Mom holds her cell phone in the air near Dr. Stanislovitis's face. Uncle Roger is on the line, listening. "Well, what do you think?" she asks her brother.

Uncle Roger's voice crackles over the bad connection. "I spoke with Dr. Dykema last night, and we agree this is the best thing."

"The best thing is to just yank this icky thing out of my leg and let me get back to cheerleader practice," I say with great force in my voice. "I have to make it to camp."

Dr. Stanislovitis sits on the edge of my bed. Her warm brown eyes appeal to me, calming my nerves with their gentleness. "I wish it were that easy, Hayley. See, we have to determine first exactly what type of cancer you have. There are so many varieties that we have to make one hundred percent sure that we not only evacuate all of the mutant cells, but that we put you on the most effective follow-up treatment for your certain disease to minimize the chance of recurrence. I know you're anxious to get back to your life, and I want nothing more than that for you. I'm just asking that you keep working with us and continue to be patient."

I let out the breath I've been holding. Damn . . . this woman has good bedside manners. Must have taken Elements of Persuasion in college.

My head falls back into the bulky pillows, and I tug at my long hair, bringing several strands up to my lips as I contemplate everything. It's not like I have a choice. There're "mutant cells," as she said, "invading my body." They have to come out.

"Let's do it," I say with a weak smile.

Dr. Stanislovitis pats the bed. "That'a girl. We'll get the second biopsy scheduled for Wednesday."

"Four days from now?" Mom asks before I can.

"Nan," Uncle Roger breaks in. "That's perfectly normal. They'll need to run more tests, possibly do another MRI, and just keep a watch on the lesion before the second biopsy."

Great . . . I get to be poked, prodded, and drained of more blood. Not to mention radiated again and again. That can't be a good thing, even though they have been putting a lead apron on me to protect my "womanly parts" during all X-rays and tests.

"Thanks, Mrs. Matthews, Dr. Swonsky," Dr. Stanislovitis says. "We'll see you later."

"Roger, I'll call you later," Mom says into the phone, and then clicks it off.

Just as the resident and her team of interns exit, Ginger slides into the room toting a gargantuan bouquet of white roses—a dozen it appears—accented by green leaves and baby's breath.

"These are for a Ms. Hayley Matthews in room 211."

"Wow! Those are totally amazing!"

"I wonder if they're from Mother and Daddy. Or the church."

Ginger shakes her head. "Someone's got an admirer, I'd say," she teases. "Sorry, I peeked. I'm a snoop."

My pulse quickens. My fingers tingle. All good things in anticipation of finding out who sent these. I know who I *want* them to be from! The sweet-smelling aroma of the arrangement wafts over to me and lifts my spirits off the floor. I forget all about another week in the hospital, another surgery, still not knowing what I've actually got . . . and dive forward to retract the card:

> THINKING OF YOU, MISSING YOUR
> SMILE, AND HOPING YOU'RE BACK ON
> YOUR FEET SOON.
> XO, DANIEL

Swoooooooooooooon!

"From Daniel?" Mom asks.

"Ooooo . . . a hot guy back home?" Ginger asks, and I blush profusely.

"Football player," Mom notes.

Ginger giggles as she heads out the door. "Of course he is."

"Aren't they beautiful?" I say, fluffing the arrangement and setting it on the bedside stand so I can get a good look at it.

"Very thoughtful."

"I have to thank him, like now," I say, reaching for my BlackBerry.

I text his number right away.

> U R AMAZING!
> HEY HAY!

```
I GOT UR FLOWERS. OMG!
MY MOM HELPED PICK THEM OUT
THEY R GORGY!
WISH I COULDA BRAWT MYSELF
THAT'S OK
COACH HAS US DOING 2-A-DAYS
YIKES. I'M SURE
HOW MUCH LONGER U IN?
A COUPLE MORE WKS.
:(
SAME HERE :(
MAYBE I CAN GET AWAY
THAT WOULD B AWESOMEM
I'LL C WHAT I CAN DO
SWEET. THX.
WE'RE ALL PULLING 4 U
THX DANIEL
TXT ME L8R
WILL DO. BYE!
```

"Everything good?" Mom asks, the worry lines starting to show on her lack-of-a-good-night's-sleep face.

"It's all good," I say with a smile, and gaze adoringly at my flowers.

Knowing that Daniel is thinking about me is all I need.

* * *

"I NEED A BREAK!"

Tossing my e-reader to the rolling table next to my bed, I feel as if I'm going to literally expire from boredom. It's Tuesday. My second biopsy is tomorrow. The interns come in every afternoon to question me. No new news. Very few texts. It's July. People are starting to forget about me as I atrophy here on the seventh floor of UAB Hospital.

Mom jerks up from her knitting. "Are you okay, Hayley? Are you in pain?"

I wave my hands around. "Mental anguish," I say in a perfect teenage whine. I despise the sound of my own voice. I need a vacation from myself.

Actually, I need to get back to my life.

"Why don't you take a shower?" Mom suggests.

"Good idea." I slowly ease out of the bed and hobble to the bathroom, holding on to the wall and the nearby chair. Mom moves to hand me the crutches, but I want to do this on my own. Besides, the bathroom isn't far. The five stitches in my leg itch and sting like all get-out and make me feel as though my skin's going to tear apart. The "lesion" still throbs with a dull ache. My leg will never be the same. Tomorrow, there will be a bigger slash. More stitches. Less of me.

After a long, hot shower, I towel off, put on my PHS cheerleader shorts and a Patriots T-shirt, and head back into the room. I'm surprised to see Cliff and Lily standing there grinning like they've committed a crime.

"What?" I ask, my eyes wide.

"Get dressed," Cliff says.

"Um . . . I *am* dressed."

Lily smacks him on the arm. "Ignore him, Hayley."

"I've been trying to do that my whole life," I say with a giggle, and then stick my tongue out at my brother. He swats at me playfully, and, for a moment, the world is all right.

Cliff sits on the chair and tosses me my tennies that are on the floor. "Seriously. Get presentable for the outside world."

My hopes soar. "We're leaving the hospital?"

"Busting you out, kid!" Cliff says with a laugh.

Mom just smirks from across the room. "I told you to be patient."

"What's going on? Where are we going? Home?"

Lily helps me get my left shoe on since it hurts to bend my leg too much. "We've got a wonderful surprise for you. You have to trust us."

I don't care if they're taking me to the zoo and leaving me in the cage next to the lion. I'm busting out of here. Sunshine! Blue sky! Fresh air!

Fifteen minutes later, I have an afternoon pass from the hospital from Dr. Dykema and I'm waiting outside on the curb while Cliff brings his SUV around to pick us up. Mom hops in the front with Cliff and Lily sits in the back with me; my crutches on the seat between us.

As we weave through the streets of downtown and up into the mountains, I roll down my window and let the sticky-hot July sunbeams shine on my face. My long hair blows in the wind and into my eyes, blocking my view of the stores, shops, billboards, and traffic.

"We're almost there," Cliff announces.

I roll the window back up and sit back, excitement trilling my pulse and making my toes wiggle.

My brother turns the SUV in to a long driveway that leads up to a bunch of large buildings. A sign reads "Welcome to Birmingham High School, Home of the Patriots."

"Oh, my gosh! It's the school where Emma and the other cheerleaders are from."

Lily reaches for my hand. "Wait! There's more."

Cliff turns right into the circular drive around the school. An expansive—expensive—marquee lit up with scrolling information for the students. "First Day of School August 21 . . . Band Camp August 14 . . . Patriots vs. Lakewood Warriors, Friday, August 25 . . ."

Mom sees it first and gasps.

I'd do the same if it weren't for the lump of emotion in my throat.

I watch as the red dotted letters scroll . . .

"Welcome, Hayley Matthews, Honorary Patriots Cheerleader!"

CHAPTER TWELVE

I have always depended on the kindness of strangers.

—Tennessee Williams

Emma and the rest of the squad surround my brother's car as we pull up to the Patriots' gymnasium.

"Hey, Hayley!" they all call out when I open the door. I carefully swing my bum leg out and hold it up as I put my weight on the crutches.

"Y'all are amazing!" I screech out.

"Lily and Miss Lynda, our sponsor, talked, and agreed you need a break from the hospital," Emma says. "So, we thought it would be cool for you to come to a practice."

"It's beyond cool!"

Mom, Lily, and Cliff sort of fall into the background as I'm surrounded by the BHS varsity squad. They set me on the first row of the bleachers in the gym while they get to work. My eyes nearly pop out of my head watching their tumbling passes and funky dance routine to a fast-paced Hip-Hop/Dance mix. They execute the moves like they've been working together for years. Pop. Lock. Clap. Slap.

"That was awesome!" I call out when they take a quick break.

Emma, trying to catch her breath, plops down next to me and hands me a bottle of water. I accept it and immediately quench my thirst.

"I love the pyramid y'all do at the end of the tumbling run. That girl with the braids can really fly," I note.

"That's Serena. She's my little sister. Freshman and first year on the squad."

"Are you hard on her?" I ask, thinking of how Chloe rides me because I'm new.

Emma nods and takes a long sip. "I have to be; otherwise people will think I'm giving her special treatment. She has to prove herself early on if she wants this to be her squad one day."

"That makes sense," I say.

"So, Hayley," Emma says, turning to me, "are you a flyer or a base?"

"A base," I say.

"Me too. There's no way you'd get me up toward the top of a pyramid like that."

We laugh together, and then I have an idea. "Hey, you know how your two end girls just did splits?"

"Yeah," she says, listening.

"You should pair them up with the two girls in back who lifted the flyers into place. They could do a shoulder sit or stand and bridge their arms to your sister and that other girl on top."

Emma thinks it out, and then her eyes light up. "I think that's a great idea, Hayley!" She stands and then tugs on my arm. "Come on over and help us."

"I shouldn't—"

Tug, tug. "You should."

Feeling the muscle in my left leg tighten and stretch, I balk again. "I can't—"

Laughter bubbles from Emma. "Hell you can. If you're going

to overcome all this surgery, you need to have a positive attitude and just do it. Don't ever say 'can't.'"

Shocked in place for a moment, I shake it off. Her words are like darts tossed at a balloon at a carnival, on target and popping my negative attitude. It's like a spotlight of understanding has been turned on for me. "You're right. So right. I can do anything I want." I reach for my crutches and adjust them under my armpits. "Show me to the team."

"Awesome!" Emma says, leading the way back to the pack. "Hey, y'all, Hayley's got a great idea for our routine. Tell them."

Just like that, I do.

* * *

MY EXCITEMENT IS AT an all-time high when Cliff and Lily return me to UAB Hospital. Even though I'm hopping along on my crutches, I feel like I'm walking on clouds.

"They were actually asking *my* opinion," I say to Mom. "I mean, they let me show them that move that Ashleigh and Madison have been working on. Emma's little sister, Eva, is really tiny, and they can toss her really high into the air with a basket toss."

Mom hugs me to her side and kisses my temple. "I was so proud of you today, Hayley. You blended in with those girls perfectly and were practically one of them."

"They made me feel needed," I say, rounding the corner on my floor. I nod at Ginger and Rochelle and the other nurses as we pass by their station on the way to my room.

"Ms. Matthews," Rochelle calls out. "Y'all had a visitor a few minutes ago. Good-lookin' young man here to see your daughter."

I thought Daniel texted me that he *couldn't* come see me. But maybe he made it so.

"I don't know his name, but he's still here," Rochelle says, clicking her ballpoint pen rapidly with her thumb. "He either went down the hall for a soda or he's in your room."

Moving as fast as I can with one leg up off the floor, I propel myself down the hall and push open the door to room 211, expecting to see Daniel's smiling face.

Instead I see a welcome, friendly face.

"Hey, Gabriel. What are you doing here?"

He knows he's not the one I was hoping to see, although he's kind enough to smile through the awkwardness we're both sensing.

"My dad had to come up for a business meeting, and I asked him if I could ride along so I could check on you."

Disappointment melts away into complete appreciation for my old friend—my once-again friend. "That's so sweet of you, Gabriel."

I scoot past him on the crutches and flop up onto the bed, being careful not to hit my leg against anything. He moves to take the supports from me and then leans them against the wall just within my reach.

"Hello, Gabriel," Mom says when she enters the room. "What a nice surprise."

"Hey, Mrs. M.," he says, and then reiterates to her why he's in town. "So, I had to stop by."

Mom eyes a bundle wrapped in tissue paper on the table. "What do we have here?"

"Oh, right." Gabriel stands, crosses the room, and then brings the package to me. "I picked these at my grandfather's farm."

I unwrap the paper to see a couple of fistfuls of wildflowers in pink, red, yellow, and a lot of green. Honeysuckle permeates the room, and I breathe in the fragrance of . . . home.

"Thanks so much," I manage to say. "Mom, can you put them in water?"

She takes the flowers and nods at me, as if that was some sort of secret code. So not! "I'll be back. You kids chat."

I roll my eyes at her. Honestly, could she be a bit more obvious?

"Sit, sit, sit," I say to Gabriel.

He does, on the edge of my bed toward the end. I finger the TV remote next to me, but decide to leave the set off so we can just talk.

"How's the food here?" he asks.

"Meh. The meat loaf was really gross the other night. But the breakfasts are good. They give me these awesome, buttery grits every morning."

His eyes meet mine and he chuckles. "Remember that time your grandmother made cowboy grits for us?"

I screw up my face and cock my head to the side. "Um . . . no . . ."

"Sure you do," he says. "We were in the yard playing and were, like, eating sand, pretending they were grits."

"Oh yeah! I remember now," I say, laughing at the silly memory. "You dared me, if I remember correctly."

"Probably," he says with a shrug. "Sounds like something I'd do. Your grandmother found us and washed our mouths out. We thought we were in such big trouble!"

"Oh, for sure! It wasn't as if we were doing anything horrid or immoral, like playing doctor."

Gabriel slices his eyes over to me and suddenly I'm hot with embarrassment. Fortunately, he steps around my verbal mess and continues down memory lane.

"Yeah, right. Instead of yelling at us or punishing us for being stupid kids, she made us some cowboy grits."

I bob my head up and down. "Grits, milk, butter, cheddar cheese, and Worcestershire sauce all baked together."

Now he turns his head. "Seriously? Worcestershire sauce? That's her big secret?"

"The one and only," I verify.

He laughs deep. "I just remember it was the best thing I'd ever had in my life. I don't know if it's because I was so hungry from eating dirt or if it was because I was with—" The sentence hangs between us like leftover Mardi Gras parade beads in the trees. I breathe. He does, too. He shakes out of the thought and then continues. "You know, having a good time with my friend Hayley," he finishes.

I smile and glance down at my leg. "We had a lot of fun growing up. Lots of running and biking and just being goofy. I hope I can run, bike, and be goofy when all of this is done."

"You will. I know it," he says with more confidence than the group of interns that corral in my room daily.

I think back to the fun times we shared being silly little kids. My lungs tighten when I remember the day I took my new radio-controlled car down to his house and not only saw the For Sale sign in the lawn, but discovered that the Tremblay family was . . . gone.

Swallowing hard at the car wreck of emotions zuzzing through me, I ask, "Why did you just move?"

"I didn't have a choice," he says softly.

"You didn't even say goodbye."

"I know. I'm sorry about that." Silence surrounds us momentarily. Then he says, "But I'm back, and I'm here for you, Hayley."

My chest feels heavy and my body feels weak. Maybe I exerted myself too much today. Or, perhaps I'm merely gloomy for the lost innocence of children who used to think you could eat dirt and that was fine. Or "swim" in the monkey grass that surrounded the tree in our front yard. Now, I'm faced with . . . reality.

"Thanks, Gabriel," I manage to say in a whisper.

"You can beat this, Hay. I know you can," he says firmly. "You *will* beat this. Believe in yourself, hang in there, be tough, and above all, keep a positive attitude."

"Are you speaking from experience?" I ask him.

His back straightens. "I've never had cancer."

I press. "But you've had a challenge?"

He shakes his head. "It doesn't matter. I'm just saying, Hayley. Be true to yourself."

"That's all I can do."

Something tells me there's a lot more to Gabriel Tremblay than what's on the surface. I won't press him . . . not now.

He stands and steps forward. "I'd better go. Dad's meeting will be done soon."

I sit up and stretch my arms out. It just feels like the right thing to do. Gabriel hugs me like the long-lost friend I am, and then he messes my hair when we pull apart.

"Thanks again for coming. And for bringing the flowers."

He winks at me as he heads toward the door. "Give 'em hell, Matthews."

After the day I've had, I honestly think I can.

* * *

OPENING MY EYELIDS IS like passing an act of Congress.

I force them up with all the strength I can muster, which isn't saying much.

Where am I?

What day is this?

The sound of my own heart beeping across the monitor next to me knocks me in the brain.

Right . . .

It's Wednesday.

Second biopsy.

My teeth chatter together and my face feels wet.

I'm crying?

Yes. Wet, salty tears flow down my cheeks, pooling on the . . .

Oxygen mask?

I'm in recovery. Recovering. This was not how I saw my summer unfolding when Mrs. Ingram announced that I'd placed on the PHS squad. Lying helplessly flat on my back while people hack away at my limb isn't what I'd call the ideal.

"Hayley? Can you hear me?" a female voice asks from above.

I squeeze my eyes shut in a halfhearted response.

"I'm Rayanne," she says. "Can you talk to me?"

"I hurt," I say through the annoying oxygen mask.

"Where?" she asks me. She must be a nurse or something.

I think to say, "All over more than any place else," a favorite expression of my dad's. Instead, I muster up all the fortitude I have to lift my right arm out from under the covers and push the oxygen mask away from my face. Away from my tears.

Rayanne's wearing pink scrubs with pictures of bunnies all over the front. Her smile is bright and friendly, even though she's missing two teeth on the side. I'm not judging her by that; I'm just noting it. Details matter now to help me climb back to consciousness.

"Hurt," I repeat.

"It's going to hurt, darlin'," she says while making notes on a chart. "The doctors had to dig a little deeper into that tumor of yours to get the samples they wanted."

Interesting choice of words. "Tumor of yours." Like it's a pet I went and picked out especially for myself at the shelter. I shudder at the thought.

The woman replaces the oxygen mask on my face. "Now, darlin', you have to leave this on."

"Don't want to," I mutter, and the tears continue, flowing all by themselves. I have no control over them. The fiery pain in my left leg must be triggering them.

"Now, now. Be a good girl," she coos to me as though I'm six again.

"No," I say in a moan, not even knowing why. I shove the oxygen mask away a second time.

Rayanne's by my side to retrieve it once again. "There, there. I know this is all foreign to you, but with each step, things are only going to get better."

My eyes close at the thought, and I have to wonder if that's really, honestly, true.

CHAPTER THIRTEEN

*It is in moments of illness that we are compelled to recognize
that we live not alone but chained to a creature of a different
kingdom, whole worlds apart, who has no knowledge of us and
by whom it is impossible to make ourselves understood: our body.*

—MARCEL PROUST

LOOK WHO DECIDED TO wake up," Dad says when our eyes
meet. He's standing over me, watching me sleep. There's stubble
on his face, and I can see he hasn't been sleeping well.

"I'm sorry, Dad," I manage to eke out.

"For what, Little Kid?"

"All of this." I gulp down a dry lump in the back of my throat.
"You're missing work. This is costing money."

He sets his index finger on my mouth. "Shhh . . ."

His smile says one thing, but I know my dad. Dark shadows
pool underneath his eyes. There's a sadness in his face that's, of
course, understandable. However, it pains me that I'm the cause
of his concern and worry.

"How long can you stay?" I ask.

"Only a little while longer. I have a lot going on at the store
tomorrow."

My head throbs at the thought of what my medical bills must
be racking up to be. I'm sure my parents have some sort of supple-

mental health insurance or what have you . . . who knows these days? It's not exactly something they discuss with me over dinner. Does insurance even cover what's going on with me? Is a private room more expensive?

I burp rudely and expel some of the gas that was used on me during my three-hour surgery.

Dad makes a joke out of it and waves the air around him. "Give me a little warning next time."

I try to giggle, but the movement shakes me infinitesimally and my leg cries out from the newly stitched area. "Sorry." My eyes close again. "So sorry," I mutter.

Dad's strong fingers find their way onto my forehead and he rubs, smoothing back my in-need-of-washing hair. "You have nothing to apologize for, Hayley. Your mother and I are making sure you have the best possible care. So is your Uncle Roger. He's watching every move from San Francisco, talking to the doctors, and getting detailed reports on you. We're fighting this all the way, baby."

"Will I be able to cheer?"

"You'll be able to do anything you want to do."

Eyes still closed, I can barely hear the words I'm asking. "How did I get cancer, Dad?"

His hand strokes even more gently. "We don't know, Little Kid. It really doesn't matter. We just have to figure out how to get rid of it."

I lick my dry lips and then tug my eyes open. "I hope it doesn't take much longer."

* * *

I DON'T HAVE TO wait very long.

After a heated canasta battle with Mom Friday afternoon

(which she won in the end, mostly because I wasn't paying attention due to texting with Daniel), Dr. Dykema enters my room with his team of interns and a sullen look.

Seriously . . . do they teach them that facial expression in medical school?

Dr. Tanner Dykema pulls an empty chair up next to my bed and stretches out in it. He's quite tall, and his legs seem to go on forever.

I try to lighten the energy in the room. "Why so gloomy, Doc?"

For a moment, I think I see a crinkle of laughter in the corner of his goatee'd mouth. Not really, though. He's all business.

"Is everyone here at UAB treating you well, Hayley?"

"Yes, sir," I say politely. See, I was raised right.

"You have an excellent staff here, Dr. Dykema," Mom says. "It's one of the reasons that my brother, Dr. Roger Swonsky, sent us here."

The doctor nods. "That makes me happy."

"So, do you have news for us?" I ask before Mom can.

"As a matter of fact, I do." He removes my thick file out from under his arm and spreads it out on the bed next to me. "You see, Hayley, I don't like to jump to rash judgments about what's ailing my patients. I prefer that we explore all avenues, do the proper tests, and make sure we know what we're dealing with."

"Haven't we been doing that?" I ask.

"Yes, we have," he assures me.

Good. I thought he was going to say something like we had to start from scratch. I would not like that.

"Cancer is a stubborn competitor," he starts. "In order for us to win the war, we have to also win the battles along the way. We have to understand our opponent, what it's made of, and how we can defeat it."

I want to roll my eyes at the military references. Can't he just spit it out?

Instead, I nod and pay rapt attention.

"Hayley, from our first operation on your leg, we discovered that the cancerous cells around your left fibula were benign."

Mom puts her hand to her chest and lets out a sigh. "Benign. That's good."

"Yes, Mrs. Matthews. It's a good start." He turns his eyes to me. "Benign means the cells lack the ability to metastasize. However . . ." He pauses for emphasis, and that one word — *however* — hangs there like a white flag of surrender (to use his military reference).

Mom gasps. "Roger was right," she says in a whisper.

Dr. Dykema continues. "I spoke with your brother about this . . . yes. You see, deeper into the lesion and closer to the tibia — the larger bone in your leg — the cells have the ability to metastasize, therefore, causing us much more concern due to the malignancy of the cancer."

Benign was good. Malignant is not.

"I know cancer's not good, period. But I have, like, a half-good, half-bad cancer?"

Dr. Dykema leans forward more, his elbows resting on his knees. "The cells toward the inside of your leg are malignant, which means, if not properly treated, they can spread. Not just to your tibia, but to other areas of your body. These cells are deadly, Hayley."

My head pops to glance at Mom. She's remarkably calm . . . considering. "Your uncle explained it to me this morning," she says. "Your tumor isn't an apple, nor is it an orange. It's sort of . . . fruit salad."

Okay, I'll never eat *that* again.

The doctor explains more. "You have what is commonly referred to as periosteal osteosarcoma. I was actually one of the first to diagnose this disease back in the 1980s. It was rare back then, but, unfortunately, it's much more common today. Luckily, we know how to take care of it better. It'll require an extensive evacuation of the malignant lesion, possibly your left fibula, as well. We won't know for sure until we get in there and see how much damage has been done to the tibia. After that, you'll need chemotherapy and radiation treatment just to be safe."

"How long will that take?" Mom asks.

"We'll get her surgery scheduled for next week for the tumor resection, followed then by a week of chemo, and another week of radiation. Due to the mixed nature of this lesion, we don't want to take any chances."

"Will you take her bone out?" Mom asks.

"We won't know until we open it up and see exactly what we're dealing with."

Great . . . we're talking at least three more weeks here from the sound of it. Three more weeks? And did he say that he's taking a bone out? Is that even possible? Of course it is; otherwise, he wouldn't say it.

That means a longer recovery . . .

More time on the crutches . . .

And you can bet the farm that . . .

"I'm not going to get to go to cheerleader camp," I say mournfully. I know that's not the most important issue on the table right now, but it's pretty high up there for me. I was making it my goal to be out of here and on the bus to Pensacola for camp with the rest of the team.

Not going to happen.

I've failed Chloe. I've failed the squad.

My leg has failed me.

Mom taps me on the arm, drawing me back into the conversation. "Hayley, I know camp was important for you. Your health is what matters the most. We have to see this to the end."

"I know, Mom." I turn to my doctor, needing him to not pussyfoot around the issue. "What's the worst-case scenario?" I ask boldly.

Dr. Dykema strokes his goatee. "Truthfully, Hayley, if the cancer has metastasized to a point where we can't save your fibula or your tibia, we may have no other option than to amputate the limb to keep the cancer from spreading and to save your life."

"A-a-amputate? You mean, like cut my leg off?"

Mom reaches for me.

My breathing stops.

She's already yelled at one doctor for using that word.

"It's a *very* extreme measure, Hayley," the doctor says, "and one we don't consider likely."

"Thank God for that," I mutter, still too stunned to move.

"I have operated on this type of cancer before with extremely positive results. So, let's focus on that. Put your trust in me and I'll take care of this."

"I can only really put my trust in God, Dr. Dykema. But I'll give you some props, too."

He pats my bed and smiles at me. I have to trust him. He, like, went to college for eight years to learn how to do things, and he's been a doctor longer than I've been alive. Uncle Roger sent me here because this guy is the best.

My chest pangs with an adrenaline-filled anxiety much like what I experienced when Mrs. Ingram announced that I'd placed on the varsity squad. Only this ache is mixed with a powdery trepidation. I block out the worst case. It's not a possibility. I won't let it be.

Nope. Not going to happen.

Thoughts of another surgery, pain, stitches, sutures, needles, and X-rays. Am I going to glow after this? I have no choice in this matter. I'm helpless to the cellular attack consuming the bones of my left leg. Nasty, gooey, lesions that have wrapped around my bone and . . . what did the doctor call it? Metastasized? That just sounds so . . . wrong. I tamp down the hot, salty tears that threaten to spill from my eyes. What's the point? It is what it is. What good would crying do? I need my wits about to me understand what's happening inside me and how we're going to make this right. I'm not letting cancer defeat me.

No way. No how. Hell no.

The doctor directs his comment to me. "I'm sure you have questions, Hayley, and I'll do my best to answer them."

I'm sure he's prepared to respond to all sorts of emotional queries. There'll be time for that later. Right now, I need to let the experts do their job, so I can get back to mine.

"No, sir," I say, and then let out a gush of air. "I won't make it to camp. Fine. I'll get over that. I trust you to get me back on my feet in time for the first football game at the end of August."

"I'll do my best, Hayley."

I have a new goal.

CHAPTER FOURTEEN

Love cures people—both the ones who give it and the ones who receive it.

—Dr. Karl Augustus Menninger

THAT NIGHT, MOM IS stretched out on her cot fast asleep.

I'm wide awake. It's only nine thirty p.m.

I draw my laptop up onto the bed and settle into the sheets.

Double-clicking on the Skype button, I wait to see which of my friends might be online. I'm thrilled to see my partner seems to be available. I move the mouse over her name and wait.

On the third ring, her happy voice fills my headset and her smiling face fills my computer screen.

"Hayley! Oh my God! It's so awesome to talk to you," she says. "Look at you!"

I'd showered earlier in the day and washed and dried my hair, so my appearance is decent. I even have some makeup on, thinking it would help me feel . . . *like a normal person* . . . instead of the sick girl in the hospital with periosteal what'cha-call it.

I return a vibrant smile. "Hey, Lora! What's going on?"

"I have so much to tell you," she starts. "Practice has been killer. Chloe got this choreographer from Maxwell State to come help us out on our dance routine. He's been running us ragged with all these new dance moves. Holy crap, you'd think he was making us try out for the Pussycat Dolls or something."

Missing out. Missing out. Missing out.

"Can you video it and e-mail it to me so I can start memorizing the moves?"

"I'll get right on it," she says.

I change the subject. "How are things going with William?"

"Perfect," she says, literally beaming at me. "We've been out four times. He is the best kisser I've ever known."

Memories of Daniel's soft kisses click into my mind. "I hear that," I say.

I half listen as Lora prattles on about practice, the parties people have had, the new uniform fitting, etc. It only serves to make me feel like even more of an outcast than I ever felt before. *I* should be at home experiencing these things. *I* should be sharing these memories with her. *Why* am I stuck in this stupid bed just . . . waiting?

"So, what's going on with, you know . . . your leg and stuff?" she asks. It doesn't sound as if Lora can actually bring herself to say the *C* word. I understand. Saying it out loud makes it real. Gives it power. Spreads the word.

I take a deep breath. "It's cancer, you know, and that can mean a bunch of stuff."

"Like what?"

"Like more surgery and"—I swallow hard—"and I suppose if they can't fix it, I could lose my leg."

My ears ring just hearing the words. Syllables I never thought I'd utter.

"Oh, Hayley . . . don't say that. It's not going to happen," Lora screeches.

I lay out the details of what Dr. Dykema told us about the

surgery and follow-up treatment. Lora's face is ash white even on the computer screen as if she's taking it worse than I have.

"It's not a big deal," I stress, trying to believe the words myself. "I found it, they X-rayed it, they'll take it out. Voilà . . . and I'll be back in business in time for the first game."

"I really hope so, Hayley! Chloe's been bitching about the 'vacant spot' on the team. I've just been working with Tara and Ashleigh on stunts and things, so I'm cool with stuff."

"What do I tell the team?" Lora asks. "Everyone's asking how you are. Have you seen all the posts on Facebook?"

I smile weakly at the camera. "Y'all are great. Just keep praying for me."

"You know, if there's anything you need from me, I'm here for you."

I smile at my friend. "Thanks, Lora. I'll be back in my cheerleading shoes in no time!" I have to be. It's not an option.

"Oh, speaking of shoes," she says. "Get this. You know my Uncle Ross? Ross Scott, who owns Game On sporting goods?"

"Yeah, you've mentioned him."

"He donated new sneakers to the whole squad. Any name brand we want!"

"That's fantastic," I say. "Was there a vote?"

She nods. "Chloe got overruled. She wanted the Reeboks, but we found some Nikes with red swoops that will look awesome. Especially with the new uniforms."

"I can't wait! Make sure you get some shoes for me."

"Size seven?" she asks.

"Seven and a half," I say, smiling. "Why did he donate them?"

"He went on some massive mountain-climbing thing in Tibet. He said it was like a spiritual calling for him to do something for the team."

I snicker at the thought of anyone from Maxwell, Alabama, going to Tibet. Maybe I should take a journey there myself.

Just then, my Skype rings out.

"Daniel Delafield is calling. Answer?"

Hell yes!

"Lora! It's Daniel . . . Can you hold on?"

"No way, girlfriend," she says with a giggle. "Go talk to him. I'll keep praying for you."

"Thank you!"

I straighten up in bed and foof my hair, bringing the long tresses over my shoulder to cover up the mint green hospital gown. This is the medicine I need. A strong shot of Daniel.

"Hey, Daniel," I say, nearly bouncing in the bed.

"Look at you," he says back. His hair is wet, like he's just gotten out of the shower. I can almost smell the shampoo and soap on him.

"Look at you!"

"I've missed you, Hayley."

His words make my chest contract and expand. I drop my eyes down as I feel a blush sneak up on me. "It's nice to be missed."

"Have you talked to the doctor lately? When can you come home? Anthony's having a pool party second week of August when his parents are out in Reno on vacation."

"Man, I hate that I'll miss it," I say. Then, I tell him about my upcoming surgery, leaving out the part about possibly losing my leg. It's not that I think he's shallow or anything, but he's a boy and they don't get things like a girlfriend does. "So . . . another surgery and they'll take it all out."

His voice softens and his eyes drop. "Damn, Hayley . . . I'm so sorry you're having to go through this. It totally sucks."

"Yeah, it does," I agree. No matter how many times I tell the prognosis to friends or family, regardless of how I spin it, it's still one thing: cancer. It has to be defeated before it conquers me.

"Please say a prayer for me," I ask softly.

Daniel's eyes are soft and full of concern. "You know I will."

"Maybe we can do something when I get home. Before school starts."

He leans at the camera. "They're opening this new Japanese steak house on the north end of town near the Video Mart. Whattaya say it's a date?"

"Awesome!" I say with a bit too much rambunctiousness.

Mom stretches and sits up. "Everything okay, Hayley?"

"Sorry, Mom. I'm on Skype with Daniel."

She raises an eyebrow, but then she smiles at me and lies back down.

"Then it's a date," he says.

"I'd better run," I say, not wanting to end the conversation. However, I'm bone tired and want to sleep for a week so that I'll wake up and all of the tests, X-rays, and surgery will be over.

"G'night, Hayley."

He kisses the webcam, and I turn to goo. I do the same, actually closing my eyes as I press my lips to the cold glass as if it's really Daniel.

"Night," I say, and then his window disappears.

From her position on the cot, Mom chuckles.

"What?"

"Things have certainly changed from the days when your father and I dated."

"Yeah, well, you've got to roll with the times, Mom."

And that's what I've got to do. Wait out one more week. One more surgery. A little chemo. Some radiation. Then I'll have my life back.

Making that first football game.
Cheering in my new shoes.
Going to dinner with Daniel.
Having that perfect, unforgettable senior year.
At least I hope it's that simple.

CHAPTER FIFTEEN

Courage is not the absence of fear, but rather the judgment that something else is more important than fear.

—AMBROSE REDMOON

TUESDAY AFTERNOON, THE DAY before what Dr. Dykema refers to as "the big surgery," I push aside the ham and cheese sandwich and tomato soup the orderly brought for my lunch.

Ginger and Rochelle come in to check on me. Rochelle sticks out her lower lip when she sees I've merely picked at my food. "Hayley, you've got to eat, girl."

"I'm not hungry," I say, returning the pout. I'm so over this hospital. I'm so over this process. I'm so over being angsted about everything.

Because yesterday, I texted Chloe with the news that I wouldn't make it to cheerleader camp with them.

She's texted nothing back in reply.

Ginger retrieves the tray and clicks her tongue at her coworker. "Leave her alone, Rochelle. She can't eat too much leading up to tomorrow's surgery."

"That's just it," her partner says. "She's going to wish she'd eaten."

"Well, we have something better for her to focus on," Ginger says. The nurse disappears out of the room momentarily while Rochelle checks my IV, takes my pulse, and adjusts my pillows.

When Ginger returns, she's carrying shiny red and blue metallic poms, just like we use at PHS. "Hayley Matthews, have I got a surprise for you!"

She steps aside, and I nearly lose it when I see my fellow Polk High School cheerleaders come bouncing into my room. They're all wearing the brand-new white uniforms and the awesome donated Nikes. They're all here—Madison, Lauren, Tara, Samantha, Ashlee, Ashleigh, Brittney, Hannah, Melanie, Lora, and Chloe. Everyone made it.

"H-A-Y-L-E-Y . . . Shout it loud, shout it high!"

I clap along as my girls surround me, shaking the poms, and clapping for me. Lora moves forward and hugs me tight. "We just had to come see you."

"How did you get here?" I ask, brushing at the water on my face.

"Lora's Uncle Ross chartered a luxury limo, and we all came up together," Ashlee says, kissing me on the forehead.

Just at that moment, Mom walks in and bursts into tears. Behind her is a young guy in his early thirties. Very handsome, tall, and athletic. "Hayley, isn't this amazing?" Mom says. "This is Ross Scott, Lora's uncle. He brought the team all the way up here from Maxwell just to see you."

"I know! It rocks."

Mr. Scott moves forward and draws his hand from behind his back. It's the PHS spirit bear that is passed down from one class to the next. "Lora's told me all about you, Hayley. I know the girls wanted to see you, so I made it so."

"You're awesome, Mr. Scott!"

"Call me Ross."

Lora rolls her eyes. "Call him Ross . . . whatever. Open your package!"

Tears of joy fill my eyes as Lora hands me a wrapped box. I rip it open like it's Christmas morning and then I gasp at what's inside—a new, white PHS uniform. Not just any uniform. Not one that was passed down to me when I made the squad. This one is *mine,* made especially for me and worn by no one else. Underneath the freshly sewn outfit is my pair of complimentary Nikes. I clutch everything to my chest and hug them tightly. No one can take these away from me.

That's when my eyes meet Chloe's. She's standing toward the back of the room leaning against the wall. She's participating, yet not.

I gulp down the lump in my throat. "I'm so sorry that I won't be at camp with you," I manage to say through the emotional swell. "I wanted nothing more."

Lora squeezes my hand. "It's okay. We reworked the routines, and it'll be fine."

"Just as long as you're back for the first game," Ashlee says.

"You couldn't keep me away," I say through my tears.

The girls sit around for about a half-hour, asking me questions about the tests, X-rays, and surgery, and I do my best to fill them in on what I know. Chloe diddles with her iPhone, seemingly uninterested in the conversation.

For a moment, Satan pops up on my shoulder and whispers evil thoughts at me. Why didn't this happen to Chloe Bradenton? Why isn't she the one lying here in the hospital while we're all cheering her on? As quickly as the negative thoughts enter, I tamp them down. It's not right to wish anything bad on someone, even if it is Chloe Bradenton. I simply don't understand why people like her never suffer or struggle. Not that I wish that on her. Just that I wish it *not* on me.

Chloe taps her watch impatiently. "We should get going if we're going to make it back to Maxwell before dark."

"We just got here," Tara says.

"I'm just saying."

There's a collective groan in the room, yet I understand it's a three-hour ride.

"I can't believe y'all came up here. This is the best thing ever!"

One by one, the girls hug me and wish me well on my surgery tomorrow.

Lora's next to last, and she squeezes me the tightest. "Don't give up the good fight, Hayley."

"I won't," I whisper to her.

Chloe approaches me and pats her hand on the bed. "Get well, Hayley."

"Thanks, Chloe. Good luck at camp! Let me know how it goes."

"Oh, I will," she says a bit snarkily. "You'll be hearing from me soon."

Ross waves at me. "Take care, Hayley."

"Thanks for everything Mr. . . . er . . . Ross."

He flashes me a movie star grin, and I want to bolt out of the bed and hug him for making this happen. "I'm happy to help. I'm an athlete myself, and I know how hard it is to come back from an injury. It's well worth the work when you get back to your sport."

"What happened to you?" I ask.

"Blew my knee out in college and lost my football scholarship. I made up for it, though," Ross explains. "I had surgery, excellent rehab, and now nothing holds me back. I mountain climb, race bikes, water and snow ski. I've done eight marathons, and two triathlons." He points to his skull. "It's all up here. It's all mental."

"Wow, that's so amazing." He owns a large sporting goods

chain as well, so he's not just talking the talk. He's walking the walk. "Thanks for the encouragement."

He shakes my hand and then heads out the door.

"I'm just going to see them out," Mom says in Ross's wake.

After everyone leaves the room, I am beyond super-juiced. I have my new cheerleading shoes, my new uniform, and a specific timeline as to when I can get back to the squad. My teammates came to visit me and they care. I truly felt the love from all of them. And Lora's uncle is way cool.

I swing my legs off the bed and stand carefully. I need to stay limber, so I nab my crutches and head out the door of my room for a little up-and-down in the hospital corridor.

When I crutch past the nurses' station, I hear voices raised around the corner toward the elevator.

Is that . . . *Mom?*

"I won't let you," she says.

"Hayley's left me no choice, Mrs. Matthews." It's Chloe. "I'm the head of the squad, and I have to do what's best for the whole group. It's nothing personal. I'm just doing my job."

"Kicking my daughter off the spot she earned is not an option," Mom says sternly.

What?

I nearly lose my balance and have to grab onto the wall to keep from falling.

"I'm really not trying to be mean here, Mrs. Matthews. I'm doing what I was chosen to do as captain. The team voted whether or not to keep Hayley on the squad. I want to get an alternate to step up and go with us to camp. There's a transfer student from Florida named Kristin Powell who just moved in across the street from me. She was on her squad in Destin and could easily slip in to take Hayley's place."

I want to run.

I want to scream.

However, I'm cemented to the hospital's tile floor, unable to breathe, think, or move. I don't know whom I hate more—Chloe or this Kristin Powell person who wants my spot.

"You would do that to Hayley?" Mom asks my captain.

"I would do what's best for the PHS varsity squad," Chloe says. "Thing is, the girls voted me down, but I have the final say. If we go into camp a man down, we won't win."

"This is about Hayley, not about winning," Mom stresses.

I chew on the inside of my cheek to stave back the tears that threaten to reveal me. My breathing is labored as I strain to hear every word.

"It's about the team, Mrs. Matthews. Hayley is just one cog in the wheel. When there's a cog missing, the wheel can't function properly." Chloe stops for a minute as if searching for the right words. "I know everyone's worried about Hayley, and I get that. I'm concerned about her, too. But I had plans this season, you know? Big plans. I was going to be the first captain in PHS history to win first place at camp. That's a huge deal. If one of my squad members is down, then we can't accomplish that." She points to her chest. "*I* have dreams, too, Mrs. Matthews."

I've never heard Chloe talk like this before. For the first time, I "get" her a little more.

Mom doesn't, though. She only cares about protecting me. I see her take a few steps forward. She is totally in Chloe Bradenton's face. The ire in her voice is apparent. The tone authoritative.

"Listen here, missy. I don't care about what you want or what your dreams are. I have to think about my child. You can*not* take cheerleading away from my daughter. It's what's keeping her going. It's what's keeping her mind off the malignantly cancerous tumor growing in her leg. It's taking her mind off the possibility that she might not walk again once they remove her bone. Or at the very least, she'll have a limp for the rest of her life. Being a cheerleader and getting to that first football game even if she's on crutches is what's keeping her going. You will *not* take it away from her. I won't let you."

There's total silence.

I hold my breath.

It seems that Chloe does, too.

"I understand," Chloe says meekly.

You go, Nan Matthews!

You would have thought my mom was a cheerleader in her time instead of a mere clarinet player. I'm glad she's my cheerleader now. I've always loved my mom, but I've never loved her more than I do at this moment. Little red-hot fire engine that she is! I back away slowly and quietly and hobble back to my room so they won't know I was listening.

Damn right I earned this.

Damn right I'll make a comeback.

This spot is mine. No one's taking it away from me.

Especially not Chloe.

CHAPTER SIXTEEN

*The golden moments in the stream of life rush past us, and we
see nothing but sand; the angels come to visit us, and we only
know them when they are gone.*

—GEORGE ELIOT

I'VE JUST SETTLED INTO my nest of pillows following the last
Diet Coke I'll have for a while when Dr. Stanislovitis walks in
with two interns in tow.

"Hi, Hayley," the doctor greets me. "Mrs. Matthews," she says,
nodding at Mom.

Mom springs up from her place next to me where she's been
playing chess on my e-reader. As always, she has a look of apprehension across her tired face. Poor thing. She's spent every night
next to me on that cot without one complaint.

"Good afternoon," Mom says. "Tomorrow's the big day."

"Yes, it is," Dr. S. says. "That's why we're here. We need to ask
Hayley several questions about her medical history."

"Her father and I did that when we originally checked her into
the hospital."

"I understand, Mrs. Matthews," the doctor starts. "But

these are things we need to discuss personally with Hayley. You understand."

From the crease in her brow, Mom certainly does *not* understand. Nor do I.

"If you'll just give us a few minutes," the resident requests.

"Certainly," Mom says, and then turns to nab her purse. "Hayley, I'm right outside in the hallway if you need me."

"Yes, ma'am," I say in a bit of a squeak.

When the door shuts behind my mother, the doctors gather around me with clipboards in hand.

"Now, Hayley, there are things we must absolutely know about you before Dr. Dykema can perform surgery tomorrow. These are very personal and somewhat intrusive questions. You must understand that this has to be done, so please don't be offended by anything."

"Um . . . okay." It's not exactly as if I have anything to hide.

Dr. S. slides to the end of my bed and begins her questioning. Nothing too pushy. Height. Weight. Last time I had a period. Any medication I'm on for allergies or conditions my family doctor prescribed. Geesh, they had to kick Mom out of the room for this?

Then the questions turn.

"Hayley, are you involved with anyone? A boy or a girl?"

What? "Um . . . I went out a couple of times with Daniel Delafield, who's on the football team back home."

Dr. S. smiles nicely at me. "What is the nature of your relationship?"

Nature? "We went to a party and the movies and—"

"Your sexual relationship," the doctor interrupts.

I sit up high in the bed and feel the blush completely cover my body. *Wow, let's be forward, why don't we?*

"We don't *have* a sexual relationship, unless you count making out a little."

"Have you ever had a sexual relationship?"

"No!"

"Oral or anal sex?"

"Yuck! No."

"I'm sorry, Hayley. These questions aren't meant to be offensive. We have to know your complete history." The doctor continues. "So, have you ever had an abortion?"

"I thought that was pretty obvious. No sex. No baby." This is, like, ridiculously embarrassing.

"Have you ever done illegal drugs?"

"I took a Claritin-D from my friend Shelly one time from her prescription."

The doctor snickers and so do her interns. "That's not what I'm talking about. Any cocaine, heroin, meth, acid, marijuana, ampheta—"

"None of that," I snap. "I'm an athlete. I don't need any of that stuff. I get 'high' from cheerleading."

"We have to ask."

"No, you don't," I say. "I've never had sex, I don't drink, smoke, or do drugs. I'm really boring and proud of it. Besides kissing a few boys during party games and a couple of dates with Daniel, I'm pretty squeaky clean. What does this have to do with my surgery?"

Dr. S.'s eyes soften. "We just have to know anything and everything that your body may have been through or is going through. It's important to the doctors to know any substances or surgeries. I do apologize for the questioning, but it is necessary."

"I guess," I mutter, feeling completely violated.

A few more questions about my menstrual cycle, when it started, how long it lasts, and have I ever missed a period, and the interrogation ends. Honestly, I want to get up and take a hot, cleansing shower. Hospital stays really do strip you of all your dignity and privacy.

Mom returns to the room and rushes to my side, wanting to know what they asked me. I'm very honest with her and fill her in on both the queries and responses. Tears fill her eyes for like the eightieth time since I was admitted here. My heart thuds down to my toes and back up for all the pain and anxiety I'm putting her through.

In a tiny voice, I say, "I'm sorry, Mommy."

She sits on my bed and throws her arms around me. "You're sorry? *I'm* sorry!"

As we hug, she rocks me back and forth. "Why are you sorry?" I ask.

"Because I couldn't protect you from this."

"Oh, Mom, how could you—"

"You're my child, and I'm supposed to keep you from any danger. I'm supposed to protect you and keep you safe and not let you get . . . cancer."

"Like any of us had a say in this."

She pulls back and braces her hands on my shoulders as she gazes at me. "I would switch places with you in a second, Hayley," Mom says with great conviction.

Words of appreciation clog together in my throat. I swallow so I can speak, but the emotional lump is nearly as massive as the cancerous one in my leg.

I finally find my voice and take Mom's hands. "It'll be okay, Mom."

We sit like that for a moment in silence, each of us, no doubt wondering if it truly *will* be okay. To me, the real angst is the fear of the unknown. What will happen tomorrow when Dr. Dykema cuts my leg open? What will he find? How long will the surgery take?

Most of all, will I ever be the same?

* * *

BEFORE I GO TO bed that night, Ginger and Rochelle note all of my vitals and make sure my IV is secure and flowing properly. Even though I'm not allowed to eat anything presurgery, they bring me a dinner tray . . . for Mom. Bless her heart. Bless their hearts.

"We'll see you tomorrow after you're out of surgery, Hayley," Ginger says to me.

Rochelle tightens the blanket around me and pats the bed. "We're all pulling for you, sweetheart."

"Thanks for everything," I say.

I toss and turn for a while, trying to settle my brain from the conglomerated mess of information swirling around inside. Words to cheers. Convos with Daniel. All the texts, e-mails, and calls that came in throughout the day from friends, relatives, and acquaintances. So many good wishes. So many prayers. Surely God will hear the large outcry on my behalf and take care of me during the procedure.

I finally doze off while watching some cooking show demonstrating how to make gourmet cupcakes. I don't know how long I've been asleep when I'm suddenly pulled out of my dream about different-colored cupcake frostings to find an African American woman standing at the foot of my bed. She's not someone I've seen in the hospital before, but she could be a night-shift nurse who checks on patients while we sleep.

She's wearing white and her hair is cut short to her chin. From the moonlight cascading through my window I can see her smile is vibrant and warming and her eyes dark and caring.

Our eyes meet and she lifts a finger to her lips in the "shush" motion. Then, I see her begin to pray. Her right hand reaches out over my covers, and she lightly touches my left leg. I don't hear her words, but her lips move slowly in reverence. My heart pounds away under my hospital gown and will most certainly set off some sensors at the nurses' station.

At this moment, Mom sits up in her cot. "Is everything okay?"

The nurse doesn't seem concerned with my blood pressure, temperature, or pulse. Rather, she just stands there at the end of my bed, finishing her prayer.

Mom watches with wide eyes and then swings her legs off the cot.

The woman stops her with a hand and a smile.

Again, Mom asks, "Is everything all right?"

The nurse puts her hand back on my leg and smiles Mom's way. "Everything will be just fine. Now, you go back to sleep, shug. It'll all be okay."

Almost trance-like, Mom nods at the woman. I do the same.

She finishes her prayer, pats my left leg, and winks at me. With that, she turns and walks out of my room, closing the door behind her.

Mom bolts off her cot and rushes to the door. I watch as she glances left down the hall and then furiously back to the right . . . and to the left again. Then, she heads off in the direction of the nurses' station.

"What's going on, Mom?" I ask when she returns.

She closes the door behind her and leans her back against it. "The hall was completely empty."

"You mean, that lady just disappeared?"

"No trace of her."

"What about at the nurses' station?"

"It was that older woman, Joyce. She was reading a book."

My left leg tingles slightly where the mystery woman had patted me.

"Go back to sleep, Hayley," Mom instructs.

As my heartbeat returns to a normal cadence, I wonder if I was just touched by an angel.

The thought comforts me as I fall back into a deep sleep.

CHAPTER SEVENTEEN

We must embrace pain and burn it as fuel for our journey.

—KENJI MIYAZAWA

I COME OUT OF THE bathroom the next morning to find Mom and Ginger discussing our visitor from last night. Part of me thinks the woman was just a dream that Mom and I shared, and the rest of me . . . well, I'm not sure what to believe.

"She's an angel," Ginger says with great confidence.

"An angel?" Mom repeats.

"A lot of patients see her before their surgery."

I can't believe it. "No way!"

Ginger smiles at me. "Believe what you'd like. I'm just telling you what others have said. Same description. Same interaction."

Mom puts her hand to her chest. "It's a blessing, Hayley. We have to look at it that way."

"Pretty cool." And I nod.

Literally . . . touched by an angel.

Suddenly my apprehension over what's to come today subsides like a wave pulling away from the beach. There's a zinging sensation up and down my spine, and I'm really not frightened of the surgery. It has to be done. Then I'll be better and can get back to Maxwell . . . to cheerleading . . . to Daniel . . . to life.

The door creaks open, and in walks my support posse of Dad, Cliff, and Lily. Of course, Lily has some sort of baked goods in a box with her.

"Do I smell chocolate chip cookies?" I ask with my empty stomach growling away.

"They're for when you're out of surgery," Lily says.

While Mom regales everyone with the story of our angel visit, I zone out a bit, thinking about Lily's simple words.

Out of surgery . . . like saying "when you're out of the shower."

But it is that simple, isn't it? It's not as if I can do anything other than lie here while all of this circles around me. I'm helpless to this . . . *thing* . . . growing inside my body. The doctors are here to take care of me. All I want is to get back to the summer I had planned out. This wasn't supposed to happen. This . . . this bump—literally—in my road.

"You all right, Little Kid?" Dad asks, knocking me back to the here and now.

"Hey, Dad," I say, smiling and stretching my arms up to him.

He leans down to hug me and plants a kiss on my cheek. "You're going to be just fine."

"I know I will be, Dad."

His eyes meet mine. Dark on dark. Confidence on trepidation. Who wears what is a toss up. Mostly love on love. And that's really all I need to get through this, right?

"Dr. Dykema says you may have a long road of rehabilitation ahead of you," Dad tells me.

My shoulders lift, then fall. "I'm a cheerleader, Dad. *That* will be my rehabilitation, believe me."

"I know you think that now, baby, but we don't know what today's surgery will bring."

I flatten my lips. "Are you trying to scare me, Dad?"

Mom steps up. "No, Hayley. We're just all here for you. That's all you need to know, right, Jared?"

"Right," Dad says. He seems so tired and stressed out.

"Is everything okay back home?" I ask him. "You know, with the store and everything."

He shakes his head and smiles. "That's not anything you should worry about."

"Dad, I—"

Ginger strolls back in with her arms full. "We need to get you prepped for surgery, sweetie."

"Do we need to clear out?" Cliff asks.

"No," I say quickly. I'm not ready to be without my support group yet.

"Fine with me," Ginger says.

She removes the covers from me and places towels under my left leg. Using soap and water, she carefully shaves the leg hairs that have grown over the last few weeks. She slides the razor gently over the protruding bump on my calf. I glare at the spot—the damn lesion that's trying to stop me in my tracks. Just when I'd hit the pinnacle of my high school life, this stupid, effing cancer had to pick me of all people to attach to. I'm glad I'm having this surgery. Take the icky thing out. Take out the bone. Take out whatever you have to—just make me *me* again.

The nurse pulls out a swab and wipes it up and down the length of my leg, turning it a yellow-red hue.

"Damn!" I exclaim, unable to halt my reaction. "That's cold as crap!"

"Sorry," Ginger says. "That's why I brought warm blankets for you."

"What's that stuff?" I ask.

"Iodine rinse to help sterilize."

Ahhh . . . wonder how long it will take for that to wash off. She finishes up and then covers my leg with the towels. After that, she spreads the toasty covers over me and I burrow into the mattress for warmth, protection, safety. I shudder a bit—I don't know whether it's from the coldness on my leg or from nerves. Could be that I haven't eaten in twelve hours.

Mom tucks the covers up around my chin since she can see my teeth chattering. "Not much longer."

"It's just all so . . . surreal," I say to my parents. "I've watched so many medical shows on TV. I just never thought I'd be starring in my own episode."

Cliff snickers. "You always wanted to be an actress."

"When I was nine!"

We all laugh together, and it feels good.

Ginger instructs me to remove my earrings. I pull my hands from under the covers and tug the pierced sterling posts out and plop them into my mom's outstretched hand for safekeeping. I don't have any makeup or nail polish on because the nurses told me the doctors have to be able to monitor my status by looking at my eyelids and nail beds. Besides the hospital gown covering me, I am as naked as the day I was born. *Au naturel.*

According to the clock on the wall, it's only seven thirty in the morning. I feel like I've been awake for hours.

My other nurse, Rochelle, joins Ginger, carrying a new IV bag and another syringe. "Good luck to you, Hayley," she says with her bright smile.

"Thanks." I watch as the two nurses connect the fresh glucose to the silver tower attached to my bed that's feeding me nutrients.

"We're going to give you a slight sedative, Hayley, to soothe your nerves before you get to the operating room."

I nod my thanks and lift my eyes to the spot on the IV tube where Rochelle inserts the needle. She presses her thumb on the top of the syringe, and the clear liquid empties into the tube. I count, waiting until I can feel the effects.

Eleven . . . twelve . . . thirteen . . . fourteen . . . oh yeah . . .

"Are you okay, Hayley?" Dad asks with distress in his eyes.

I bob my head up and down. My eyes flutter closed momentarily to let the soothing sensation dance over my arms and legs. I'm feeling somewhat rubbery and flexible like a bendy doll. The throbbing in my left leg fades away as I luxuriate in the comforting blankets that cover me.

I feel Dad's firm hand stroke my forehead and hair. He rubs in rhythm to the pounding of my heartbeat. A soft kiss. Words of love and encouragement. Mom's soft hand joins in. Prayers and wishes. Blessings.

"The orderlies are here to take Hayley to surgery," Ginger says.

"Ohhhkay-alll-righty," I say in my floaty haze.

The loving touches retreat, and suddenly I'm chilled again. Large hands grip me and slide me from my hospital bed onto the gurney. Ginger instructs the two men to keep me covered and warm. I don't understand why I'm this cold when it's mid-July in the Deep South.

I'm moving now, toward the door and out into the brightly lit hospital corridor.

As the gurney begins moving, I hear a voice calling out my name. A familiar one. One I never hear other than on those obligatory phone calls on holidays and birthdays. The voice I've missed so much. I had wondered why she hadn't come to see me. But now she has.

"Wait!" the voice calls out. "That's my little sister. I have to see her before her surgery!"

A light of recognition emblazons me. If I had the strength, I'd jerk the covers up, fly off the gurney, and run down the hall to my big sister. Instead, I lie still as she comes to me.

The orderlies move aside, and soft brown eyes smile down at me. It's Gretchen. My big sis. The black sheep of our family who never comes home and whom no one really speaks about. The long-lost relative who retreated from our home to make her own in Boston, Massachusetts. But she's here. Now. Holding my hand and kissing the top of it. The big sis I looked up to so much when I was a little kid, so much so that I'd wear her clothes and jewelry and pretend to be her when she wasn't around. Now, she's here with me. Tears pool in the corners of her perfectly lined eyes, and she tightens her lips together.

"Mom called me yesterday," she whispers to me. "I got here as fast as I could."

My eyes flutter shut in blissful delight. "Gretch . . . you came."

"Nothing would have stopped me, Hay."

CHAPTER EIGHTEEN

*You gain strength, courage, and confidence by every experience
in which you really stop to look fear in the face.*

—ELEANOR ROOSEVELT

THE GURNEY IS MOVING again.

I watch as the ceiling panels pass by overhead; a fluorescent
light breaking up the tiles every now and then. We stop, and I
hear the *ding* of the elevator.

"We gotta go," one of the orderlies says.

"We love you, Hayley." Mom kisses me.

"I've got my watch set, Little Kid. I'll see you when you get
out." Dad squeezes my hand.

Cliff and Lily layer kisses on my forehead.

Gretchen stretches out over my chest and hugs me to her. "I
love you so much. Everything will be fine, Hay. I'm here for you."

Our hands entwine, and I sense the energy and love from
her pouring into me. Fingers drag smoothly against each other
as we're finally separated. The wheels begin moving, and soon
the tang of my sister's sweet perfume is but a memory. My skin
tingles in a good way. I'm still covered in my family's love like an
additional blanket on top of me.

Everyone has told me it's going to be all right. Why should I be worried, then?

When the elevator reaches its floor—*did we go up or down?*—I am being wheeled down another long corridor and into an area where a sign says Hospital Personnel Only. Double doors automatically open for us, and I'm pushed into a room full of people dressed in aqua scrub suits, masks, and hats. Gloved hands begin handling me, sliding me from the gurney onto the operating table.

"It's so cold in here," I say through chattering teeth.

A nurse with lots of mascara around her hazel eyes smiles down at me. "We have to keep the temperature low for sterile reasons. Don't worry, we'll get you more blankets."

I hear the clang of instruments being placed on the metal tray. Knives and stuff that are going to be slicing into me. Gack . . . Why am I thinking of things like that? Is there going to be a lot of blood? How will they clean it up? What will they do with it? Will I need a transfusion?

These are all questions I *should* have asked Dr. Dykema—or at least Dr. Stanislovitis—when I had the chance. Stupid me!

My eyes shift up, and I squint hard at the intensity. Gigamonic circular lights shine down on me. It's like a dentist's light on acid. I blink as I try to stare past it. Nothing but gray and white walls, hospital staffers, and the antiseptic smell of sterile cleansers.

My arms are shaking. My legs are quaking. My body quivers from head to toe.

The trembling isn't just from the temperature. I'm downright scared. Shitless. It's all finally hitting me. The first two surgeries were a simple piece of piss. This one is major.

What happens if Dr. Dykema opens up my leg and the tumor has taken over too much? Will he really take my leg? The nerves? The bones? I never thought of it before, but will I be able to walk again? Will I be able to cheer? Why hadn't I pressed these issues more? Was I truly in *that* much denial?

The nurses attach sticky pads with cords on them on each of my boobs and one right under my left one. Then they roll me to my side and place them on my back, as well. Some sort of monitors. There are so many of them now that I can't keep them straight. I just want them to keep putting blankets on me.

My pulse trills against my temple. My eyelids twitch in anticipation. When I'm back in place on the stretcher, I do my damnedest to slow down my frenetic heartbeat that now I hear echoing throughout the operating room.

I try to focus on what the angel said last night.

Everything will be just fine.

Similar words my sister whispered to me.

Everything has to be fine, and I'll be cheering again in no time.

I've earned this. I can't lose it before I've experienced it.

Fear shifts in my veins to utter frustration. This is the stupidest summer I've ever experienced. And it's absolutely the most ridiculous thing I've ever had to deal with. Cancer? At seventeen? Are you kidding me? I'm not going to be one of those people who has to have a benefit for them to raise money so they can get back to their regular life. I'm a cheerleader. I will cheer myself up. I *will* overcome this!

The angel said I would.

I know Mom and Dad had to sign a form giving Dr. Dykema permission to "do whatever is necessary" to save my life. However, no one is taking my leg.

No. One.

The medical staff flits around me connecting this, that or the other tube or wiring. Machines beep, whir, and hum. Are they all attached to me? So much technology.

My nose twitches. A fiery itch.

I pull my hand from under the covers and scratch away.

"Don't do that, Hayley," the nurse instructs in a calming voice.

"I have to . . ."

A rubber-gloved hand comes down on my nose. "I'll do it for you." She scratches for a moment and I'm fine.

It returns, though, and so does my hand, scratching away at the annoyance of this whole procedure. Fidgety frustration. Itchy irritation.

"I've got it," the nurse says, removing my hand once again.

The third time I reach for my nose, another person steps in to strap my hand down to the operating table.

My brain screams!

Echoes of panic fill me like I'm those caged animals at the zoo. Let them be free. Let me be free. Don't tie me down.

Yet the words won't leave my mouth. My tongue is heavy with the sedative.

I don't want this to be the end for me.

I don't want to lose my leg.

I don't want to . . . die.

I want to run. To escape. To bolt as far away as possible.

I will my feet to move and my legs to carry me out of here.

Nothing.

My body has betrayed me.

Or perhaps it knows what's best.

How can losing a bone, or, God forbid, a limb, be best?

What is the lesson in all of this?

Why me? *Why me, God?* Why not Chloe Bradenton?

No, I shouldn't think that. Why anyone?

I want to run. I want to escape. I want to disappear to a deserted island where no one can threaten me with surgery, chemo, amputation, cancer. The salt air will heal me.

In my mind, I'm fighting the hospital staff tooth and nail. I'm flailing about, screaming for my freedom and insisting that the diagnosis is incorrect. It really *is* just a calcium deposit exactly as Dr. Colley first said. I'm shaking, I'm screaming . . . but only in my head.

In reality, a small groan escapes my parched lips.

Before I can even wrap my muddled brain around this procedure any further, a masked man with amazing crystal blue eyes leans toward me. Even though I can't see his mouth, I sense that he's smiling at me. Then, I see the darker eyes of Dr. Dykema, so confident and assured in himself.

"Good morning, Hayley. We've got a long day ahead of us," the doctor says. "You just go to sleep, and I'll take care of everything."

I think I nod at him. I'm not sure.

The blue-eyed doctor tells me, "I'm going to put you to sleep now, Hayley. Just relax."

Easy for him to say. He's not the one strapped to an operating table.

He continues in a comforting voice. He almost sounds like Dad, which makes me take a deep breath and release the tension in my muscles. Dad is near. Mom is near. Cliff and Lily are with them. And Gretchen came home. They're all waiting for me.

Dr. Blue Eyes continues. "I want you to count slowly from a hundred to one. Can you do that for me?"

Another nod. *I think so.*

The overhead light reflects brightly on the tip of the silvery needle he holds up. The syringe is full of a clear liquid that is headed into the tube on my hand.

"Hayley, you're going to feel a slight burn, but it's nothing to be worried about. Start counting."

"Ahhhh-hundruuuud . . . ninnney-nine . . ."

"Good girl."

Searing heat moves into my hand and up my arm. It's as if the liquid has on a new pair of cleats and is running through my body as fast as it can . . . going where?

"Ninnney-ayyyyyyte . . ."

My ears ring from a phone call I cannot answer.

Buzzing. Darkness coming.

The magic elixir closes the curtains around my eyes. I am helpless to stop it.

God, please take care of me.

The blackness encompasses me.

CHAPTER NINETEEN

Pain is inevitable. Suffering is optional.

—BUDDHIST PROVERB

*U*_{gh}.

Where am I?

Owwwwwwwwww . . .

There are no words to describe the excruciating pain ripping through my body. Okay, so *excruciating* may be good enough. I try to wrap my brain around which particular adjectives my English teachers would want me to use here: agonizing, unbearable, terrible, awful, severe, sharp, painful, and just down right *hurting*.

Oh right. I'm in the recovery room.

I have no idea what time it is.

Or what day it is.

The oxygen mask is, again, tight on my face. My face is wet again. Tears, no doubt—tears I don't realize I've even shed.

I go to lift my hand; it feels as if it weighs fifty pounds. My fingers brush against the annoying oxygen mask, sweeping it off my face and away to the side. A nearby nurse places it back over my mouth and nose. I go through this dance with her a few times before she tucks my arms back under the covers and scolds me.

"This helps you wake up."

Wake up. From a dreamless sleep.

It seems as if only moments ago I was being told to count down from one hundred, and now I'm here.

I try to move. Anything. Nothing reacts to my brain waves.

Am I paralyzed?

No, I lifted my hand before.

I attempt to send a message from my mind to my legs. However, there's a heaviness weighing me down.

A man appears next to me pushing a bulky machine. I can't exactly describe it except it's gray and ominous looking. He moves my covers aside and they block my view of what he's doing to me. Whatever it is, it sends roaring pain through all of my extremities.

"Ouch!" I cry out. A lead apron is draped over me.

The nurse is at my side. "It's okay, sweetie. He's just taking some new films."

"Oh . . . okay . . ."

It's anything but okay. Tears cascade out of my eyes, dripping down into my hair.

Hummmm . . . click.

Hummmm . . . click.

Hummmm . . . click.

So many X-rays. It must be good, though, if he's taking pictures. My leg has to still be there, right?

He slides the machine away, removes the apron, and covers me back up. I think I pass out from the pain.

When my eyes lift again, I don't know how long it's been. I'm in a perpetual fog. A density that surrounds my senses from smell to sound to sight. To my left, the moans and groans of another patient fill the air. I wonder what this person is in for. Is he okay? Will he survive? I've survived to arrive at this point.

Of course, I'm breathing and alive, but am I whole?

My stomach plummets like a falling elevator. I remember the waiver my parents had to sign, and I begin to tremble uncontrollably. Slowly I slide my hand down the left side of my body, inch by torturous inch. A groan escapes from my windpipe as I try to lift myself. There's a mound of blankets over me, warming me, yes, but weighing me down and keeping me from shuffling about.

My hand only reaches to my kneecap . . . which is still there. My thoughts scatter, and I can barely keep them organized from the metronoming of my heartbeat.

Okay . . . I've got to get a message down to my left foot.

Move.

Move!

I'm telling the toes to wiggle, but are they doing it? Are they even still there?

Terror fills my lungs. My heart hammers away in my chest to the point where I feel as if the next beat could be the last. I breathe in the antiseptic aroma of the room through my nostrils, overtaking the freshness of the hissing oxygen.

Sheer panic takes over. Flashed images of living life in a wheelchair or hobbling around on a prosthetic leg amp up my dread. I can't cheer if there's nothing to cheer about.

My chest heaves up and down and my groans increase. I know I'm freaking out; yet I can't calm myself. I take the oxygen mask and chuck it across the room.

"Help me! Please . . . I want my leg back! Please . . ."

The nurse rushes to my side with the abandoned mask in her hand. "Shhh . . . there, there now. You're just fine. Just fine."

Through my uncontrollable sobs, I manage to get out, "My leg. I can't reach down far enough. Is my leg there? Please . . . please tell me . . ."

The kind nurse smooths my hair away from my face and dabs my tears with the back of her hand. "Shhh . . . you're just fine,

Hayley. Your leg is still there. You came through the surgery just fine. Dr. Dykema removed the tumor and your fibula. Now just calm down and breathe."

Your leg is still there.

Her words flit through my head.

I still have my leg.

I'm going to be okay.

Exhaustion and relief coat me in yet another blanket of warmth, and I relax into the bed, secure in the fact that I'll be able to cheer after all.

Thank you, God. Thank you for saving my leg.

* * *

"THERE'S MY GIRL," DAD says to me, who knows how much later.

I lift heavy lids to find my dad standing over me. I'm back in my hospital room where everyone is watching me and waiting. I try to form words, but my throat is arid. Instead, a long sigh releases from my chest.

Dad waves his hand in front of his face. "Phew! I'm going to pass out from all that gas on your breath."

I try to laugh with him. Everything hurts too much. Even my eyelashes feel sore.

"Hey, baby," Mom says from the other side of my bed. I crane my neck to meet her gaze. Her hand moves to mine and our fingers entwine instinctively.

My mouth opens. Nothing. I lick my lips and swallow hard at the dry clot. "Wh-wh-what time is it?" I finally eke out.

"It's almost five thirty," Dad reports.

"Seriously?"

"Your surgery was six hours and then you were in the recovery room for about an hour," Dad continues.

"Dr. Dykema came out to see us," Mom tells me. "He said he got the entire tumor out; however, he had to remove your fibula and part of your periosteal nerve."

She's speaking Swahili to me right now, although I did get the part about the tumor being gone.

"You're gonna be okay, kiddo," Cliff says from the end of my bed. Lily stands wrapped against him, smiling at me. I lift the corners of my mouth in recognition.

Someone's missing, though. Or was that just a sedative-induced dream? "Where's Gretchen?"

"I'm here, Hay." Mom adjusts to make room for my big sister. Gretchen takes the hand Mom's been holding and she squeezes tightly. "I'm here, Hay. I'm not going anywhere."

"Thanks," I say quietly.

Looking about, my entire family has aged while I've been under the knife. I feel like shit causing them such worry. Crinkles from loss of sleep surround Mom's eyes. Dad's beard has a day or two's growth. Cliff and Lily seem as if they haven't eaten a good meal all day. And Gretchen. She looks like the beautiful big sis I've always known, although it's been about three years since I've actually seen her in person.

"You came."

"As soon as Mom called to tell me what was going on. Had I known, I would have been here sooner." I'm not too groggy that I miss the exchange between my mother and sister that shows my sister's utter annoyance at being kept out of the family informational loop.

"Did you see my uniform?" I ask dreamily.

"Yeah! Mom said you're a varsity cheerleader. You'll be jumping and tumbling in no time," my sister says with such confidence in her eyes.

Yes. My leg was saved.

However, I'm minus a bone.
And part of my nerve.
My leg has been saved.
Thank you, Lord.
The question remains, what in the world is next for me?

CHAPTER TWENTY

My help cometh from the Lord which made heaven and earth.
He will not suffer thy foot to be moved: he that keepeth thee will
not slumber.

—Psalms 121: 2–3

I SLEEP THROUGH THE NIGHT and wake up the next morning to find Gretchen, not Mom, sleeping on the cot next to me.

"Good morning, sunshine," she says with a yawn when our eyes meet.

I stretch awake and feel less like I've been run over by a Mack truck. I still can't move my leg since it's all wrapped up in gauze and Ace bandages to keep it protected. It seems to be twice its natural size and feels like it's made of cement every time I try to lift it. I'm not complaining, though, because it's still there. Two tubes peek through the gauze where fluid is draining from my surgical area. I can't look at it as the thought of something still stuck in my leg like that skeeves me out. Thank heavens I've been asleep when the nurses have come in to empty them. The only thing I can see on my left side is my big toe poking out of the bandage. It just stares at me, unmoving, like it's not even mine.

Gretchen's eyes follow mine, and she moves to grab her purse. She pulls out a bottle of vibrant pink nail polish and moves to the foot of my bed. Slowly, she spreads the shiny paint onto my big toe, bringing it to life.

After it dries, I giggle when she takes a Sharpie and draws a smiley face into the pink.

"There," she says. "That's a whole lot better."

Rochelle sweeps into the room with a tray in her hand. "Now, I bet y'all someone in this room is powerful hungry."

"That would be me," I say in a hoarse voice.

"Oh no, sugar," she tells me. "You can't eat just yet. It's too soon. We had a tray ordered already, so I thought your momma or sister would like it."

I slump. "Oh. Sure."

The nurse sets the tray on my rolling table. Then she presses a few buttons on the bed to raise me up into a sitting position. Each squeak and hum of the bed makes my body ache at the motion.

"We need to get you up walking the hallway soon," my nurse tells me.

"I'll help her," Gretchen says.

Rochelle nods.

Gretchen sets about uncovering the plates. "Do you mind?"

"Go ahead," I say, wishing I couldn't smell the food. It's just too soon after my surgery for me to eat. There are scrambled eggs, grits, and apple juice. She salts and peppers the eggs slightly and stirs butter into the grits. Taking the spoon, she dips it first into the eggs and then into the grits and holds it up to her mouth to blow.

"You still like all of your breakfast food mixed together?" she asks.

I smile. "You remembered."

"I remember," she starts, "that we did that family breakfast at the church one Easter morning, and Cliff fussed at you for mixing your eggs, grits, and bacon all together."

"Yeah, it embarrassed him somehow." A bubble of laughter rises from me. "I told him it all gets mixed anyway."

Gretchen loads another spoonful. "Exactly."

I study my sister's face while she eats in silence. I remember the small mole on the side of her nose. It's covered with makeup. Her dark eyes are lined, and mascara touches her long lashes—lashes I always envied. Her brows are perfectly plucked, just like mine, since she's the one who taught me how to pluck them when I was ten years old. There's a tiny white scar at her hairline where she cut herself on a diving board when she was my age. She's twenty-seven now. Ten years older than I am. Worlds apart.

I finally break the silence. "Why have you been away so long, Gretch?"

She fingers the plastic wrap over the apple juice. "Oh . . . you know . . ."

"Actually, I don't. I haven't seen you since I was fourteen."

"I know."

"You stopped answering e-mails."

"I know."

"And you don't call me anymore."

"I know!" she says, tossing down my spoon. "I'm sorry, Hay. It's not you."

"Then what is it?"

"It's family stuff, you know?" Her chin drops, and she studies the juice where it rests on the table. "Stuff I did when I was young and stupid and influenced by the wrong friends."

"That was a long time ago," I say. "What happened to bygones being bygones?"

Her eyes lift. "It's not that simple, sweetie."

"Well, it should be. I think y'all are all being stubborn asses."

"Hayley!"

I watch Gretchen take the fork from the tray and scoop up

more eggs into her mouth. I hope her appearance here at the hospital isn't merely temporary. I want my sister back in my life. I need her—and the rest of my family—to help me get through the next phase of whatever this cancer has done to me.

"Where's Mom?" I ask.

"She went to Cliff's to get some sleep and to be with Dad. They texted that they'll be here in an hour. They're giving us some time together." She opens the bagel and takes a bite, chewing thoughtfully. "I'm sure it's been hell for Mom sleeping on that cot while you've been in the hospital."

"She hasn't left my side," I note.

"Because that's the kind of mother she is."

"I know."

"She feels it's her fault," Gretchen says.

"I know . . ."

"That she should have protected you better."

"So you two are talking?" I ask.

"While you were in surgery. We . . . talked for a little bit, mostly about you."

Something in Gretchen's eyes tells me she regrets the distance between her and our parents and how whatever dirty laundry is there has put a wedge in our own relationship. The words don't need to be spoken.

Gretchen moves the half-eaten breakfast away and pours me ice water in a plastic cup with a straw to help me keep hydrated. She then comes back to sit on the edge of my bed.

"Why don't I wash and style your hair for you. I bet you feel gross, huh?"

I tug my hand through my greasy tresses. "Yeah, a little."

"I'll fix you up," she says with a wink. "Let me go get a wheelchair and we'll get you in the bathroom."

My sister moves to the door and I feel her absence immediately.

"Gretch?"

"Yeah?"

"How long will you stay?"

Her eyes touch mine. "I'm not leaving until you're out of here."

* * *

LATER THAT AFTERNOON, THE nurses bring in water bottles that I have to blow air into, making the water go from one bottle to the next. It's supposed to help clear the anesthesia from my lungs so I won't get pneumonia. It's pretty funky and a little hard to do, but it has to be done. The last thing I need after all this time in the hospital is to get some other stupid illness that slows me down even further.

I'm working on the bottles for the third time with Dad supervising when Dr. Dykema and his team enter my room.

"There she is," he says in a cheerful way, quite different than his usual holier-than-thou attitude. "Have you been up walking around yet, Hayley?"

"Um . . . no. I can barely move as it is."

He comes over and checks the drains. "These can come out this afternoon, and then I want you up on your crutches walking the hallway."

"You got it, Doc," Dad says.

"So, what's the prognosis?" Mom asks. Of course, she's already consulted with Uncle Roger who's told her what to expect, but she's held off telling me anything and instead is letting me hear from my doctor.

"Yeah, when can I break out of here and go home?" I ask with great anticipation.

The doctor scratches his goatee, which means he has something very important to say. "I wish it were that simple, Hayley.

You see, your tumor was malignant to the point where it had reached your tibia. I scraped the side of your tibia, but in order to be sure we got all of the cancerous cells, we'll be following up your surgery with chemotherapy and radiation treatment."

I sigh. Dad presses my shoulder to calm me.

I'm thinking my newly set goal of making the first football game may be a pipe dream.

"We have you scheduled for five days of chemo, followed by five days of radiation." He flips through some notes on my chart. "Also, your recuperation and rehabilitation could take some time. I have a physical therapist arranged for you, and our team of psychologists is here for you in case you need to talk about any mental demons you're facing."

I can't help but snort my laughter. "Dr. Dykema, the only problem I have is that PHS's first football game is in two weeks."

"You're not going to make the first game," Dad says.

My face falls. Tears threaten to pour from my eyes.

Mom's face scrunches up. Dad speaks up again. "Do you think you'll really be up to cheering, Hayley? That's going to be very tiring for you."

"Yes, sir," I snap out. "I can do it." Then I pause with the realization and glance up at my doctor. "You're not telling me I can't cheer, are you? Because you can't tell me that. You can*not* tell me that."

Dr. Dykema frowns at me. "I didn't say that. I believe the exercise will be very good for you. However, I don't want you running or jumping on that leg."

"That's hard not to do if you're a cheerleader," Mom says.

"That's cool," I assure them. "I won't run and when I jump, I'll do everything on my right leg." I continue pleading my case. "Can't I do rehab stuff back home?"

Dr. Dykema nods. "Your parents and I will talk it over and work something out."

"They have a great gym at her school and a new conditioning coach for the football team. I'm sure he can help," Dad says. "Maybe we can talk to a physical therapist, and then we can put her on a work out regime there."

"That's possible," the doctor says.

"How are you feeling after the surgery, Hayley?"

I look at my doctor, unsure of the proper answer to this question. "Um . . . sore. Tired. Hungry. Impatient."

He gives me a long blink over his reading glasses. "All very valid feelings. I'm talking more about depression, anger, and those sorts of things."

I have had moments of depression and self-pity. Who wouldn't in this situation? I always seem to talk myself out of it, though. What more could a psychiatrist do for me? "No, sir. Honestly, I just want to get home and back to my life. That would be the most awesome therapy for me right there. This—this thing is now out of me, so the best thing for me to focus on is being able to walk and run and jump again."

"I have to be very honest with you, Hayley. I had to resect a portion of your periosteal nerve as it was woven into the tumor."

"What's that?" I ask before my parents can.

"It's the nerve that aids in lifting your foot and moving it from side to side. There's no guarantee that you'll be able to walk normally again."

I hold my hand up. "I'm not hearing that," I say sternly. "I will walk just fine. All I need to do is exercise and stuff. I will walk, and I'll do it like I always have."

Dr. Dykema actually smiles at me, and then he turns to my parents. "You have a very strong girl here. We'll work with you on a fitness schedule for at-home rehabilitation. Our therapists are available twenty-four/seven if you ever need them."

"Thank you, Doctor," Mom says. "We'll keep that in mind."

Not that I'm perfect or Miss Goody Two Shoes or think it's bad to talk to a professional or anything—that's not it at all. I merely want to get back to my life. It's *really* that simple. I could scream or cry or throw things. That's not going to change anything.

"Two more weeks, huh?" I ask.

He nods.

"I'm going to miss cheering for the first game. That totally sucks."

"It can't be helped," the doctor says.

"It's an away game, Hay," Mom notes. "You'll be there for the first home game, though, and that's more important."

"I suppose," I say, trying to breathe through the pain of actually missing a game.

Dr. Dykema pats the bed. "I am working to get you out of here. In the meantime, follow your nurses' directions and get moving up and down the hallway."

"Yes, sir," I say.

"I wish all of my patients had your attitude, Hayley. Recovery is mostly a mental thing. You're going to need to keep up that positive attitude to fully recover."

It sounds like a compliment, but there's also something ominous in his words.

"I'll do what I have to."

CHAPTER TWENTY-ONE

Every tomorrow has two handles. We can take hold of it by the handle of anxiety, or by the handle of faith.

—HENRY WARD BEECHER

WE'RE MOVING YOU, HAYLEY," Ginger tells me Sunday afternoon.

I look up from my laptop where I've been rewatching a YouTube video that Lora sent me of the routine the squad took to camp. Sadly, I'm not with them, but thankfully there hasn't been any more talk about replacing me on the squad.

"Where am I going?" I ask.

"They're moving you off the orthopedic floor to the general hospital area."

My bottom lip pokes out. "Does that mean I'm losing you and Rochelle?"

She cocks her red head. "You'll be fine. They've got a great staff down on the fourth floor."

This totally blows. I love my nurses, and they've really been here for Mom and me. It's a move in the right direction, though. I'll get this chemo and radiation over, and then I can get home. I won't even think about that first game against Emmanuel High. It's on their turf, anyway. This way, I'll make my debut on our home field. I'm already memorizing these dance moves in my head for when I can start performing them.

"They're moving you, Hay," Gretchen reports as she bursts into the room.

Mom rushes in behind her and shoves a Hallmark card in front of me. "Here, sign this. I also got a lovely box of chocolates from the gift shop for Ginger and Rochelle for all their wonderful help."

"Awww, that's sweet," I say as I nab my pen. I write a gushing thanks to my nurses and sign my name and a smiley face.

Gretchen and Mom pack up my few belongings and all of the get-well cards scattered around the room. I gather my e-reader, computer, cell phone, and all of my other personal items into my backpack, ready to move to the new room. Mom does the same with her stuff, too. Soon, an orderly shows up with a wheelchair to take me to the new digs with Mom and Gretchen in tow.

I say goodbye to the room that's been my home for the last month. At the nurses' station, Ginger and Rochelle both give us hugs and thank us for the candy. A lump surrounds my throat as I'm being wheeled away; emotions clogging and choking me. I want to cry, but I don't know why. It's not that I'm sad to leave the room. It's just that so much has happened to change me and the course of my life in the last few weeks. I haven't worried about pool parties, tan lines, or college applications this summer. This has been some heavy shit to deal with, even if I haven't allowed myself to truly let it sink in.

If I do dwell on it or slush around the details too much, I might actually need those psychologists Dr. Dykema has set up for me.

Positive. Focus on the positive.

It's hard to, though, when I replay the dance video in my head, marveling at how awesome the squad looks. My pulse trips up a notch knowing they're at camp without me. I wonder, too, if I'll be able to return to tumbling. Will I have the same flexibility I did before? Will I still be able to lift Lora over my head? And what about this whole thing about some of my nerve being removed? Dr. Dykema never talked about that before. Is that going to keep me from cheering? It can't!

Nothing can.

Seriously. I've come this far. What more do I have to endure?

Once I'm settled in my new bed—the room's layout is the mirror image of the room I was in before—I get to hear more of what's to come for me when Dr. Stanislovitis walks in with another doctor. This guy is tall, completely good-looking (in an older-guy way), and has chocolate brown eyes.

"Hi, Hayley. I'm Dr. Sampson. I'll be administering your chemotherapy."

"Okay," I say, smiling at him. Cheekily, I think he can administer anything he wants to me.

He takes the chair next to me, and I sense there's about to be a flirting buzz kill.

Mom moves to my side, as does Gretchen. I watch as my sister lowers her eyes at Dr. Sampson, too, in a totally flirtatious way. I hope we can concentrate on what he's here to talk about.

Dr. Sampson goes through the motions of explaining what they're going to do.

"We'll insert a needle into your aorta artery in your groin area and thread a tube down to your knee so the chemotherapy is directed right at the spot where your tumor was."

I cringe at the words "groin area" and the thought that doctors and nurses will be examining me . . . there. How mortifying! Heat spreads across my face at the mere thought.

"And that will drip in her for five days?" Mom asks.

The cute doctor nods. "We'll check it at three days to see if the full course has gone in. Five days is standard, and then you can check out of the hospital."

Energy bolts me upright. "Like go home?"

"Well, you'll have your radiotherapy as an outpatient."

I slump again. The calendar has flipped. Time is running out. School is about to start.

"Now, Hayley," he begins, "I must talk to you about the side effects of the chemotherapy."

I gulp down. Oh right . . . side effects. Like . . . bad shit.

My hands begin shaking and the pain of the incision on my leg intensifies momentarily. I've been good about not asking for too many pain shots, but I just might need one now.

Dr. Sampson continues. "The most common side effects are depression, extreme fatigue, nausea, diarrhea, constipation, vomiting, dehydration, and most of all, hair loss or hair thinning. You can also experience brittle nails, acid reflux, dry mouth, dry skin, infertility, headaches, weight loss or weight gain, and other symptoms."

Ack! He sounds like one of those commercials on television for this, that, or the other drug that has horrendous side effects to the point where you wonder why anyone would actually take it. While I hear him list everything, I can't wrap my mind around the reality of each symptom. I'm on information overload and I just want to run screaming from the room, from this cute doctor, and from everything I have to face. But that would be running away from my reality.

Besides, I'm not actually in the most optimal flight condition.

"We can monitor you and medicate any of these issues as they arise. Most side effects take place a few weeks after your treatment is completed."

What can I say? I have no choice. My cancer was malignant, and they have to be sure it doesn't spread anywhere else. That's the important thing.

I shrug my understanding. "So, we'll get started tomorrow?"

"That we will," Dr. Sampson says. "We'll see you in the morning."

I'll see what happens then.

* * *

THE PROCEDURE TO GET the chemotherapy tube inside me was humiliating!

Not only was cute Dr. Sampson doing it, but a not-so-nice nurse named Mae with long fingernails shaved my . . . er . . . private area before the doctor made the incision in my groin area and slid the tube into place. Thank heavens I couldn't feel it moving inside of me. Now *that* would have been too out-of-a-horror-movie creepy for me.

Now I sit in my bed, unable to move too much because of the potent chemicals pouring into my leg.

My new nurse, Rachel Mary, comes and checks on the fluid levels several times a day, in addition to checking my vitals and making sure I'm doing well, in general. I'm glad she's taking care of me instead of Mae with the claws.

On that long list of side effects, I'm totally experiencing the nausea and upset-stomach part.

"Can you eat some soup?" Rachel Mary asks.

I shake my head, cringing at the thought of eating anything. The smell of the noodles makes me want to puke. I gag at the salty smell, and the nurse moves quickly to get me a bedpan.

Ugh . . . not pretty.

She just smiles, hands me a wet rag, and cleans up my mess.

God love her—and all of these nurses—for taking care of me. Did I mention I'm using a bedpan because I can't get up? Seriously, there's no way to be modest when you're in the hospital.

It's Wednesday afternoon, and I'm bored shitless. If I watch one more talk show, I'll go ballistic. Soap operas are stupid and badly acted. I refuse to watch the news and hear other people's sad stories. Mine is pathetic enough.

I'm starting to think this positive thinking isn't going to work. Anger creeps down my arms, causing my hands to fist. The powerful chemical zipping through my blood system is changing me, eating away at me, taking a piece of me with it as it attempts to cleanse.

"What's wrong, Hayley?" Gretchen asks. She's got a Diet Coke for me. I hope I'll be able to stomach it.

Irritation, rage, and resentment are my bedmates, and I sense my boiling point has been reached. "What's *wrong?* What the hell is right?"

My sister's eyes widen, and I can see she's taken aback.

"What's right in my life? I'm immobile in a hospital bed three hours from home. Two hours from where cheerleader camp is going on as we speak. But no, I'm not there, participating with my squad like I always dreamed of. I'm in a fricking hospital bed, puking my guts up because I have *cancer!* Cancer! How stupid is that? Cancer!"

Gretchen attempts to smooth out the situation. "Calm down, sweetie."

I slam my fists to the bed. The IV bags rock back and forth on their perch.

"Calm down? I've been calm since the moment this was discovered. I've handled this the best way I can, but today, I am pissed. That's what I am. Pissed off. Pissed off at whoever or whatever gave me this. Pissed off at all the doctors and nurses. Pissed off at this frickin' chemo that's making me feel this way. I haven't eaten, and my leg hurts like holy hell. I just want this over with!" I don't even realize how loudly I'm speaking. Gretchen's face is ashen as she has no idea how to handle me right now.

I don't know how to handle me right now.

I want to lash out. I want others to hurt. I don't want to be the only one in pain.

"And you . . ." I say to my sister, turning my ire on her. "Why did it take frickin' *cancer* to get you home? Would you have even come back in May for my graduation? Or just for the heck of it? Why did it take a family disaster to get you out of Boston?"

The nerve in Gretchen's neck twitches. "Hayley, I'm here for you. I know you're going through a horrible thing, and I just want to support you because you're my little sister and I love you."

"You have a horrible way of showing it," I snap.

"I apologize for being absent and not keeping in — "

"Absent? It's like no one knows anything about you or your life. I don't even know what you do for a living. Do you even have a job? A boyfriend? I know nothing about you."

Tears fill my sister's eyes, and I've got my sick wish. Someone else is hurting. However, I'm the cause. Damn this medicine churning through me and fueling my bad attitude.

"I'll tell you anything you want, Hayley," Gretchen says with a sniff. "I can't change the past. All I can do is make the present bearable and be here for you."

I drop my head, and my long hair surrounds my face in a curtain of shame. I want to cry, but I don't think my body is hydrated enough to produce tears.

"I'm sorry," I say in a whisper.

Gretchen is on the bed with me, hugging me tightly to her and rocking us back and forth.

"You have nothing to be sorry for, kiddo. You're going through hell. No kid should have to go through this at all. You have us, though." She takes my hands in hers. "You have *me*."

The words are so quiet that I almost don't know I've said them. "Please don't leave."

"I won't, sweetie."

We hold each other, and I let a few tears of frustration and humiliation fall onto my sister's designer shirt. This is how Dad finds us when he comes into the room.

"Everything okay here?"

My sister and I pull apart. "Just some sisterly bonding," Gretchen says, and steps away.

Dad replaces her and runs his hand over my forehead. "How are you feeling, Little Kid?"

"Nauseated, yet hungry."

He reaches into his pocket and withdraws a slightly smushed Snickers bar. "I read online that chocolate is a good thing to fight off the nausea. Wanna try?"

"Should I?"

Dad waggles the chocolate bar at me, and a smile takes over on my face, replacing my dour behavior. I snag the treat, rip open the packaging, and take a bite. The sugary sweetness crashes together with the saltiness of the peanuts and gooey goodness of the nougat and caramel. I moan my pleasure as it goes down nicely into my stomach and doesn't cause World War III. It's very simply the most delicious thing I've ever eaten in my life.

"That's my girl," Dad says with a smile.

"It's not making me sick."

"That's a good sign. I'll sneak in some more for you."

"Thanks so much, Daddy," I say with a mouthful of candy. "You're the best."

God knows the sacrifices he's making being here this week. I don't even ask who's watching the store or feeding Leeny. Dad's the man. He's doing it all. Working. Traveling. Probably gobs more that I don't even know about.

He's taken care of everything. He's taking care of me.

A lot of kids in school have problems with their parents, that is, if both of them are even around. Ashlee's mom is an alcoholic and her dad forgets to make regular child support payments. That sucks for her. Skipper O'Rourke's mom died from heart failure when he was eleven. Shelly's 'rents are divorced. Even my partner, Lora, and her mom are by themselves. That's why she's so close to her Uncle Ross. I guess family is what you make it. Mine's not perfect, but they're there.

I always took for granted that Mom and Dad were there for me, reliable, and just parents.

I look at Dad now as he takes my empty Snickers wrapper from me and tosses it over to the garbage can like an NBA player.

I'll never take my parents for granted ever again.

CHAPTER TWENTY-TWO

Courage is being afraid but going on anyhow.

—DAN RATHER

FRIDAY CAN'T COME FAST enough.

Not only does Dr. Sampson remove the tube out of my aorta, but Rachel Mary removes the *sixty-three* staples from my leg. Ouch! No wonder my leg hurt so much. I'll admit, though, it didn't hurt when she flipped them out; rather, it tickled like all get-out.

I finally get a good glimpse of the slicing and dicing of my leg. The scar runs from next to my kneecap all the way down to my ankle. There are smaller scabby scars where the two drains had been inserted. My calf muscle is about half the size it used to be. Dr. Dkyema had to cut out some muscle along with everything else. The skin is tight and pulls whenever I try to flex, so I guess I won't do that.

While I'm walking the hallway with Rachel Mary carefully monitoring my progress, I decide to try and put some weight on my left side.

"Son of a—owwww!" Yeah, not a good idea.

My foot touched the ground, but soon the hot, searing pain

shot up my leg all the way to my stomach. It feels as if my leg will split open right down the fresh seam.

Rachel Mary steps in. "Oh, honey, now don't you be putting any weight on that leg until you're told to. We just need you up and moving in the hallways with your crutches."

I nod at her words, feeling idiotic for pushing myself too hard. It'll have to be done one day, though.

When Rachel Mary and I make it back to the room, Mom has my things packed up and Dr. Sampson is there reviewing the chart.

"How's your groin today?" he asks, in reference to the suture he made.

"Fine, how's yours?" I ask, not even thinking.

OMG! I totally made this man blush. He pretends not to hear what I said, which is probably better. I don't know what got into me. Maybe knowing he's currently filling out my walking (or hobbling, rather) papers has me giddy from head to toe.

I slip back into bed and lift my leg up onto the blanket. Gretchen and Lily redecorated my big toe last night using blue polish and drawing silvery fireworks with sparkly glue-on beads. It's quite fabulous for a single-toed pedicure.

I dress in the same pair of shorts and T-shirt I wore the day I checked in. My leg is still wrapped in an Ace bandage for protection, and my crutches are more than likely going to be my constant companions for a while. I thank Dr. Sampson and Rachel Mary for all their help and slide into the wheelchair that awaits me.

The orderly wheels me down the corridor and to the elevator. It's an amazing feeling to be going down into the massive hospital structure instead of to one of the various examining or operating rooms on the higher floors.

Cliff is waiting for us at the patient loading and unloading zone in his Jeep Cherokee. Mom and Gretchen hop in back and let me take the front seat.

"Wow, this is the first time I've been out since I went to Birmingham High School's cheerleader practice."

"It's been a while," Mom says from the back seat.

Cliff pulls off into traffic and turns on to the interstate toward his apartment. I squint up at the bright August sun beating down on us. I feel like I should shield my eyes from it like a vampire who's been caught in the light after dawn.

Ten minutes later, we're at Cliff's apartment, which is fortunately on the first floor. I settle into the couch as Mom, Gretchen, and Cliff bring my stuff in. I hate being this helpless, but there's not exactly anything I can do about it at this point.

"Why can't we go home?" I ask.

"Since you start your radiotherapy on Monday, it just made sense to stay in Birmingham," Mom says. "Your dad's also on his way up. He's about an hour away."

"He must know I-65 by heart now," Cliff says, handing me my backpack and purse.

I hear my phone beep and see several texts from Lora:

WHAT UP?
SCHOOL STARTS ON MONDAY
MISS U
TXT ME!

My heart sinks to my one painted toe and slowly rises back to pound out my fretfulness. I don't understand why we couldn't have gone home to Maxwell even for the weekend. I should just be happy that my brother lives so close to the hospital and we have a free place to stay.

"Hayley, you'll sleep here on the sofa where you'll have more room to stretch. Your father and I will take the guest room, if that's okay."

"Mom, you've been sleeping on a crappy hospital couch for weeks. Of course it's okay," I say.

Instead of wallowing in self-pity and thoughts of why couldn't we do whatever, I nab my phone and text my partner.

```
OUT OF HOSPITAL FINALLY!
HEY U! CONGRATS!
HOW WUZ CAMP?
2ND PLACE BEHIND JOSIAH HILLCREST
BLECK.
WISH U COULD B @ SKOOL MONDAY
ME 2. RADIATION STARTS THEN
DANIEL ASKED @U
OH YEAH?!?!?!?!
ASKED WHEN U'D B BACK
Y DIDN'T HE TXT ME?
SAID HE DIDN'T WANT 2 BOTHER U
OMG WHAT A DORK
I NO
I'LL TXT HIM.
OK. CALL ME L8R IF U WANT!
HUGS!
```

I scroll into my address book and find Daniel's number. I choose Send MMS Message and start typing:

```
GUESS WHO'S OUT OF THE HOSPITAL? :)
HAYLEY!
DANIEL!
```

R U HOME?

NOT YET

WHEN R U BACK?

1 MORE WK

R U MISSING THE 1ST GAME?

:(

THAT SUX

:(

HOW WUZ SURGERY?

GOOD. I'M ON THE MEND

AWESUM

HOW'S FOOTBALL PRACTICE

AWESUM. WE'LL KICK ASS THIS YR

CAN'T WAIT!

CAN U CHEER?

TRY TO STOP ME

C U SOON!

CAN'T WAIT

And I can't! Everything is falling back into place. My leg is on the mend, I'm finishing up my treatment, and I'll miss only one week of school. Not bad.

"Mom? Can I finally try on my new uniform?"

"I don't see why not," she shouts from the kitchen.

"I'll get it for you," Gretchen says.

Using my crutches, I swing down the hallway to Mom's room so I can change in private. Gretchen brings me the white uniform and lays it on the bed. It's so crisp and fresh and new. Made just for me. I trace my fingers over the double-stitched "PHS" on the front. The blue and red mesh together perfectly, as do the swishes of color trim around the neckline. The skirt is short and has a flair that's been starched and ironed. My pulse begins to race just thinking of actually performing for the crowd in this outfit.

"How exciting," my sister says.

"Totally."

"Listen, Hay," Gretchen says. "Now that you're out of the hospital, I've got to get back to Boston."

"Why?" I say in a high-pitched whine.

Gretchen steps toward me. "I've got my job. My life. I can't be gone forever."

"What do you even do?" I ask, not able to remember what job she has these days. I remember she was a waitress for a while in college, then a bartender in a club. She worked for an airline for a year or two, and for a computer company.

She snickers. "I manage mutual funds for Reliable Financial. We don't get a lot of vacation time, but my boss understood that I had to be here for you."

"That was nice of him."

"Her."

"Whatever," I say, hanging my head. I was just getting used to having Gretchen here, and now she's buzzing off again.

Her finger finds my chin, and I glance up into the face I wish I could see more. "Hey . . . I'll be back, okay?"

"When?"

"Thanksgiving. How's that?"

My eyes widen. "You're actually going to come to a Matthews' holiday event?"

"For you, anything," she says with a glowing smile.

I can't help but ask. "Are things better with you, Mom, and Dad?"

"We didn't murder each other." Her laughter chokes her up.

"That's a start."

She spreads her arms. "You know I love you. And you can call me *any*time — day or night — seriously."

Warm in her embrace, I merely shake my head up and down.

Gretchen kisses me on the head and lets me go. "You're going to be an awesome cheerleader."

"Thanks, Gretch. Thanks for being here."

She blows me a kiss and closes the bedroom door.

It takes a bit of effort on my own, but soon I'm decked out in my PHS Patriots uniform. The top fits me perfectly in the boobage and midriff area. The skirt is a little loose because I've lost weight in the hospital. No worries, that bulk package of Snickers bars I've been noshing will help take care of that problem.

I glance in the mirror and scrutinize my appearance.

From the knees up, I look perfectly normal. Dark brown eyes staring back at me, long brown hair brushed straight to my elbows, and a smiling face — an excited grin meant for cheerleading. Then my eyes shift — down past my knees, down to the bandage-encased leg that's seen so much attention these past two months. In my new shoes, courtesy of Lora's Uncle Ross, I stand tall, putting all of my weight on my right leg and holding my left foot just up off the ground.

I hop.

Once.

I wince.

I try again.

Another wince.

Falling back onto the bed, I rip at the Ace bandage, unwinding it away from me until I can see my left leg in its entirety. It's scrawny, scarred, scabbed, and I have very little feeling from my ankle to my toes.

"Bleck," I say to no one. I look horrid, as though I just got out of the hospital. How am I going to cheer like *this*?

I sigh and then take a deep breath to calm my frustration. I'll make this work. I *have* to make it work. I promised the doctor I wouldn't run or jump on my left leg, so I won't. That puts the onus on my right side.

What will I do with my crutches?

I suppose I can keep them nearby when I cheer.

I throw my hands up in disgust and stick my tongue out at myself in the mirror. Sure, from the knees up, I look the part of a perky cheerleader. From the knees down . . . *sigh.*

This is a disaster.

I suddenly remember how Lora's Uncle Ross told me how he took lemons and made lemonade out of his college injury. The guy messed up his knee and now he runs marathons. Thing is, I'm not exactly a lemonade fan.

I don't know how I'm going to make this work, but I will do my damndest.

CHAPTER TWENTY-THREE

Life's a voyage that's homeward bound.

—Herman Melville

DAD ARRIVES THAT NIGHT in time for burgers and dogs that Cliff grilled out on the balcony and to say goodbye to my sister. They hug reluctantly, and then she pulls away. With a wave and blown kisses, my sister is gone. I hope it's not three years before I see her again.

"Something smells delicious," Dad says to break the silence. He seems overly tired, and the stress lines in his forehead seem a bit deeper. I have to remember that he just put in a three-plus-hour drive, in rush hour.

"Burger or hot dog?" Cliff asks.

"Both," Dad says.

"Me too," I echo, knowing it will be a miracle if I can eat anything. The chemo really nauseates me beyond belief. Very little seems appetizing except the chocolate bars from Dad. Even though the smell of most things now makes me gag, I reach for a grilled wiener and put it on a bun. I pour some ketchup on and then layer on some mayonnaise to make it just right.

Dad sits next to me at the table and slides a Diet Coke in my direction. "I went to the school yesterday and got your class schedule for you." He reaches down into his bag and withdraws a manila folder.

"Oh wow! Thanks!"

Seeing the official PHS crest with my classes is the equivalent of the light at the end of the tunnel. I'm *almost* out of it. I glance over what my senior year will be like: AP English Literature, French II, AP Economics, AP Chemistry II, Journalism, and Cheerleading/Physical Education. It's a schedule worthy of any college application and enough to keep me busy and challenged.

When we finish eating, we all retire to the den and spread out on Cliff's large sectional sofa. I take the end with the chaise so I can put my leg up on the cushions. While the rest of my family tunes in to some reality show du jour, I crank up my laptop for some Facebook catching up.

It's a bit depressing reading everyone's status updates. They're talking about school, buying new clothes, or taking final vacations. Like Daniel.

His Facebook reads, "Headed to PC with the boyz for final summer weekend."

Hmm . . . PC means Panama City, which is only an hour and a half away from Maxwell. I hope Daniel doesn't find some cute girl there who isn't scarred from surgery and walking on crutches.

My lips pout even more when I see pictures Lora posted. Apparently, Ross just completed some mountain-climbing hike of Mount Rainier in Washington with a group Game On sponsored. It's not his group's healthiness or feat that saddens me; rather, it's Lora posed by the convertible Beamer Ross gave her when he got back. Seems he's driving a Hummer now and the BMW was wasting away in his garage. After all the money Mom and Dad have more than likely spent on my hospitalization, I dare not even hope for a car of my own for senior year or to go off in to college.

Stupid fricking cancer.

Then my mind shifts to Ross talking about being positive. He's one crazy adventurous guy.

When I'm fully recovered, I want to do something awe-inspiring like him. I want to climb a mountain or go skiing down a black diamond run or go parasailing over shark-infested waters—something just to prove I can do it. And I *will* do it.

I decide to post a status:

"Out of hospital, on the mend, will be home next week to cheer the Patriots on!"

There. Something positive.

Within seconds, I have four "likes" from Lora, Tara, Ashlee, and Madison and a few "Awesome" and "Cool" comments. My spirits lift with each post, and I can't wait to see my friends again.

Suddenly, a chat box pops up from Gabriel Tremblay:

GABRIEL TREMBLAY: HEY HAY!

HAYLEY MATTHEWS: HEY G!

GABRIEL TREMBLAY: COOL THAT YOU'RE OUT OF THE HOSPITAL

HAYLEY MATTHEWS: YEAH, I THINK I WAS GETTING BED SORES. LOL!

GABRIEL TREMBLAY: I CAN IMAGINE

GABRIEL TREMBLAY: WILL YOU BE AT SCHOOL MON?

HAYLEY MATTHEWS: NO. RADIATION STARTS.

GABRIEL TREMBLAY: BUMMER. YOU WON'T MISS MUCH. LET ME KNOW IF YOU NEED ME TO E-MAIL YOU HOMEWORK OR ANYTHING

HAYLEY MATTHEWS: THAT'S REALLY SWEET. THX

GABRIEL TREMBLAY: WHAT HAPPENS
AFTER RADIATION?
HAYLEY MATTHEWS: I COME HOME!
GABRIEL TREMBLAY: WHAT ABOUT REHAB?
HAYLEY MATTHEWS: I'LL DO IT MYSELF.
GABRIEL TREMBLAY: GOOD ATTITUDE.
I CAN HELP YOU WITH A WORKOUT IF
YOU NEED IT, SINCE I'LL BE DOING IT
FOR THE FOOTBALL TEAM, TOO.
HAYLEY MATTHEWS: THAT'S COOL OF
YOU. I'LL TAKE YOU UP ON IT.
HAYLEY MATTHEWS: HEY, GABRIEL, I
NEED TO RUN. NEED TO HEAR WHAT MY
PARENTALS ARE DISCUSSING.
GABRIEL TREMBLAY: SNEAKY?
HAYLEY MATTHEWS: A BIT. ☺ TTYS!
GABRIEL TREMBLAY: TAKE CARE OF
YOURSELF, HAY!

I close the lid of my laptop and reach for the TV remote to mute the rerun of some cop show. Cliff left earlier for Lily's, so it's just the three of us. Mom and Dad are sitting at the dimly lit dining room table with their heads bent together. I swear I see Mom wipe away tears from her eyes. Is something wrong? Something about my surgery? Something they're not telling me?

I scooch over on the couch, staying low, and straining my ear to listen. I hate eavesdropping like this, but if it has to do with me, I deserve to know. Peeking through the cushions, I watch as Dad scrubs his face with his hands.

"I don't know what else to tell you, Nan. I had to let Kirk and Jamaal go. The business just isn't bringing in enough revenue for me to keep them on full time."

"Which means we'll now have to pay their unemployment," Mom whispers.

"It is what it is, Nan."

"Why is this happening now?" Mom pleads.

"The economy sucks, and people aren't shopping in small towns anymore. Helen Cargill at the fabric store next door put a For Sale sign up in the window of her store yesterday. Mom-and-pop businesses are the way of the past, and I can't compete with the corporate giants in Montgomery, Dothan, Birmingham, or even as far as Atlanta. Everyone wants things quick and discounted, and Matthews Hardware isn't about that. Sales are down across the board."

Mom starts to speak, but she spots me. She quickly shifts into Happy Mother Mode and calls out to me, "Everything okay, Hayley?"

"You tell me," I say back.

"Fine, just fine. Your dad and I are catching up on things." Hmm . . . she's never been a good liar. I can see right through her. I'll let it go for now. "Everything's just fine," she repeats.

Fine. Really, Mom?

Is it?

* * *

BRIGHT AND EARLY MONDAY morning, Mom and I use Cliff's car to go downtown to the Lurleen B. Wallace Radiation Therapy and Cancer Institute at UAB where I'm going for my outpatient radiotherapy.

Radiotherapy—what a weird term, like I need help listening to the radio or something.

Where these thoughts come from, I have no idea!

Mom holds the door open for me as I swing through on my

crutches. We wander around the state-of-the-art treatment center named for the only female American governor to die while in office. Poor woman had something like three kinds of cancer that her husband and her doctors hid from her at first because back then you just didn't talk about things like that. Honestly! Thank God my parents and I didn't play games with each other.

We climb into the elevator and hit the button. Mom lets out a rather choppy sigh, and I stare at her.

"I feel like I'm descending into hell," she says.

"We're going up," I say, trying to break the tension.

"Figuratively, Hayley."

We reach the proper office and sign in. They promise the wait time won't be very long—famous last words in a doctor's office. I don't know why they bother actually scheduling people for a set time, because they can't ever stick to it.

The waiting room is full, and I'm clearly the youngest patient in the area. All eyes turn to me as I swing on my crutches over to a small couch that Mom and I share. The TV is muted, and everyone seems to be thumbing through magazines in the most uninterested manner. These are my fellow sufferers, though; my kinsmen. Everyone is here for radiation treatment of something. Will we all survive? Are there those among us who won't?

I bite my thumbnail as Mom fidgets in her seat. If I know her—and I do—she's finding it hard *not* to strike up a conversation with a total stranger. That's just how she is.

Sure enough, after a moment, Mom turns to a grandmotherly type woman who sits across from us clutching a rosary.

Mom leans forward. "Have you been waiting long?"

The old woman looks up with soft hazel eyes. "My husband is in right now," she says. Her gaze shifts to me and my bandaged leg. "You poor thing. Cancer?"

I shrug like it's no big deal. "They took it out. This is just follow-up treatment."

"God bless you, sweetie." She looks around the room at the other patients. "How in the world do you even get cancer? I don't understand what causes it."

I'm sure if Uncle Roger were here, he'd regale her with all the proper medical points. I don't have the first freaking clue. I'm still asking myself the same question.

A man in overalls speaks up. "I smoked for twenty years. The doctors suppose that's how I got lung cancer."

The old woman shakes her head. "No . . . that's not it. My husband doesn't smoke at all."

A woman close to Mom's age says, "My husband drank a lot. I'm sure that had something to do with his cancer."

Again, the old woman isn't satisfied. "See, my husband doesn't drink at all. Never has."

"I've been angry most of my life," a third person says. His face is red as he says it, probably pissed off at the cancer itself. "They say anger and stress can harm your body. Maybe my constant irritation with everything caused my tumor."

The old woman gives another dismissive head bob. "My husband is the most kind and gentle soul. He never gets angry at anyone. That can't be it."

I can't stop myself. "Ma'am, if you don't mind my saying"—I smile—"I think I know what caused your husband's cancer."

Her eyes widen. "You do?"

"Yes, ma'am. I think his halo is on too tight."

There's dead silence, but only for a millisecond. Then everyone in the waiting room bursts out into healthy laughter. I giggle at my joke, and the old woman chuckles heartily into a tissue until her eyes are filled with tears.

"Good one," the smoker man says.

"I needed that," another woman says.

The old woman gives me a look that tells me I shouldn't have said that, but she loves me dearly for it. "You've got a clever girl there," she says to Mom.

"Sometimes a little too much," Mom says. Her cheeks are three shades of crimson.

Saving me, a woman on staff comes out and announces, "Hayley Matthews?"

"Good luck, everyone," I say, and follow the woman wearing scrubs with SpongeBob SquarePants on them. The old woman waves to me.

"I'm Tracy," she says, escorting us back into the radiotherapy room.

Like pretty much every other room I've been in at the UAB hospital, it's frickin' freezing in here. Chill bumps dance across my bare arms and down my legs, not only due to the massive air conditioning, but also the trepidation tripping through my system. I'm entering yet another alien world.

Using a small step stool, I climb up onto the black table covered with a thin quilting top. In front of me in the sterile room is something I can only describe as an overgrown Mr. Coffee on steroids. Seriously! It's humongoid! Only, the place where the coffeepot should go is where I'll be lying down. *That's* going to shoot me up with radioactive waves?

I must shudder noticeably, because the technician seeks to soothe me.

"It's a little intimidating, isn't it?" Tracy asks with a laugh. "Don't worry, Hayley. I'll explain everything to you before we do any of the radiation. I want to make you as comfortable as possible."

"I don't know if you can," I say through gritted teeth.

Tracy slides a couple of chairs up next to the small desk in the room. "Please." She indicates the seats with her arm spread. Mom takes the first one and I lower myself to the second. Tracy puts her elbows on the table and begins to explain what's about to happen to me now.

"External radiotherapy is also known as external beam radiation or teletherapy where you have your treatment here in the hospital's radiotherapy department, but you're not an inpatient. Beams of radiation from this external machine"—she points to the institutional-size coffeemaker—"are focused on the areas of concern, according to your physician. We'll target the surrounding tissues from where your tumor was removed and any other areas of your leg affected by the cancer."

"So, I, like, lie under that huge thing?" I ask with a hitch in my breath.

"It's called a simulator," Tracy tells me. "I know it can be a bit intimidating, but you really have nothing to worry about. You can't feel a thing."

A bit?

I scrunch up my face as I gaze at the electronic beast beside me. "It looks uncomfortable," I say, trying not to sound like a complainer; I'm only making an observation.

Tracy smiles. "That's the main complaint about radiotherapy—the couch is a tad lumpy."

Glancing around the room, I feel as if the machine is waiting for me—to consume me and keep me from getting to my cheerleading. "If Dr. Dykema removed the tumor and my bone, and then Dr. Sampson put all of that chemotherapy in me, I don't understand why I have to do this, too?"

"It's all part of the total therapy," the technician tells me. "We'll do your radiotherapy treatment every day this week at eleven a.m. starting today, Monday, and going until Friday. The doctors have only called for one week of treatment, so that's good."

"I suppose," I say, peering down at my big toe that's now painted in a white and red French manicure style.

"The radiotreatment is painless, Hayley. I promise you, it only takes a few minutes out of the day."

Tracy stands and then points to the "couch," as she referred to the black table. It's certainly not anything I'd want to stretch out on to watch a movie. Still, I do as I'm instructed.

"Mrs. Matthews, why don't you wait outside the room? You won't be allowed to stay once the machine is activated."

"Oh, of course," Mom says, and gathers her purse.

Sure . . . Mom can leave, but I get to be in here for five days as this machine fries my insides.

I slip off my sandals and stretch out on the table. At least the pillow is fluffy.

Tracy unravels the mass of Ace bandages and sets them on a nearby table. "I'm going to make a pinprick tattoo on your leg so I'll know how to line up the machine." True to her word, she pulls out a thick purple pen and draws a dot right in the center of my leg; the spot that was operated on three times. From there, she begins extending the lines in all four directions. Ugly purple marks crisscross my fresh scar like a mad scientist writing on a white board.

"Will that come off?" I ask.

"In time," Tracy says. "Please don't wash them off this week as we'll be using these guidelines every day."

I nod, but I really wish she'd used a red or blue marker so at least the lines would match my school colors. Oh well.

"Make yourself comfy," she tells me.

I squiggle around a little to find the softest spot on the table. Not gonna happen. "I'm good," I report.

"All right, Hayley. I'm going to leave you alone for a few minutes. I'll ask you to take a deep breath and hold it. There will be a silence, a click, and then a hum. As I said, the treatment will *not* harm you. You won't feel a thing. You must, however, lie very, very still for the few minutes it takes to treat you. While the machine is on, I'll be able to hear you in the next room through the intercom if you need me for anything."

Breathe. Hold it. Don't move. So much to take in. So much to remember.

She positions me on the table and squares the above light to focus on her grid. She takes a roll of medical tape and secures it over the top of my foot and across to both sides of the table. "Since it's your first time, this is only for good measure."

With a pat on my knee, Tracy the tech in her SpongeBob scrubs disappears behind a swinging door into an observation room. Her voice comes across the crackling intercom.

"Are you ready, Hayley?"

"Yes," I say instead of nodding. I'm so paranoid trying to *not* move that I feel like I *am* moving. Good thing she taped me down.

"Okay . . . Take a deep breath . . . Hold it . . ."

Click.

Whir.

Hummmmm.

The sound is muffled by the staccato beat of my heart apparently trying to start its own rhythm section.

A red hue covers my leg for what seems an eternity. I don't blink for fear that even that slight motion could cause the radiation to kill off good cells in my leg. As soon as the light comes on, it fades away and the machine silences. The mighty monster is satiated for the moment, so it returns to its dormant state. I'm totally going to have nightmares about that thing.

"Good . . . Now breathe."

A gush of air escapes me, followed by somewhat of a pant.

I did it. I got through it. At least the first treatment.

"See? It was easy," Tracy says when she comes back into the room.

Sure, it was a piece of cake for her. She stood behind a lead wall and pressed a button.

I sit up and rewrap the Ace bandage around my scarred and purple-marked leg. I slip my shoes back on and crutch out of the treatment room to where Mom's waiting for me in the hallway.

"Well?"

I muster up a bit of a smile, mostly glad that I made it through and didn't mess up or make things worse for myself.

"One treatment down. Four to go."

* * *

MONDAY NIGHT, I SLEEP like a baby. We're talking out like a light before eight p.m.

Tuesday afternoon, I'm nauseated like all get-out. I throw up water and can't stomach the tomato soup Mom places before me.

Wednesday after dinner (spaghetti that I can't eat), I fall unconscious on the couch watching TV. It's as if someone gave me a sleeping pill.

Thursday morning, Tracy tells me "extreme fatigue" is a side effect of radiation therapy.

"It's very common. It's your body telling you it has to rest. That'll be gone about three weeks after your treatment is completed."

Perfect. So now I'm narcoleptic.

Thursday night, I can't get through reading e-mails or checking people's Facebook. I'm sick as a dog, and now the skin on my leg is so massively dry that even the most intense Jergens skin lo-tion won't help. I manage to eat two Snickers bars so I can bring my blood sugar levels up before I crash hard at eight thirty.

Friday morning, I'm dead to the world and can barely come to consciousness when Mom rattles me on the shoulder.

"Wake up, sweetie."

"Nuh-uh," I mumble into the pillow.

"This is it, Hayley. Last treatment and then your dad's coming to get us. We're going home."

This sparks in my brain like a clanging alarm clock and three cups of espresso.

Home. Back to Maxwell. Back to my life.

It's really the only thing that forces my limbs awake and into action. Since I slept later, I forgo a shower and grab the last Snickers bar on my way out of Cliff's. Mom has our bags packed for when we return from UAB.

For the first time all week, I'm not overanalyzing my position on the therapy table. I easily slide up onto the pad and stretch my leg out into position. Tracy, noticing my confidence, even skips taping my foot down before she slips away into her protective room.

One last click, zoom, and hum of the simulator.

I sit perfectly still.

But in my mind, I'm running free. I haven't a care in the world weighing me down. I'm running down the sidelines of the football field, cartwheeling, and doing back handsprings. There's nothing holding me back. I can do anything. I'm unlocked from the medical shackles that have held me back all summer.

My goal is in sight.

I'm going home!

CHAPTER TWENTY-FOUR

The soul would have no rainbow had the eyes no tears.

—JOHN VANCE CHENEY

HEY, LADIES, NEED A ride to Maxwell?" Dad asks when he pulls up in the truck outside Cliff's apartment. He just drove three hours to get here, and now he's turning around to do it again. He must be as relieved as I am that I'm done with this.

"Yes, please!" I say enthusiastically.

We load our things into the truck, and Dad helps me up into back seat of the cab.

He's brought a pillow along that he places on the seat and hefts my foot up on it. "There. Buckle up and make yourself comfortable."

I do as he says, clicking the shoulder strap around me.

Mom climbs into the front, and we're off.

Soon, the skyline of Birmingham is nothing but a faded memory. Dad weaves through Friday afternoon traffic heading south on I-65. I lean my head back and let out a long, deep sigh, one that's been stuck in my windpipe since the day I discovered that nasty-ass growth in my leg. I can't believe that was only six weeks ago. In some ways, it feels like yesterday; in others, it feels like years.

Mom turns in response to my massive exhalation. "Are you okay, sweetie?"

"Just thinking."

"About what?"

I give her a "you've got to be kidding me look," so she adjusts forward in her seat.

Cancer.

It's something old people get. People who smoke or drink too much get afflicted with it. It's inherited. Millions of people walk in charity fundraisers to combat it. Telethons are held for it. Pink is now the color that represents cancer prevention.

I've always liked pink. So why couldn't I prevent it?

Cancer.

An uncontrolled growth of abnormal cells.

I remember my church did a fundraiser a few years ago for Ralph Rodgers when he was diagnosed with lung cancer and needed help paying for treatment. I've put spare change in the cans in the grocery store for the American Cancer Society. I've seen the billboards on the highway with pictures of sick kids.

I'm one of those sick kids.

Rapidly, my pulse begins to pick up, seemingly matching the seventy-five miles per hour Dad's doing. My breath hitches in my lungs. For a second, it's as if I've had the wind knocked out of me, just like the time when I was twelve and was skateboarding down the hill in Ashlee Grimes's yard and busted it big-time. The air returned eventually then. Now, I'm not so sure.

Dr. Dykema's rough voice rings clear in my head as I'm hearing an echo of the side effects of chemo and radiation.

Nausea.

Diarrhea.

Dry skin.

Abnormal menstrual cycle.

Brittle nails.

Extreme fatigue.

Loss of appetite.

Nerve damage.

Hair loss.

I gasp in air as these symptoms tumble around in my mind like wet towels in the dryer.

As I tug the end of my long hair, the realism of what I just went through sinks in. Am I going to lose all of this? I hadn't even considered going bald a possibility. I mean, I've watched TV shows where the characters have cancer and never get their makeup smudged let alone lose one hair on their head. But this is reality—my reality.

Oh my God. It's really *hitting* me.

>>BLAM<<

Like a thick two-by-four smack against my forehead.

Reality sets in.

Understanding coats me from head to toe.

I don't know why it took this long to comprehend the breadth and depth of my diagnosis.

I had cancer.

Like cancer cancer.

Real, live, not made for television cancer.

Malignant cancer that dared to attempt to take my leg. Take my *life!*

Cancer that thought it could beat me.

Cancer that thought it could defeat me.

Fucking cancer.

Yeah, well, fuck you, cancer!

I try to calm myself. It's over and done with. I won. *I* defeated *it.*

It's gone. Cut out, burned with chemicals and zapped with radiation.

Take that!

Where is the cancer now? In some jar in the pathology department at UAB so doctors can study it and learn from it.

Where am I? On my way home to get back to school, get back to cheerleading, get back to life.

Damn straight. Fuck you, cancer!

I glance down at my left leg stretched out on the back seat and propped up on the pillow my dad lovingly brought from home. My leg is still covered in an Ace bandage only to provide protection for the very delicate skin still healing from the surgery and still stained with the purple radiation guidelines. I'm healing. I'm overcoming. I'm winning.

I'm going to have one hell of a scar and an interesting story to tell for the rest of my life.

It is what it is.

An absurd thought enters my mind, causing a bubble of laughter to sneak up through my lungs and burst out in the silence of the car.

Dad jumps. Mom spins around.

"Hayley! What's wrong?"

I can't stop laughing. It feels amazing.

"I was just thinking," I say between giggles. "You know, with a scar like this, I think I can pretty much rule out that future career as a *Playboy* centerfold."

Mom's face breaks into a broad grin, and her hearty laughter joins mine. Catching her breath, she says, "You can still do it, Hayley. They'll have to photograph you from the right side, though."

Our conjoined laughter over my ludicrous joke soon alters to me crying.

Big, chubby tears that roll down my cheeks and land on my T-shirt.

Mom starts crying, too — a catharsis for both of us perhaps.

I let the tears flow, heavy and hard, from the swirling emotions. Relief. Anger. Uncertainty. Thankfulness. Irritation. Gratefulness.

Mom laces her fingers through mine and squeezes. It says she loves me and is proud I'm dealing with this. Her face blurs from the window of tears cascading from my eyes. It's okay, though. This outburst was a long time coming.

This is the first time I really cry.

* * *

"MEEEEEEEOOOOOOOOWWWW!"

My kitty, Leeny, sits just inside the kitchen door as Mom, Dad, and I walk in. It's like she knew I'd be coming home today and wanted to be the official welcome committee.

I lean the crutches up against the kitchen table and bend to scoop up my beloved pet. Immediately, her motor boat of purring starts, and she rubs her head against my chin. It's the best homecoming anyone could ever ask for. I kiss her on her furry head and then return her to the floor.

Dad hauls our bags in; Mom brings the two plants I got while I was in the hospital.

"Now, Leeny, don't you dig or pee in these plants," Mom says to our pet. Like Leeny cares.

Nabbing the crutches again, I make my way down the hallway to the base of the staircase. Dad stops me before I can start climbing.

"Your mother and I were thinking that we can give you our room downstairs and we'll take your room upstairs so you won't have to climb."

It's the sweetest thought but not necessary.

"Dr. Dykema told me not to run or jump. He didn't say anything about not climbing stairs."

My parents exchange glances.

"It's up to her," Dad says to Mom.

"It'll be good for me. Good exercise."

Mom widens her eyes. "Please promise me you'll be careful."

"Duh . . ." I say with a laugh.

It takes a good ten minutes to climb the twenty-six stairs — steps I usually take two at a time in a few seconds flat. Dad, bless his heart, spotted me the whole way up as I cautiously climbed toward my room.

"Phew!" Leeny bounds up the stairs easily and passes me to head right into my room. "Showoff," I call out to her.

"Good job, Little Kid," Dad says. "Promise me that's how you'll always do it."

"As long as I have to," I say. "I'll be bolting up them in no time."

"That'a girl," Dad says, tugging my hair. He heads back downstairs.

I round the corner, past my bathroom, and smile as I walk into my room. Mom has already brought stuff up and left it on the dresser. There's a large box overflowing with get-well cards, the cheer basket the BHS cheerleaders brought me, and the two plants. On the far wall, a "Welcome Home, Hayley" banner is pinned to my curtains.

"Your dad printed that out at the store," Mom notes.

He's the sweetest thing, ever!

Other than that, everything is pretty much how I left it. My canopy bed is made up and all my stuffed animals are in place among the pile of pillows. There's an indentation in the red satin comforter where Leeny has, no doubt, been sleeping. She leaps onto the bed and curls up there to prove me right.

"Leave the clothes from your suitcase out in the hallway and I'll wash them for you."

"You don't have to do that, Mom."

"I want to. Anything to help."

I lower myself to the bed and sigh as I sink into the familiar surroundings.

Mom kisses me on the head and then leaves me to myself.

I'm home.

In my room. Back on my turf.

The smell of freshly laundered sheets and the Lysoled bathroom.

The crunch of a small piece of kitty litter on the carpet that Leeny must have been playing with.

The safety and security of the familiar.

And I couldn't be happier.

CHAPTER TWENTY-FIVE

When the Japanese mend broken objects, they aggrandize the damage by filling the cracks with gold. They believe that when something's suffered damage and has a history it becomes more beautiful.

—BARBARA BLOOM

THE MOMENT I STEP (okay, swing) into the door at Polk High School, chill bumps dance up and down my forearms.

Eyes are all over me. Jovial smiles fade, replaced by curious glances. Conversations stop and whispers begin.

A sea of students parts to make room for me to pass. The girl on the crutches.

The girl who had . . . *cancer.*

Are they judging me? Feeling sorry for me? Poking fun at me?

My pulse triples its cadence as I make my way through the school.

Beads of perspiration spring up on the back of my neck.

Nerves jitter under the surface of my skin.

Faces and expressions mix together in a tossed salad of anxiety.

I never expected a welcoming party when I slid through the glass doors of PHS, but I'd hoped for a wave or a grin or two instead of this scrutinization. It's not like I'm the first student to ever be hobbling down the hall on crutches. Just last year, Keegan Bryce wrecked out hard on his mountain bike and had a cast from ankle to hip.

Maybe I'm simply being paranoid.

"Hayley!" a familiar voice calls out to me in the hallway.

Lora Russell bursts through the crowd and hugs me with all her might. "I'm sooooo happy to see you! I would have come over this weekend, but Mom and Uncle Ross and I went to Gulf Shores to his condo. We went jet skiing and it was so much fun." Her pretty face falls. "I'm completely insensitive. Who cares about me? You're here! You look awesome, and it's so good to have you back."

I hug her the best I can while balancing on my right leg. "I missed you, too."

"We're sharing a locker," she says, pointing to number 227 on the wall of gray. "I snagged a top one so you don't have to stoop down."

"You're the best," I say as I attempt to unwind the knotted ball of nerves inside me and pretend I'm just another student stashing books and notepads. Still, the stares of passing students brush against me like a ghostly figure. "Does everyone, like, know what happened to me this summer?"

Lora's eyes shift about. "That you were in the hospital? Yeah, I guess. You're a cheerleader, so you're kind of in the spotlight, you know?"

"I suppose." The life of a PHS Pop is still something I'm getting used to as much as learning to walk straight again.

"Oh, look what I got you!" Lora nearly bounces in place with her excitement. She tugs out a navy blue L.L. Bean canvas backpack with the initials *HAM* embroidered on it. (Yes, my initials are *HAM* for Hayley Ann Matthews.) "It's so you can carry your books to class while you're still on crutches."

She's the sweetest thing ever, and I hug her again, holding tight to her like an anchor in these tumultuous waters.

"I'm scared, Lora," I whisper to her.

"Don't be," she says quietly into my hair. "I'm here for you."

"I'm here for you, too," a male voice echoes.

I push away from my partner and see Gabriel, my good, old friend, standing behind Lora and smiling from ear to ear.

"It's good to see you upright, Hay," he says teasingly.

I spread my arms wide, careful to hold the crutches in my armpits. "What can I say? I'm a modern medical miracle."

Gabriel's dark eyes smile out at me. "I'm sure you will be. Remember, I'm here to help in any way you need me."

"I'm taking you up on that, Gabriel."

"Hayley! You're here!" Hannah, Melanie, and Tara join us at the lockers, and they attack hug me. It's a cheerleading reunion. "We missed you so much," Tara says.

"I missed all of y'all," I say through the emotional lump in my throat. These are my peeps, my comrades in cheerleading arms, the chicas I spent so much time with this summer before everything changed. They are the same ones I let down with my absence from camp, but the very ones who voted against the captain to keep me on the team.

"You heard we kicked Emmanuel's ass on Friday night, right?" Melanie asks.

Hannah grabs my hand. "It was amazing. Daniel caught a sixty-eight-yard pass in the beginning of the fourth and ran it in untouched for a touchdown to put us ahead."

My heartbeat picks up at her description. I wish I could

have been there to see Daniel triumphantly soaring into the end zone.

Chin up, I say, "He'll just have to do it again this Friday against Highland High. I know I'll be there on the sidelines."

A collective whoop arises from my teammates, and my body comes alive. I'm okay. Despite my lengthy absence, I'm still part of the group.

Then reality crashes in a bit. "Can you cheer while you're still on crutches?" Tara asks.

At that moment, the energy around our group changes as the spicy orange scent of Chloe Bradenton's expensive perfume wafts into our circle. We part like the Red Sea.

"Yes, Hayley, how will you cheer when you're"—her eyes slide over my crutches and settle on my bandaged leg—"well . . . still incapacitated."

She says the word as if it's a witch's curse.

I foster up a good strong ounce of courage and square my shoulders. Chloe is very definitely out to get me, so I kill her with kindness.

"Hey, Chloe," I say forcefully. "Great to see you. And don't you worry about me. My doctor said I can't run or jump on this leg, but the rest of me can do anything. I'm back in business."

She starts to sneer at me. Lora's voice interrupts with, "Isn't that great, Chloe?"

Chloe smiles a saccharine-sweet one for the gathered crowd. "It is. Nice to have a full squad again. We're so happy to have you back, Hayley. We're all behind you one hundred percent."

"Thanks, Chloe." And I honestly believe she means it. I'm sure it was hard trying to compete at camp without a full team. I know we didn't win, and winning was Chloe's dream as captain. My chest tightens knowing I prevented someone else's hopes from happening. I'm here now, and I plan to make up the loss not just to Chloe, but to the whole team. "I can't wait for practice," I say excitedly.

"Definitely," Chloe says. "Three p.m. sharp."

"Absolutely," Hannah says, too.

Another looming figure joins the melee in front of my locker. "There's my girl," I hear, and my heart does that zippy roller coaster thing down to my stomach and back up.

Daniel pushes through the crowd and reaches out for me, gathering me to him. I'm literally consumed in his broad chest and I take in the freshly showered smell of his skin. It's been so long since I've been near him, felt his strong muscles, and relaxed into the comfort of his arms.

I hug him the best I can as I balance on the crutches. "Here, lean on me," he says. Then he adjusts his stare at Chloe and says, "It's great to have Hayley back in the cheerleading lineup. We're going to need all the school spirit we can get if we're going to go undefeated this season."

My flirt gene comes out of its long hibernation stage. "I heard you had quite a night Friday. Hate that I missed that."

"No worries," he says with confidence. "I'll score a touchdown for you this week."

I'd probably melt into a puddle of goo if both Daniel and my crutches weren't holding me up. His hand finds its way into my hair, and he strokes the strands with conviction, as if to say he's serious about his promise.

I feel less of an anomaly and more like a regular girl starting her senior year.

Lora winks her approval at me. Even Chloe nods as she turns to go off to her class.

Daniel lowers his mouth close to my ear. "I'm here for you. Whatever you need. Just let me know."

A blush tickles my cheeks, and I smile up at him.

The bell for first period rings out, and our small tribunal disperses.

Daniel squeezes my shoulder. "See you at lunch."

As I begin shuffling down the hall, Gabriel joins me. "AP English?"

"Yeah . . . you too?"

He cocks his head to the right. "This way."

My school year has begun.

* * *

PEOPLE SERIOUSLY DON'T KNOW how to treat me.

Even the teachers seem knocked off their game.

Mrs. Joseph, the AP English Lit teacher, certainly doesn't have any kind of poker face when I hobble into the classroom with Gabriel.

"Oh my God, Hayley Matthews!" she shouts out at me. "I was so sorry to hear about your" — she scans the room to see if anyone's listening and then she whispers the word — "*cancer.*"

"It's okay, Mrs. J. It's all gone. Cut out. Chemo'd and radiated."

"It's just such a sad thing for a teenager to go through." She emphasizes her words with her hand to her heart.

Gabriel steps in. "It's a horrible thing for anyone to go through. Hayley's gonna be all right, though. She's tough."

I smile up at my friend. Yeah, I guess I am if I've made it this far.

The teacher continues to whisper. "I'll keep you in my prayers, Hayley."

"Thanks for that." I don't really get why I need prayers now. The cancer is gone. What else can happen? I'm still me, only minus a bone and some nasty, icky lesion.

"Take your seat, dear. If you need to leave for any reason during class, just do it. I'll understand."

"Um . . . okay."

Gabriel grins like crazy. "Carte blanche, my friend." Then his face grows serious. "You know I'm here for you, too, right?"

"Thanks, Gabriel. I appreciate that."

"I'm not kidding. I won't mollycoddle you or treat you differently, no matter what." He speaks with such conviction, I feel he's talking from some sort of experience. He leaves it at that, though.

"Thanks. Everything's going to be fine now. I just have to work out and get my leg in shape while it heals. I'm meeting with Coach Carnes this afternoon to show him what the physical therapist in Birmingham suggested I work on."

"Cool," Gabriel says, then adds, "Hey I've got P.E. last period, and I'm training the football players on their workouts. Tell Coach Carnes to get me a copy of the exercises and I'll help you out on the machines. I know some good stuff to help build your strength back up."

"Awesome." I smile at my friend who not only wants to help me, but he's treating me the same as he always has.

I sit back and take the syllabus Mrs. Joseph hands to me. Should be an interesting class. There's poetry from W. H. Auden to William Butler Yeats, drama from Edward Albee to Tennessee Williams; fiction from Kingsley Amis to Virginia Woolf, and expository prose that includes Ralph Waldo Emerson and even Norman Mailer.

Good. Back to my education. Rounding out my senior year with the last advanced placement classes to impress colleges. I can't believe how excited I am to delve into all of this reading, analysis of the words, and composition. Same with my economics, French, and other classes. Being back on the terra firma of the PHS school grounds makes me feel much more myself now.

I'm the senior, the cheerleader, the normal girl finishing up high school.

"This should be fun," Gabriel notes, seated next to me in the second row. "My old school didn't have the AP classes like here, so I'm glad to get this on my record."

"Where do you want to go to college?" I ask quietly as Mrs. Joseph flits about the room.

Gabriel shrugs. "I want to study engineering, so I have a lot of choices. Cornell, Carnegie Mellon, MIT, Georgia Tech, but those all cost an arm and a leg, which is no surprise."

"Tell me about it," I say. I think Mom and Dad used to have a small savings account for my college fund. However, after my medical bills, I have no idea if any of that is left.

"I'm applying to a bunch of places for financial aid and scholarships, so we'll see what happens. Where are you applying?"

What do I even want to do when I grow up?

"Bama as my first choice. Miami or maybe UGA as backups."

Gabriel grins. "All party schools."

"All football schools." What can I say? Girlfriend loves her college gridiron. Both of my parents went to The University of Alabama, and crimson is in my blood. I want to be a part of that community. As for what I want to do as a career, I guess I need to start figuring that out.

In good time.

For now, I'm happy to be one of the many schmucks here at PHS just trying to make it through the day. No more medical drama or feeling sorry for myself. I'm finally where I want to be.

Mrs. Joseph says, "Let's start with some Emily Dickinson this morning, why don't we?"

Ah . . . the queen of dashes and unconventional capitalization.

With that, I'm back in the groove.

* * *

LAST PERIOD, I HEAD to the gym, slip into the girls' locker room, and change into a PHS Varsity Cheerleader tank top and blue shorts. After my meeting with Coach Carnes, he delivers me to the weight-training area and hands me off to an eager Gabriel. He immediately gets me working on some very gentle leg curls for starters.

"Yikes," I say through gritted teeth.

"What?" Gabriel asks, ever much the concerned coach.

"There's all sorts of pulling and burning in my left leg."

He nods. "Coach Carnes said that's going to happen. You're working those muscles for the first time in a while. Trust me, it's necessary, though, to get you fully back on the road to recovery. Just take it easy."

"If you say so," I say, and concentrate on the exercise.

A while later—I must have lost track of time—Chloe comes over and jabs her hands to her hips. "If you don't mind, we need you at cheerleader practice, now that you're actually here."

I slide off the weight machine and reach for my crutches. "Coach Crane has me doing my PT the first fifteen minutes of the period."

The captain rolls her eyes. "Okay, well, it's been twenty. We need you over here now."

I turn to Gabriel and nod my thanks.

He flips Chloe the bird finger behind her back and then laughs. Wish I had the guts to do that to her face. I follow behind her, watching her ponytail sway from left to right as she walks along. I glance down at her shoes and mentally put myself in them for a moment. Sure, Chloe's a bitch. That's a well-known fact at PHS.

But she also has the responsibility of heading up our squad. It's not an easy job, especially when a lot of times we'd rather gossip, text, and rest instead of putting our all into the practice and routine.

I silently vow not to pose any problems for Chloe and make sure I get back up to speed immediately so there's no further hole in the team.

The rest of last period, Lora and I work on our partner stunts. With my crutches close by, I focus on putting all of my weight on my right side and only using my left for balance. The first time Lora runs up on my shoulders, I splay out face first on the gym floor.

"Holy shit!" my partner screams. "I'm so sorry!"

The other girls freeze in their various positions and Chloe just shakes her head.

My body groans from every pore, yet I grit my teeth and smile through the pain. I'm laughing instead of crying. "Now you see why my brother and sister call me 'Grace.'"

My teammates laugh and go back to their own stunts.

"Are you really all right?" Lora asks with concern.

"I'm kosher like a dill." I'm determined to make this work. I can't show any signs of weakness; otherwise, Chloe will definitely boot me off the squad. I ignore the pain and get ready to go at it again. "No, no, I slipped," I say, glancing at the sweaty spot where I landed on the parquet. "Let's try again."

On the third run up, I manage to support Lora's weight and assist her in performing a perfectly executed star pose—on the right side, of course.

"Good job, y'all," Ashlee compliments.

Chloe claps her hands together. "This is going to be a full and busy week. Practice after school Tuesday, Wednesday, and Thursday. We have a dance routine to learn for the pep rally, signs to make for the game, and spirit prizes to determine from last week's game."

Melanie speaks up. "Did you see Furonda Garrison, one of the majorettes? She was cheering her ass off. She should definitely be up for spirit person."

"Totally," Brittney agrees.

Funny, I used to win the spirit person prize every now and then. Now I'm helping decide who gets it.

"Fine with me," Chloe says. "We'll discuss it more at practice tomorrow."

The captain then turns her cold stare at me. "Are you going to be able to keep up?"

Someone behind me, possibly Samantha or Lauren, gasps noticeably at Chloe's snarkiness.

Thanks for understanding, you insensitive cow. Nope, can't say that. Instead, I respond "I'm here to do my best and whatever is needed of me."

Lora speaks up. "If we're doing the routine from camp, we can make a few adjustments to accommodate Hayley until she's completely off her crutches."

Chloe's cell phone rings, and she walks away from the group, dismissing us with a wave of her hand.

"She's such a bitch," Lora mumbles. "You need a ride home?"

I bite my tongue and reach for my crutches. "Sure, that would be great."

I follow my partner out of the gym with my bag slung over my back. Gabriel waves at me from the corner, and I smile back.

"Look who's here!" Lora shouts as she holds the gym door open for me. "Uncle Ross!"

"Hey, Lora!" the older man says. "Hayley, right?"

"Right. Hi, Ross."

"What are you doing here?" Lora asks.

He pulls off his sunglasses. "I closed a new deal this afternoon with the Muscle Up company. Just doing some PR with all of the local sports teams to drum up some business. Coach Blumentritt over at Maxwell said I should visit Coach Gaither to give some samples to the team. You know, to see if they want to place orders."

"Orders for what?" Lora asks.

Ross dips back into the front of his Hummer and retrieves a huge box with a logo of a ripped bicep on it. "Protein shakes, protein bars, energy drinks." He sets his sunglasses to the top of his head. "You think the cheerleaders would want to try any of these products?"

"What for?" Lora asks.

He explains. "Protein's essential for anyone's diet, but athletes need more than the average Joe to replace nutrition lost during intensive workouts. Your body needs protein to build healthy muscles, bones, and skin."

"Maybe Hayley should try them," Lora suggests.

Ross smiles. "What a great idea!"

"Me?"

"Sure. You've got to work on building your muscles after your surgery, right? It'll help with your stamina and strength. I'm sure my niece isn't easy to lift up over your head," he says with a smirk.

"Uncle Ross!" Lora whines.

I giggle because he's right.

He hefts a box of samples up onto his shoulder. "Where's your car, Hayley?"

"Um . . . I'm riding with Lora." My mouth drops open. "You're giving *me* all that stuff?"

"Absolutely," he says with a Hollywood grin. He stashes the box in the back seat of Lora's BMW convertible. "I've got plenty more in the back. It's all promo stuff. You take this home, read the directions, and protein up!"

"Isn't he the coolest?" Lora says, knocking me with her elbow.

"Yeah, he is."

With the help of so many good people, I am definitely not going to need these crutches much longer.

CHAPTER TWENTY-SIX

*Keep your dreams alive. Understand to achieve anything
requires faith and belief in yourself, vision, hard work, determination, and dedication. Remember all things are possible
for those who believe.*

—GAIL DEVERS

GETTING AROUND SCHOOL ON crutches and making it to each
classroom on time during my first week is a feat, but I do it.

I'm getting settled in all of my classes and the teachers are
starting to treat me like simply another student. I guess they all
had to get over the shock of what happened to me and how to
"handle" me. Mrs. Kiaurakis, the guidance counselor, sent me
an e-mail Tuesday after school telling me she's "there" for me if
I need to "talk." She referenced having brochures and websites I
could read about surviving cancer and rejoining society. Like I
left it? Geesh, she's as bad as Dr. Dykema and his team thinking
I would need a bunch of psychiatrists to hash over how I "feel"
about having cancer. They cut it out; it's in a jar; I'm done. End of
story.

The workouts with Gabriel are extra helpful. He's not easy on
me, either; expecting me to follow his directions and training.
I started using one of the machines that strengthens the upper

body. Turning backwards on the bench, I lift the weights from behind to simulate working with my partner. The weights are set for one hundred and ten pounds, a smidge more than what Lora weighs.

"Good, Hayley," Gabriel says, noting the sweat rolling down my face. "You're doing a great job."

I let the weights fall back into place and take the towel he tosses at me.

"That's hard as hell."

"No pain, no gain," my friend says.

I rub my sore arms and wince. "Oh, there's definitely pain."

Gabriel smirks. "The trainer I worked with last year told me to chant 'hurts so good' over and over in my head when things get bad. We're not doing anything too straining on you, Hay, so be patient and go slow. You've come a long way in three days. It's all in the consistency."

"Yes, sir, Mr. Tremblay," I say with a really serious face.

He starts laughing, and I throw the towel back at him. Gabriel makes that he's going to tickle me, and I squeal like the girl I am.

"What are you doing to my girl, Tremblay?" Daniel asks, sauntering up.

He's wearing a tight gray T-shirt that reads "Property of PHS Athletic Department." He's all sweaty from some physical activity, and he looks absolutely amazing.

Gabriel's mood changes and he clams up. "Workout regimen to get her back in shape."

Daniel winks at me. "I like her shape just fine."

I really need to stop blushing like all get-out every time he flirts with me. Daniel's going to think I have rosacea.

"You have practice after school?" Daniel asks.

"Yep, and we're making the run-through sign for the game," I explain.

"I'll give you a ride home after. Okay?"

"Perfect," I say.

* * *

PRACTICE IS ROUGH FOR me.

The aches.

The inner moaning.

The tug of my scar.

The biting of my tongue so no one knows how much it hurts.

It's more physically demanding than my physical therapy.

I do my best to perform all the dance moves in rhythm to the rest of the girls. Chloe's got me on the back row. Hide the problem. Cover it up. No one will notice. I suppose she's right, though. No need for me to be front and center.

I make it work. I shift my balance to my right side and listen to the beat of the music. I concentrate on the moves and not the pain stretching up and down my leg.

Punch. Clap, clap, clap.

Punch. Crunk. Crunk. Crunk.

Pop. Lock. Pop. Lock.

Step, step, step. *Ouch. Hurts so good.*

Swing left. Swing right.

Turn. Turn. Lunge. *Ouch. Not good.*

Pop. Punch. Crunk.

Swish to left. Swish to right.

Clap, clap. Punch, punch.

Hurts so good.

Hurts so good.

"Not bad," Chloe says to me when we're done. Then, surprisingly, she adds, "You okay?"

I struggle to catch my breath. "Um . . . yeah, thanks."

Wow. She actually complimented me.

Double-wow. She actually showed concern.

Maybe Chloe does have a soul deep down.

I don't take something like that for granted at all.

My muscles are singing a song of pain and suffering. But, as Gabriel said, "Hurts so good."

We get the run-through sign painted—a large sheet with a Patriot bringing a fist down on a Highlander's head, squashing him into the ground. That's what I hope we do to Highland High tomorrow night.

Chloe goes through a checklist as we finish up. "Uniforms for school and pep rally tomorrow are the white shirt, vest on the red side and the red, white, and blue skirt. Game uniform is the new white uniform. Hair in a high ponytail. No exceptions."

I glance over at the bleachers where Daniel and a bunch of the football players have gathered, all sweaty from their practice. He rolls his eyes at Chloe.

Chloe finally closes practice, and I grab my things. Lora tosses me my silvery poms, and I shove them into my bag.

"Do you need a ride?" she asks.

"Daniel's driving me."

"Go for it, g'friend."

"Here, let me get that for you." Daniel takes my bag and slings it over his shoulder. I pull my crutches up under my arms, glad to be off my leg and the pain emanating from underneath my bandage. I'm totally taking a long, hot, bath when I get home. I keep scrubbing at those stupid purple marks that are still on my leg from the radiation.

Daniel helps me up into his truck and then places my crutches underneath the seat. He comes around and climbs in himself, revving the engine and then backing out of the parking spot. It's about a ten-minute drive through Maxwell to get to my house.

The setting sun provides an amber glow on Daniel's handsome features. He is so fricking gorgeous, it's not even funny. All I want to do is reach out and touch him to make sure he's really there and that I'm really here. I want to open my heart to him and tell him all my hopes, dreams, and fears.

He's quiet and distant, though, so I break the silence.

"Everything okay?"

He jumps a little as he stares at the red light in front of us. "Huh? Oh, yeah. Fine."

"You seem distracted."

"I'm just thinking about Coy Parker."

My brows knit together. "Who the hell is Coy Parker?"

"All-state outside linebacker for Highland High. He's a real mother. Tough bastard. Put a guy in the hospital in their first game. I don't want him to do the same to me."

I sit up. "What did he do to him?"

Daniel's wrist dangles over the steering wheel as he describes the play. "It was perfectly legal—the hit, that is. Tackled him midfield and flattened him. Bam! Dude's made of solid muscle, can run like a scalded dog, and I hear he's mean, too."

I reach my hand over. "You'll be great. You're one of the best players PHS has ever had. You've broken, like, three school records. No one can stop you. Not even Coy Parker."

Daniel turns his smile on me. "I've got my own personal cheerleader."

"Well, yeah," I say, squinting my eyes at him.

He stares at me for a minute . . . an hour . . . a day—who knows how long? That is until the minivan behind us honks the horn and snaps us out of our gaze. He lifts his hand in acknowledgment and guns the truck. A few minutes later, we turn on Willow Hollow and stop in front of my two-story house. Mom's car is parked in the driveway; Dad's not home yet.

Daniel kills the engine and moves to face me. Is he going to kiss me? I sure hope so! It's been too long.

"Listen, Hayley," he begins. "Coach Gaither says we've got to stay really focused this year. We seniors, especially, are gunning for the state championship we missed out on last season."

"I know."

"Right. So, I can't have any . . . distractions . . . this season."

The strong-willed animal in me gets my haunches up. "Are you saying *I'm* a distraction?"

"No, no, not at all. I just know you're sick and are still getting over cancer and—"

"I'm *not* sick, Daniel. I had surgery and treatment and I'm over it," I say, pleading my case. "The cancer is gone. There's nothing wrong with me."

He scrubs his hands through his hair. "I know, and I didn't mean it like that. There's a lot of pressure on me."

This time, my hand touches his when I stretch out. "Look. You're going to be awesome. You're an amazing athlete, and every college is going to be drooling to hand you a scholarship. Don't get so freaked out over the pressure that you don't enjoy it, you know?"

And with that, he relaxes. Boys are like that. They need to know how cool and special they are.

"Thanks, Hayley," he says with a smile. He squeezes my hand and rubs his thumb on top. "You really are a great cheerleader."

"Yes, I am. Wait until tomorrow night!"

* * *

EVEN THOUGH I'M ON crutches, it's totally cool walking the hallways of PHS in my cheerleader uniform. People I barely know turn and wave or say "hey" to me. I finally feel like I'm *someone,* which sounds kind of pathetic. I don't mean it that way. It's just that for the first time since I've been in high school, a lot of people know my name and who I am.

I think that's cool.

My first pep rally is even cooler.

Although I come in on my crutches, I prop them up nearby and limp along, trying not to put too much pressure on my left leg as I walk on my tiptoes. The nice new Nikes are firm, supporting, and helpful.

"Let's have a vic'try tonight!" I scream with the rest of the squad. "When you're up, you're up!"

"When you're up, you're up," the students in the gym repeat.

"When you're down, you're down! When you're up against the Patriots, you're upside down! Hey, hey, mighty Patriots . . . let's have a vic'try tonight . . . hey!"

The adrenaline pumping through every vein in my body has me feeling no pain. If my leg is hurting, I certainly don't know it. But I still put all of the pressure, weight, and responsibility on my right leg as I execute the cheers.

I glance down at my armband with the pep rally schedule written on it. It's made from athletic tape we got from the trainers. I remember when I was a freshman at PHS, I got Jordan Gardner's wristband from her after my first pep rally. I wore it to the game that night, and PHS totally kicked butt. I wonder if some freshman girl will come up and want mine when we're done.

Lora rushes to the microphone and introduces the team captains for the Highland game. "Let's give a big cheer for seniors, Skipper O'Rourke and Anthony Ricketts!"

I nab my silver poms in my fists and brush them together as the gym goes crazy for our captains. Skipper, tall and lanky, steps to the microphone. Anthony follows behind him with a small black case in his hand.

When Lora returns to stand in front of me, I ask, "What's Anthony got there?"

She shrugs and turns back to the players.

"We just want to thank everyone who traveled with us last week to the Emmanuel game. It was awesome seeing so many fans on our side," Skipper says, peering up through his long side-swept blond hair. "We're really dedicated to winning the state championship this year, and we'll do anything to get there."

The students cheer crazily, and I hop on my right leg, raising my poms high over my head to egg everyone on. To my left, Chloe executes a perfect pike jump while Melanie does one herkie after another. The gym is electrified with so much school spirit. The kinetic energy alone could power the stadium lights for tonight's game.

Skipper motions for everyone to be quiet. "My cousin plays football out in Colorado. Last year, the whole team decided to shave their heads as a symbol of their unity and toughness. And you know what? They won the championship!"

Anthony opens the medium black case he's been holding, revealing an electric clipper with all the comb attachments. My brother used to have one just like it and managed to give himself a buzzcut because he didn't use the right comb.

"That's right, y'all," Skipper says as he points to the clipper. "We're gonna do it, too!"

Everyone goes ape! It's so loud in the gym that I can't hear myself think. I'm amazed as I watch Anthony load a comb onto the end, switch on the device, and then run it over Skipper's thick mop of hair. Blond strands fall in a pile on the floor while everyone cheers them along. When Skipper has nothing but a thin layer of peach fuzz on his head, he holds his hands up high, pumping his fists in the air. Anthony's next, buzzing off his short cropped black hair. Over the next few minutes, the rest of the players gather around Skipper and Anthony, breaking out more electric razors.

"Oh my God," Tara shouts over to me. "This is freaking amazing!"

Everyone buzzes his head. Hair is everywhere. The student body is pumped by the frenzy. Even Coach Gaither pulls off his baseball cap and shaves what little hair he has left. Gabriel and the two other trainers bend down and off comes their hair.

I gasp when he turns to me and gives me a thumbs-up.

I shake my head back at him and raise the poms in his direction.

Lora points to her wristband. "We certainly didn't have *this* on the schedule."

"Seriously!"

All of a sudden, there's a murmur in the crowd, and I hear Skipper on the PA say, "Come on, Delafield. Don't be a chicken."

Daniel still sports his shaggy mop; really standing out as the only red-shirted guy in the gym who's unshaven. "I can't. My mom'll kick my ass."

LaShawn "Scoop Dogg" (known for scooping up fumbles) Carter throws his hands up. "Man! You're messin' with our flow."

Clearly embarrassed and torn over what to do, Daniel rocks back and forth on the heels of his feet. A hissing boo arises from the students, and Daniel waves them down.

"I'll do it! I'll do it!"

Scoop Dogg moves in with the clipper, and Daniel stops him.

"I'll do it, man."

"Whatever, dude," Scoop Dogg says.

I hold my breath as Daniel digs through the comb attachments and snaps a new one into place. He moves the clipper over his scalp, and a good portion of his hair joins the pile on the floor. It isn't *nearly* as short as the rest of them, but at least he made the effort and everyone seems to be happy enough.

The music kicks on, and we cheerleaders fall into our dance routine. I'm pumped beyond reason, and I've never experienced such intense school spirit.

Boy, Highland High is going to be in trouble tonight!

CHAPTER TWENTY-SEVEN

Once you choose hope, anything's possible.

—CHRISTOPHER REEVE

DAD ESCORTS ME DOWN the concrete steps of the stadium and onto the football field. The home crowd of students, parents, alumni, teachers, and boosters is already gathering, and the familiar smell of chargrilled burgers and fresh popcorn fills the air.

I take that first step onto the green grass and head over to the area in front of the fence where the cheerleaders traditionally stand in front of the band and the student section. My feet are rooted to the soft sod as I'm still trying to take in that I'm actually here in my new uniform to cheer in front of the home crowd. Madison Hutchinson and Lauren Compton are already in place, doing some warm-up stretches a few feet from me. Madi waves.

"Are you okay, Hayley?" Dad asks.

"Yeah, great, in fact."

"You look great, Little Kid."

I believe I do. My long hair is pulled up into a high ponytail, as requested—demanded, more like—by my captain. I have on the new white uniform that Mom took in a bit in the waist to fit me better. My makeup is simple: powder (which I'll just sweat off), waterproof eyeliner and mascara, and a touch of sparkly blue

MAC eye shadow on my lids. I even went as far as putting on some lip gloss, which will last about as long as the powder does. But I'm here. Front and center. Actually, on the end . . . still. I'm ready to cheer on the Pats.

"I'll set your crutches here," Dad says as he leans them against the fence. My purse gets stashed on the ground next to them. I limp/hop over to my cheer spot and place my blue and red metallic poms on the ground.

I'm as ready as I can be.

Moments later the rest of the cheerleaders arrive, and we begin to put up the signs we'd made during the week. Members of the Pep Club help by taking banners down to the end zones and hanging signs there for the players — and opponents — to see clearly.

Lora bounds down the stairs and lands in front of me like she's just parachuted out of an airplane. "I've been calling you since after the pep rally. Where have you been?"

"At home. Napping. Showering. Getting ready."

She smacks me on the arm. "I was going to give you a ride to the game. You know, so we partners could arrive together."

"Oh, sorry! Mom and Dad are here, so I rode with them."

She twists to scan the stands. She sees my mom and waves up at her.

"Well, you're hanging with me after the game. Anthony's having a victory party at his house. Food, beer, swimming, making out," she says with a wink. "William is expecting me, and I suspect Daniel will want you there, as well. You can spend the night at my house so you don't have to worry about curfew."

"Sure. Sounds awesome!" I guess Mom and Dad will go along with this plan.

Chloe and her partner, Melanie, arrive last. Chloe is fresh from the salon with perfectly sculpted nails done in red, white, and blue. Her hair is shiny, clean, and pulled into a ponytail. She surveys the signs and how we've hung them on the fence.

"Who has the run-through sign?" she asks clippishly.

Hannah points to the large, folded painted paper on the bench next to the fence. "Ashlee and I brought it down."

"Great." Chloe moves her eyes to me. "So, Hayley, you going to last the whole game?"

Bitch. "I plan on it. I just won't be able to run across the field with y'all to greet the visiting cheerleaders."

Before Chloe can speak, Lora adds, "Hayley can get the Gatorade and sodas taken care of while we do that. How's that?"

The captain shrugs. "Whatever."

Off in the distance, I hear the familiar cadence of the band; the drum beats, bass, and bells chiming out the march into the stadium. For a moment, I pause to see if I have any weird feelings about not being in the band. Hmm . . . nope. It's simply a "been there; done that" sort of thing for me. How far I've come from being hidden under the plumed hat to being on display in front of the entire school.

We cheer for the band as they file into their rows on the bleachers. The majorettes are wearing unbelievably skimpy sequin and satin uniforms that make them look like Las Vegas showgirls. All five of them wear the uniform well, though. I also note the color guard has new flags with our Patriots logo in shimmery fabric.

"Come on, y'all," Chloe indicates. "The team is coming."

I limp slowly behind the rest of the squad, trying not to overdo before the game even starts. We spread the run-through sign out on the field and then await instructions from Chloe. She points to Tara and Brittney and then to Lora and me. "Y'all shoulder up and hold the sign. Everyone else spread out on each side for the guys to run through. Poms in hand!"

Lora fist bumps me, yet I don't know if Chloe's rewarding me for my first game or trying to shame me, thinking I'll fall flat on my face in the turf or get mowed down by the team. I'll show her.

Tossing all of my body weight over to the right side, I lunge over for Lora to run up onto my shoulders. She does so with ease, and I hold my breath as I balance her weight on me. I have to thank Gabriel for the workouts this week. I can totally feel a difference in my muscles. The rest of the girls hand the sign up to the flyers, and I hold on to it with my left hand.

Next thing I know, the Marching Patriots sound out the school fight song and the crowd roars. I hear the pounding of feet coming toward me like wild buffaloes, and I brace for the contact.

Bust!

Riiiiiip!

All that work drawing and painting only to be torn to shreds by the guys in two seconds.

When the last player, trainer, and coach rush past us, Lora dismounts. She then executes three textbook back handsprings while others on the team do the same. I feel like a total dumb-ass just standing there with a leftover handful of the sign. I've got to do something.

"Don't run or jump on that leg," Dr. Dykema said.

Favoring my right side, I wind up into a cartwheel. Basic, yes, but it's the best I can do. The first one is great. The second one is elementary and wobbly. Okay, maybe it's too early to start doing stunts. I wince on my next hobbled step and hope no one caught my pained facial expression. Lora must have, because she rushes over to my crutches and nabs one for me. In no time, she's at my side and we're making our way back to our cheer spot.

"You can't do shit like that yet, Hayley."

"I'm okay," I insist.

Chloe's too busy leading the cheers to comment on my stunt, so I slide into place and join in on the chant she's started. The teams line up on the field, and I spot the jersey with number eleven and "Delafield" on the back. I send good thoughts his way for a powerful performance. He did, after all, promise to score a TD for me.

The game progresses with a swapping of downs. In front of us at the gate are a bunch of little girls in mini Patriots cheerleader uniforms. They aspire to be what I am, a varsity cheerleader.

During a time-out, I sit on the bench and down half a bottle of water. One of the little girls stares at me through the chainlink fence.

"What's wrong with your leg?" she asks. "You've got a bandage on it."

I don't want to frighten her with the *C* word, so I just say, "I had surgery this summer."

"You're still a cheerleader?" she asks with sweet, innocent eyes.

I beam a smile at her. "Yeah, nothing slows me down."

Through a semitoothless grin, she says, "You're cool."

"Thanks, I think you're cool, too."

Halftime comes, and I'm totally exhausted. Not that I'll admit that to anyone. Not to Lora. Not to my parents. Certainly not to Chloe. Instead, I man the drink table and pass out Gatorade, Coke, and Diet Coke to the visiting Highland cheerleaders. They're nice enough and cheer on our band as they perform their program. I watch the familiar steps that I spent three years doing. When the band slides into the final formation and blares out our fight song, we take to our feet and clap for them as they file back up into the stands.

Then the game is back on with Highland accepting the kickoff. We nail them on the fifteen, and the third quarter is off.

"Push 'em back, push 'em back . . . waaaaaaay back, hey!"

"Defense!" Clap-clap. "Defense!" Clap-clap. "Defense!" Clap-clap.

"I said it's great to be a Polk High Patriot! I said it's great to be a Patriots' fan!"

Nevertheless, there's a strange niggling inside of me that tells me something's not . . . right. I sense eyes are on me. I'm doing my best, but are people whispering about me, wondering what I'm doing out here with a bandaged leg and crutches nearby?

Are there mothers in the crowd wondering why their daughter wasn't given the chance to replace me on the squad?

Do my fellow band members think I should be back in the brass section?

Jesus, is paranoia another side effect of chemo and radiation?

Seriously. I don't need these stupid thoughts.

I don't need any kind of darkness to overcome me and get me off track.

I shake out of the funk and spin to refocus on the game. I shouldn't be making up dramas in my own head. Save that for my English compositions.

The third quarter isn't a good one. Coy Parker, the defensive guy Daniel was concerned about, is all over the field, nailing our running back, Marquis Richardson, and sticking him into the dirt. The poor runner can't gain an inch, much less a yard. Add to that, Highland manages to tie up the score at twenty-one each.

"We've got to change our offensive strategy," I say to Lora.

"Go tell Coach Gaither," she says with a laugh. She spins back to the crowd to start a cheer, and I join in.

"Whattaya want?"

"TD!"

"What's that?"

"Touchdown!"

We hold up our hands with four fingers showing when the last quarter starts, and we begin chanting, "Fourth quarter's ours!"

It's a major defensive battle back and forth, and I fear we may have a loss on our hands. I can't worry about my leg or who's staring at me or what Chloe thinks of my performance tonight. We simply can*not* lose this game — not the first home game. That would muck up the entire rest of the season.

Just like in any college or pro game, everything turns on a dime in football. All my negative thoughts are erased when Daniel breaks free of the man-to-man coverage Coy Parker's putting on him and he hauls in a twenty-six-yard pass from Skipper. Daniel tucks the ball and sprints into the end zone for the touchdown. He hands it off to the ref in a very sportsmanlike manner, although there's a little chest bumping on the five-yard line with some of his teammates.

As time ticks down, the guys on the sideline storm the field. We've won! The Patriots are two and oh. We cheerleaders are right behind them, mixing in the melee of tired players. I propel myself like a marathoner on my crutches as I move through the sweaty, dirty crowd of Patriots and Highlanders congregating at midfield.

Then, I hear my name, and I'm scooped up into the strong arms of number eleven. My crutches fall to the ground, and I hold on as I'm swung around. Daniel is stinky and dripping wet; yet I don't care. He sets me on the ground and kisses me right there in front of everyone on the field.

"How'd you like that?" he asks.

"Fantabulous!"

"I scored that for you, remember?"

I nod, unable to speak.

He places his hot forehead against mine and whispers, "My own personal cheerleader."

* * *

"COME ON, HAYLEY!" LORA calls out to me in the locker room.

"I have to finish with my hair!" I was so nasty hot after the game that I had to take a quick shower. Afterward, I attack a Conair, blasting it at maximum high as my wet hair flies about. I've got to get my ass in gear for Anthony Ricketts's party.

Five minutes later, I pull my purse-size travel flat iron through my mostly dry hair, watching the steam rise as I drag it through. The iron snags on my hair and jerks out several strands. Yikes! Lora's going to kill me as it is. I tap a smidge of powder to the deep chickenpox scar on the side of my nose and spread it across the rest of my face. I'm lucky I'm not more scarred, considering how badly I got the disease last fall. Mom gave me her long, white evening gloves from her prom days and made me wear them so I wouldn't scratch myself. Good thing she did.

"Come onnnnnnnnn . . ." Lora whines at me. "Meet me at the car."

"Be right there."

Okay . . . I step back and check myself out in the mirror. My uniform is still clean, albeit a little damp from exertion. I actually look pretty good despite the crutches and bandage.

Outside the gym, Mom and Dad are getting into the truck. "So, you're going to a party and then spending the night with Lora," Mom reiterates.

"*Oui.*"

"No alcohol, Hayley," Dad says firmly.

"Dad, it's not that kind of—"

"I'm serious."

"Yes, sir." He's so old-fashioned.

"And if Lora drinks, you call me and I'll come get you."

I kiss his cheek. "Thanks, Dad."

Before they issue any more rules or edicts, I hop into the front of Lora's Beamer.

The party is going full blast when we arrive. The music blares from the backyard. Good thing Anthony lives outside the city limits so there aren't any neighbors who might complain.

Lora hooks her arm through mine and leads me into the back-yard filled with tons of people. To the left, a barbecue grill is fired on high, grilling burgers, dogs, corn, and chicken. To the right, lounge chairs are strewn around the custom-made swimming pool. There's a keg, a DJ, and even laser lights. Man, Anthony doesn't mess around. Even though the food smells heavenly, I don't dare eat anything. My nausea is back, and I wish I had a Snickers bar in my purse.

Damn . . . I'll be glad when these side effects are over.

I watch as William tips his cup in Lora's direction. He is so totally into her. Why not? She's pretty and she's a genuinely nice person.

I pour a Diet Coke into a cup so people can't see what I'm drinking. I can pretend it's alcoholic. It's not that I'm a prude or anything—and I am underage, after all—I just want my wits about me this evening. Besides, my post-chemo tummy doesn't need any intrusions. It would be just my luck to take a few sips and then puke all over the place. I stick out enough as it is already without adding on that stigma.

Man, if this is how we party after winning the home opener, I can't wait to see what happens if we get to the state championship. A zip of excitement zings up my back at the thought of making it that far.

Lora points out over the lawn where most of the PHS Patri-ots roster is scattered about playing volleyball in a sandpit (aren't they tired from the game?), chugging beer or roughhousing in the swimming pool.

Before I know it, a volleyball comes flying toward me and re-markably, I'm able to half herkie myself into the air—landing on my right foot—to avoid a smash that would have smarted like all hell.

"Dude, watch it!" someone shouts.

Daniel rushes over to my side. "I was going to ask if you were okay, but after that bit of gymnastics, I'd say you're just fine." He loops his arm around me and hugs me to him. When he touches me, I nearly jump away from the shock of the contact. I'm still not used to Daniel Delafield being into me.

"Seriously, are you all right?" Daniel asks, caressing my arm.

"Totally fine."

"Throw the damn ball back, Delafield!" one of his teammates shouts out. He does as he's asked.

Daniel cracks a crooked smile at me and then leans down toward my shoulder. Hot lips meet my skin in a surprising sizzle when he kisses me. He straightens and then lifts his eyes to me.

A smile paints across my face. "Oh, I think you can do better than that."

There are a few catcalls around us as Daniel takes my hand and leads me into the house. People are everywhere, dancing and drinking and eating. Daniel weaves us down a long hallway and into a darkened room where several couples are making out to the light of the TV.

He indicates an available couch in the corner. "Over there."

Next thing I know, we're making out. Daniel is fiery hot and kisses like a professional. His tongue touches mine, and I feel as if I'll explode into a million miniscule sections. His hands work themselves into my hair, and he strokes at the freshly shampooed length.

He breathes deeply and then whispers, "I love your hair. The way it feels and smells. Mmm." Then he nibbles his way down my jaw line and neck to my ear. I am going to explode.

Daniel pulls back when his massive class ring gets snagged in my hair. I try to untangle us, but next thing I know, he's holding a clump of brown strands.

"Eww . . . what's going on here?"

"Damn, Daniel, you pulled my hair out."

He examines the knot and then tosses it over toward a silver garbage can. "Sorry, babe."

"It's okay."

Without another thought, I press my lips back to his.

CHAPTER TWENTY-EIGHT

Just when you think it can't get any worse, it can.
And just when you think it can't get any better, it does.

—Nicholas Sparks

Two saturday mornings later, I wake up in my bed with a pile of hair on the pillow and stuck on the mattress. This has been happening little by little the past couple of weeks.

This is more, though.

A lot more.

My hands crawl across the sheet to make sure it's actually mine.

It's mine.

No doubt about it.

I sit up, and my heartbeat stammers my panic.

"Son of a bitch!" I scream out in a mixed cocktail of fear, anger, and disbelief.

The doctors all told me one of the main repercussions of chemotherapy is hair loss. Any idiot knows that. Since it didn't happen immediately to me, I thought I'd sidestepped it.

But you can't dodge the Grand Canyon of side effects.

I've pretty much been ignoring the clumps of hair in my brush by flushing the wads of evidence down the toilet. I have thick,

thick hair to begin with, so maybe I didn't really notice it was thinning.

Since ponytails are the "thing" for the varsity cheerleaders, I've just taken to wearing my hair up all the time hoping people wouldn't notice how the thickness was diminishing. By game time last night, only I knew how bad it really was when I tugged my hand through my hair only to pull back a fistfull of chestnut strands equal to what Daniel had caught in his ring after the second game.

I stare at the rat's nest underneath me in the bed and sadly call out. "Dad!" I run my hands into my hair and there's an even bigger knotted mess on the crown of my head. "Dad!"

I don't know why I think to call for him instead of Mom. He bounds up the stairs two at a time.

"Are you all right, Little Kid?"

"Look," I say, pointing to my mattress.

Dad's face falls for a moment, then he tries to soothe me. "The doctors said hair loss was a possibility."

I tamp down my dread by swallowing hard. Fiery heartburn flames up my throat, threatening to consume me. "It's been four weeks since my chemo. I didn't think I'd lose my hair."

I sniffle a bit as Dad goes to my dresser in search of my paddle brush.

"I'll take care of that knot."

He sits on the bed and I put my back to him so he can get a good angle. He carefully tugs the brush through my long hair, working at the knot on the back of my head.

"Remember how I used to brush your hair when you were a little girl? You'd sit in front of me as I'd watch the news."

I nod. "I always loved it. Why did we stop doing that?"

He snickers. "You grew up and learned how to brush your own hair."

I let out a muffled laugh and languish for a sec in the memory. "I guess you're right," I finally say. "Thanks for doing this now."

I sit quietly as Dad gently strokes through the mess on top of my head. Five minutes later, Dad speaks to me, barely above a whisper and a quiver in his usually brave voice.

"I'm so sorry, Hayley. It couldn't be helped."

My chest aches from the massive hammering of my heart against my ribs. First, I shift so I can see the brush. It's full of my brown hair and there's also a substantial pile in Dad's lap. I'm almost afraid to turn and look in the mirror.

I have to, though.

I have to face myself.

The reflection I see is not me.

It's an image of a girl I don't recognize.

One whose eyes are ripe with horror and doubt.

But this girl is me.

Through some miracle of the moment, I find my voice.

"I-i-i-it's gone . . ."

"Not all of it," Dad says in a hushed tone.

Not even his tender voice can salve this wound.

"Enough of it's gone," I say. "Like, you can see my head . . . everywhere."

My shaky hand reaches up to find only a few stray wisps of hair remaining on my scalp. My bald, white scalp.

Is this really me?

I thought I was past everything and back to my life. Now *this*?

I've seriously lost all my long hair?

Before I can stop them, tears stream from my sleep-filled eyes. I can't halt them any more than I could keep the roaring river from tumbling over Niagara Falls.

"Oh, Daddy," I cry out.

A torturous shriek fills the space of my room and I realize it came from deep within me.

"I know, baby."

Dad pulls me into his arms and kisses my forehead. We hug each other tightly; our tears mingling together.

This is the second time I cry.

At least my daddy is here to comfort me.

* * *

I HIDE OUT IN the house all day Saturday, avoiding Lora's texts. She wants me to go shopping with her later, but it's the last thing I want to do. I know I'll eventually have to go out in public, but why rush it?

I tell her I have horrific menstrual cramps, which she buys, and leaves me alone.

The day is spent downloading historical romances to my e-reader so that I can escape into the fantasy of the ladies in lace and hoop skirts and their hair up in perfectly coifed chignons. Whatever the hell those are.

Leeny doesn't leave my side, obviously sensing my anguish. She got sprayed by a skunk two years ago when she escaped the house one time. The vet had to shave off her thick gray fur to get the stink out. I suspect she knows what I'm going through.

Sunday morning, I avoid going to church. Quite frankly, I'm a little miffed at God for what I'm going through. Or maybe I should be pissed off at Satan. Honestly, I don't know who to blame. I don't think it's God's fault, per se, that I contracted cancer, but why couldn't he have protected me? I've been baptized. I take Communion regularly and pray (almost) every night when I don't fall asleep first. I've been going to Sunday school religiously—no pun intended—since I can remember, and I've been a member of Methodist Youth Fellowship and choir. I totally believe in God the Father, the Son, and Holy Spirit and that I will spend my life in heaven with them when I die. But why can't my earthly life be better?

Why am I going through this?

I thought everything was over when the tumor was cut out.

The only obstacle was to walk without a limp.

Now this.

Baldy McBalderton the varsity cheerleader.

Fuck this noise.

By six o'clock that night, Mom won't let me sulk in my room any longer. She insists that I come to the dinner table even though my eyes are swollen from crying and blowing my nose nonstop.

"This is *not* God's fault," Mom snaps at me, knowing what I'm thinking apparently. "He spared your life, Hayley, by allowing you to find that tumor in time to take care of it."

I pick at my baked chicken and rice, feeling sorry for the fowl that had to sacrifice its life so we could eat tonight. Poor bastard.

I don't want any part of it.

I push the plate away.

No food sounds interesting or appetizing.

A chalky aridness coats the inside of my throat.

Nothing—and no one—can cheer me up.

Doubt is my closest friend and most detested enemy.

Stupidity surrounds me.

Right at the peak of my high school social life. Right when I have an amazing, popular boyfriend. Right when my crowning achievement is being a varsity cheerleader.

I'm frickin' bald and I have to go to school tomorrow.

I'm bald . . .

I'm bald . . .
I have no hair . . .
I look like an . . .

Mom slams her utensils to the table, knocking me out of my pity party. "Hayley Ann Matthews. Stop the damn pouting right now!"

I jolt up in my seat, not believing the insensitivity my mother is showing at this moment.

"Mom, in case you haven't noticed, I'm *bald!*"

"Big deal, Hayley. Hair grows back. Instead of wallowing in self-pity and trying to place the blame on God, you should thank Him—and your doctors—that you still have a leg to walk on. You have been so upbeat and positive up until now. You *can't* let this defeat you."

Dad reaches out to stop her. "Nan, don't you think you're being a little—"

"I will *not* have her doubting her faith, Jared."

"I don't . . . really," I say meekly. "I just thought I was through everything. Through all the bullshit." I bite my lip. "Sorry. How do I go to school looking like this?"

Dad smiles at Mom and then turns to me. "You'll go like you do every other day. You'll walk in the door, go to your locker, say hello to your friends, and go to class. You're still the same person, Hayley. There's more to you than just your hair."

Mom chimes in, calmer now. "You're alive, sweetie. That's what's important."

I suppose she's right. One day I'll look back on all of this and realize my parents knew what they were talking about. Still, it doesn't make going to school tomorrow any easier.

I'm trying *not* to feel sorry for myself, but it's pretty damn hard not to.

There's very little sleep that night and in the morning, my getting ready time is significantly less since I have nothing on my head to style. I stare at myself in the mirror, trying to find myself in the image somewhere. The features are still the same, albeit a bit sadder.

Leeny rubs up against me, purring and meowing. She still loves me. Just the way I am. Mom and Dad do, too. I should love myself.

"Hair grows back," I say to the mirror.

There's a deep, cleansing breath for confidence, and I grab my purse, backpack, and crutches and head out the door.

Mom lets me take her car to school . . . I suppose in the event that I need to flee. I won't let that be an option, though.

When I walk in through the glass doors, there are noticeable gasps, sideway glances, and unspoken judgments regarding my bald pate. I ignore them and instead head straight to my locker. I stash the books I don't need right away and pull out the AP English Literature textbook.

There's a sobbing cry beside me. My partner stands there stock-still as her mouth hangs open. "When did it happen, Hayley?"

"Saturday morning," I say quietly.

"Oh my God," Lora says. Then she wraps her arms around me. I need this support more than anything right now. Staving back tears that I refuse to shed at school, I hug her back and try to laugh about it.

"It's my extreme makeover."

Water pools in her eyes. "I'm glad *you* can laugh about it."

"What's my choice?"

"You rock, girl," Lora says. "I don't know if I'd have the guts to walk into PHS like that."

I had to. Mom's right. I can't let the shit get the best of me.

"Again, what choice do I have?" This time, I snicker even harder, really starting to feel the meaning of the words.

The whispers and eyes of fellow students dance and swirl around me. I refuse to let them consume me, though. Mentally, I shield myself in a barrier of protection to knock down any negativity or criticism. I have to in order to get through this. The worst part is behind me. I have to keep my eye on a brighter, healthier future.

Still, I'm fully aware that I'm the talk of the school and not in a good way.

"Wow, would you look at Hayley Matthews," I hear from a distance.

Leave it to Gabriel Tremblay to save the day. Without missing a beat, my friend with the shaved head strides right up to me and rubs my head. "Look at this! A PHS cheerleader has so much school spirit that she shaved her head, too."

A smile cracks on my face.

Kids nearby murmur among themselves with some oohs and ahhs here and there. Do they honestly believe I'd do that?

"Well, that worked," he says to me. He scrubs his own severe buzzcut and smiles. "You're one of us now, Hayley."

For a moment, I'm almost no longer self-conscious about my lack of hair.

That is until my boyfriend passes by.

Daniel sees me and immediately bursts out laughing. "Hayley! Holy shit! You shaved your head? What the fuck? You had such gorgeous hair."

Thanks . . . I know . . .

Lora moves to chastise him. "Daniel, don't—"

"Wait, wait," he continues. "Is that some sort of makeup skullcap thing? Some sort of joke?"

Gabriel grinds his teeth together. "Dude, are you seriously this insensitive?"

Daniel's clueless. "What? What did I say?"

His laughter pierces my soul and echoes through my brain. I want nothing more than to crack him in the knees with my crutches just to shut him up. I muster up the courage I so need at this moment and snarl out at him.

"I had chemo and radiation, you asshole. *That's* why I lost my hair."

Awkwardly, Daniel steps back, and embarrassment is written all over his face. He advances on me and pulls me to him. "Oh, babe. I'm so sorry. I am an asshole."

His hand moves up and briefly touches my scalp, but he quickly moves it away, as if burned by the skin.

"Everyone's going to react differently," I say. "I know I freaked out."

"You're still adorable," Lora says. "Right, Daniel?"

He stares down into my face, and I know he has no idea what words could make this right. "You're the cutest," he manages to say. The words seem a little flat. Or maybe I'm just reading too much into it.

The bell for first period rings and we disperse.

Lora walks beside me and says it's going to be my "signature look." "I'm going to make you some head rags to wear. We'll sew sequins on them and make them to match the cheerleading uniforms."

"That's a perfect idea," Gabriel says. I hadn't even realized he was still hanging with us. I have him to thank for being able to breathe normally at this point.

A sigh of relief escapes my chest, and I head off with him as Lora goes to her first-period class.

"You're gonna be okay, Hay."

* * *

I MAY BE, BUT Chloe Bradenton certainly isn't.

At practice, she's horrified.

"We have a *look* on this squad."

"I understand," I say. "Like I planned this."

She softens when she seems to realize what a class act bitch she's being. "I'm sorry, Hayley. I know all of this has been difficult for you. But I have to think of the squad. First, you're limping and using your crutches, and now you're . . . you're . . ."

"You can say it," I interrupt. "I'm bald."

"We have a look," she reiterates, like I'm stupid.

Hands on hips, I stare her down. "What do you suggest I do?"

Chloe thinks for a moment, glancing around at the other girls. Then she snaps her fingers. "I've got it! Have you thought of getting a long wig?"

* * *

AFTER SCHOOL, I GO pick up Mom, and she and I drive forty-five minutes south to Dothan to do some wig shopping. I'm not exactly thrilled about this. I want to keep my spot on the squad. I just don't know if hiding myself under synthetic hair is the answer.

We park the car and walk into the mall. I've passed this store a hundred times before when Mom and I've been shopping for school clothes, although I never pictured myself shopping here.

Roxanne's WigWam.

The corniest name ever for a wig shop.

The front of the store looks like a tepee. I can't believe I'm coming in here.

An older, chubby woman asks if she can help us. She's totally wearing a wig, à la Carol Brady from *The Brady Bunch* reruns on television. She wears it well, but I don't think I'll be ordering up that look today.

"My daughter underwent chemotherapy and has lost her hair, as you can see," my mom explains.

Mrs. Brady gasps and pulls her hands to her mouth. "Cancer? In someone so young?"

"Yes, ma'am," I say politely, and appreciate the woman's reaction. Surely she's met a lot of cancer patients in her line of work? Right?

Then she sits me down in a wicker chair in front of a simple mirror. "I have several looks that might interest you, young lady."

I point at her retreating form. "I already know what I —" but she's disappeared in the back.

"Trust her," Mom says. "She does this for a living."

I relax into the creaking chair and await Mrs. Brady's return.

Mom can't help but snort when she sees the choices on the plastic mannequin heads before me. First, Mrs. Brady brings me this ridiculously long, blond wig. She lays it on my head and proceeds to tell me, "It's you. It's so you."

Tugging it off, I set it back on the fake head. "Only at Halloween, I'm afraid."

Next, there's a thick, black, curly wig. Totally not me.

A short red bob might work if I'm ever in the witness protection program.

Finally, the sales lady reaches to a top shelf and pulls down a long wig made of soft mahogany-colored hair with stylish bangs. The lady fits it over my head and begins fussing with it.

"Now, this one is called 'Lavish,' and it's from the Raquel Welch collection."

"Rachel who?" I ask.

Mom rolls her eyes. "Raquel. She was an actress back in the 1970s."

The sales lady gushes over me. "Oh yes. The Raquel Welch wigs are top-quality designer wigs. This look offers the ultimate in a natural front hairline. You can see this sleek cut includes a tapered front and sides that blend with the long, straight layers that fall all the way to the middle of your back."

"I like it," Mom says. "How much?"

"This one's on sale for one hundred and ten dollars, and you get a free wig stand with it."

Just what every high school senior wants in her room. A wig stand. And a free one at that.

I survey myself in the mirror, moving it around my head to glance at all the angles. The hair is pretty enough and I sort of look like myself again. I attempt to gather it up into a ponytail, but the whole thing just pops off my head.

"Holy crap."

"Hayley."

"Mom, this is silly."

The saleswoman senses my hesitation. "It's totally you, my dear."

"Actually, it's *not* me at all, ma'am."

It's not her fault I'm completely against this entire shopping excursion.

Mrs. Brady literally crams the fake hair back onto my head, squiggling it down over my ears and again picking at the bangs to set them to the left. I stare past her into the mirror.

Just as before in my room when I saw my bald pate for the first time, I don't recognize myself.

My eyes are sunken into my face. Sad. Lost.

The real me — the Hayley who doesn't let shit get her down — is hidden behind this wall of synthetic fibers.

I feel like a fraud. A farce. Someone wearing a façade.

Like I'm ashamed of what I went through.

Like I can just stick this, this, this . . . thing on my head and cover up the fact that I had cancer.

Like I can tuck the surgery and scars, chemo and radiation up underneath a wig so no one can see them.

Besides, is the wig for me to feel better about myself or for other people not to feel sorry for me?

I'm not going to do it.

I politely swipe Mrs. Brady's fidgety hands away from me and remove the "designer" wig.

"Thank you so much for your help, ma'am. I'm all set."

She balks. "But—"

"I am who I am," I say to both her and my mother.

The woman gathers the plastic heads and huffs off into the back.

My eyes meet Mom's in the mirror. She places her hands on my shoulders and gives me a supportive squeeze.

"I can't do it, Mom," I say quietly as the emotions reach a boiling point within me.

"I understand, sweetie."

"It's just not me." I spot myself in the mirror one more time. My brown eyes shine out at me, glistening with the tears I'm about to shed. "They can take me as I am or not at all."

And with that, the teardrops roll lazily down my cheeks.

This is the third time I cry. Mom and I sob quietly together. Then we dry our eyes and leave the WigWam hand in hand.

CHAPTER TWENTY-NINE

*Neither do men light a candle, and put it under a bushel, but on
a candlestick; and it giveth light unto all that are in the house.*

—MATTHEW 5:15

WHEN I WALKED OUT of the house this morning, Mom told
me not to hide my light under a bushel. It sounded corny at the
time, but as I cruise the hallway at school, I realize that if I put
off positive energy and confidence in my state of baldness, that
"light" that I emit will spread.

People still give me the once-over, and I hear whispered words:
"bald"; "cancer"; "cheerleader." Yeah, well, tell me something I
don't know. I simply smile and find my locker to stash my books.

I hold my bald head up high and pretend it's the absolute hottest look for the fall season.

Gabriel appears next to me with a large shopping bag from
Macy's. "Look what I've got for you."

I screw up my face. "You went shopping for me?"

"Nah, I raided our storage at home." Peering into the bag, I see
a bunch of baseball caps. "You remember my big sister, Camille,
right? She's in school at UGA in Athens. Two years ago, she went
through this hat stage. Mom and I thought you could use these."

My heart warms as I rummage through the bag. There are several NFL caps including the Falcons, Dolphins, Jaguars, and Saints. There are also a well-worn Georgia Bulldogs hat and a brand-new black and white hounds tooth one for the University of Alabama. I find a Diesel, a DKNY, a Mickey Mouse hat, and a floppy straw beach hat.

I hold the straw hat up and giggle. "I don't think this one's appropriate for school."

Gabriel pushes the bag into my hand. "They're yours to do as you see fit."

"Thanks, Gabriel. This is totally sweet."

For good measure, he rubs the top of my head like he's shining a bowling ball, and then he points to his own shorn look. He's taken to doing this a lot to me. I don't mind in the least. "Don't worry, hair grows fast."

I've noticed many of the football players who shaved their heads are sporting some new growth. Most look like they've returned from military boot camp.

Two depressing Virginia Woolf reads later, Gabriel and I pack up our books and head out of AP English Lit.

"I think the hounds tooth would go great with your black shirt and jeans today," Gabriel says with a smile.

"Oh yeah? Well, I am a Crimson Tide fan."

"See you sixth period. Be prepared for the workout of your life."

I salute him and head back to my locker to retrieve the Bama cap. He's right. It looks *très* cute.

* * *

LATER THAT DAY, I discover Gabriel wasn't kidding when he said he was going to test my limits.

I grit my teeth as I push the leg press forward.

"Grrrrr . . ." I grind out. "Damn, how much weight do you have on there?"

He moves to check. "Fifteen pounds. Again. Three sets of ten. You can do it."

Can I?

I have to.

This is my rehabilitation.

I push again and feel as though the scar on my leg is going to rip open.

"Arrrrrrrggghhh . . ."

"Remember . . . no pain, no gain."

"I honestly want to smack the person who came up with that," I say when the weights fall back into place.

Gabriel keeps encouraging me. "What's the mantra?"

"Hurts so good . . . hurts so good."

"Good girl. One more set and we'll move along."

I count the final set in my head.

Eight . . .

Nine . . .

Ten . . .

"Phew!" I reach for the towel and mop the sweat off my face. I giggle for a moment as I swipe the fabric over my head.

"What's so funny?" Gabriel asks.

"I don't have to worry about messing up my hair now."

We chuckle together and it feels good. He's not poking fun or laughing at me. Hell, *I'm* laughing at myself. He's enjoying the moment with me, and that means the world.

"Yo, Tremb," Skipper O'Rourke calls out. "Spot me, dude?"

Gabriel looks over to our star defensive back who is stretched out on the free weight bench. "Sure thing." Back to me, he asks, "You good over here?"

I give him a mock salute. "Yes, sir!"

I concentrate on my upper-body strength now, working on three different machines to exercise the deltoids, pectorals, and trapezius. Gabriel's a good coach, teaching me the different muscle groups and how they can help me when I'm lifting Lora. With the firmness I have in my upper body, it doesn't matter that I can't run or jump. I can toss any of our flyers and help anyone get to the top of our pyramids and stunts.

"Who's the new guy?" I hear Daniel calling out. He then stops next to me on the bench press and makes eye contact. "Oh, Hayley. I was only kidding."

Ouch. "You'd better have been."

"Smooth, Delafield," Skipper notes, flat on his back.

Daniel reaches out to run his hands through my hair as he's become accustomed to doing, only there's nothing there to stroke anymore. Awkwardly, he pulls his hand away and instead rests it on my shoulder. "So . . ."

"So . . ."

"Do you have practice after school?"

"Every day," I say with a smile. I try to read his thoughts, but I'm not exactly psychic and he's not particularly demonstrative when it comes to emotions.

"Meet me after and I'll give you a ride home."

Now, that's the Daniel I'm used to. Maybe my lack of hair won't put a wedge between us after all.

Following two hours of dance practice and a new pom routine, I gather my things and plop down on the tailgate of Daniel's truck. I toss a Dolphins baseball cap on my head, turning it backwards with the bill pointed at my back. I'm sure I look ridiculous. I was never a hat person before chemo, and something tells me I'm not exactly one now. But I appreciate that Gabriel made the effort to try and make me feel better.

The sound of heavy football pads hitting the flatbed startles me to attention.

"Ready to go?" Daniel asks. His face is red from exertion.

I climb into the truck and adjust the air conditioner vent to blow directly in my face. Daniel does the same, and then we get going. We pretty much ride in silence through the fast food strip of Maxwell until he pulls into Crower's Fried Chicken. Usually, I salivate at the thought of their chicken nuggets and special sauce with the poppy seeds. However, the odor of the hot grease that floats in the air surrounding the restaurant makes me want to gag.

"You want anything?" Daniel asks.

"Diet Coke?"

"That's it? I have money if you want food."

I cover my nose and mouth and try not to wretch. "I'm okay. Still nauseated from my treatments."

Fortunately, it's a quick transaction, and Daniel passes a very large soda and straw to me. I gulp down the cola and try not to let the smell of his food make me ill.

Soon, we turn down my street, and Daniel parks in front of my house. It seems as if he wants to talk. I wonder if this is the breakup speech. I guess I wouldn't blame him for not wanting to date the bald chick.

Finally, he looks at me and says, "I'm sorry about your hair. I feel really, really bad for you."

Annoyance boils under my skin. "I don't want your pity, Daniel."

"I wasn't pitying you, I promise."

Maybe I'm too sensitive, but I can't help saying, "It sure sounded like it."

"Not at all."

I lick my dry lips with my even drier tongue. "I need your support, Daniel."

"I understand." He lowers his voice. "It's just that you had such pretty hair."

If I agree with him, I sound like a self-aggrandizing bitch like Chloe Bradenton. I sit quietly for a moment and gather my thoughts.

I swallow hard and spill my guts to him. "You have *no idea* how hard it is to wake up each morning knowing I have to go to school looking like this." I point to my scalp for good measure. "Not only that, I have to retrain the muscles in my leg to work again. There's no nerve there anymore to tell my foot when to lift up and down. I'm literally having to learn to walk again. I feel like an idiot."

I can see he's a bit ashamed. "I had no idea, Hayley."

"My only goal is to live a normal life and not melt into a little pile of goo every day."

"Seems you're handling things pretty amazingly so far," he says, and smiles.

"I'm trying. Really, I am." I glance at his hand on the seat, and I so much want to take it. It's his move, though. Mustering up a strong breath, I say, "I need to know if you're going to be there for me."

He stretches his large hand out and weaves my fingers into his. "Don't worry, Hayley. You can count on me."

* * *

WEEK FIVE INTO SCHOOL, I'm sitting in French II, mentally walking through the pep rally routine we'll be doing Friday instead of reading about famous Francophones and deciding who to do my oral essay on. French is the last thing on my mind when the Patriots are still undefeated. It's up to us cheerleaders to keep school spirit at an all-time high to keep the players and coaches supported and motivated.

The intercom rings out, and Mademoiselle Saunders, my teacher, instructs us to listen up.

It's Mr. Parish, our principal. I know exactly what could be so important as to interrupt third period. According to Mademoiselle Saunders's wall calendar—the one with the large pictures of the Eiffel Tower—it's mid-October, which means one thing.

Homecoming court nominations.

I bounce a bit in my seat in anticipation. Homecoming's not for two weeks, but it's an unspoken tradition at Polk High that the varsity cheerleaders are a shoe-in for nominations. I don't know if there's ever been an instance in PHS history where that hasn't happened. Cheerleaders *always* get nominated.

My pulse picks up, and I'm breathless with anticipation. Of course, I don't expect to actually make the court or anything, but like any Oscar nominee will tell the press, being nominated is an honor in and of itself.

"Attention students," Mr. Parish says over the PA system. "In recognition of PHS's upcoming homecoming celebrations, I'm pleased to announce this year's homecoming court nominees. Starting with the freshman class . . ."

I listen up to names I don't really recognize until he says, "Madison Hutchinson." Awesome, little Madi is the first cheerleader on the list.

"Next, our sophomore nominees are Lauren Compton, Samantha Fowler, Paige—"

I tune out as Mr. Parish mentions the other three nominees, all of them non-cheerleaders. The tradition continues.

I'm certainly not surprised when Ashleigh, Tara, Hannah, and Brittney complete the ballot for the junior class. That just leaves us five senior girls to fill the nominations for the twelfth grade.

I sit tall in my seat and smooth my sweaty palms on the sides of my pants. The only other time I've heard my name on the loudspeaker was last spring when Mr. Parish listed the new squad.

This is truly a moment to remember and to cherish, so I tug out my BlackBerry, scroll to the Voice Note function, and press Record. Why not?

With my heart ticking away like a time bomb in need of diffusion, I listen closely to the principal.

"And the nominees for the senior class, the list of which will include those girls eligible for homecoming queen are . . . Chloe Bradenton, Lora Russell, Melanie Otto, Ashlee Grimes, and . . ."

And me!

Say it . . . Hayley Matthews!

"Furonda Garrison."

Who? What?

The breath rushes out of my body, and I fear I'm going to slide to the floor in a massive heap of disappointment. I hear a snicker behind me as if someone else noticed that my name wasn't on the list.

Furonda Garrison's a nice enough person. Pretty. Head majorette.

She's not a cheerleader, though.

I am.

I was supposed to be nominated.

So much for school tradition.

Eleven of the twelve varsity cheerleaders are on the nomination ballot.

I'm the only one left off.

Gulping down my pride, I raise my hand to get Mademoiselle

Saunders's attention. She nods in my direction. "May I please go to the bathroom?"

The teacher clicks her tongue at me and waves her finger. *"Veuillez le dire en français."*

Say it in French. Right.

"Oh, um . . ." I think quickly and stumble over my request as I do my best to keep the hot tears that are building behind my eyes from falling in front of my classmates. "Um . . . *est-ce que je peux satisfaire vais la salle de bains?"*

"Oui, vous pouvez."

Since the period is almost over, I gather my belongings and stow them into my backpack. Expeditiously, I crutch my way out of the room and down the abandoned corridor to the girls' bathroom. I seek out the farthest stall on the end and hang my crutches up on the hook behind the door.

I sink to the toilet seat and cover my face with my shaking hands.

The flood gates open, and the one-woman pity party resumes.

This is the fourth time I cry. I cry all alone in the bathroom until my eyes are puffy.

CHAPTER THIRTY

We cannot direct the wind but we can adjust the sails.

—Attributed to Bertha Calloway

The absence of my name from the list of homecoming court nominees isn't acknowledged by my fellow cheerleaders. It's the white elephant in the room no one wants to recognize. Instead, at practice we throw ourselves into learning a new pompom routine.

I'm beyond exhausted when Lora drops me off at home. The whole ride, she was talking to William on the phone, so neither of us had to discuss the homecoming court dissing. I guess I understand how the rest of the student body wouldn't want a cancer patient representing them. I only wonder if people are ashamed that I'm front and center cheering for the Patriots each week. Is it an embarrassment to the PHS community for me to be all bald, leading cheers?

I don't want to overthink this, which I'm so good at doing. I earned the spot, and I am going to cheer, come hell or high water. I'm getting stronger each day, my leg muscles are developing more, and I have more school spirit than the other eleven girls put together.

I wave and blow a kiss at Lora as I step out of her car at my house. She tinks the horn and pulls off, still chatting away with her boyfriend.

Now, I'm sitting at the kitchen table reading my AP Economics book about supply and demand, an economic model of price determination in a market that concludes that, in a competitive market, the unit price for particular goods will vary until it settles at a point where the quantity demanded by consumers at the current price will equal the quantity supplied by the producer, resulting in an economic equality of price and quantity. Phew . . . I totally memorized that.

Apparently the supply of available cheerleaders for the homecoming court didn't equal the demand from the student body, resulting in my economic disparity. God, it's a horrible, horrible analysis. My teacher, Mrs. Hildegard, would probably give me an instant F for such an asinine comparison.

I throw my yellow highlighter across the kitchen table, watching as it lands in the container that holds the pink packets of Sweet'N Low.

The back door bursts open, and in walks Mom carrying a bulky, white plastic shopping bag.

"Oh good, Hayley, you're here," she says, a bit out of breath.

"What in the world do you have in there?" I ask.

I move to help her, but she waves me off. "No, no. I've got it."

"Yeah, but what *is* it?"

In one fell swoop, she upends the plastic bag, and hair products and other various items spill across the table.

"I went to the Hair Cuttery and talked to my hairdresser, Tommy. You remember him. Tommy Shaw, lovely man."

Impatience blankets me, especially after the disappointment of the day. "Point, Mom?"

Mom puts her hands on her hips. "What's with the attitude?"

"I'm sorry," I say, closing my textbook. "Lots of homework." I don't want to upset her by telling her I was the only cheerleader who didn't get nominated for the homecoming court.

"Well, this is homework, as well." She starts stacking the products in a line of obedient hair care soldiers. "I spoke with Tommy about growing hair."

I'm too stunned to speak.

"There's no secret formula or magic bullet, but there are things we can do to encourage growth. The average person only has six inches of growth in a year, so I figure that's a jumping-off ground for us."

I peruse the products on the table. There's a bottle of henna shampoo and a whole slew of vitamins: B-6, biotin, folic acid, magnesium, sulfur, silica, zinc, and vitamin E.

"Wow—that's a lot to swallow. Literally."

Mom ignores my bad pun and continues. "Tommy said the henna shampoo will promote growth, and the vitamins will help strengthen the follicles and speed growth." She then pulls papers from her purse—stuff she's printed off from the Internet about aiding hair and nail growth. My nails have become brittle and started splitting, too. "Here," Mom says when she sees me checking out my fingers. "Gelatin capsules will help."

"I'm supposed to take all of this?" I ask, not in a complaining way but more to note what my new daily regimen will need to be.

"Yes! We'll get one of those pill dispensers from the drugstore and we'll lay everything out—what you need to take when and how often."

I nod my head in agreement.

"Oh, and from now on, you'll be eating a diet that's rich in protein, which stimulates hair growth, as well."

"Right, that's the same thing Ross told me. You know, Lora's uncle."

Mom's eyes brighten with recognition. "Oh, the nice man who brought the cheerleaders to Birmingham. That was very lovely of him."

"He gave me some protein bars and shake mixes that I've started using."

"That's very nice of him. Did you write him a thank-you note?"

"No, Mom. I just told him 'thank you.'" She's so old-fashioned sometimes.

I get the motherly eye roll, and then she disappears back out the door. I hear her fumbling around in the car. I'm hobbling out to help her when she hands up four bags of groceries to me from the bottom step. "Take those in the kitchen, if you can. I'll get the rest."

I begin unloading everything onto the counter: two dozen eggs, several different kinds of cheeses, steaks, burger meat, cottage cheese, peanuts, peanut butter, black beans, green beans, chicken breasts, tuna, bacon . . . Wow, she's really gone all out.

"This fell out in the car," Mom says when she returns. She tosses me a can of something that looks like hair mousse.

"Rogaine? Isn't that for guys?"

"It's for anyone with patterned hair loss. How can it hurt?"

I snicker at it, but I'll try anything.

"I know this is hard for you, Hayley, but you have to be patient. This is going to take time. We'll do all we can to make it work."

I cross the kitchen slowly to hug her and kiss her on the cheek. "Thank you so much, Mommy." I don't have to be a rocket scientist to figure out this can't be easy on her. "I appreciate all you're doing for me. I really do."

She wipes away a tear and says, "When your chick is hurting, you hurt, too. I just want to do anything I can for you, Hayley."

"You're awesome."

She plants a kiss on my forehead and goes about putting away groceries.

"You're okay?"

I nod. "I assure you, I'm fine."

I let out a sigh and return to my homework.

I don't like lying to my mom.

* * *

WE HAVE A BYE week Friday night, which means no football game. Saturday night, Daniel picks me up to take me to a party at Bryan Cousin's house. He's the president of the senior class and the Student Government Association.

I'm sporting a new pair of jeans and a shimmery black and silver top I got on sale at H&M. I wear my black boots, but I need my crutches since I'm still limping and unable to put all of my weight on my left side.

Daniel waits in the foyer, where, thankfully, he's left alone. Mom's in the kitchen fussing over dinner, and Dad's on his way home from the hardware store. The poor guy works his ass off, and I've barely seen him these days. I hope he's not pushing himself too hard or making himself sick.

I emerge down the staircase—slowly and carefully—and I meet Daniel's stare. He smiles at first and then his mouth shifts into a frown.

"What?" Is my makeup smeared? Do I have food stains on my new clothes?

"Don't you want to wear a hat or something for your head?"

My spirit deflates like a soufflé when the oven door is slammed.

He knows he's screwed up. "Wait! No! I didn't mean it in a bad way. Shit. I meant, in case you get cold or anything."

"Daniel, this is who I am, and I'm fine with the way I look."

It takes a moment; then he says, "Me too. Let's go."

When we arrive at the party, Gabriel's the first one to greet me. He rubs me on the head for good measure, just like he does every day at school. Some people think he's being cruel because he's not treating me any differently. But I appreciate that about him, and it's better than the others who don't know how to start a conversation with me.

"I'm feeling some growth there, Hay."

My hand skips across my skull and I smile. Sure enough, wispy, tiny, soft hairs like those of a baby are barely peeking out and starting to sprout. "Whattaya know?"

Gabriel nods and holds up his cup of beer to salute me. "It's a good thing you're not wearing a wig. It would probably stifle all that new growth."

Daniel tugs on my arm. "Later, Tremb. Let's make the rounds, Hayley."

"See ya, Gabriel," I say to my friend.

Daniel leads me around, high-fiving a teammate here or fist bumping another one there. Scoop Dogg and a few of his buddies approach Daniel.

"Yo, it's Dandelion-field."

Daniel blows up. "What the fuck is that supposed to mean, LaShawn?"

The muscular defensive safety is in Daniel's face. "Some of us have been talking about your commitment to the team. All of us, we shaved our heads straight out." LaShawn indicates his shiny dome. "But you, man, you opted for more of a buzzcut."

"I did the best I could," Daniel says in his defense.

Anthony Ricketts joins in the prodding. "Y'all know Delafield's too much of a pretty boy." He and Daniel are good friends, so more than likely it's the alcohol talking.

"Piss off, Ricketts."

Anthony tries to hug him. "Awww . . . come on, man. You're my bro."

LaShawn laughs heartily, almost a snort. "Dude, your girl-friend has more balls than you."

"I didn't voluntarily shave my head, LaShawn," I say, correcting him.

"I know, sweetheart. You had the Big *C*." He stretches out his fist at me. "Respect."

My chest aches with pride at someone recognizing my challenge. I return the fist bump and say, "Thanks."

"I got your back anytime," he says to me.

The banter is interrupted with the high-pitched whine of an electric razor that Anthony holds over his head like the hammer of Thor.

"We can take care of the rest of it, Dela," he says with an evil grin.

I step in to intervene. "Y'all are too drunk," I say, laughing.

Daniel grits his teeth and hisses at me. "I don't need you to fight my battles, Hayley." He turns to his intoxicated teammates. "Y'all know I'm with the team two hundred percent. I cut my hair as much as I could. My mother would have disowned me."

Wrong thing to say. It only makes matters worse.

Scoop Dogg and his buddies, along with Anthony, start cat-calling and razzing Daniel. I can tell he's majorly pissed off. He throws his hands up in the air and takes a few steps back. "What-ever."

Anthony can barely stand up. "Don't be like that. We're just messin' with you, man."

Daniel flips them the middle finger and then grabs my arm. "Let's get out of here."

Lora catches my eye from across the room and furrows her brow. I shrug and retreat from the party with my boyfriend.

Outside, Daniel drops my arm and storms off to his truck. "Fuck them! They're a bunch of shitheads."

"They're your friends," I say, following him as fast as I can on the crutches.

"They're assholes."

When I catch up, I say, "Daniel, they're drunk."

His face hardens. "That's not an excuse."

"It's a reason."

He jerks open the door of his truck, helps me in, and then slams it behind me.

Uh-oh . . .

When he slides in, he just sits there a moment catching his breath.

"Do we really have to go?" I ask quietly.

"I'm not dealing with that. I've scored eight touchdowns this season. Eight! In five games. Scoop Dogg's had one fumble recovery. And Anthony. Did you see the tackle he missed on Henderson High last weekend? Almost cost us the game."

I nod in understanding, trying to be the supportive girlfriend. "It's okay," I say.

His eyes darken. "Oh, it was fine for you. Scoop Dogg's all like, 'I got your back, sister.' What the hell was that all about?"

I lift my shoulders. "I don't know. I barely know the guy." There's a long pause, and then I say, "It was nice of him to recognize what I've been through."

"And I haven't?" Daniel asks in a bit of a growl.

"I didn't say that!"

He pounds his hands on the steering wheel. "Dammit, Hayley, I'm so frustrated."

"About the team?"

He shakes his head. "No . . . the hell with them. I don't know what to say to you."

I press myself into the seat. "What?"

"Yeah. I'm so afraid of saying the wrong thing to you. You're in this delicate state. I mean, LaShawn knew what to say and I just stood there."

I snicker. "First of all, I'm not in any kind of 'delicate' state. I'm one tough cookie, if you haven't already noticed. Shit happens . . . and boy, did it happen to me."

"What can I do, though?" he pleads. I appreciate that he's trying. However, it shouldn't be this hard for us.

I scoot over next to him and bravely put my hand on his knee—not exactly something I've done before. I seem to be a new Hayley, though.

"Look. Just treat me like you did before I got cancer."

He shines a brilliant smile at me and says, "I'll try."

I run my hand over his chest, up his neck, and around his head. With a gentle tug, I take the reins and pull him toward me. It's a sweet kiss at first. Chaste and friendly. I let him know that I want more. I deserve passion and caring from him.

We make out heavily for a few minutes, parked right in front of the party, and I hope I've gotten through to him.

When we separate, he asks, "Are you hungry?"

Not really, but I'll feign it to stay with him. "Sure."

As he starts the truck and drives off, I try to look on the positive side, but something's just not right.

CHAPTER THIRTY-ONE

Oh, my friend, it's not what they take away from you that counts. It's what you do with what you have left.

—HUBERT HUMPHREY

AT FRIDAY'S PEP RALLY, three freshmen girls approach me, asking if they can have my wristband after the event. They literally raced one another to get over to me, but Janell Armstrong was first and I promise it to her. When the music cranks, I fall into line and perform our funky dance routine as if nothing's wrong with me, smiling through the discomfort in my leg. Most of the routine has me doing moves in the back where I don't have to walk around a lot. At least Chloe choreographed it that way for me.

Hurts so good . . . hurts so good . . .

Friday night at the game, I'm decked out in the one-piece red and white uniform with a large "P" on the front, just like the other eleven girls. I leave the crutches on the bench and do my best to get along without them for the duration of the game.

The game is a real barn burner, as my granddaddy would say. Daniel catches six dump passes and one screen pass in a row right before the third quarter plays out, with Marquis Richardson punching it in from the two-yard line to put the Pats up.

Lora hugs me and we squeal like little girls.

The band cranks up the fight song, and we break into our dance. The adrenaline is rushing through me. With only three or four measures of the song left to go, I forget and put my weight on my left side, scream bloody fricking murder, and collapse onto the grass. Tara and Ashlee rush to help me.

"Hayley!" Tara screams out.

"I'm okay." I lie. The white-hot ache creeps from my knee to my numb toes.

Damn my leg! Damn this cancer!

When the song's over, Lora turns to help brush grass off me. She smiles and laughs. "Nice move, Grace."

We laugh together, although I really want to cry.

How embarrassing to fall like that in front of everyone in the stadium, in front of my friends and my . . .

"Hayley Ann Matthews! What are you doing?" Mom shouts from the gate. "You're not supposed to be jumping on that leg."

"I know, Mom. I slipped. Okay?" I lower my voice. "Please don't make it any worse."

I note the agony in her eyes, remembering how she said when her kid hurts, she hurts. The last thing I want to do is to cause her more pain.

Looping my thumb and forefinger together, I give her the okay sign. She reluctantly returns to her seat in the stands, but I sense her eyes constantly on me.

Chloe glares at me. I've messed up her perfect squad once again. However, instead of reacting to her judgment, I simply hold out the ends of my cheerleader skirt and do a curtsy to her and then to the stands. I get a rousing round of applause. Or maybe it was for the extra point that Philip Bradenton just kicked. Depends on how one wants to interpret it.

We win the game by a touchdown to remain undefeated for the season. I get my crutches and take to the field in search of Daniel.

"Awesome game!" I say as I come up to him.

Instead of acknowledging me, Daniel steps over to the retreating referee—actually, one of the back judges—and points at number thirty-six of the opposing team. "That asshole's held me all night."

"Game's over, son," the man says. "You won. Take your victory home."

Daniel jerks away and mumbles under his breath.

"The ref's right. It doesn't matter. We won," I say.

"Whatever," he says.

I think about kissing him, but he's in too icky a mood, so I leave him alone as we walk off the field together.

Chloe sidles up to him, all bouncy and happy. "Great game, Daniel!"

A smile actually forms on the corner of his mouth as he looks down at her. "Thanks, Chloe."

Oh what? He's nice to her? WTF?

"I'm having a party out at my farm. You're invited, of course," she says to my boyfriend.

Thank heavens Daniel includes me. "Whattaya say, Hayley? Up for a party?"

"Sure, Hayley, you're invited, too. Of course." Chloe's voice is sickly sweet. "It's a pool party, though." Her eyes slide down the length of me to rest on my bandaged leg. "You're not exactly able to swim, are you?"

"I don't see why not, but it's October. Won't we freeze our tushies off?"

She rolls her eyes at me. "It's heated . . . hello."

"Yo, Dela," Skipper yells out at Daniel. "Postgame meeting in the locker room."

"Be right there!" He turns to me. "Get a ride to the party from Lora and I'll meet you there later." Then he runs off to join his teammates.

Chloe sneers at me. "Guess I'll see you there."

Oh hell yeah, you'll see me there.

Lora and I do a quick run by our respective houses for bathing suits, towels, and a change of clothes.

"Must be nice to have a heated swimming pool," I say as Lora steers her BMW into the gravel driveway of Chloe's farm.

"Her parents are made of money. They have horses out here that they pay some guy to take care of, but it's mainly a party place for her family. I've heard her father has a poker ring that operates out of here."

I snicker. "You make it sound so Mafioso for south Alabama."

Lora turns to the right and parks under a large pecan tree. "That's just what Uncle Ross has told me. He got invited to a blackjack night one time, but he had a business trip the next day or something and didn't go."

Lora and I get out of the car and walk around—I crutch around—to the back of the ranch house. It's totally packed with people. There's a huge swimming pool filled with teeming blue water that sparkles from the lights shining down on it. Steam rises in inviting, swirling fingers. Fellow students can't resist cannonballing and diving into its depths. A water slide sits in one corner, and people are already lined up to zip up the ladder. There's a diving board in the deep end, and I see Ashlee Grimes preparing to hurl herself into the warm water.

Squinting off at the low-lit deck that leads into the ranch house, I ask Lora, "Is that . . . a waiter?"

A guy is carrying a plate of sandwiches around, offering them to people.

Lora sets her stuff down on a chaise lounge. "The Bradentons have more dollars than sense."

"You can say that again." I pause for a moment and change the subject. "I don't understand exactly what Chloe's problem is with me. We used to be friends in middle school. I mean, just last year, we talked civilly to each other, and I took her homework to her when she had her chickenpox. Now, she treats me like I'm pond scum under her feet."

Very matter-of-factly, Lora says, "Hayley, it's obvious. She's jealous of you."

I can't suppress the snort. "Chloe? Jealous of me? Oh sure, let's be jealous of the bald chick who had cancer and is still hobbling around on crutches. You know, the *one* cheerleader who didn't get nominated for homecoming. Yeah, I'd be jealous of me, too. Not."

"Sarcasm doesn't look good on you, my friend," Lora says with a laugh.

"It doesn't make sense."

Shifting toward me, Lora explains. "It's simple. You've taken the attention away from *her*. It's always been about Chloe . . . since, like, birth. She's always been popular and pretty. People just don't say no to her. She's one of those girls. A cliché. But clichés are clichés for a reason."

"Exactly. But why lash out at me?"

"Hayley," Lora says, rolling her eyes, "you've stolen her lime-light."

I'm so confused. "What limelight?"

"You're an inspiration to people as you stand on the field and cheer. Don't you get that? People aren't looking at the pretty captain in all her glory. They're watching the brave cancer survivor who's cheering her heart out for her team while she has no hair on her head and a long scar on her leg."

My pulse races under my skin at her words. Had anyone else said this to me, I might have told them they were crazy. But Lora doesn't play games. She doesn't bullshit. "Wow. I never tried to do any of that."

"Exactly," Lora says, and then wraps her arm around me.

As her words sink in, I try to process all of it. I never wanted to be a role model or an example to anyone. I just wanted to cheer.

Our interlude is interrupted by a friendly face. "Having fun, ladies?"

"Yo, Tremb," Lora says. "How's it going?"

Gabriel lifts a beer and a half sandwich and smiles. "No complaints from me. Y'all want anything?"

The hoppy smell of the beer churns the nausea in my stomach. "I'm not drinking."

Lora jumps up. "Well, I am. I see William over by the keg . . . so I'll BRB."

Gabriel replaces Lora on the chaise when she leaves. He retrieves something from the pocket of his long, baggy swim trunks. "Here, maybe this is more your speed."

I glance at his palm and see five mini Snickers bars. My smile widens as I snitch them from him. "How'd you know?"

"I notice things. Besides, there's a big bowl of candy over there."

I pop the delicious chocolate into my mouth and suck on it, allowing all of the layers to break down in my mouth one by one.

"So what's with prince charming?" Gabriel asks.

"Who?"

"Delafield."

"Oh, Daniel. He had to see the coach after the game. He'll be here."

Gabriel points over to the hot tub. "He's already here. I meant what's with him all up on Chloe?"

My head snaps, and I swallow the mouthful of candy. Over in the corner, Daniel is sitting on the edge of the hot tub with none other than a bikini-clad Chloe Bradenton massaging his shoulders. Okay . . . maybe she's jealous of more than just the attention I'm getting. Maybe she's resentful that I'm dating the hottest guy in school.

I sense steam rising off me much like off the pool. Only mine is fueled by anger, not by the nippy weather. "Crutches, please."

Gabriel silently obeys, and I take a swinging stroll to the other side of the backyard.

"Hi there," I say, surprising both my boyfriend and my adversary.

Chloe smirks at me and then slowly removes her hands from Daniel's shoulders.

"Hey, babe," he says nonchalantly. "I didn't know you were here."

"I didn't know *you* were here," I retort. "You know, I could do that for you . . . babe." I emphasize *babe* in a way that tells her to back off and him that he's being an ass.

"Of course you can, Hayley," Chloe says. "It's too bad you can't really enjoy the party."

I glare at her, trying not to let my hatred for her haughtiness show too much. "What do you mean?"

"You know—you can't really swim, what with the crutches . . . the bandage . . ."

Is this some sort of dare? A gauntlet being thrown down at my feet?

Well, screw her.

I turn on my crutches and return to where Gabriel is sitting.

"Hayley, don't let her get to you."

I bite down on my bottom lip, trying to channel my rage into something useful. "Too late."

I lay the crutches down, flip off my shoes, and bend down to unwind the bandage from my leg. The purple marks have finally faded and there's nothing but a pinkish-red scar and a large scab at the point where the doctors cut me open three times. I don't need the bandage anymore. I have nothing to hide from anyone anymore. I'm not ashamed.

I grit my teeth as I take four hobbled steps to the diving board. Hot, shooting pangs of agony elevator up and down my leg, but I climb the ladder in spite of it. I'm walking. Well, climbing. One unsure step . . . then another. It hurts like blue-blazing hell, but I do it.

Gabriel cheers me on, as do Lora, Tara, Hannah, and Ashlee, who've all gathered around to watch what's going on.

Daniel dives into the pool and emerges through the steam, smiling about ten feet in front of the diving board. He holds his arms out. At least he's trying to help me.

I move to the end of the diving board and wiggle my toes on the edge. Using my right leg to push off, I springboard myself up, spread my legs out, touch my toes with my hands, and then plunge into the warm, awaiting water. I catapult to the bottom and then push off with my right foot. As I swim upward, a special victory washes over me, purifying me of the hatred and resentment I feel for my cheerleading captain who should be a hell of a lot more understanding. I break the surface and take a deep breath. Water sluices down my bare head and face. Several people applaud. Daniel swims to me and gives me a bear hug.

To the side, Chloe flattens her lips, and I swear I hear her harrumph.

Whatever. If she's got a problem with me, then *she* needs to get over it.

Like Neil Armstrong, I've taken one giant leap.

I *will* walk without those crutches, come hell or high water.

CHAPTER THIRTY-TWO

I have heard there are troubles of more than one kind.
Some come from ahead and some come from behind.
But I've brought a big bat. I'm all ready you see.
Now my troubles are going to have troubles with me!

—Dr. Seuss

Ever since i started high school, I have adored homecoming week.

Everyone has a common goal, and the school spirit is off the charts. Now it's the perfect distraction to all that troubles me.

Issues bounce around in my head, but I refuse to stop and deal with them. There's simply no reason to dwell on the bad things like no hair, a scarred leg, no homecoming court nomination. Instead I pay attention to making senior memories, wearing my cheer spirit on my sleeve, and being with my boyfriend.

There is so much going on this week leading up to our game with the Jeff Davis Prep School Lemurs, one of our biggest rivals. (What a 'tarded name, though. They used to be the Confederates. Then the name got changed to the Generals, and a few years ago, they went with Lemurs. I'm glad "Patriots" isn't politically incorrect.) Each day this week, we have different dress-up days to get the school spirit at an all-time high. Monday is "Going to War with Jeff Davis Prep," so everyone comes dressed in fatigues. Lora and I hit the Army-Navy supply store Sunday afternoon and got pants and T-shirts in the desert colors. I tied camo bandanas on my crutches to add to the effect.

Tuesday is "Lasso the Lemurs," so all of the classes are decked out in cowboy attire with big Stetsons, jeans, boots, plaid shirts, overalls, and suspenders. I found a pair of soft camel-colored high-heeled boots in the hall closet that used to be Gretchen's. Surprisingly enough, when I wear them, the heel elevates my foot and I don't limp as much. Who knew?

Wednesday is "Fake a Jeff Davis Lemur Injury Day." I like this one because all I have to do is put my Ace bandage back on my leg and use my crutches. Anthony Ricketts wears his head in a fake vice, and David Avery in the freshman class actually makes himself an oxygen tent to sport around in. (The teachers make him come out of it for each class period.) Lora and I use makeup to put fake bruises on our faces and arms. Marquis Richardson and Scoop Dogg got their hands on some pre-Halloween fake blood that they keep squirting on everyone. Even Mr. Parish, the principal, gets into the spirit by driving around the school on a Rascal scooter all day.

Thursday is "Trash Jeff Davis" day. Students are encouraged to fashion clothing from garbage bags. Fortunately, the cheerleaders planned ahead on this one. Ashleigh Bentley's mom made these vests and skirt covers out of Hefty cinch sacks to go over one of our uniforms so that we could all match. They're actually pretty fashionable, if I do say so myself for polyethylene.

And, of course, Friday is the day to show your true Patriotic spirit. Red, white, and blue regales the hallways, and every student and teacher at PHS sports the school colors. We in the squad wear our navy blue sweater with the white and red stripes around the waist and the small "Polk" lettering over the right breast. I've been waiting all season to don this outfit.

It's an exhausting week because the cheerleaders not only help to keep the school spirit high and people motivated, but we're also responsible for overseeing the door competition. Each class decorates its homeroom door in the theme of "passion for the Patriots." Each homeroom competes to come up with the most creative, positive, and original door decoration using any items that don't "disrupt the learning environment." (Gotta love rules from the school handbook.) The cheerleaders get to score the final pieces from one to five on creativity, theme, originality, positive attitude, attention to detail, and school spirit.

The last thing we get to help out with is the shopping cart displays. Since we're such a huge school and we're trying to go green, lawn displays and parade floats were voted down as waste. (I heard that three years ago, the senior class used four hundred sixty-two rolls of toilet paper in the lawn display.) However, in order to have something in their place, the student government came up with the idea of shopping cart displays. The local Food World loans us carts for whatever groups, classes, cliques, or individuals want to participate. The carts are decorated to represent patriotism and school spirit and will be paraded around at the pep rally on Friday. Then, they'll be placed at the front of the stadium Friday night, and attendees of the homecoming game will vote by putting money into each of the carts. Proceeds will go to the local food bank in the name of the school.

It's totally a win-win sitch all around.

We really go all out. Each day at lunch, there are activities, as well. Monday, there's a special hot chocolate fountain to "Scorch Jeff Davis Prep." Tuesday, there's a dance contest where all the hip-hop kids face off in amazing action to the sounds of a DJ. Everyone in the lunchroom gathers around, cheers, and then votes. It's our own version of homecoming *American Idol*. Wednesday is PHS trivia day, Thursday is karaoke and also the roller chair races.

The race traditionally uses rolling chairs from the teachers' office. The chairs are placed in a row in the caf with teams of two racing around the obstacles of chairs, tables, the food court, and trash cans. One rides; the other pushes.

Gabriel and I partner up for this event since Daniel's off doing something with Coach Gaither. He's been a little distant all week, but I chalk it up to this being a mondo-big game tomorrow night. Rumor has it even some college scouts will be there.

"Ready, Hayley?" Gabriel asks. He cracks his knuckles and assures me we will win.

I plop down into the large chair that could only be Mrs. Quakenbush's. She's quite . . . um . . . rotund and has to have a special chair for her . . . er . . . girth. I sit in it cross-legged and hold on to the arm rails.

Gabriel gets all scientific on my ass. "This one's got a light mesh to the back, so air will flow through as we race around."

I giggle and shake my head. "Just run *fast!*"

Our cheerleader sponsor, Mrs. Ingram, blows the whistle, and we're off.

"Gooooo!!!" I shout.

Gabriel pushes me past the Future Farmers of America kids, a group of freshmen, and Skipper O'Rourke, who is hanging off his chair. We zip past the computer science geeks. I duck low in the chair, hoping to cut wind resistance as we round the lunch tables at the end. We certainly don't have to worry about hair from either of us slowing us down. In the home stretch now, Gabriel avoids an overturned lunch tray of splattered yogurt. The FFA kids aren't as fortunate, and they slide out of play. Lora and Lauren run beside us as we're racing for the finish line, cheering us on. We cross the toilet paper string before anyone else and are declared the winners.

Gabriel spins my chair around and around until I think I'll be sick from laughter.

Honestly, school shouldn't be this fun.

The lunch bell rings and we disperse back to our afternoon classes. I settle into my desk in journalism class, but I know we won't be talking about press releases, media ethics, or the power of the press just yet.

It's time to vote for homecoming court.

My journalism teacher, Mr. Wannstedt, places a lock box on his desk at the front of the room and then hands the ballots off to Amanda Leftkowitz to pass around. Once I have mine, I flip over the paper and read the names. Tamping down the desire to feel sorry for myself for not being on the list, I let out a sigh and decide who'll get my vote. Freshman attendant is a no-brainer for me, and I check the square next to Madison Hutchinson's name. Lauren Compton gets my vote for sophomore attendant, Tara Edwards is my pick for junior attendant, and, in the section for the seniors, I find myself staring for a moment at the names.

I swallow hard to dispel the lump in my throat at seeing the proof in writing that I'm the only cheerleader missing from the list. For one nanosecond, I'm half-tempted to write my name in. I squash that idea immediately as I have nothing to prove. If my classmates left me out because I'm bald . . . well, the hell with them. If they left me out because they'd rather have me on the field cheering . . . well, that's easier to live with.

I know who I'm going to vote for.

I also know who I'm *not* going to vote for.

Each PHS student gets two votes in the seniors section. The one with the most votes will be the homecoming queen and the second-most vote-getter will be the attendant. I check mark my friend, Ashlee Grimes, and, of course, my partner, Lora Russell, and then limp up to the front of the room to add my ballot to the lock box.

When sixth period starts, I head to the gym and don my workout clothes. The football players are practicing in the gym on drills and strengthening. I try to catch Daniel's eye, but he looks right past me. One of his teammates smacks him on the arm and then points at me. I wave and smile. He nods back.

Ohhh-kaaaay.

"He's thinking about the game," Gabriel insists, obviously seeing the exchange.

"Yeah. We haven't talked a lot all week. Mostly texts and IM-ing at night."

Gabriel scrubs his hand through his growing, thick hair. "It's a big game tomorrow night. Then you guys can celebrate at the dance, right?"

I hiss a quick intake of air. While it's been *assumed* that Daniel and I would be homecoming dates, we haven't exactly formalized it. It's not like we can sit with each other at the game and hold hands or anything. I don't even need to buy a special, fancy outfit because I'll be in uniform. There is a school dance afterward, and nothing would thrill me more than being in Daniel's arms and letting him move us around the parquet to whatever the DJ is spinning.

"Yeah, sure," I say, and then move away to attack the leg press.

For thirty minutes, I concentrate on giving the heave-ho to the weights and extending my left leg as far as it will go. Under Gabriel's tutelage, I try something new. I bounce the apparatus up and down in small beats with just the balls of my feet. The muscle burn runs all the way up my body.

"You'll really feel it in the back of your legs," Gabriel instructs.

"I do . . . I do . . . but it doesn't hurt as bad as it usually does."

"It's because your muscles are strengthening, Hayley. You're getting there." Gabriel's face grows all serious for a moment. "I'm really proud of you," he says with a soft smile. "You're handling all of this like a champ."

I smile back. "What choice do I have?"

"You could be a royal bitch like some people. Or, you could be like Bridgette Sandusky."

"Who in the world is Bridgette Sandusky?"

"A girl I knew in Ohio."

"At your last school?"

He nods and makes a pained face. I wonder if she was his girl-friend. He answers me immediately. "She was a cheerleader. She went in for a physical and had an . . . um . . . abnormal . . . you know . . . thingy that girls have . . ." His blush is endearing and completely adorable. Come to think about it, Gabriel's kind of cute, too. He's really grown up since the gangly boy I used to know. He's all filled out and muscular and he's got a sweet smile. I'm surprised he hasn't hooked up with someone since coming back to Maxwell.

I shake away from my assessment of him and get back into the story he's telling me.

"Oh, you mean an abnormal Pap smear?"

He shudders. "Yeah, one of those. She was told to come back in a few days to run more tests to see if it was cancerous or what have you."

"Poor thing."

"Not really. She was a chicken shit, Hayley."

My mouth falls open, yet words don't come out. I've never heard Gabriel be so rude. "How can you—"

"She went home, wrote a long e-mail to her parents about how she didn't want to have cancer and get chemo and lose her hair and this, that, or the other, and then she chowed down her mother's bottle of prescription valium. They found her a few hours later when her parents got home from work.

My eyes pop. "She killed herself?"

Gabriel bobs his head. "All because of a test . . . and needing to get more tests. She was too vain and concerned about her appearance and what people would think that she just checked out like that." He snaps his fingers for emphasis.

I put my hands on my hips. "I'm sorry, but there is *nothing* so bad in this world that you have to take your own life." I think for a second. "Okay, if you're like a prisoner of war and are getting tortured for American security secrets, then I could see—"

"It was all for nothing," Gabriel interrupts. "Her autopsy showed no sign of cancer. The abnormal test was just that—an abnormal test."

My hands fly to my mouth. What a waste of a young life. Ended by her own ignorant, prideful hand. I glare at my workout coach. "Don't you have any happy stories?"

He smiles a toothy grin at me. "You're a happy story, Hayley."

Now it's my turn to blush.

All I can say is "Thanks."

*　*　*

"THAT'S GOING TO BE one hell of a fire," a man says behind me. I turn to see Lora and her Uncle Ross. She's almost late for the pep rally and bonfire.

"I'm sorry! My car ran out of gas and I had to call my uncle."

Ross smiles. "To the rescue." He nods my way. "You're looking good, Hayley. Working out? Taking those protein bars and shakes?"

"Yes, sir," I say. "They're really a huge help. Thank you so much."

"Anything to help out. Let me know if you need anything else," he says with a wink. "Before you know it, I'll have you signed up at Game On to go on the hike to the rainforest in Costa Rica with us in the summer."

As cool as that sounds, I certainly don't see *that* happening. "Thanks, Ross!"

He waves us off to join the squad. "I'll just hang back until this is over, okay Lora?"

"Sure thing." She grabs onto me, and we hustle — as much as I can — over to where everyone else is gathered.

"You're late, Lora," Chloe says flatly.

"She's here now," I say in my partner's defense, which surprisingly shuts up the captain.

At precisely nine p.m. on Thursday night, with Ladder Forty-Two and Engine Eleven of the Maxwell fire department standing by, the cheerleaders lead the students, fans, and football players out onto the baseball field where a fifteen-foot bonfire structure has been erected by the Pep Club.

Team captains Marquis Richardson and Skipper O'Rourke carry a large pole with a fake Jeff Davis Prep School football player strapped to it. The two of them dip it into the awaiting lighter fluid bucket, and one of the firemen steps forward to ignite it.

Fffffffooooooooof!

In the blink of an eye, the dummy is engulfed in flames, as is the wooden structure.

The crowd goes wild and the band plays the fight song as the players take their seats behind the fire. We cheerleaders slip into position in front of the blaze and begin leading the chants.

"Gimme a P! Gimme an H! Gimme an S! Whattaya got? PHS! Louder! PHS!"

My thin white turtleneck underneath my dark blue criss-crossed top is nearly choking me, and I'm sweating from the scorching inferno. I'm about to suggest that we're too close to the fire, when everyone else on the back row starts moving forward toward the gathered crowd and away from the fire.

After a couple more cheers, Chloe takes the mike and introduces Coach Gaither, who gives a quick, inspirational speech.

"We've come a long way this season, and we still have a tough road ahead of us. But we've pulled together like no other unit I've coached. We've got the best fans in the conference and the most spirited cheerleaders—no one could ask for better ones. So, let's go out there tomorrow night and show the Lemurs we mean business."

The fire pops and sparks, hissing out a victory cry for us.

I spy Daniel through the orangy glow. I wave, and he smiles back at me halfheartedly. Damn, he really is distracted if he can't just chill out and enjoy the festivities. We move into our pom-pom dance routine with the marching band playing along, and, I swear, Daniel and his friends are talking about me. Two guys point at me, laugh, and then elbow Daniel. He shoves them off and crosses his hands over his chest. They're probably commenting on my lack of hair. I could care less. The skin on my entire body has grown rhinoceros thick over the past few weeks. I finish up the routine, bouncing on my right leg, but not executing the Rockette-like kick at the end. No one notices . . . except Daniel—or so it seems when I make eye contact with him. It's like he's embarrassed by me, as though I'm not a whole cheerleader.

To prove him—and anyone else with doubts—wrong, I shift into the pyramid formation. First, Melanie Otto climbs onto my shoulders, and I lift her higher up onto Ashlee's shoulders. Then, I take Lora and put her up top, as well. My heavy lifting is over, so I hobble around front and dip down into a split. The fans go crazy, cheering as the fire swooshes behind us. A red-hot ember sizzles out of the wooden structure and lands one millimeter from my left leg. I scream and freak, so afraid of anything happening to my weaker limb. I roll out of the way as Nick McDugall, one of the drummers, runs up and stamps it out with his booted foot. I glance back over my shoulder to see if Daniel has any concern, but he has his head in his hands and his two teammates are cracking up.

When more sparks and cinders begin falling into the crowd—it wasn't just me—the Maxwell fire department steps in and says it's time to snuff the bonfire out. It was magical and brilliant while it lasted.

Lora grabs her poms and calls out, "Everyone's headed to the Burger Barn. Uncle Ross is dropping me off. You coming?"

Daniel's striding toward me.

"I've got Mom's car. I'll meet you there."

The remnants of the fire reflect in the white eleven on Daniel's jersey as he approaches.

"Bitchin' bonfire, huh?"

He tugs my arm and pulls me along with him. "You could have been frickin' maimed by that chunk of wood that fell near you."

So, he did notice. "But I wasn't. I handled it."

"Yeah, by screaming out like an idiot."

"Ex-*cuuuuuse* me? Who are you calling an idiot?"

"Hayley, look—"

"No, you look. I screamed because I'm human and it scared the shit out of me. The only people who heard me above the roar of the crowd were the few around me . . . and apparently you."

If he'd just say he was worried about me and he cared, that

would be one thing. But to be reprimanded by him like I'm some little kid—uh-uh, that ain't happening.

He shoves his hands into his thicker-than-most hair. "I can't be there *every* second to protect you. My mom said you fell at a game a few weeks ago."

"It happens, Daniel." A long sigh escapes him as people file past us.

"That's embarrassing," he says quietly.

"To me or to you?" We're standing in the subdued hue of the quenched fire, yet I'm burning mad. "Spit it out. You have something to say. You've barely talked to me all week. It's like you're avoiding me. What's your glitch?" I ask bravely.

Silence sizzles on the night air as Daniel glances about to see who might be watching. God forbid I cause a scene or give the Pops something to gossip about on the PHS message boards or text messages.

He stares at his sneakered feet. "I don't think I can do this anymore, Hayley."

"Do what?"

He spreads his hands wide. "This. Us. See, I'm just not . . . I'm not good with being around sick people."

I can't help but chortle. "I'm not sick, Daniel." Not anymore. Not that I ever really *felt* sick. My body was ill; I was fine.

He continues to shake his head. "I can't handle the responsibility of being there for you. Not with football season and trying to get a college scholarship. It's too much stress."

I shove my poms into my purse and rest my weight on the crutches. If I were a dragon from some mythical story, I would be snorting fire at him, chasing him through the forest, because that's what's churning inside me. Trying to calm my resentment, I say, "You said you'd be there for me. You promised."

"That was before . . ."

"Before *what?*"

He takes a deep breath. I hope he chokes on it. "Before all of the side effects of your surgery and treatment and stuff . . . just all of it, Hayley. I thought everything was over when you got out of the hospital."

"Yeah, well, cancer sort of takes time to get over," I say sternly. He's totally flaking. Just like a guy. Just like a stupid, selfish, immature high school guy who thinks only of himself. "Is it because I don't have any hair?"

He shrugs. "Sort of. Maybe. Or not really. I don't know."

"What *do* you know?" I snap.

"I don't know!" he growls back, and then stops himself.

I am on him like white on rice. "Well you know what, Mr. Football Star? Cancer creeps in uninvited and totally fucks with your life. I can't help that I lost my hair. I sort of had what they call 'radical' chemotherapy and massive doses of radiation. And now, I'm trying to train my boneless and nerveless leg how to *walk* again. Not just for tomorrow, but for the rest of my life. So, I'm sorry if my 'illness' doesn't fit into your ideal image of what someone's senior year should be like. It's not like I went online and ordered this for myself."

My chest heaves up and down as I'm gasping for breath. Never in my life have I ever had it out with someone like this. A little part of me is secretly dying—that part of me that allowed Daniel Delafield to be more than a crush. I suppose it's because my heart was really falling for him and he just dropped back five yards and punted it away.

Finally, he speaks, not meeting my stare. "I just can't deal with it. It's such a . . . downer."

As if I didn't lose my shit before, it takes all the strength in my body *not* to wind up my fist and smack him right in his smug nose. My wrath gets the best of me, and I scream at him as if he's just scored the winning touchdown for the Patriots in the state championship game.

"Yeah? Well screw you, Daniel! It's not about *you!* It's about *me!* It's about getting on with my life the best I can and not letting this kind of bullshit get me down or get the best of me. I'm lucky to even have a leg. I'm lucky the cancer didn't spread. Do you know I'll have to get checked for cancer regularly now? For the rest of my life? What do you have to do?"

He reaches for me, but I pull away. "It's just so hard for me to handle, Hayley."

"You egomaniac! It didn't happen to you. It happened to me. And if you can't be there for me . . . then the hell with you! Go play football and hang out with your buddies who laugh at the bald cheerleader behind her back. Go wait for your precious college scholarship. I don't need you!"

"Hayley, don't be—"

"Go Away!"

I tromp off, letting my crutches carry me away as fast as I can. I make it to Mom's car in a surprising flash and stash my stuff in the back seat. I slam the door, crank the ignition, and speed away from PHS before Daniel can catch up with me . . . if he was even trying.

At the bottom of the hill, there's a red light where Patriots Drive meets the highway. This is where the flood gates open, the ones I've held closed so long from this emotional tsunami. I pound my fists against the steering wheel repeatedly, like it's going to make a difference. As if it's going to change anything—make my scar disappear, make my nerve regenerate, make my hair grow faster. Make Daniel understand and want to be there for me.

"Dammit! Dammit! Dammit to hell!" I scream at the top of my lungs, knowing no one but God can hear me. "Why? Why?

Why?" I don't understand. Why is all of this stupid shit happening? This should be the best year ever, and instead it's just totally fucked.

"Oh, Hayley's so strong," I say, mocking what people have said to my parents.

It's all a disguise, a mask I've worn to fit in and be normal. I'm not, though. I'm completely different, and everyone knows it. I might as well be doomed to wear a big red *C* on my clothing forever to remind me and everyone else about the disease that has mucked up my life.

Cars whirl past me on the highway, some honking, others flashing their lights.

Here I sit.

All alone.

My hazard lights flash red outside the car, illuminating my emotional emergency.

Swimming in tears and angst, dampening my uniform.

Death grip on the steering wheel, I know I've got to keep going.

Forging ahead.

Continuing.

I have to.

I must.

I will.

But not until the racking sobs ease or at least ebb.

This is my final release.

A long time coming.

The light turns green. A Jeep behind me honks its horn.

I wave at it and then swipe the tears off my cheeks.

It's done. The crying jag, that is.

I can move forward now.

This is the fifth time that I cry—*and it's going to be my last.*

CHAPTER THIRTY-THREE

A friend drops their plans when you're in trouble, shares joy in your accomplishments, feels sad when you're in pain. A friend encourages your dreams and offers advice—but when you don't follow it, they still respect and love you.

—Doris Wild Helmering

I turn the car onto the highway and make it through all of the green lights of the fast food strip to head toward my house. I opt against meeting up with everyone at the Burger Barn. What's the point? So Daniel and his friends can ridicule the bald chick? So I can watch as he scouts out whom he'll take to homecoming instead of me? No, thanks. I'm hot, tired, angry, spent. I just want to go home, curl up with Leeny on the couch, and eat ice cream.

Yeah, I definitely have an appetite for some ice cream . . . which is good.

The music from the CD player is cranked, a strong techno beat that helps drown out the instant replay of the showdown with Daniel that my mind loves to cue up every second. I focus on the 808 beat, the whir of the synthesizers, and the repetitive keyboard riff. When I pull into the driveway, I shut the car off and sit for a while, absorbing the musical flow around me, seeping into my veins, and re-energizing me.

My melodious therapy is interrupted when my BlackBerry goes off. It's Lora.

> WHERE R U?
>
> @ HOME
>
> Y?
>
> DON'T WANT 2 TALK @ IT
>
> HAYLEY!
>
> DANIEL BROKE UP W/ME. OK?
>
> Y?
>
> BCUZ HE'S A DUCK
>
> A DUCK? LIKE QUACK?
>
> A DICK!
>
> WHAT DID HE DO 2 U?
>
> WILL TELL U L8R.
>
> COME HANG OUT
>
> DON'T WANT 2
>
> WANT ME 2 COME OVER?
>
> THAT'S SWEET
>
> I MEAN IT
>
> NO, I'M GOOD HAVE FUN
>
> U SURE?
>
> YEP :)
>
> HUGS
>
> C U 2MORROW HOMECOMING QUEEN
>
> RIGHT! IN MY DREAMS
>
> TTYL

A knock on the driver's window scares hell and four dollars out of me.

I don't know which one of us jumps more, Gabriel or me.

Rolling the window down, I snark at my friend. "You scared the shit out of me!"

He smiles. "If your music weren't so loud, you would've heard me."

"Thank you, Nan," I say when he sounds like my mother. I peer into my rearview mirror and see Gabriel's car parked in front of my house. Did he follow me here from the bonfire? Oh God, did he hear me screaming at Daniel?

I get out of the car and shove my pompoms at him.

"These don't really match my outfit, Hay," he says jokingly.

Jerking open the back door, I reach for my crutches. "Look, I sort of hate all guys right now."

"I didn't do anything to you."

"Doesn't matter. Your species did."

A final tear escapes from my lashes. Gabriel's not dumb. He reaches out with his thumb and slides it away. "I overheard the whole thing. You can talk to me, you know?"

I push his hand away and downplay the incident. "Nothing to talk about. Just another day in the life of Hayley Matthews."

He stops me with his hands on both of my shoulders, forcing me to look him in the eyes.

"Listen, Hayley. There's nothing funny about judging someone because of something they have absolutely no control over."

I don't blink and neither does he. His words are said so firmly and with such conviction.

My brows crease. "Are you speaking from experience?"

He lifts his shoulders up and down, giving me a typical boy shrug. I roll my eyes at him and say, "You know, when I'm in charge of this world, boys won't be allowed to answer pointed questions with shrugs."

"Maybe you shouldn't ask pointed questions," he says, and then smiles. "Do you need help getting everything into the house?"

"Like me?" I ask as I place the crutches under my arms.

"Like your bag and your cheerleader crap."

Adjusting my purse on my shoulder, I ease the crutches forward onto the rock path to the front door.

"You don't need those anymore, Hayley," he says.

I glance at the silver poms still in his grasp. "I'll need them tomorrow night," I say.

"No, Hay. I mean the crutches. You're a lot stronger than you think you are."

Boy, is that an understatement.

Oh, he means physically . . .

"You've been totally awesome to me. All of the workouts on the weights and exercises you've been giving me have really worked."

His smile beams out at me as we walk together toward my house. "Give yourself credit, Hayley. You could have bitched, moaned, and complained. But you didn't."

"Thanks, Gabe. I mean, Gabriel."

"It's okay. Old habit . . . right?"

The moonlight—or maybe it's just a streetlight—shimmers in his dark hair, or what there is of it. Gabriel's really been there for me when others haven't been. He hasn't treated me with kid gloves or mollycoddled me. Rather, he's treated me just the same: kidding with me, teasing me, and picking on me in a friendly way. There's always been a kindness and connection between us since we were kids and watched out for each other. It's nice to see some things don't change.

"I'm sorry Daniel turned out to be such a dick," he says. "Can't say I'm surprised, though. Jocks, you know."

This time, I shrug, breaking my own rule. "It is what it is," I say, trying to convince myself with the words. "He couldn't deal. Plain and simple."

"He's an ass, then."

I giggle, because I have no tears left. Even if I did, I wouldn't shed another one for number eleven. Not when a true friend is in my presence. "Hey, Gabriel, I've got an idea."

"What's that?" he asks, looking down at me.

"Do you want to go to homecoming together? You know, as friends . . . to hang out and have fun."

He thinks for a moment, and I pray he won't shoot me down, too.

Then he says, "I wasn't really planning on going to the dance—"

"That's okay, I understand if you don't—"

"But why not? Sounds like a good time."

I straighten, and I'm sure there's a look of surprise on my face. "Seriously?"

Gabriel drags his hand across my head. "Sure thing, peach fuzz."

A welcomed bubble of laughter rips from my throat. "Awesome, see you then."

Gabriel opens the front door for me and waits until I'm in before closing it behind me. He stops right before it clicks and then jerks it back to him. "Hayley, don't beat yourself up over that asshole. He's not worth your tears."

The door closes between us, and I smile. He's absolutely right. Daniel's not worth my tears. I'm still having ice cream and kitty cuddle time, though.

* * *

FRIDAY MORNING, I FILE to the stadium with the rest of the school to watch the announcement of this year's homecoming court. I don't really have anyone to sit with because all of my cheerleading friends will be on the field with their escorts.

"Hayley!" I hear someone call out. "Come sit with me."

It's Shelly, whom I haven't hung out with in forever.

"Your hair is really starting to come in," she says, and then stops herself. "I'm sorry."

I take a seat next to her on the bleacher. "Sorry for what? It *is* starting to come in."

"I hate what you've had to go through, Hayley. I mean, you worked your ass off practicing and stuff to make the varsity squad, and then . . . wow, like, cancer."

A weak smile crosses my lips. "Wow. Like, cancer, is right."

"Do you know how you got it?"

"Not really," I say. "I've got an appointment in Birmingham next week, so maybe I'll find out more."

Shelly lays her hand on my arm. "You've handled it in a cool way. Everyone says so," she tells me.

"You don't have to say that, Shell."

"I'm serious. Mom and Dad have commented to me about how freakin' awesome it is that you're down there cheering."

My cheeks warm, and I don't know how to handle the compliment. Fortunately, Gabriel bounds down the steps at just that moment and plops down next to me. "Can I join y'all?"

The ceremony starts, and, one by one, the homecoming nominees are escorted down the concrete steps and out onto the football field. Freshmen to the far left. Sophomores to the far right. Juniors to the immediate left. Seniors to the immediate right. Parents and family members crowd the stands as Bryan Cousin, the SGA president, acts as emcee, introducing all the candidates for the homecoming court.

When everyone is in place and all the digital pictures snapped for the yearbook and posterity's sake, Bryan makes the announcement.

"This year's freshman attendant is . . . Stephanie Keller."

I watch my fellow cheerleader, Madison, slump a bit when her classmate's name is called, and then she claps heartily. I don't really know Stephanie that well, other than knowing her big sister, Sarah, is the band's drum major.

"The sophomore attendant is . . . Samantha Fowler."

"Whoooohooo!" I shout out to my squad mate. I hear Samantha's squeal from the football field as she steps forward to join Stephanie and her escort.

"Junior attendant this year is . . . Ashleigh Bentley."

Gabriel, Shelly, and I clap hard. "Way to go, Ashleigh!" I cheer out.

Gabriel leans over and whispers. "Are we going to have to endure Chloe as our queen?"

Shelly answers before I can. "Oh, honey, she already is the queen — the queen bitch."

I snicker and then elbow both of them.

Bryan's voice echoes out, "Our senior attendant is . . . Chloe Bradenton."

Whoa!

I don't know who's more surprised — Chloe or the entire freaking student body.

Moving slowly, Chloe fakes a smile and steps up to join the other homecoming court members. For a moment, I feel sorry for her as her face totally falls flat despite her attempt to grin and bear it. Someone like Chloe dreams of being the homecoming queen . . . and why not? She's the cheerleader captain and Ms. Popularity, though not as much as she thought, apparently. Right now, I'm sure she's feeling pretty shitty on the inside.

To her credit, though, Chloe shakes it off and beams out a perfect grin to the student body.

Shelly puts her hands together in mock prayer. "There *is* a God!"

"Be nice." I elbow her again, not believing I'm taking up for Chloe.

"So, who's gonna be the queen?" Gabriel asks.

"Shhh!" I cross my fingers on both hands and then cross my arms in front of me. There's one person who's most deserving.

Bryan says, "And this year's homecoming queen is . . . Lora Russell."

Everyone cheers, and I stand up to start the ovation. Lora bursts into tears. Chloe claps politely enough when Lora joins the other winners. Samantha and Ashleigh attack hug her; then Chloe joins in reluctantly.

I seize my crutches and do my best to push past all the people crushing the homecoming court to congratulate them. I hug Samantha and Ashleigh and shout out congrats to Stephanie Keller.

"Huge congrats, Chloe," I say with a genuine smile.

"Thanks," she says, and then turns to accept a hug from her partner, Melanie. I do honestly believe this might be the first time in Chloe's life she didn't get what she wanted.

At some point, we all have to learn that life isn't fair.

"Coming through . . . coming through . . ." I say, scooting through the crowd surrounding my partner. Lora sees me and wraps her arms around me. "I am soooooo damn proud of you!"

"I can't believe I beat Chloe," Lora whispers to me. "You think they miscounted?"

Shaking my head, I say, "Get over it! *You* are the homecoming queen."

"Oh my God, I am!"

Lora's mother and Uncle Ross press through the crowd. Her

mom, Lorraine, has tears streaming down her cheeks. Ross hands her a small packet of tissues he must have brought for the occasion.

"Oh, Mom! I'm shocked."

"I'm not, sweetie," Miss Lorraine says as they hug.

Ross stands next to me and leans on my shoulder. "Will we ever be able to talk to her again?" he teases.

"I don't know," I say in agreement. "You know what they say rhinestones do to a girl."

Lora laughs and pokes at Ross and me. "Y'allllllll!"

Ross steps forward, and his niece hugs him with all her might until he screeches in pain. "Damn, girl, that's a tight grip you've got there."

Lora pulls back. "Did I really hug you that hard?"

He twists his waist a bit and presses at his ribs. "Yeah, I'm wicked sore under my ribs."

His sister chimes in. "I'm sure it's from one of your many adventures. Did you know Ross is headed down to Barbados to go zip lining?"

He stops rubbing his side and shrugs. Ugh, another shrugging boy. This is a man, though, and he's totally amazing. "You have no fear of anything, do you?" I ask.

"What's to fear?" he asks as if it's the most ridiculous question he's ever heard. Then again, the man climbs mountains, jumps out of airplanes, and goes zip lining. "Life's an adventure to be lived to the fullest. You know that, Hayley."

I snicker. "I guess I'm learning that." One day, when I'm grown up, I want to be just like Ross Scott.

"Uncle Ross," Lora interrupts, "after your ribs heal from my hug, will you escort me tonight during the halftime ceremony?"

Miss Lorraine's eyes fill with tears. Ross puts his hand to his chest and beams at my friend. "I would be completely honored, sweetie."

* * *

LATER THAT AFTERNOON, I'M dressed in the navy blue uniform with the silver and white trim on the skirt and the tank top. It's time for the homecoming parade through Maxwell.

The Shriners in their fezzes have their go-carts lined up at the front, and the fire truck is around the corner to bring up the rear. The Maxwell State University band joins the parade, as well as all of the little girls currently enrolled in Miss Kathy's Dance Academy. The PHS Marching Patriots lead the parade with our majorettes decked out and the color guard sporting new silver flags. The parade also consists of the entrants into the grocery cart display, and Smith's Tractor Company pulling a flatbed truck with hay on it that the football team rides on. There are three convertibles that hold the five homecoming attendants: Stephanie and Samantha together in one; Ashleigh and Chloe in another; and Lora in the last car wearing a red sash with the words "Homecoming Queen" spelled out on it in sparkly letters. She won't get her crown until halftime of the game tonight.

Tara steps up next to me. "She certainly didn't waste any time swooping into your territory."

"Who?"

"Who else? The runner-up."

I glance around and then see Chloe over by the flatbed where Daniel is sitting up front with his long legs dangling off. She's laughing up his way and slanting her body toward him. He doesn't seem to mind at all as he returns a smile at her.

"She can have him," I say to my friend. "I told him to 'go away' last night."

Tara seems impressed. "Well, Hannah said Daniel asked Chloe to homecoming."

"I thought she was dating that Delta Theta Psi at Maxwell State."

"I think he transferred to UT Chattanooga."

"Whatever. Really . . . I don't care." She's got plenty of hair that Daniel can play with. In fact, rumor around school is she wears extensions, so she can probably give him a few he can take home and play with.

Mean Hayley . . . mean. Not my usual style. I guess the bitter taste is still in my mouth from last night's encounter.

"You're better off," Tara says, and then hugs my shoulder.

I guess Lora was right when she said Chloe was jealous I was with Daniel. She can totally have him. The bitch and the dick — a perfect match.

I turn my attention back to the fun activity at hand. It's homecoming. It's a parade. It's a celebration. And I intend to enjoy every minute of it. Sure, I've marched in this parade with the band the last three years, but this is different. People will actually see me. My parents won't have to count over three rows, six people deep.

Before climbing into the convertible that awaits her, Chloe steps away from her flirting to address the eight of us who will be leading the cheers tonight, since we've lost four girls to the homecoming court.

"Since I'm the captain and Lora is the co-captain and we'll be sitting in the stands tonight, you'll need to vote on a leader for the game," she says. "I'd like to recommend Melanie."

I resist the urge to roll my eyes. Of course she'd suggest her partner — not that I don't like Melanie . . . still . . .

"I think it should be Hayley," Ashlee Grimes pipes up. Funny, I was just about to suggest her.

"Hayley?" Chloe repeats, a touch of disdain in her voice.

"Great idea," Madison says. "No one knows the game of football better than she does. She's always starting the best cheers at the right time."

I swallow hard at the compliment.

"Definitely Hayley," Tara agrees.

Chloe's eyes land on the crutches I'm leaning on. "I'm not so sure Hayley should even be marching in the parade since she's still dependent on her crutches." She addresses the other girls, not me. "You should make another choice. Hayley's got to watch out for her leg and use her crutches. We need a captain tonight who's on top of everything."

Does this beyotch not remember how I tossed my crutches aside at her pool party?

Of course, *I* haven't abandoned them as I should.

Gabriel even told me I don't need these damn things anymore. He's right.

It's time for me stop using these crutches as a—well, a crutch. Yeah, it's going to hurt to walk for a while, but there's no time like the present to get headed down that path.

Without acknowledging Chloe and her disparaging remarks, I allow my adrenaline to get the best of me. It's pumping so hard through my system that I could probably knock out any heavy-weight champ and swipe his big shiny belt from him. I take my crutches and lift them over my head. Over to the far left is a city Dumpster. With all my might, I chuck the crutches as far as I can. The first one hits the Dumpster and disappears into its depths while the second one bounces off the lid and hangs on top. I wipe my hands together as if to say, "It's done."

While all the other cheerleaders hoot and holler, Chloe stands stunned, her mouth hanging open.

I advance on her while I still have the guts to do it. "*Nothing*—not you, not those crutches, not anything—will keep me from marching in this parade right now or from cheering tonight or any other night." I witness the looks of my stunned teammates. They are shocked in a good way, that someone finally stood up to the queen. Oh wait, she's not the queen; she's just an attendant. "I'd be honored to be captain tonight."

The rest of the squad, including the girls in the cars, cheer for me, and I nod and smile.

I won't be a victim of this cancer anymore.

I won't let it stop me.

I won't let people like Chloe and Daniel win because I'm physically weaker.

Actually, I'm not physically weak at all. Gabriel has seen to that. I can't wait to hang out and party with him tonight.

I am mentally tough, and that's what counts.

"You've got a car to get to, Chloe," I say sweetly. "And we've got a parade to march in. Let's line up!"

"Yes, ma'am," Tara shouts out, and follows me into formation.

Although there's a profound limp, I march the entire parade through downtown Maxwell, cheering my school and executing our pompom routine, all the while smiling through the pain.

It truly does hurt so good.

CHAPTER THIRTY-FOUR

*I owe much to my friends; but, all things considered, it strikes
me that I owe even more to my enemies. The real person springs
life under a sting even better than under a caress.*

—ANDRÉ GIDE

I'M STILL RIDING THE high from the parade and from having
finally ditched the crutches. I probably shouldn't have left them
in a city Dumpster, but oh well. In a way, I owe Chloe thanks for
pushing my buttons and getting me to chuck those things once
and for all.

"Mom, I'm home!" I scream out when I burst through the
back door.

She comes running in from the den and scoops me into her
arms. "I am *soooooo* proud of you! You're off your crutches. And
you marched the entire parade route." Her eyes fill with tears;
happy ones, I assume. "Are you okay?"

"Yeah, I'm fine."

I briefly share the tête-à-tête with Chloe, and I can see Mom is
even more pleased with me.

"Don't let anyone tell you what you can and can't do, Hayley."

"I know, Mom. I know. I handled it."

Dad walks in and slips off his boots. "I saw the parade come by the store, but I couldn't come out. Sorry I missed it, Little Kid."

Mom swoops on him. "Jared, she did it without her crutches."

Dad lifts an eyebrow at me. "Did it hurt?"

"No more than usual," I say. "Besides, Dr. Dykema told me I needed to strengthen my muscle in that leg. No better way to do it than to get off the crutches."

"I'm so proud of you," Dad says, and then hugs me to him. When I pull back, he reaches into his coat pocket. "Got you something."

Another Snickers bar.

"Thanks, Dad. My appetite has actually started coming back. I'm not constantly nauseated."

He tweaks my nose and tells me to keep doing what I'm doing. "Now, Hayley, run along upstairs and get ready for the game. I have some things I need to talk to your mother about."

"Nothing bad, right?"

Dad smiles. "Nothing for you to be concerned about."

I swing my purse onto my shoulder and limp off down the hallway to the staircase. I hear my parents whispering to each other, so low that it makes me beyond curious. I stop at the bottom of the steps to see if I can hear anything.

I must have sonar hearing like a dolphin or something, because I hear bits and pieces.

" . . . business is horrible. I don't know what to do."

" . . . should sell . . ."

" . . . medical bills are rolling in . . ."

" . . . insurance won't cover fully . . ."

" . . . don't let Hayley know . . ."

My parents are keeping important adult things from me. All parents do that, right? It's normal. However, most families aren't faced with a two-month hospital stay with three surgeries, chemo, and radiation. I know we have insurance, but did it cover me and all of my procedures? Guilt coats me; an ugly fashion statement. Have I caused my parents to plunge into a dire financial situation?

"What's wrong?" Dad asks me. I hadn't even heard him approach in the hallway—so much for that dolphinlike sonar.

"Um . . . just . . . um . . . concentrating on going up the stairs without my crutches."

He nods, believing my quick fib. "Do you want me to follow you up?"

"Okay."

I take the steps one at a time and am surprised by how easy it seems to be. Sure, my leg still hurts, but it's going to. I just have to work around it and deal with it. At the top, Dad pats me on the back.

"Good job. You'll be taking them two at a time again before you know it." His smile says he's hiding something—something deep and important.

"Is everything okay, Dad? I mean . . . with the family and business and stuff?"

"Why would you even ask that?" he says. "You worry about school, cheerleading, and a full recovery. Mom and I will worry about the petty adult stuff."

He kisses me on top of the head and returns downstairs.

Thing is . . . Dad is *such* a bad liar.

* * *

THE HOMECOMING GAME ITSELF with the Jeff Davis Prep School Lemurs is lackluster, at best. Six to six is the boring score. It's a battle of the field goal kickers and nothing more. Our guys look flat and uninterested and, quite frankly, so am I.

However, the halftime ceremony has me in tears.

Lora, escorted by her Uncle Ross, looks gorgeous in her black cocktail dress. The red satin banner crossing her body shimmers under the stadium lights, really showing off the glitter. I zap tons of pics on my cell phone from my place on the sidelines. Lora waves at me, as does Ross, who's looking a little pale tonight.

Felicia Johnston, last year's homecoming queen, is back here at PHS to crown Lora with the lovely, sparkly rhinestone tiara. I'm so happy for my partner that I could burst into song.

When everyone exits the field, I give her a big hug, almost smashing her bouquet of roses. Both her mom and mine are there at the fence and snap some pictures of us together. I try to pull Ross into one of them since he was her escort, but he waves me off.

"I'm not feeling very well," he says. "I think I need to go home and lie down."

"Ross, you should eat something. Come sit with me and we'll get burgers from the concession," Miss Lorraine says with concern.

He puts his hand to his stomach. "I don't feel like eating, either. Really, Sis. I'm just worn out. It's been a long week." He leans down and kisses Lora on the cheek. "It was an honor escorting you."

"Thanks, Uncle Ross," she says.

As he passes by me, he takes a swipe over the top of my head and smiles. "Those protein shakes are working, Hayley. Keep at it."

I mock salute him and then watch him leave.

Lora notices the small wrist corsage that I'm wearing and she gasps. "Did Daniel finally come to his senses and ask you to homecoming?"

The football team arrives back on the field at that exact moment, and I give the death stare at Daniel as he runs by.

"Hardly," I say. "He's taking Chloe, didn't you hear?"

"No, I didn't. I've sort of been in a fog since the announcement this morning." She looks at my corsage again. "So who gave you that?"

"My parents," I say. "I know it's pathetic, but they wanted me to have something."

Lora's smile is as vibrant as her new crown. "I think that's very special."

"I do have a sort of date to the dance." I pause as her eyes widen. "Gabriel and I are going . . . just as friends."

"Yeah, right," Lora says with a cackle. "He's been in love with you since you hit him in the head with the piñata stick at Ashlee Grimes's birthday party."

My mouth falls open. "We were ten!"

"It's been that long," Lora reports. "Come on, everyone knows it . . . except you. And him."

Gabriel? In love with me? I doubt it.

But I can't shake the conversation the whole rest of the game. I pay attention and start the appropriate cheers when we're on offense or defense, but I can't help looking for Gabriel on the sidelines. He has a white towel slung over one shoulder, and he carries a tray of water bottles for the players when they come out of the game. I also watch as he makes notes on charts and gets whatever Coach Gaither needs to do his job. Gabriel's as big as the other guys, and probably more muscular. I wonder why he isn't playing the game as he did when he was younger and was on the peewee team.

As I'm pondering this, Marquis Richardson breaks free of a tackle up the middle and high steps it down the field. The crowd goes nuts, propelling him toward the goal line with our yells.

"Score!" I scream out, and jump up and down on my right leg.

The players on the sideline rush past us as Marquis makes his way to the thirty, twenty-five, twenty, fifteen . . . *BAM* . . . The strong safety for the Lemurs nailed him on the eleven-yard line.

I glance up at the clock. Under a minute to go in the game. Still tied. A berth in the state playoffs on the line. Thoughts of Gabriel and whether he does or doesn't like me fall aside . . . for the moment.

"Get your poms and let's go," I shout out to the girls.

"What are we doing?" Melanie asks. I see her dart a look up into the stands at Chloe. I'm in charge tonight, though, and we're going down to the goal line to help the team.

Melanie and I join hands. She helps pull me along the remaining thirty-ish yards so that we're standing on the edge of the field. No one seems to mind, so the eight of us line up, poms secured in our fists.

"Oh my God! We've got to score!" Ashlee screams out next to me.

I start cheering. "Shove that ball across the line . . . Shove that ball across the line . . . Shove that ball across the line . . . Shove it! Shove it, Patriots, shove it!"

First down, Skipper's in at QB as a mixup. He fades back to pass, but it's a fake. He hands it off to Marquis or runs right, and then he hands it off to Daniel. It's a reverse!

"Go, Daniel!" I scream out. I don't care if he is a dick; he's still on my team.

The Lemurs are onto the play and pile their linebackers and defensive backs on the left side, planting Daniel into the sod.

"That's okay! That's okay! Second down!" I yell.

Daniel made three yards on the play.

Second down, Marquis Richardson runs up the middle off

tackle. He gets a couple of hard-earned yards and then he's down.

Hannah runs her hands up into her hair, nearly tugging her ponytail down. "I can't take this!"

I start another cheer as we stomp side to side off to the side of the goal. "Our defense will dazzle, our offense is hot stuff. We're the mighty Patriots and we're tough, tough, tough."

Lauren screams out the next verse. "Sugar and cream . . . sugar and cream . . . what's the matter with the other team? Nothing at all . . . nothing at all . . . they just can't play football."

A little persnickety, but we're talking playoff potential here.

Melanie Otto starts up another, and we all join in. "Time is ticking off the clock! Give it all you've got! Score, Polk, Score!"

Third down, Skipper fades back to pass. Coverage is man-to-man. The offensive line holds. I see Daniel break free from his man into the back of the end zone. Skipper lets the pass fly from his wrist, sailing precisely toward the space between the two ones on Daniel's chest.

And he drops it.

"Son of a bitch!" Hannah screams out.

Lauren and Melanie collapse to the field on their knees. Ashlee is stunned.

"What do we do?" she asks me.

"Fourth down, we're on the five, and there're eighteen seconds left," I report like an ESPN anchor. "If I were Coach Gaither, I'd bring in Phillip to kick."

Hannah shakes her head. "Hand it off to Richardson up the middle. He can power through."

Ashlee says, "Don't you think Daniel deserves another shot at it?"

I look at him pacing around the huddle, smacking himself on the helmet. It was a perfect pass. He just . . . dropped it.

A whistle blows and Coach Gaither motions for the offense to come in. He's sending out the kicking team.

Hannah smiles at me. "You know your shit, Matthews."

"I've got an idea," I say. "We're going to kneel at the goal."

"Awesome!" Lauren says. "I've seen the Maxwell State cheerleaders do this."

Lining up, we all move to our knees, grip our poms in our fists, and lock arms with one another. The silvery-red poms shaking mightily over our heads flicker in the lights above, and we start our cheer.

"Make that kick! Make that kick! Make that kick!"

Phillip—the good Bradenton—trots out onto the field and lines up the view of the short field goal. Skipper takes a knee and calls to the center to hike the ball. Suddenly, everything is in slow motion. The ball spins end over end until Skipper snatches it out of the air and then plugs it down to the ground, supporting it with his index finger. Phillip winds up his leg and slices it downward to connect with the pigskin. The ball sails through the air, just over the outstretched fingertips of one of the Lemur linemen, and then splits the uprights.

Everything speeds up—almost on fast-forward. I bow down before the team on the sideline, pulling Melanie down with me. She does the same to Lauren and on down the line. We do this a couple of times in celebration as the clock ticks down to zero.

"We won!" Melanie screams at me, and then hugs me.

The cheerleaders huddle together, jumping up and down, and acting as though this was our first victory of the year. Behind us, the linemen have hoisted Phillip up on their shoulders since he accounts for all nine of tonight's points.

Hannah shakes me and dies laughing. "That was awesomely awesome! I loved bowing at the goal line. We're totally going to have to do that every time we kick a field goal."

"I don't know what Chloe will think about that," I say.

"Who cares? We won!"

We did indeed. Everyone floods the field. I limp out and pat passing Patriots players on the back or helmet with my poms. I can't even get anywhere near Phillip, the hero of the game.

"We're gonna party tonight!" Phillip yells out.

I catch up with Gabriel, who's gathering towels and bottles together on the sideline. "Wasn't that amazing?" I ask.

"Best game of the season," he says. "Everyone played his heart out."

Out of the corner of my eye, I spot Daniel. He's still got his helmet on, and he's not celebrating the victory at all. If I know him—which I do—he's beating himself up for not catching that pass. Serves him right for being such a pompous ass to me. Let someone else enjoy the spoils of victory.

Daniel turns and looks at me. I don't dare move. I don't blink, smile, motion, or acknowledge his existence. He knows what I think of him, because right now, it's what he thinks about himself.

"See you in about half an hour?" Gabriel says.

"The dance! Yes! Do you think a girl like me can get ready for a homecoming dance in half an hour?"

Gabriel stands and contemplates. "Well . . . it's not like you have to do your hair or anything."

I burst out laughing and smack him with my poms. "Meet you in the gym."

Yeah, this is going to be a fun night.

* * *

TWO HOURS LATER, I'M having the time of my life. I'm dancing. I'm partying. I'm hanging with my friends.

"This is the best DJ ever," I say above the music mix to Gabriel.

He's an awesome nondate. We have a great time kidding around and hanging out. There are mostly up-tempo songs that everyone's grooving out to and very few slow songs. We just head over to the soda and snack table when those happen. I'm having such a good time that I don't even stop to notice Daniel and Chloe slow dancing. Okay, so I notice, but I don't care. Now he knows what it's like to be judged and stared at by the whole stadium. Dropping a pass isn't exactly cancer; however, it can ruin any chance of a college football scholarship if he continues to make stupid errors like that.

The DJ begins spinning a funky House/Techno number, and Lora and Ashlee run up to me.

"We have to steal her, Gabe," Lora says.

The cheerleaders line up in the middle of the dance floor and start doing the routine we (they) took to cheerleader camp. As we line up, Chloe slices her eyes on me.

"You should sit this one out, Hayley, since you didn't do the routine with us at camp."

"Like hell I will," I say with a smile. I watched the video of this dance so many times, I can do it in my sleep.

"Chill out, Chloe," Lora says. "It's homecoming, not a competition."

I slide into the lineup and snap into the first dance move to prove the captain wrong. Every beat of the music pulsates through me. I'm stoked as I move along in unison with the rest of the girls. Gabriel stands in front and claps me on. I smile at him, at the crowd . . . at everything. It feels amazing to be free of the crutches. There's still a little pain in my leg, but it's nothing bad. It is what it is.

When the song ends, we huddle together and cheer out, "Patriots Number One!"

Gabriel holds out an icy soda to me when I'm done. I gladly accept it and down most of it in two gulps.

"You rocked it out there, Hay."

"I'm starting to feel more like myself."

He reaches over and rubs my head. "Hmm . . . the peach fuzz is starting to turn into real hair."

I chuckle at how he's always feeling my head. It's not weird at all. Sort of our own private ritual. His smile is genuine, and he's not staring past me to see if there's a better conversation or someone more important to impress.

My chest aches in a sweet way. Maxwell wasn't the same after Gabriel and his family left. Now, the sun shines a little brighter with him back in town.

I can't stop staring at him—his close-cropped hair, his deep brown eyes. Am I seeing him—I mean *really*—seeing him for the first time? My earwig warrior . . . my trainer . . . my friend.

"What?" he asks with a smile. "Do I have something on my face?"

I giggle. "No, Gabriel. I've just . . . missed . . . this."

"This?"

"You. Our friendship."

He wraps his arm around me and escorts me slowly back to the dance floor where the music has shifted to something slow and romantic. He turns me to face him and then places his hands on my waist. "I'm not going anywhere."

With that, I place my hands on his shoulders and let him lead me around to the sexy melody. There's an ache in my chest momentarily that I can't quite pinpoint, and then I'm back to normal. "I'm glad."

Another hour dancing and then an hour feeding our faces

with burgers, fries, and shakes at the Burger Barn, and Gabriel drives me home.

"I had a great time," he says.

"Me too," I agree. "Thanks for going with me."

"Any time. You're a great dancer."

He steps out, comes around, and opens the door for me. Together, we walk in silence to my front door. Mom and Dad have left the porch light on. I move to hug Gabriel at the same time he moves to—oh my God! Was he going to kiss me? I laugh nervously, and then we do the awkward cheek kiss thing like complete idiots.

"G'night," I say, and then slip into the house before he sees how discombobulated I am.

I float off upstairs (okay, hobble mostly) feeling super-juiced over such a wonderful homecoming.

In my room, I snap on the light, disturbing Leeny who's curled up at the foot of my bed.

I turn and look at myself in the mirror, not afraid of what I'll see.

Instead of looking at a bald chick or a girl stricken with cancer, I view someone I haven't seen in months.

Me.

And I'm happy.

CHAPTER THIRTY-FIVE

*I got the bill for my surgery. Now I know what those doctors
were wearing masks for.*

—JAMES H. BOREN

JUST WHEN I THINK my life is turning a corner, *more* shit happens.

It always does.

But the last week of October, before Halloween, two things hit
the fan and splatter.

I come home from school the Monday after homecoming to
find our postman trying to shove a bunch of stuff through our
mail slot.

"Hey, Mr. Sayner," I call out. "Can I take that from you?"

"Hello, Hayley. Yes, you sure may. Quite a lot of bills from
Birmingham in there," the old man says, like it's any of his business. I bite back the urge to ask him if he'd like to pay them, and
I don't pose the question. Instead, I take the mail and thank him.

Once inside, I spread the plethora of various correspondences
out on the kitchen table.

There's one from Dr. Tanner Dykema.

Another from the University of Alabama Birmingham Hospital.

A separate statement from the anesthesiology department at UAB.

Tons of envelopes from Home Health Providers, Mom and Dad's insurance company.

Bills from the radiology department.

Oncology.

An orthopedic group.

Pathology.

I can't take anymore *ologies!*

I reach my fingers up to cram into my hair, only remembering that I don't really have any. I rub at my head, massaging the throb that has now settled over my left eye. Dare I even open any of these to see the damage my hospitalization, surgery, and treatment have cost and are costing my parents? They have insurance, so shouldn't those greedy bastards be paying for everything?

It's bad enough that I know Dad is struggling to keep Matthews Hardware afloat in this economy. Now this? Geesh . . . with so much debt, how will I be able to go to college?

I hear Mom coming through the back door, obviously on her cell phone. "I picked up a bucket at Crower's Fried Chicken along with some sides for dinner. If you're not home in time, I'll leave it in the oven. Then we can talk about — " She freezes in place when she sees me at the kitchen table. "Jared, I'll call you back."

Mom places the chicken dinner on the butcher block in the middle of the room and slowly walks over and sits down next to me. Her eyes shift downward to take in the bills from all of the ologies and such. Quietly, she gathers the mail into a neat stack and slips everything into her purse.

"You shouldn't be concerning yourself with all of these," she says softly.

"Mom! That's a shitload of bills . . . all because of *me*."

"Language, Hayley. I raised you better than to use words like that."

I slam my hands to the table. "You also raised me not to lie. Which is what you're doing right now."

"What have I lied about?"

"Semantics, Mom." I point at her purse. "Those hospital bills. There are a ton of them. I had no idea how much I was costing y'all as I was going through all of those tests and procedures, X-rays and surgeries and—"

Mom's lips flatten before she interrupts me. "Hayley, your father and I made the decision not to burden you with our financial situation. What were we supposed to do? Let you lose your leg?"

My hands tremble as I try to remain calm. "I think I deserve an explanation. Why isn't our insurance paying for all of my bills?"

Sitting back, Mom takes a deep breath. "The insurance is paying for some of it. Not all of it."

"Then that's a crappy insurance plan."

Now it's Mom's turn to slam her hands down. "Yes, it is. That's been a problem for several years. We simply haven't been able to afford a better plan. We have had severe financial problems in this family since your sister . . ."

Mom stops and puts her hand to her mouth.

"Gretchen? What does she have to do with this?"

Mom gets up and walks over to the refrigerator. She pulls out a bottle of water and quickly gulps it down. I don't know whether she's walked away from me or if she's doing this in preparation of the truth.

"Mom? Please . . . I'm not a baby . . ."

Her eyes are full of tears when she turns to me. "You're still my baby. Your father and I have done everything we can to protect you."

I walk over to her and take her hand. We walk down the hallway of the house and into the den. As we are sitting on the couch together, I press her to tell me everything.

She takes a deep breath. "During her senior year of high school, Gretchen got involved with the wrong crowd. She was doing drugs, drinking underage, and generally getting into a lot of trouble."

"I don't remember this," I say.

"You were too young and we shielded you from it."

I'm glad she's not shielding me from it now. "Go on."

"We had a lot of medical expenses due to Gretchen and her addictions. We put her in rehab, but that didn't work. We had her in therapy, but that didn't help, either. Finally, things got so bad that our insurance carrier canceled us. We gave Gretchen an ultimatum that she was to straighten up her act or get out."

"That's when she left home," I say.

Mom nods. "She left home . . . yes . . . and she cleaned out our savings account and a mutual fund that my parents had been building for years for the three of you to go to college. We had to settle on a less expensive insurance carrier to save money, and we've been scraping by ever since."

"How did she do this?" I ask incredulously. "Was her name on the account?"

With a shrug, Mom answers, "She got the user name and passcode somehow."

My blood boils and my head feels as if it will explode. I can't believe Gretchen would do something like that. Not the sister I remember growing up. The one who played Barbies with me and the one who would judge my stuffed animal beauty contests. The sister who taught me how to pluck my eyebrows and wear eyeliner. I have trouble matching her up to a money-thieving drug addict/alcoholic who left home.

"Your father is going to be very angry at me for telling you this."

"I would have been more pissed off if you hadn't."

"Hayley . . . language."

I feign a small laugh although I'm feeling anything but happy.

"How did I never know this?"

Mom smiles. "We're good protectors. Cliff got a scholarship for college, and we've been trying to save for yours, so it wasn't an issue."

"It's an issue when I don't have my big sister in my life. Did y'all talk at all when she was in Birmingham?"

Mom spreads her hands out and then lays them on her lap. "Very basic stuff. We mostly talked about you."

I sigh long and hard. "So, let me get this straight. Y'all have virtually no savings—"

"Some."

"There's a stack of medical bills that could possibly be growing—"

"Possibly."

"And the hardware store is losing money because no one is shopping mom-and-pop stores anymore, especially since Hometime Hardware built out on the highway."

Mom nods her head.

"Do I need to get a job at the Burger Barn or somewhere after school?"

A comforting arm comes around me. "No, sweetie. That won't really help."

"But all of the medical bills. They're from *me*. From my stupid cancer." I choke on the words in my throat. "I—I—I didn't mean to cause y'all financial problems."

"Hayley, stop. It's not your fault. You didn't decide to have cancer and to stay in the hospital for a couple of months. Your father and I will find a way to take care of it."

I shake my head, trying to knock the bad information out so it won't hurt so much. "Gretchen's okay now. She's got a good job and has to make decent money to live in Boston. Why won't she pay you back?"

Mom pulls her hand back and grabs one of the throw pillows to place in her lap. "We've never asked her to. It's something *she* needs to offer on her own."

"Oh, for goodness' sake! I'm calling her!"

"Absolutely not," Mom snaps at me. "Stay out of it, Hayley. It's between your sister and us."

"No, it's not," I say forcefully. "She made you lose your good insurance. She took all of your savings. She's the one who can make this better for all of us."

"Let it go," Mom says. "Besides, I've had a couple of interviews for work. Chenowith, White, and Bell needs a legal assistant, and I had a very good conversation with them. I have two more administrative assistant jobs to look into, as well."

I know the last thing Mom wants to do is go back to work. She's, like, getting old and stuff . . . almost fifty years old. She shouldn't have to compete with younger people in this job market to get work. There's got to be an easier solution.

"I'm sorry," I manage to say.

"For what?"

"For getting sick."

"Stop it," Mom says. "The Lord never gives us more than we can handle. So, we'll deal with our financial situation the same way we've dealt with everything else."

"I still feel bad. And I'm mad as hell at Gretchen."

"So am I, sweetie. But what is a mother to do?"

Since I'm not one, I don't know the answer to her question. All I know is there's got to be some way to make it all right.

* * *

TUESDAY AFTER CHEERLEADER PRACTICE, Lora and I drive over to the Burger Barn for chocolate milk shakes. We're in line at the drive-through when a car behind us beeps. I turn and see it's Will Hopkins, Lora's main squeeze, and none other than Daniel sitting in his passenger's seat.

Lora grabs her cell phone and texts Will.

"What are you saying to him?" I ask.

"I said, 'Daniel ruined our foursome. Call me later.'"

"That sounds kinky," I say with a laugh, unable to muster any real emotions.

I haven't spoken to Daniel since that fateful night in front of the bonfire. He's passed me in the hall and I saw him at lunch yesterday, but I honestly want nothing to do with him. He really hurt me by flaking out, and I just want to forget all about him and concentrate on getting stronger.

"Here y'all go," the Burger Barn lady says as she hands us our drinks.

Lora passes my large chocolate shake to me and I stab my straw into it.

"He's not worth it, you know?" Lora says.

"Daniel? Don't I know it. You really learn a lot about a person in times of trial."

She sips her drink and winces from the apparent brain freeze. "And nothing happened to him."

"That's what I told him," I say between sips of my own.

Lora steers back onto Main Street and stops at the traffic light for Highway 223. "Will told me Coach Gaither reamed Daniel a new asshole for missing that catch Friday night. Daniel blamed it on y'all being down on the goal line cheering."

"What? That's crap! We were doing our job."

"That's what Coach Gaither said."

I place the straw in my mouth. "Whatever. I'm tired of talking about him."

For a moment, I listen to the steady click of her turn signal as we wait for the light. The smooth chocolatey goodness cools my throat and my temperature from the long afternoon workout.

Lora steers to the left and then slips a CD into the car stereo. I close my eyes and enjoy the music, the shake, and the friendship. I appreciate my friends—Lora, Gabriel, Ashlee, and the other girls. I'm happy that I have cheerleading and the opportunity to be a part of the football season. I'm grateful that my hair is growing back and that I'm getting strong and stronger each day.

"What's Ross up to?" I ask Lora.

"He's leaving for Costa Rica in a few weeks," she says. "Some trek in the jungle and the rainforest. I swear, I don't know how he does it all."

"One day, I'd love to do stuff like he does. He's fearless."

Lora smiles. "He's a great guy. Since my dad died, he's really stepped in to take care of Mom and me."

And he's taken to supporting me, as well.

"You wanna go shopping at Beck's before I take you home?" Lora asks.

I feel guilty spending $1.89 on a chocolate shake, much less any money on new clothes. "Nah, I need to get home. I've got a bunch of homework." There's a buzzing next to me. "Your phone's going off."

Lora rolls her eyes and reaches for her Android. "Ugh . . . probably Will upset at me because I blew him off back at the drive-through."

I snatch it up from the middle console for her and glance at it.

"Lorraine Russell," I report.

"Mom? She doesn't usually call me when she's at work. Put it on speaker."

Since Lora's driving, I click the button and say, "Hey, Miss Lorraine, Lora's driving."

There's a moment of silence and then recognition. "I need Lora home immediately."

"What's wrong, Mom?" my friend asks.

"Just get here fast."

Her mom hangs up, and I'm left holding the phone.

"That's messed up," she says. "Mom is never like that."

Instantly, Lora whips her BMW through the parking lot of Captain D's and heads back in the direction of her house. I don't even ask her if she's going to take me home. Something is happening in her world and since I'm her partner, I need to be there for her just as she's been there for me.

Five minutes—and two run stop signs—later, we pull into Lora's driveway. Her mom's car is there, as well as Ross's hybrid.

We both leap out of the car and head up the walk to the house. I stop her with my hand on her arm. "Do you want me to wait out here?"

She takes my hand in hers and squeezes, giving me the answer.

When we walk through the door of her house, she calls out for her mother.

"Mom? Ross? What's going on?"

"We're in the kitchen," I hear Ross say.

We round the corner from the living room and both stop in our tracks. Miss Lorraine and her brother are sitting at the kitchen table, very somber and quiet. Are they dealing with financial difficulties, too? Certainly not; Ross has money coming out of his ears.

I hang back as Lora crosses the room and takes the chair opposite her mom. "What's going on? You're scaring me."

Miss Lorraine looks at Ross. His head is down and his hands rest on the tabletop. The vein in his neck bulges. He's very upset—angry, in fact.

"You know how Ross wasn't feeling well the other night?" Miss Lorraine says. "He went to the doctor yesterday, and we got some very bad news today."

I swallow hard, knowing I shouldn't be hearing this.

"What is it?" Lora asks as tears of fear begin to cover her eyes.

"Stop trying to candy-coat it, for God's sake, Lorraine." Ross glares forward, seething. "I've been diagnosed with a very advanced stage of fucking leukemia."

CHAPTER THIRTY-SIX

I know God will not give me anything I can't handle. I just wish that He didn't trust me so much.

—MOTHER TERESA

I STAND FROZEN AS THE words leave Ross's mouth.

It's the last thing I expect him to say.

Leukemia?

The simple definition is cancer of the blood, although there's nothing simple about the disease. I remember from physiology class that it can get into the bone marrow and can also make you anemic. People have been known to lose liver function because of it, too, not to mention their life. How I remember these scholastic details at a time like this is beyond me, but I know the road ahead for Ross is not going to be an easy one.

"How? When?" Lora manages to ask.

Ross's eyes are unmoving as he stares ahead at the coffee mug Miss Lorraine set in front of him. A low growl resonates from his chest. "I don't have time for this shit. We've just taken Game On public, and the investors expect a certain level of dedication, time, and travel on my part. To be out there upholding the image of the company and to expand into other markets in the south."

Lora stammers again. "But—but—but how did you *get* this?

You're, like, in better physical shape than anyone I've ever known. You don't smoke or drink or do drugs or eat fast food or anything like that. You never get the flu or anything. You've got super immunity."

He snorts. "Lotta good all that does me now."

Lora won't let up. "You're not supposed to get sick."

I wasn't supposed to get sick, either. Cancer doesn't discriminate. It doesn't care. It doesn't give a shit who it attacks and when. It targets young and old alike. It preys on politicians, movie stars, sports figures, housewives, grandmothers, garbage men, accountants, high school cheerleaders, and even CEOs of companies.

He puts his head in his hands. "My life is over."

"No, it's not!" Miss Lorraine fusses at him.

"It might as well be," Ross says with a resigned sigh. Bitterness cascades off him like a tidal wave battering the shore to smithereens. "The signs were there and I didn't pay attention to them. I've been so busy and on the go. I didn't know . . . fatigue, pain in my ribs, bruises on my arms and legs for no reason, loss of appetite."

I remember the story Gabriel told me about the cheerleader at his old school who killed herself over the thought of being sick. And now, Ross Scott, someone I really admire and look up to, is copping the same attitude. Only, he's a grown man and should know better. Right? Aren't adults supposed to handle this kind of stuff better than a kid? Maybe no one knows how to handle this. But I feel I need to speak up. To help.

I don't know, though. I don't know if it's my place.

"I haven't been feeling . . . right," Ross continues.

Miss Lorraine speaks up. "I made him go to the doctor and get some blood work done."

I watch as Ross lifts his head toward his sister. "I'd rather have not ever known."

"That's ludicrous," Lora shouts out. "And what? Not gotten treated? You've found it now and the doctors can take care of it."

"It doesn't matter," Ross snaps. "It's *acute* leukemia. My white blood cells don't work anymore. Every breath I take, the leukemia cells are rapidly taking over. I'm completely fucked!"

Miss Lorraine is horrified. "Ross! Stop that. You don't know what this means yet."

The usually confident and calm Ross Scott pivots his head in her direction. "I most certainly do. It means I don't have very long. Everything I planned for is over. Everything I dreamed about doing . . ." He trails off.

Lora bursts into tears, and her mother moves to comfort her.

"You can't have that attitude, Ross," I finally say firmly, knowing I'm overstepping my boundaries.

His normally soft eyes slant. "Can't I? My entire career is based on sports, adventure, and convincing others to take risks and accept challenges. I can't do that from a hospital room hooked up to machines. I can't be the spokesperson of Game On when I'm getting chemo and radiation." His eyes stare off for a moment. "It's not only about my career and taking a hike—it's the inevitability of this outcome. Only five fucking percent actually beat this disease. Five!"

Miss Lorraine reaches out. "Yes, dear, but you can be among that five percent."

"Yeah, Uncle Ross. No one fights like you."

"Statistics are just that," I say. "Numbers on a piece of paper. You're a real human being who can beat the odds."

"You have to try, Uncle Ross," Lora begs.

"You do, Ross," his sister adds.

"I thought I couldn't be a cheerleader. But I'm doing it."

He's on his feet, and I'm afraid he's going to take his frustration out on me. "This is the real world! This isn't some high school pastime, Hayley. This is my life!"

I recoil as his anger smacks me down.

"Ross, do sit down, dear," Miss Lorraine says, trying to rein him in. "Hayley, he doesn't mean anything against you. We all know what you've been through."

"Right," I say quietly, knowing I have to get this out. "But you can't have a negative attitude and be all 'woe is me' and stuff. That's the worst way to be. It means you're going to let the cancer win. You have to fight this, Ross."

He shoves his hands through his hair and lets out another sigh. "It's hard to fight something I didn't even know I had. It's *acute* leukemia, which means it could already have spread to my organs. What's the point in getting chemo and radiation, only to go into remission and then hope that the doctors can figure something out?"

"You have to fight it," I repeat. "Like I did."

Ross's smile is one of frustration. "You're just a kid, Hayley. You've got the rest of your life ahead of you. Me, I've got an investor's meeting next Thursday in Chicago. I've got a board of directors to report to. I've got a mortgage and car payment. You've got homework and football games and school dances. It's not the same thing. I have to take a leave of absence from the company I created so I can go lie in a hospital and have chemicals pumped into my body."

I flatten my lips together, not buying his argument at all. "Just like what I went through this summer."

"Listen to her, Uncle Ross. She knows what she's talking about," Lora begs. "You can't get all pissed about this. You have to fight it. People do beat leukemia."

He sneers. "Do you know that in the year 2000, two hundred and fifty-six thousand people — children and adults — came down with leukemia? Do you also know that two hundred and nine thousand of them died? That's eighty percent. Eighty percent!"

"That's not today, Ross. Statistics change," Miss Lorraine says. "Your own doctor said they can get you into treatment and get you on the road to remission."

I look at my partner's uncle, my friend. This is the man who so unselfishly arranged for my cheerleading squad to drive three hours to Birmingham to visit me in the hospital and cheer me up. This is the man who gave me protein bars and shakes from his store to help me with my own recovery and rehabilitation. He's only in his midthirties, yet looking at him now, he suddenly seems so much older — aged from his diagnosis and weary over what to do next.

Tears seem to be lurking at the base of his eyes. I certainly can't blame him. Crying is a release; a way of shouting out your frustration and anger at the universe. I cross the room and take the chair next to him, feeling very much like the adult in this situation. I lift my hand and place it softly over his. He turns his head and looks at me, more than likely taking in my weak smile and my fuzzy-haired head from my own loss. He has rich, thick blond hair that I fear will come out, too, once he gets into treatment. When he looks at me, does he see himself in the future? Or do I somehow represent hope to him? I pray it's the latter.

"You've got to try," I whisper. "For yourself, for your family, for your company, and for everyone else who's had cancer."

His hand flips over and he grips mine tightly. His eyes squeeze shut, and the tears gush out and down his cheeks in a release he so needs. His voice trembles when he speaks. "I don't know if I'm strong enough . . . as strong as you."

"You're strong enough to climb mountains. You're bold enough to trek through rainforests and jump out of airplanes," I say, smiling with my eyes.

"Those are adrenaline rushes," he says.

"You're only as strong as you want to be." I point my index finger to my head. "It's all up here. Mind over matter. I could have easily crawled into a hole after they found my tumor. If I had, I might not be here now — in the least, I wouldn't have a left leg to walk on. I never let the cancer get into my head. I never let it tell me I couldn't beat it. I never listened as it mocked me." I don't know where the words are coming from, but they sound good, and I hope he believes me. "Your doctors know what they're doing and they can help." I squeeze his hand. "Don't give up, Ross. Don't give in. Even if you have to battle it for years. Fight it."

His tears become racking sobs to the point where it's breaking my heart. Miss Lorraine comforts him on one side and Lora comes up from behind and wraps her arms around his neck. The four of us stay that way for a moment — or an eternity, who knows?

"Fight it, Ross," I whisper.

Then he nods. Small at first. "I will."

"What?" I ask, making sure I heard him correctly.

"If you can do it, Hayley, I can, too."

I don't know how long we sit like that — a supportive knot of hugging — but we finally breathe a sigh of relief and separate. Miss Lorraine hands him a napkin, and he wipes his face.

"When does the treatment start?" Lora asks.

"Immediately," Ross responds. "The doctor said he can get me into Maxwell Memorial Hospital on Monday."

"Shouldn't you go somewhere that specializes in leukemia?" I ask.

"I have to stay near the business. Maxwell Memorial has a good rep."

"It's going to be a long road, dear," Miss Lorraine says. "We're all here for you." She smiles up at me and winks her thanks.

"I'm going to need it," Ross says.

I get up and walk over to the counter for my purse. Digging inside, I locate the item I'm searching for and grab it in my fist. I present Ross with what has been so helpful in my own recovery.

It brings a small laugh from him. "A Snickers bar?"

"Trust me, it's going to become your best friend."

CHAPTER THIRTY-SEVEN

A kiss is a lovely trick designed by nature to stop speech when words become superfluous.

—Ingrid Bergman

I stopped at the hospital this afternoon," I tell Lora as we drive up the hill to school Halloween night. The annual PHS Halloween carnival starts in about fifteen minutes.

"Oh yeah? Was Ross still telling all of the nurses what to do?"

I giggle. "Nah . . . he was good. I took him a big box of Snickers and some sudoku books. I think I've got him hooked on them."

Lora nods. "Something fun for him to dwell on instead of financial spreadsheets and stuff from Game On."

"Who's running things?" I ask.

"Uncle Ross . . . remotely. He's got his computer and his cell phone. His head of sales, Franklin Dean, will do the more out-there appearances over the next few weeks."

Poor Ross. I know how frustrating this must be for him. "He seems in good spirits."

"All because of you, Hayley," Lora says. "You really helped him get over the negative attitude. He's going to do just fine."

"I pray for him every night," I say.

Lora steers her car into one of the few remaining parking slots in front of the gym. "That's all any of us can do."

We walk into the school that is teeming with students, teachers, and families crowding around for the annual festivities. PHS really goes all out and no space goes to waste. Tons of prizes have been either donated by local merchants or made by students and their families. There are darts, pick-up ducks, go fish, face painting, henna tattoos, a best costume contest, a haunted house, hayride, a cider station, pumpkin carving contest, a monster mash dance-a-thon, bingo, fake roulette, and a country store full of homemade jams, candies, bread, and cookies made by teachers and staff. I'm carrying in a red velvet cake that my grandmother made for the cake walk in the library, where Lora and I are assigned to work for an hour.

I love the cake walk and have ever since I came to my first Halloween carnival here at PHS when Cliff was in school. They clear out the tables in the library and then put large pieces of masking tape on the floor. Each piece of tape has a number written on it in a random order. Whoever's working the event plays a CD of music for a few minutes. When the music stops, a number is drawn. Whoever is standing on that number wins the cake of his or her choice. And boy howdy, are there a ton of them. Angel food, devil's food, ones iced with vanilla, chocolate, coconut, strawberry, a couple from the local bakery, and a few fancy ones where people tried their hands at fondant decorating. There must be more than fifty cakes sitting here on the tables.

Lora and I have the shift for the first hour. We herd people into the library so they can grab a spot on a number before the music starts. We're dressed as zombie cheerleaders, wearing one of our uniforms, but sporting fishnet stockings that are torn at the knee, pale white makeup with dark circled eyes, and a ratty cape to keep us warm in the October chill. All of the cheerleaders decided to do this, but when I see Chloe Bradenton walking by outside the library, I see she didn't go for the zombie makeup part. Whatever. Like she can't be seen in any kind of ugly way.

She really needs to get over herself.

Lora gets ready to cue the music up, and people flood the library to take their turn at winning a homemade confection. I walk around the circle, taking tickets from everyone standing on a number.

A little girl points up at me and says, "Mommy! Look! She has no hair."

The mother pulls the child to her and apologizes. "I'm so sorry. Please don't get upset with her."

Even though I'm still self-conscious about my appearance, I smile. "It's okay. I'm used to people staring."

"What happened to you?" the little girl asks.

"I was sick and I lost my hair." I rub the top of my head for good measure. "It's growing back, though."

"You don't look sick."

"I'm not anymore," I say.

The mom turns six shades of red. "Kathryn's just a little thing. Please don't mind her. We're all so proud of you and how you've handled this."

You are? I don't even know who this woman is, but her compliment warms me.

"Thanks," is all I can manage to get out before Lora cues up "The Purple People Eater" for everyone to walk around to.

When the music stops, Lora pulls a number from the basket. "Forty-two."

"That's us, Mommy!" little Kathryn shouts out.

I slip over to verify the number. "We have a winner."

"What do we do?" the girl asks.

"Pick any cake up there and it's yours."

She smiles a wide, toothless grin at me. "Did you make one?"

I point to the one with the cream cheese frosting. "My grandmother baked that. It's red velvet."

"I want that one, Mommy."

Her mom smiles, and Lora hands the cake to her.

When they walk off, Lora says to me, "You really have no idea how many lives you've touched, do you?"

I scoff. "What are you talking about? I did what I had to."

"Exactly," she says with a huge grin, and starts the music again. And off to work I go.

* * *

MRS. QUAKENBUSH SITS OUTSIDE the haunted house — aka the boys' and girls' locker rooms — taking tickets. "Two, please."

"We're seniors," Lora says.

She looks over the top of her glasses and then reaches for a clipboard with the names of the seniors. "And you are?"

I want to roll my eyes, but I just smile in my zombie makeup instead. Lora gives her our names, and she lets us pass through the black curtain.

"Honestly, it's not a national security matter," Lora says with a laugh.

We trudge through the entrance, which is basically black sheets hung from ceiling to floor to make it like a maze. We hear the cackles of our fellow classmates in character as they attempt to scare the patookie out of us. Strobe lights flash, leading the path through the attraction. Lora grabs my arm in pure terror, as if any of these clowns in here are going to do us any harm.

Deeper inside, we push into a forest area where we're chased around by a couple of werewolves, a vampire here and there, and someone — is that Phillip Bradenton? — with a fake chain saw grinding out. Lora screams like a little girl, but I can't help but laugh. I guess when you've faced cancer, some theater makeup and sound effects don't frighten you.

The Monroe twins, Jayne and Jessica, are dressed as zombies, coming at us with psychotic looks on their face. Someone's dressed as a demented clown, and a botched operation is happening on the right.

"Who is that?" Lora asks of the body laid out on the table covered in phony blood.

"I think it's Furonda."

She rises from the table and moves toward us. Again, all I can do is laugh.

In the vampire forest, we're surrounded by classmates dressed as the nighttime predators. A black light allows their teeth to glow in the dark. At some point, Lora and I are separated.

"Hayley! Where are you?" Lora cries out.

"Over here, cornered by a guy from my journalism class."

He rolls his eyes at me and continues to the next victim behind me.

There's wispy smoke from a dry ice machine, and several fans blow black curtains around in confusion. I search for the exit in vain. It's just too dark in here, and the screams of fellow PCHers drown out everything else.

"Lora? Where are you?"

No answer. Great. I've lost her.

I slip through the fog and find a seam in the sea of curtains. But my pathway is cut short when a dark, cloaked figure, surely meant to represent the Grim Reaper, backs me into a dark, dark corner, blacker than the rest of the room.

His hands are strong on my arms, but not frightening at all. His breath smells sweet, as if he's been eating the divinity candy from the carnival's country store.

"Hayley," he whispers to me.

"Who is this?" I ask, trembling, but not due to fear.

"I think you're amazing," he whispers.

And then he kisses me.

A soft, feathery kiss on my lips.

Who? What? Huh?

I can't move from the shock. I can't breathe from the stolen moment.

Just as quickly as the Grim Reaper appeared to me, he disappears. He fades back into the props and confusion of the haunted house.

My hand moves up to cover my lips, still warm from the contact.

"Hayley?" Lora calls out again.

"Over here," I barely manage to get out.

She grabs for my hand and pulls me to her. "Let's get out of here."

"I couldn't agree more," I say.

I don't tell Lora what just happened, simply because I don't exactly know what it was myself.

How to describe it?

A dream?

An apparition?

A secret admirer?

A delicious encounter that has my senses reeling?

I have no clue.

And I have no way of figuring it out.

CHAPTER THIRTY-EIGHT

An apology is the superglue of life. It can repair just about anything.

—LYNN JOHNSTON

I WALK THROUGH THE MOTIONS the rest of the night, my skin still buzzing from the mystery kiss. I win at the rubber duck pond and get a bag of toys and stuff at the fishing booth. However, I can't keep my mind from dwelling on what happened inside the haunted house.

My heart is pulsating in my chest.

My hands are tickly and tingly.

Adrenaline flows through me in a river of questions.

People don't just kiss me randomly.

Nor do they tell me I'm amazing.

Chills tiptoe up my spine at the memory of his soft words and tender kiss.

Then doubt creeps in.

Was it a joke?

Part of a prank? Or a dare?

How do I unravel this mystery?

When the carnival comes to a close, Lora and I join up with Ashlee and Tara to take some pictures of us all in costume. One of the yearbook photographers snaps us, as well. The smell of popcorn and cider is prevalent in the air, so we stop on our way out to raid the leftovers. Mrs. Ingram hands us free servings as they're trying to clean up. I try to concentrate on the salty goodness of the snack, but my lips still buzz from the kiss.

We head out of the school and into the parking lot where the last hayride unloads right in front of us. That's when I see him.

It's Daniel. He's wearing a black cape with a hood, just like the Grim Reaper. Could it have been him who kissed me? You'd think I'd recognize his kiss, even though it's been a few weeks since we broke up. Hell, we haven't even spoken since that fateful night at the bonfire.

But was this his way of apologizing?

Does it mean he actually cares about me after all?

Why do guys have to play such asinine games?

Will Hopkins, dressed as a vampire, climbs down off the wagons after Daniel and comes over to Lora. "Where have you been all night?"

"Working," Lora says. "Bite anyone interesting in the haunted house?"

Exposing his plastic fangs, Will moves to nibble at Lora's neck and she squeals.

Daniel actually makes eye contact with me and sort of smiles. "Hey."

"Hey," I say, not able to form any other words.

"What are y'all doing now?" he asks.

I don't respond, not knowing exactly what our status is at the moment.

Ashlee says, "I've got to go home. Trig test tomorrow."

"What teacher gives a test after the Halloween carnival?" I ask.

"Quakenbush."

"'Nuff said," Daniel says with a laugh.

Byron Burke, a fellow senior and one of the offensive linemen on the football team, pulls up in his Jeep. "Y'all wanna go riding around? See what trouble we can get into?"

I glance at Lora. "I don't have to be home until eleven."

"Me either."

Lora and Will climb into the back of the Jeep with Lora sitting in his lap. Byron's driving with Phillip Bradenton in the front seat. Daniel awkwardly stares at me and then motions for me to get into the back of the Jeep before him. I slide in next to Will, and then Daniel squeezes into the small space left. We're totally smashed together and touching from shoulders down to our knees.

"You got enough room?" he asks.

"Yeah . . . I'm fine." I swallow hard, not knowing what to say to him after what we've been through. And after that mysterious kiss in the dark.

Byron lets out a loud whoop and slams the Jeep into gear. We speed down the PHS driveway. I pull my thin cape around me for warmth and hold on to the roll bar overhead to keep from flying into Daniel's lap.

Before I know it, we've driven all through Maxwell and into a residential section over behind Maxwell State University. We weave through the quiet streets and then turn onto Gravity Way.

My grip tightens on the bar, and I grit my teeth.

"Get ready!" Byron shouts, and then slips the Jeep into low gear.

Gravity Way is this huge downward steep grade that I've heard about people racing down, followed by a sharp upward incline.

"Gun it!" Will shouts. Lora hides her face in his vampire cloak.

"Do it!" Daniel yells, and puts his hands up in the air.

The chilling night air whooshes around us as we speed down the hill. I'm trying to enjoy the thrill, but I'm torn between the sheer terror of what if we flip or crash, or what if one of Maxwell's finest is waiting at the bottom of the hill to ticket the crazy kids out causing trouble Halloween night.

Fortunately, neither happens, and we make it up the hill safe and sound.

"Do it again, dude!" Daniel says.

Boys.

"Naw man, check this out," Byron says as he turns left onto this tiny gravel road. It's darker than dark, and the treetops provide a leafy tunnel that we drive through. The Jeep's headlights touch on a wrought-iron gate at the end.

"What is this place?" Lora asks.

I see an overgrown sign that reads Restful Grove.

"Oh my God," I say, breathless. "We're at a cemetery?"

Byron turns and laughs. "It's the oldest one in the city. Isn't even on the maps." He pulls the Jeep all the way up to the gate and shuts off the engine. "Let's go explore."

Lora and I exchange panicked looks. This is so *not* cool, but I don't want the guys to think I'm freaked out. Guys love it when girls freak out.

Byron, Phillip, and Daniel force the gate open, and Lora, Will, and I slip inside. The place is very run-down with broken headstones, piles of leaves, and tall grass and weeds covering the area. It's no bigger than my grandmother's backyard; yet it has a total creepiness factor.

"I don't like this, Hayley," Lora whispers. "I'm scared."

I try to reassure her while comforting my own tripled pulse rate. "It's okay."

Is it, though?

Daniel and Byron start dueling with long tree branches they found on the ground. The rest of us wander around checking out the old graves. Some date back to the mid-1800s with a lot of unmarked, unknown, or sunken-in tombs. The hairs on my arm stand at attention and not from the cold. There's an eeriness here that crawls over me, and makes me feel like something is watching us. Not that I necessarily believe in demons, ghosts, or spooks, but this just doesn't seem right.

My instincts couldn't be more dead—no pun intended—on when I hear Byron scream out to Daniel, Will, and Phillip.

"Dudes . . . run!"

Will drops Lora's hand that he's been holding and takes off toward the gate with his football buddies. Lora screams like a banshee and bolts after her boyfriend. I can't exactly run and am totally screwed.

"They're trying to leave us!" Lora yells.

"No shit, Sherlock!" I cry back.

"Will! Don't do this to me!" my partner begs as she's running fast. Guess he forgot she ran track in the spring.

I can't run, though, and can only watch as Byron squeezes back through the gate, followed by Phillip, and Will pulling up the rear. Lora catches up to him, screaming and waving her hands. The Jeep starts backing up, and I see Lora dive into the back seat, wailing away on her boyfriend as he laughs and fends her off.

Oh my God. They're leaving me. WTF?

Daniel's the last one of the pack to make it to the gate; his black cape flapping in the wind. However, his cell phone comes flying out, and he pauses to get it.

This is my chance!

I have no idea where I get the energy, strength, or even the ability to close the distance between the two of us. Daniel straightens from picking up his cell phone, and that's when I tackle him like a lineman on fourth and short.

"You're not going anywhere," I growl out.

He struggles with me in the dirt and leaves that we're rolling around in. "Hayley, what are you doing?"

"Y'all aren't ditching me! If I'm left, so are you."

He wrestles away from me, but my sudden Wonder Woman strength keeps him pinned on the ground.

The squeal of tires on gravel catches my ear, and I realize the deed is done.

"Great! Just great!" I yell, climbing off him.

Daniel slams his fists into the ground, sending leaves flying everywhere. "Fuck!"

I stand up and pick remnants of broken shrubs, twigs, and grass off my uniform. My teeth begin to chatter, so I wrap the thin cloak around me, hoping Byron will come back soon. What an asshole!

I give Daniel the death stare as he dials his cell phone. He obviously gets Byron's voice mail. "Yo, Burke. What the fuck, man? That wasn't the plan. Girls—we were ditching the girls, you retard! You'd better get your ass back here ASAP!"

I hiss through my teeth, trying to cap my anger. "Are you serious? You idiots planned that? What . . . strand the cheerleaders in the cemetery . . . for what purpose?"

"It's Halloween," he says. "You do shit like this."

"Yeah, well, I don't."

I turn my back and walk away from him. I cross over to a crumbling mausoleum covered with vines and clumps of mud. At least there's a little overhang to protect me from the extreme cold. Why hadn't I thought to bring my coat tonight? Oh, I know—because I didn't know I was going to get left in a freaking cemetery with my ex.

Pulling my knees up in front of me, I wrap my arms around my legs and pull the cape over myself. The torn fishnet stockings do very little to keep me warm.

I sit like this for at least fifteen minutes, wondering if our ride will ever come back. It's not like we're near anything or could walk to a house and ask for help. Daniel can't call 911 because we're totally trespassing and the cops would *not* be happy.

Several feet from me, Daniel keeps calling and texting Byron to no avail. If he were a cartoon character, steam would be spewing from his ears.

No words are exchanged as he paces back and forth near me. At least he has long pants on and a thicker cape — a cape similar to the person who kissed me. Was it Daniel? And if so, why is he being so distant now? Shouldn't he be comforting me or something?

Hell no. He's too concerned about himself, as usual. My fists ball up, and I dig my fingernails into my palms. Irritation rushes through my veins, and I become passionately outraged on the inside like a bubbling volcano about to burst.

I can't take it anymore. I erupt.

"You know," I call out to Daniel, "you're a real jerk."

Quietly, he shuffles through the leaves and makes his way over to me. He hangs his head and then sits down next to me. His eyes meet mine, and I see regret overcome him.

"Yeah, I know it," he acknowledges.

Ahhh . . . victory. "At least you admit it."

Silence surrounds us again as the night wind curls around our feet. An owl hoots in the distance, and I quake.

Daniel moves closer and wraps his cape around me in a nice gesture. The one streetlight, coupled with the moonlight, bounces off his face. I see his Adam's apple bob up and down as he's about to speak.

"I'm sorry I flaked on you, Hayley."

I don't know what to say, so I just nod and listen.

He sighs. "Cancer is just too much for me to handle."

"Tell me about it," I say sarcastically.

"It's high school, you know? Senior year. Final blowout. Not real life."

My own sigh releases. "Well, it's real life to me."

He pulls me closer, and I appreciate the shared warmth. "I know."

We sit like that for a few more minutes—how many, I don't know. We're friends comforting each other. Nothing more.

After a while, I see the headlights to Byron's Jeep approaching. They're waving and laughing like they've just pulled off the cleverest gag of all times. Whatever.

At least I had this time with Daniel—the real Daniel; not some jock trying to impress his friends.

I forgive him in my head for being such a stupid boy.

Deep, deep down in my female intuition, I know he wasn't the one who kissed me in the dark.

The question remains . . . *then who was it?*

CHAPTER THIRTY-NINE

Attitude is a little thing that makes a big difference.

—WINSTON CHURCHILL

I CREEP INTO THE HOSPITAL room and find Ross sitting in bed with tons of paperwork in front of him.

"Mobile office?" I ask.

"Hayley, what a treat," he says, smiling. "Come sit."

I pull the chair up next to his bed and hand him the gift bag I brought for him.

"What's that?"

"The real treat."

Ross opens it and then laughs. "Snickers bars. Honestly, kid. You should buy stock in the company."

I bob my head. "It was the only thing I could stomach during my chemo."

"It sucks," he says. "You know, to be technical about it."

"Yeah, it did."

He seems older, more worn, and very tired. His hair is definitely thinning, and there are bruises all up and down his arms. He's been in the hospital three weeks now, and I can tell he's fidgety and frustrated.

He shifts the paperwork aside and reaches into the bag for one of the candy bars. Ripping into the paper, he takes a bite and then moans in pleasure. "That works."

I lace my fingers together on my lap. "So, how is everything going?"

Ross lays the chocolate on the tray in front of him. "Day to day, you know? Seems that in order to kill the leukemia cells, a lot of my healthy cells and tissue get damaged. I'm starting to lose my hair, my nails have all broken off, and every time they stick a needle in me, I bruise like I've been in a prize fight."

I shake my head, realizing how "simple" my treatment was in comparison. "I'm sorry, Ross. But you have to do this to get well."

"That's what they tell me," he says. He fakes a smile at me, but I know better.

"I'm so tired, Hayley. I've never been this exhausted in my life," he says. Frustration underlines his words. "I've climbed mountains with less effort. Now, all I want to do is sleep and not throw up. You know what I'm talking about."

"I do," I say quietly. "I don't know what I can do for you, but I'm here."

Ross reaches for my hand. "That's priceless. That and the chocolate bars."

I tighten my grip to encourage him. "I know this is hard. Believe me, I do. You have to trust that God has a plan for you and that the doctors can take care of this so it won't get worse."

He chuckles. "You should bottle that positive attitude and sell it on eBay, kiddo."

My cheeks heat from the compliment. "It's how I get up every day and go to school. I *have* to stay positive."

He points to my head. "Just as I'm losing my hair, yours is coming in nicely."

I scrub at the short soft growth on my scalp. "It's coming in darker. It's almost black now instead of brown. The doctors told me the texture can change, as well."

"Cancer perm," Ross says. "I heard all about it. Sometimes you get a wave or curl when it grows back."

"That would be cool," I say, smiling.

The nurse knocks and enters the room. "Sorry to interrupt, but I've got some medicine for you, Mr. Scott."

Waving her off, Ross says, "Mr. Scott? Mr. Scott is my father."

Standing, I drop Ross's hand. "I'll get out of the way."

"Please come see me again," he begs.

"Of course I will," I say.

"I need you to help me be brave, Hayley. I need you to share that innocence you have. That lust for life. This is hard for me and I don't admit things like that easily. I run a multimillion-dollar firm, yet, I can't control my own body."

I take his hand again. "I know it's frustrating. Been there, done that, bought the T-shirt. There's a reason for everything. We just don't know the 'why' part all the time."

"Stay as you are, Hayley."

My lips curl up into a wide smile. "I'm here for you . . . whatever you need."

"Your friendship means the world."

* * *

FOR THANKSGIVING, OUR SMALL community neighborhood takes to the street. Even though the weather's a bit nippy, we bring out our picnic tables, chairs, lawn furniture, fire pits, and we all share a massive celebration dinner before the sun sets. We've been doing this since I was about eight years old, and I'd be crushed to experience Thanksgiving any other way.

It's the same thing every year: Mom's green bean casserole with the fried onions; Mrs. Newbaum's baked yams with the melted marshmallows and toasted pecans; Dr. Johnson's deep-fried turkey; Ella McQueen's pineapple-glazed ham . . . and more.

What's different this year, is Gabriel and his folks are back in the neighborhood. His mom's apple sausage dressing is to die for, and when I heap it onto my plate I realize how much I've missed it in my life.

Gabriel sits next to me at our picnic table with Cliff and Lily opposite us. We don't talk much as we stuff our faces with the yummy delights from the many neighbors, even going back for seconds. It's great to have my appetite back, especially for this meal. I can't get enough of the fried turkey, slathered in gravy.

"Dessert?" Gabriel asks when we've finished our meal.

"Um . . . yeah! Have you just met me?"

We laugh together and make our way down the street to where the dessert table is set up. There's everything you could ever want: apple, pumpkin, blueberry, and cherry pies, cheesecake, lemon tarts, cookies, cakes, fudge, fruit—you name it.

I select a huge chunk of the pumpkin streusel cheesecake and follow Gabriel over to the lawn table in front of the Newbaum's house. Several bites into the delicious dessert, I finally get my nerve up to ask my friend the hundred-thousand-dollar question.

"Gabriel?"

"Yeah?"

"Why did your family leave Maxwell?"

"You know, things happen."

I fork another mouthful of cheesecake and swallow quickly. "No, I don't really know. Like I've said, you just left and never said goodbye. And now, you're back all of a sudden."

He wipes cherry pie off his lip with the napkin. "Is that a bad thing?"

"No," I say. "It just seems all shrouded in mystery."

Gabriel stares ahead, picking at the crust of his pie. "Don't worry about it."

I sit up and plant my feet on the lawn. "*That's* your answer? 'Don't worry about it.' Are you kidding me?"

He lowers his brows at me. "It was six years ago. What does it matter?"

"Because we were good friends. We hung out and played and you killed earwigs for me. You just . . . disappeared. Like someone kidnapped you. One day you were in my life, and the next you were gone."

His eyes touch mine. "I'm here now. Isn't that what matters?"

"Don't get me wrong. I'm glad you're back. Especially now, given how much you've helped me. I only wanted to know what happened. There's something you're not telling me."

His plastic fork drops to his plate. "Leave it alone, Hay."

"Leave *what* alone?"

He snaps. "Look. Things happened to us as a family, and we just . . . dealt with them. Same thing with you and your family dealing with your cancer. Let's drop it, okay?" He pauses for a moment or two and then stretches his legs to get up. "I think I'll try the chocolate cake."

As he strides away back to the dessert table, I know there's something he's not telling me.

Gabriel Tremblay has a secret, and I'm going to find out what it is.

* * *

SCHOOL RESUMES AFTER THANKSGIVING, and the Patriots play their final regular season game. We've miraculously survived the tough schedule and come out unscathed and undefeated.

Two playoff games — one home, one away — and we've made

it to the state championship game. This is the big enchilada, the crème de la crème of our football world. Only four quarters and one team stand between us, the title, and the humongous trophy.

It's an epic battle for the ages . . .

Okay . . . so maybe my AP English class has rubbed off on me too much. But this game is killer! Physical. Demanding. Punishing. Emotional.

My voice is nearly gone by the beginning of the second half.

"Go, Pats!" I eke out.

In the beginning of the fourth quarter, Daniel hauls in a thirty-eight-yard pass and dashes for the end zone, putting us up by two touchdowns. Since I can't scream, I wind up and do a back handspring.

Nailed it!

Oh my God! I haven't done that since this summer.

It feels freaking awesome!

Chloe even takes notice and nods at me while she executes her own perfect backflip.

Lora high-fives me, and we move into doing some partner stunts. Thanks to my steady workouts, she seems to weigh almost nothing. I hold her high over my head easily and shine my smile and spirit out to the crowd.

The clock ticks down and we win!

"We're state champs!" I scream out to Lora the best I can.

All of the cheerleaders take off into a run onto the field for the celebration. I don't run, but I move out there as fast as my leg will take me. Everyone's hugging, chest bumping, and patting one another on the back.

"Awesome job! Congrats! Way to go!" I say to the players.

Scoop Dogg runs toward me and lifts me up into the air, swinging me around. I yelp, but I'm loving it. The adrenaline rush and high from this victory are like nothing I've ever experienced. And I was a part of it.

"Trophy presentation," Chloe snaps. "Line up, squad."

We form two lines next to the players and cheer them on as the officials hand over the monstrous silver trophy to Coach Gaither. He raises it high, and the crowd goes wild. We're the visiting team for this game, but a ton of fans and parents came along on the two-hour road trip. Reporters surround the players and dozens of camera flashes blind us. I love the high of this!

The ceremony ends, and the players head to the locker room to change. Afterward, Lora, Tara, Ashlee, and I follow the football bus in Lora's car to a local steak house. Coach had arranged ahead of time for us to have our own banquet room.

"Steak dinner, baby!" Tara says when we walk in.

"Filet mignon for me," Ashlee says.

I don't care what I eat. I'm jazzed just to be here.

I'm part of this. I helped make this happen. Okay, sure, I didn't catch any passes or score any touchdowns, but I kept the crowds into the games and did all I could to encourage the players from my small place on the sidelines.

"Hey, y'all," Chloe says. "I've got something to give out."

She comes around the table and presents each of us with a small white box wrapped with blue and red ribbons. It's almost too pretty to open. But the other girls are tearing at theirs, so I do the same.

"I just wanted to thank all of y'all for such a great season. I knew we could go all the way, and we did. The guys couldn't have done this without us. This is the best squad I've ever been affiliated with, and I'm so proud of y'all." Chloe's voice catches at the end, and I'm actually touched by her speech.

"Oh my God, these are gorgeous," Melanie exclaims.

"Wow, so pretty," Madison echoes.

"My momma and I made them for y'all. Each one is personalized."

Lora's mouth drops, and she shifts her eyes to me.

I rip open the box and gaze at two beautiful ceramic combs with the Patriots' emblem and my name hand painted on them.

My first instinct is to bite my lip. I don't know whether it's to keep from saying what I'm feeling or to stop the tears from gushing out of my eyes.

Combs?

Really, Chloe? Are you kidding me?

I know I said I wouldn't cry anymore, but this is cruel and adds insult to injury.

I find my voice and speak up. "Chloe?"

She turns; her long ponytail following in her wake. "Yeah, Hayley?"

I hold up the present. "Are these meant for me?"

"Of course," she says. And then it must hit her, because her mouth drops open.

"In case you might have forgotten, Chloe, I don't have any hair."

She stops moving. "Um . . . I'm . . . oh my God . . ."

I can't let her off this easily, but my heart is ripping. "Is this supposed to be a joke, or are you just *that* mean and hate me that much?"

Her hands go to her mouth, and I don't know whether she's genuinely that insensitive or just a raving fool. "Oh, Hayley, I don't know what to say."

I'm mortified. Pure and simple. I don't want her to see how much she's upset me, but it's pretty obvious. *I'm* not a good actress. Lora pats me on the leg to comfort me. Mainly, I want to run out of the room crying and disappear from public until my hair returns to its natural state. Chloe has ruined this beautiful moment by reminding me how different I am from everyone else.

"You most certainly *do* know what to say, Chloe," Gabriel says, coming to my rescue. "How about 'I'm sorry'!"

"What?" she asks, surprised that someone's challenging her. "I didn't mean any harm . . . I—I—I thought it would give her encouragement for when she does have hair."

Gabriel points his finger in her face. "You're a bitch, Chloe. You have no idea what Hayley's been through, and you have no respect for her being out in front of people, cheering her heart out with no hair. You're the most insensitive cow I've ever known."

She recoils at his words. Obviously, no one has ever spoken to her like this before.

He's not through. "You need to have more respect for people. Especially Hayley and all she's dealt with. She's cried and suffered, yet she's triumphed. And through it all, she's cheered. Could you have done the same?"

With every eye in the banquet room on her, Chloe softly says, "I—I—I don't know if I could have." She twists to face me. "I'm sorry, Hayley. I really am."

She moves to take the combs; however, I stop her. "For when my hair comes back."

A weak smile covers her face, and she slinks away.

Whoa.

Gabriel . . . to my rescue—once again.

I smile my thanks to him, and he winks at me.

CHAPTER FORTY

Convert difficulties into opportunities, for difficulties are divine surgeries to make you better.

—AUTHOR UNKNOWN

Can i ride home with you?" I ask Gabriel outside the restaurant.

He flips his keys in his palm. "Wouldn't you rather go with your friends?"

"You're my friend."

"You're right, I am." He unlocks the doors with the press of a button. "Hop in!"

As we zip down the highway, Gabriel messes around with the radio to find something better to listen to than the seventy country music channels. We sing along together to the top-forty-hits station. It feels amazing to just . . . be.

A few miles from Maxwell, I see Gabriel in a totally different light. The reflection of the other cars' head beams shines on his face, outlining the masculine details, kind eyes, and warm smile. My earwig hunter. I'm seeing him like I never really have before. Kind. Sensitive. Caring. Giving. Not a typical guy who cares only about himself. He cares about me.

He's . . . really cute. I mean, *really* cute. When did this happen? How have I not noticed the fineness of my friend? Was I too blinded by the idea of dating Daniel that I couldn't see the perfect guy who was right in front of me? The one with the dark eyes and lashes that should be illegal for a boy.

My heart flutters underneath my uniform, and I'm suddenly feeling tongue tied, shy, and . . . nervous. Gabriel . . .

We roll up to a red light, and he turns to look at me. "What?" he asks with a smile when he catches me ogling him. "What's going on, peach fuzz?" He reaches over and gently brushes his fingertips over the soft new growth of babylike hair on my head.

I just grin at him and wait for the light to turn green so the moment isn't as intense.

"You don't mind that I don't have hair, do you?"

"Why would I?" He scowls at me for asking the question. "You're still the same person."

"My limp doesn't bother you, either."

Gabriel steers the car onto Willow Hollow. "Give it six months and you'll be good as new. Just keep working on those toe-strengthening exercises. We'll gradually increase the weight so you can—"

I reach my hand over and touch his arm. My skin ignites where it touches his and from the look on his face, he feels something, too. He slides the car in front of my house and puts it in park.

"You don't judge me, Gabe," I say.

"I know what it's like to be judged, Hay."

"You've really been there for me. Not just with the physical therapy . . . but . . . everything." Why am I only now realizing this? Was I too blinded by the glory of dating the King of the Pops that I couldn't see this amazing guy right next to me?

Without overthinking it and before I chicken out, I lean over and kiss him.

Gabriel's taken aback at first; then he pulls me into his arms and returns the kiss.

It's totally magical.

I'm sure somewhere orchestra music is swelling and fireworks are going off.

This is everything a first kiss should be.

Soft. Sweet. Spine-tingling.

One to be treasured.

One to be replayed.

One to remember always.

One between friends. But so much more.

His hands cup my face as our lips tangle together and dance against each other. I close my eyes and smile into the kiss, wanting more and more from him.

But he suddenly freezes and pushes back. "We have to stop. I can't."

Scalded by his cold words, I press my lips together. "Wh-wh-why? Are you gay?"

Incredulous, he says, "No! It's not that at all."

"What is it, then?" I ask, feeling the fool.

Gabriel puts his hands on the wheel in the ten and two positions. "I've got problems, Hayley. Problems that sent me and my family away from Maxwell in the beginning. I can't get too close to anyone."

This is the lamest brushoff in the history of brushoffs.

Problems? You want to talk about problems?

I grab my purse and pompoms and jerk the car door open. Before he can say anything, I slam it shut and rush into the house as quickly as my bum leg will take me. I don't stop to say good night to Mom and Dad who are lounging in the den watching TV. I actually take the stairs up two at a time and retreat to my room.

I throw my stuff on the floor and then fling my body onto my bed, staring up at the ivory lace of the canopy top.

What is it with me and guys?

Are they all complete jerks?

* * *

SATURDAY MORNING, MY PARENTS and I drive to Birmingham for my first checkup. I rudely wear my earbuds the whole way up with the newest Ministry of Sound CD blaring so I don't have to answer any questions about my hasty flight to my room last night.

I never thought that Gabriel would flake, too. Just goes to show what I know.

The hell with boys. I need to focus on what the doctors have to say.

I'm quickly X-rayed and scurry off to Dr. Dykema's office to wait to see him.

"Hayley, look at you!" he says cheerfully when I step into the examining room.

"I told you I'd walk again, Doc."

He flips through my chart and the notes that I'd given to his nurse about my physical therapy and exercise routine. "I'm very, very pleased with your progress. You responded well to the chemo and radiation, and, from the films we took today, there's no trace of the tumor or the cancer cells."

I let out a long sigh of relief that only lasts a split second longer than those my parents release.

Dr. Dykema peers down at me. "I'm most impressed with your

attitude and your motivation to get back on your feet. I wish all of my patients were as positive as you are."

"I had no other choice."

"You've been cheering?"

"Every game since she came home," Mom answers.

"No running or jumping?"

I try not to lie. "Not really. But I let my leg guide me."

Dad interjects. "She doesn't take any unnecessary risks, Doctor."

The doctor moves his reading glasses to the end of his nose, and then he peers over a report in my chart. "Interestingly enough, I wanted to share this with you folks. I sent the resected bone and tumor off to the pathology department for further research. UAB is a teaching hospital, after all, so anything we can learn from your case that can help others is very important to us."

"Of course," Mom says.

There seems to be a proverbial other shoe to drop here, so I listen up.

Dr. Dykema continues. "The pathology indicated what we discovered from your biopsies that the lesion was malignant toward the tibia, but benign toward the surface. What I found fascinating about the report was there were slight traces of the varicella zoster virus in the tumor."

"What is that?" Dad and I ask at the same time.

The doctor glimpses over his glasses. "You would know it better as chickenpox. Didn't you tell me you had a serious bout with chickenpox last October?"

A gasp leaves my chest and my pulse picks up to space shuttle speed. "The chickenpox gave me cancer?"

"We can't prove it, Hayley. It's just a theory. We don't always know what causes the white blood cells to divide and multiply out of control. However, with the severity of your varicella zoster last fall, it would stand to reason that your body went into overdrive to fight off the virus and simply overdid its job."

I don't hear any of the medical mumbo jumbo he tosses out at me.

All I know is Chloe Bradenton is responsible for my cancer.

* * *

"I HATE HER," I say in the truck on the way home to Maxwell.

"Hayley, you can't be like that," Mom fusses.

I can be, though. Chloe Bradenton has had it out for me since the moment the judges gave me the twelfth spot on the varsity cheerleader roster. She has never seen me as an equal or someone who even deserved to be on the squad. And *she's* who I have to thank for getting fucking cancer?

Utter hatred for her flows through my central nervous system, sparking every emotion known to God and man. "I want to get even with her." I want her to suffer. I want to shave her head and let her see what it's like to walk around with no hair. I want her to feel what it's like to be self-conscious every time you walk into a room, classroom, or the football field, knowing that people are watching, questioning, judging.

Mom swivels in her seat. "You can't be like that, Hayley. Chloe was your computer partner, and you had a lot of interaction last year when her little brother came down with the illness."

"I don't care."

"Hayley Ann Matthews, you listen to me. God did not bring you through cancer to have you bitter and full of vengeful venom."

"Listen to your mother, Little Kid," Dad says firmly.

I roll my eyes, not wanting to hear this, but knowing she's right. Tears sting the corner, and I shift my eyes to the window to watch the highway sail by.

Mom continues. "Chloe did not give you chickenpox intentionally with the hope that it would give you cancer. It just happened, sweetie."

"I know," I say meekly.

"Hating her is not the Christian thing."

"I know."

"You have to be grateful that you found that lump in time and it didn't move to your tibia. Your father and I had to sign a form . . ." Mom trails off as her voice catches. Dad reaches over, but she holds him off. "We had to sign a form allowing them to take your leg if things were too bad. That didn't happen, though. If we hadn't caught this in time, it could have spread to other parts of your body. It could have consumed you, Hayley. Because you were a cheerleader and working out so intensely, you *found* the tumor. Chloe pushed you to work hard, and that's what allowed you to discover the lump."

I hope Mom doesn't tell me that I have Chloe to thank, although I see the point she's trying to make. Still, the irony doesn't escape me, and it's something I'll have to get past.

I take a deep, cleansing breath.

One that calms and relaxes. One that encourages me to forgive.

Chloe's just a kid like me, trying to make it in this world. Someone who probably couldn't have handled what I went through.

I'm blessed in so many ways. I need to realize that and stop fighting . . . everything.

I have two legs.

I can walk.

I can cheer.

And one day soon, I'll be able to run, jump . . . leap!

Most of all, I'm cancer free.

I'm alive.

No one can take that from me.

"You're right, Mom. Cheerleading saved my life."

CHAPTER FORTY-ONE

A dollar is not worth as much as you think it is. Your honesty is worth much more.

—T. Boone Pickens

Sunday afternoon after church, I stop in at Maxwell Memorial Hospital to see Ross.

I push open the door and give him my best smile. "What up, dawg?"

Ross laughs when he sees me and then breaks into a cough. "Sorry. The medicine really makes me sick as hell. Sit, sit . . . Tell me what's going on with you."

His skin is even pastier than before and more of his hair has come out. I don't recognize the virile man who visited me in the hospital this summer.

Pulling up the visitor's chair, I regale him on the latest 411 and the chickenpox connection to Chloe.

"Your mom is right," he says when I'm done. "You have to forgive Chloe."

"I know," I reply.

Ross folds up the *Wall Street Journal* he'd been reading and sets it aside. "Chloe Bradenton is a stupid teenage girl filled with delusions of grandeur. She's had everything handed to her. She knows nothing of true strength, character, challenges, or triumphing. Like you, Hayley."

"Thanks for that, Ross."

He snickers. "I'm not trying to blow sunshine up your ass. It's the truth. There aren't many kids who could have handled what you did . . . and with such a great attitude. I don't think my own niece could have handled it with the aplomb you did. Remember, it was you who told me to get over myself and the self-pity. I don't like it any better than you liked your cancer. The thing is, we're dealing with it. Facing the challenge. It's making us better people. You're the one who told me that."

I sit back in the chair. "Wow. I really said all of that?"

"Something to that effect. At least, it's what I heard."

We laugh together, and I hand him the fresh box of Snickers bars I brought for him.

"The hospital pudding seems to help me, but these are the ambrosia."

I don't like the way he appears. He seems to be shriveling up lying in this hospital bed. The medication is really taking a toll on him. Or, perhaps, it's the leukemia itself. Acute leukemia can attack fast, from what I've read on the Internet. I just hope Ross's treatment makes him better. I so want to go with him to the rainforest of Costa Rica or zip lining in Barbados.

"How much longer on the chemo?" I ask.

Ross shakes his head. "The doctor isn't sure. It's not taking as well as he'd like, and my white blood cell count is totally fucked." He lifts his eyes. "Sorry for the language."

"I've heard the word before," I say with a small smile. "Is there anything I can do for you?"

He snorts laughter. "Wanna run my company?"

"Wish I could." I grasp his hand.

Ross thinks for a second. "I really need someone smart, and

driven, and local, with an MBA to help out while I'm stuck in here. Your father has one, right?"

"One what?"

"An MBA."

"Yeah, from Bama," I say.

Ross nods. "Maybe I'll give him a call."

Right now, I can't think about spreadsheets, bottom lines, and sales reports. My friend is sick and isn't looking any better. "I'm so worried about you, Ross."

"Shhh . . ." he says. "I appreciate the concern, but don't freak out. I'm following the doctor's orders . . . and yours. Positive mental attitude. Everything happens for a reason."

Words I sort of remember saying. Questions I still have that apply to myself.

Ross wiggles our hands. "It gives me strength to see you and know how you're doing. Just promise you'll keep coming to see me, Hayley."

"I promise."

I just hope he's here when I come to visit.

* * *

"THE BANK APPROVED OUR mortgage refinance," Dad is saying to Mom when I walk in the back door. "We can use the equity to pay off some of the bills that—"

They both turn and stare at me like children who've been caught eating cookies before dinner.

"Are we going to lose the house?" I ask.

"No, dear," Mom says. "We're just rearranging some of our finances."

"Because of me and my medical bills," I say.

Dad holds up his hands to wave me off. "Due to a lot of things, Hayley. You don't need to concern yourself with this."

I won't let him do this. I'm about to be eighteen, and I deserve to be treated like an adult. "If it concerns the family, it concerns me." Looking between the two of them, I put my hands on my hips. "Seriously . . . spill it."

My parents relent, and the three of us sit down for a financial state of the Matthews union. I had no idea how bad things are. My medical expenses are astronomical, and the insurance company is delaying payment on several claims. On top of that, the college fund my parents had saved has been depleted to pay for bills, inventory for the store, and to keep the house payments current. Homestead Hardware's new super center is killing Matthews Hardware, and Dad doesn't know how much longer he can keep the doors open.

"A master's degree in business and I can't compete with the big boys," Dad says, rubbing his eyes with his thumbs.

"Dad, it's a corporate beast. There's nothing you could have done," I say. My AP Economics class has taught me enough to know that Dad isn't a bad businessman. He's in the wrong business. "So . . . not to make it all about me, but do I even bother applying for college?"

"Of course you do," Mom says. "There are all sorts of financial aid and scholarships you can apply for. A lot of foundations and organizations out there will help provide college tuition to cancer survivors. All we need to do is fill out the paperwork."

The last thing I want is someone feeling sorry for me and giving me a free ride to college. The dam of anger and resentment toward my sister and her actions years ago completely overflows, and I have to excuse myself.

"Hayley, where are you going?" Mom asks.

"I need some air."

"Let her go, Nan."

I trudge around the house and down the road. At the end of the street, past Gabriel's house—he's still on my shitlist—there's a small park with a tiny brook that runs through it. I need some Mother Nature therapy to help ease my anxiety over so many things I can't control.

There's only one person who can make all of this right.

I tug my cell phone out of my jeans pocket and dial Gretchen's number in Boston. She answers on the third ring.

"Gretchen Matthews," she says in a very businesslike manner . . . on a Sunday.

"This is your sister," I say flatly.

"Hayley! Hey hon! I've been meaning to call and check on you—"

"Whatever, Gretchen. You haven't. I haven't heard from you since the obligatory Thanksgiving call that went straight to voice mail."

My sister pauses. "Are you mad at me?"

I grip the phone so tightly to my head that I fear I'll burst the components apart. All of my pent-up resentment toward her, toward Chloe, toward Gabriel—even toward Daniel still—to the universe for what I had to go through, and for what Ross is now going through. I brace myself for the can of whoop ass I'm about to unload on my sister.

"You know . . . Mom and Dad are struggling financially. Dad's going to lose the business, Mom's going to have to get a job, the house has a second mortgage, and I might not get to go to college thanks to you. You *stole* a shitload of money from them, and you've never offered to pay it back! Instead, you move off to the other end of the country, you never call or visit, and then you just pop up when I'm in the hospital to tell me you're there for me, only to disappear back into your world."

"Hayley, I don't know what—"

"This isn't a discussion!" I snap. "Look, Gretchen. You had your chance. Mom and Dad scrimped and saved to take care of us, and you ripped them off. I don't care whatever you were on or what you were doing, but you took advantage of them, and now we're screwed. They don't deserve this. They're good people. You wouldn't know that, though, since you've disconnected from the family. Cliff had to pay his way through college with loans and scholarships. I'm prepared to do that, too, if I have to, but, dammit, Gretchen, you had your turn and mucked it up. This is my turn!"

There's a profound silence as my chest rises and falls from unsteady breathing. I assume she's still there, listening.

"I worshiped you," I say softly. "You're my big sis, the one I looked up to. Not now. You're the problem. The hindrance. The cause of our struggles. How can you let Mom and Dad suffer like this?"

Her muffled sobs come through the phone clear as day plucking at my heartstrings. What a turd I am taking out my frustrations on her. I certainly don't hate her or anything. I just needed to let her know how I feel.

"I'm so sorry, Hayley," she finally says over her sniffs.

"Gretchen, I'm—"

"No, you're right. One hundred percent right. I had a lot of problems when I was your age. Mainly because I was trying to fit in and fell in with the wrong crowd. It was easier to drug up or get drunk and fit in than to be myself and take the risks of being accepted or rejected. I was never as strong as you, Hayley."

I choke back my own emotional swell bubbling in my chest.

"I'm going to make this right, Hayley. I promise."

"How, Gretchen? Dad may lose the store. That's not your fault. I just looped that in."

"It's okay, sweetie . . . I'll take care of everything. Don't worry."

"I'm sorry," I say, letting the tears fall.

"No, *I'm* sorry," she says. "You're the bravest person I know, and you don't deserve to have your future messed up because of me. I'll make this better. I promise you."

Now I'm quiet.

"I love you, Hayley."

"I love you, too, Gretchen. Please come home."

"I'll do what I can. Talk to you soon."

The phone clicks, and I stare at the blank screen, damp from my tears.

I don't know what Gretchen can do, but anything will help at this point. God knows, we need it. I have to put my faith in her . . . and in Him, like I've done so many times before.

CHAPTER FORTY-TWO

Hope is that thing with feathers
That perches in the soul,
And sings the tune without the words,
And never stops at all.

—EMILY DICKINSON

As if the family tension isn't enough, I've got to deal with Gabriel at school on Monday. He's standoffish to me in AP English, not even saying good morning or rubbing my head like he usually does. I don't understand what I did wrong. Was my kiss *that* unpleasant for him?

"I don't know what to do," I say, picking at my mac and cheese at lunch. I finally opened up to Lora and told her everything that happened with Gabriel after the game.

She points her fork at me and scowls. "I think you really need to exercise that new backbone you've grown. You know, the one you used to tell Chloe what a shit she is? Which was long overdue, by the way. Just talk to Gabriel and tell him how you feel."

"Progressive new concept," I say with a smile.

Why not . . . I'll try anything. The new Hayley Matthews kicks ass and takes names.

Last period, I change into a long-sleeved T-shirt and my shorts and walk through the gym. Because of the cold December chill outside, no one seems too motivated to do much of anything. Most of the girls in my class are over in the corner watching a DVD on health issues. There are five guys playing a game of horse on one end of the basketball court while a crowded volleyball game is full press on the other side. Only a handful of football players are using the weight machines, so I head over for my workout.

Gabriel is on the leg press, sweating hard. His muscles bulge with each labored breath as his well-built legs lift more than two hundred pounds. His hands grip the railings, and he breathes hard as he counts repetitions. From his look of concentration, I would say he's trying to exorcise something out of his system. I just hope it's not me.

If we can't be boyfriend and girlfriend, hopefully we can still be friends. I'd hate to think of life without him.

I cross over to the elliptical machine opposite him and punch in fifteen minutes. I slip my headphones on so I can move to the rhythm of the electronic beats. I pump and climb and churn my leg muscles, feeling the burn with every move. It's all good, though—all part of my physical rehab.

Too bad my mental rehab has taken a step back. I regret my phone call to Gretchen and how I laid into her. I don't know all of the details, and it wasn't right to stick my nose in where it didn't belong. I'm just so worried about the stress on Mom and Dad and our family's financial future. Cancer and its stack of medical bills aren't exactly something you budget for. Neither is having your oldest child clean out your savings account. Gretchen does need to make things right . . . in the very least with our parents.

I push the beads of sweat away that roll down my face. The intense workout has my blood pumping and my heart racing. For what it's worth, I'm in the best shape of my life—go figure.

When the timer buzzes for the elliptical, I step down and towel off my face. I glance around and see that Gabriel's moved on to the free weights where he's doing arm curls over his head to tone his back muscles.

Good idea.

I step over near him and select two ten-pound weights. I start doing the arm curls he showed me a few weeks ago. I'm in the third set when I see in the mirror that Gabriel is standing behind me. I'd love to spin around and attack him with a hug and a kiss. However, I don't want to cause a scene in the gym, especially if he pushes me away.

"You're doing that wrong," he says to me.

My arms drop to my sides with the weights dangling in each furled fist. "I am?"

Gabriel reaches around and lifts my left arm. "Do it this way."

Like a rag doll, I allow him to position me properly. As he moves my arm upward, our eyes meet in the mirror. We stand locked like that for what seems an eternity, and then he removes his hand from mine and backs away.

I slam the weights back into their grooved housing and turn my continued frustration on him.

"What is your major malfunction with me?" I bite out at him. A couple of the football players stop midlift and turn their attention to the drama unfolding.

Gabriel seems speechless. Or maybe he's just embarrassed by our intimate moment the other night. Either way, I lay into him much like I did with my sister. Lora's right. I'm rehabilitating my backbone, as well.

I advance on him. "I don't understand you, Gabriel. You're the one person in this whole school who made me feel normal. I thought we shared a . . . *moment* . . . the other night. Apparently not. I understand if you don't want to go out with the bald chick, but I don't want to lose you as a friend."

He retreats to the leg press and grabs his towel, swiping it furiously over his face. "You know, Hay, you've been hanging around bitches like Chloe Bradenton too long. She's made you dense as shit."

My eyes jump open and I bow up. "Excuuuuuse me?"

He slams the towel down. "You heard me." He closes the distance between us, slants toward me, and lowers his voice. "What happened between us the other night had *nothing* to do with your hair. Give me a break! Why do you think I kissed you in the haunted house?"

"Wh-wh-what?" I fight to catch my breath at the realization. "That was you?"

Gabriel notices some of the football players taking in our conversation, so he reaches over and grabs me by the hand, tugging me along with him. We climb the bleachers up to the top row where he sits and waits for me to do the same.

I can't believe he's the one who kissed me. Not Daniel. Not some phantom, wonderful mystery guy. But Gabriel. *He's* the one who thinks I'm amazing.

"Look," he begins, not looking at me. "I'm sorry about the kiss in the haunted house. I saw you, you were so cute in your zombie outfit, it was dark, and I took advantage of the situation."

He thinks I'm cute? I smile broadly at him, hoping to ease his embarrassment.

"It's okay, Gabe," I say reassuringly. "If you kissed me then, why did you push me away Friday night in the car?"

He shakes his head. "There's a lot you don't know about me, and it wouldn't be fair to burden you with my problems while you're dealing with your own."

I roll my eyes. "Oh, give me a freaking break, would you? In the least, you're my friend. A friend I've missed and one I'm thrilled to have back in my life. If there's something going on with you, I want to know." I stretch my hand out to take his. "I want to be there for you like you've been here for me."

He takes a deep breath. "Okay, here it is."

I brace myself for the absolute worst.

"Ever since I was a little kid, I've suffered from petit mal seizures, a form of epilepsy."

"Ohhh-kay . . ." I say, waiting for something worse.

"That's why my family left town six years ago."

I resist the urge to laugh. "That's your big secret? You have seizures?"

"It's a big thing, Hay. Remember how we'd be talking and stuff and I would sort of zone out? Those were seizures. The older I got, the more prominent they became, to the point where they'd last like fifteen seconds or more. I'd be in one room of the house and then come to in another one. It was freaky."

This time, I do giggle. "I remember you did that when we were watching TV one time. I was talking to you, and you zoned out for ten seconds, staring into space. I just thought you were being a boy with no attention span."

"Yeah, it was getting bad, especially in school. Mrs. Hendrix in fifth grade kept writing me up as not paying attention in class and even went so far as to tell my parents I had ADHD. My mom explained to her what was going on, but it didn't help. Maxwell just didn't have the medical personnel to help me out."

"Do you still have them?"

"I haven't for a long time," he explains. "We moved to Cincinnati because Children's Hospital there specializes in cases like mine. Thanks to the anticonvulsant medication they gave me, we could control the seizures until I outgrew them."

I play with his thumb, stroking my fingers over it as I take all of this in. "You outgrew them?"

"Pretty much." He nods. "They mostly last until you're through puberty. Last spring, the doctors weaned me off the medication, and I've been good ever since. We would have stayed in Cincinnati if my grandfather hadn't gotten sick. But I'm glad we came back to Maxwell. I'm happy I could be here for you."

His hand caresses mine; his thumb brushing over my knuckles and giving me chill bumps up and down my arms. He likes me. I know he does. That's what makes all of this so damn confusing.

I cock my head to the side and ask frankly, "So, this is why we can't date?"

He stammers for a second and then tells me, "I feel too abnormal to get involved with someone. This is, like, hereditary, and I can pass it down the line."

I laugh at his seriousness. "Gabe, we're still teenagers. I don't want to get married and have babies or anything right away. I only want to get closer to you and have fun."

His eyes soften and he peers out at me. "With everything you've been through, I didn't want to burden you."

I pull back and smack him hard on his chiseled arm until we laugh together. "It's fine." I think about Mom and Dad and all they've been through in their years as a couple, through thick and thin, hard times and good times. That's what your significant other is for — to be there with you and to share the experiences. Gabriel's been here with me since my diagnosis, supporting me, encouraging me, helping me get back on my feet — literally. "We're both survivors, Gabriel," I say to him, brimming over with happiness.

He snakes his hand out around my waist and pulls me closer to him. "That we are."

Then he kisses me. There's no hesitation this time. It's not a kiss between friends, but between two people who have so much to offer and share with each other.

When we break apart, Gabriel smiles and touches his forehead to mine. "So, you want to go to the football banquet with me?"

"I thought you'd never ask."

CHAPTER FORTY-THREE

*If you learn from your suffering, and really come to understand
the lesson you were taught, you might be able to help someone
else who's now in the phase you may have just completed. Maybe
that's what it's all about after all.*

—AUTHOR UNKNOWN

WEDNESDAY EVENING, DAD WALKS in the back door and heads
straight to the refrigerator. He pulls out a cold beer—one that's
been in there forever since he doesn't drink much. He sits at the
kitchen table and announces, "It's done. I sold the business and
inventory to Homestead Hardware."

Mom moves to hug him. Obviously she knew this was in the
works, but I'm shocked.

"Whuuu . . . huh?" I stumble out.

Dad sips the brew and relishes the taste as he closes his eyes
and sits back. "We couldn't compete anymore. They paid a fair
price for everything, and we should be okay for several months
while I start looking for my next job."

"I got a call back from the law firm for a second interview,"
Mom announces. "They're looking for someone only twenty
hours a week, so I think that'll be perfect for me."

Dad nods. "I got a call from a headhunter yesterday. Imagine the timing. They're looking for someone short-term over at Game On. Isn't that your friend, Ross Scott's business?"

I sit up and take notice. "It is, Dad! You should totally go work there. Since Ross is in the hospital, he can't run everything. I'll talk to him."

Waving me off, Dad says, "Thanks, Little Kid, but I'll take care of it. Go through the proper channels."

"It's a good lead, Jared," Mom says.

Dad reaches for her hand and kisses it. "We're going to be fine, Nan."

I know Dad basically told me to butt out. I want to help, though. I can at least put in a good word . . . something . . . anything.

"May I borrow the car?" I ask my mother.

"I was just about to put dinner on."

"That's what the microwave is for, Nan," I say with a laugh. "I really need to do something right now. Trust me."

Dad slides his keys across the table to me. "Take the truck, Little Kid."

I grab my purse and hustle out of the house. I climb up into the truck, adjust the mirrors and the seat, and then back out of the driveway.

I have one destination and one only.

Maxwell Memorial Hospital.

* * *

"WERE YOU SERIOUS ABOUT wanting to talk to my dad about working at Game On?" I ask when I get to Ross's hospital room.

"Of course I was. Since you didn't say anything, I figured he wasn't available."

"Oh, he's available. Your headhunter even contacted him," I say.

"Neal did? Excellent. Seems like it's meant to be. I'll call Neal in the morning and get him moving on the interview," Ross says.

"You'll love Dad. He's way smart and he's a good businessman. He's athletic, too. At least he used to be," I say. "We would go water-skiing up at Lake Martin, and he played tennis all the time before he started the hardware store."

Ross laughs and holds his hands up. "Sounds like we need to get Jared Matthews active again."

I carefully fling myself onto my friend's chest and hug him, being sure not to hurt him. "Thank you so much."

He chuckles. "I haven't hired him yet."

"I know. But still. You're the best, Ross."

He hugs me back, gripping me to him. "You are, too, Hayley." When he doesn't let go right away, I feel his body shake, and I realize he's crying.

"Oh my God, Ross . . . Don't . . . don't cry. Everything's going to be okay."

Ross's handsome face is splotchy from tears, and fear outlines his features. My strong friend, the man who climbs mountains and dives with sharks admits, "I'm scared shitless, Hayley. How did you get through this?"

"I had no other choice."

I get a tissue and wipe his tears away. "Don't tell anyone I lost it like this," he says. "Lorraine and Lora wouldn't let me live it down."

"We all have our moments," I say, thinking of the five major times I cried.

"The doctors will know in a week if the treatment is helping."

"Keep thinking positive thoughts," I say, trying to encourage him.

"I don't know if I can," he says softly.

"Did you not listen to what you've been telling me all along? You're the one who told me to be tough and it was all mind over matter. Ross, I'm just quoting you back to you. I'm just a kid who didn't know what in the world she was going through. You told me to believe and I did. You need to do it, too."

"I gave pretty good advice, huh?" he says with a smile.

"The best."

He really is dealing with a lot more serious shit than I did. At least, it seems that way. All I can do is be here for him and cheer him on.

"I should let you get your rest," I say.

"We'll see if your dad's a good fit," Ross says, getting his composure. "And Hayley?"

"Yeah?"

"I couldn't do any of this without you."

I smile hard. "You don't have to."

* * *

THE CHILLING WINDS OF December sweep through Maxwell, dumping a foot of snow on our lawns and giving us a beautiful white Christmas. There aren't as many presents under the tree, but we're together. Cliff and Lily drove down last night from Birmingham and brought a truckload of baked goods that Lily made for us. Mom cooked a spiral ham with pineapple and honey glaze and sweet potato casserole. The house is filled with the scents of the holiday, mixing with the spicy candles and the minty greens hanging on the mantel. Even Leeny, wearing a red bow that I put on her, seems in the Christmas spirit as she sits underneath the tree and watches us open our few presents.

Mom got a new coffeemaker, a scrapbooking kit, and a simple

gold tennis bracelet. Dad got a new job. He and Ross and the headhunter finalized everything last night, and on January first, Dad starts his new position as Associate Vice President of Management at Game On. Ross has someone he can trust, and Dad has a new lease on his professional life.

My parents deserve good things because they're good people.

I got some movie DVDs, new clothes, and the dangly vintage earrings I've been jonesing over from the antique shop next to the hardware store.

"You forgot one," Dad says, pointing to a small box toward the back of the tree.

"I couldn't see it for Leeny." I move the kitty aside and reach for the pretty blue package.

The card reads "To Hayley, from Santa."

Really? I can't help but laugh.

I rip off the bow and paper and then peel back the lid of the box. There's a mound of cotton on top and then underneath . . .

"Car keys?" I dangle the large black key with an H on it. We don't own any Hondas.

"Let's go outside," Dad says with a wicked grin.

I'm on my feet in a heartbeat. "What?"

My heart stutters with excitement as we make our way down the hallway and out the door without a coat. I scream out when I see what awaits me.

"Is that for me?!"

Parked behind Mom's car in the shoveled driveway is a silver Honda Civic.

"Merry Christmas," my parents shout out.

"But . . . how . . . how did you afford this?"

"Don't worry about it," Dad says as we all head down the steps.

I round the car and take it in. So cute. So perfect for me.

I shake my head, though. "This is too much, y'all. I don't want you to spend too much money on me after everything."

Dad tweaks my ear. "Be quiet, Hayley. Besides, we knew you needed a car for college, so we got this used for a good deal," Dad tells me. "It has about forty thousand miles on it, but it's in great condition and should serve you well."

"I can't believe . . ."

"Show her the best part, Jared," Mom instructs.

Dad opens the door, and I climb inside the black interior, squiggling into the driver's seat that now belongs to me. I glance down and see the manual transmission.

"Stick shift?"

Dad smiles. "We thought it would be a great way to exercise your leg."

I've only driven a stick a few times, but this is going to be great. I crank it up and test out the air conditioner and CD player first.

Cliff snickers. "You're such a girl. I'm surprised you didn't look to see if there's a mirror on the driver's side sun visor."

As Lily smacks him, I say, "Good call!" I flip the visor down and lo and behold, there's not only a mirror, but one with a light on it.

I crawl out of the car and gather both of my parents into one gigamonic hug. "Y'all are amazing! Thank you soooooooo much!"

Mom kisses my cheek while Dad pats me on the back.

I don't know how this Christmas can get any better.

Just then, an unfamiliar white car turns into our driveway.

"Expecting more company?" Cliff asks.

Mom tents her eyes with her hand and looks out over the glare that's bouncing off the fresh snow. The car door opens, and we all collectively gasp when we see who's here.

"Hi, guys," my sister Gretchen says.

My heart feels as if it'll burst out of my chest. I rush over to my sister and hug her with all my might. She holds me tight and then rubs me on the head. "Look at you," she says in a whisper.

"I'm so glad you're here. I'm so sorry about—"

Gretchen stops me with a gloved finger over my lips. "You were right about *everything*." Hand in hand, we walk toward our parents. "I hope you have room for one more."

Mom is reserved, but her smile is genuine. "You're always welcome here, Gretchen."

Cliff claps his hands together. "It's frickin' freezing out here. Can we have this reunion inside?"

"I agree!" I say, leading the way. I can play with my new car later.

Inside, Lily, Gretchen, and I help Mom get all the food on the table. Cliff tends to the drinks, filling everyone's glasses with iced tea for our meal. Dad carves the ham, and we're ready to eat.

"Let's pray," Mom says.

We all join hands—Dad to me to Gretchen to Mom to Cliff to Lily and back to Dad. I bow my head and listen as Dad speaks out as the head of the household.

"Dear Heavenly Father, thank you for these blessings we are about to receive. Thank you for the struggles we have overcome this year with your help and through the love of your Son, our Savior. Bless us and keep us safe this coming year. Amen."

"Amen," we all echo.

I'm in full reach of diving into the sweet potato casserole when Gretchen speaks out.

"I have something I'd like to give you," she says, looking back and forth between our parents. "It's long overdue, and I hope it will help me make my way back into your lives . . . and your hearts."

Tears fill her eyes as she passes over a white envelope to my dad. He reaches into his front pocket for his reading glasses and then peels open the packet.

"Well . . . shit," he exclaims when he glances at my sister's offering. "Gretchen, where did you get money like this?"

He passes the check to me, indicating that I should send it down to Mom. I can't help but peek at the amount.

My eyeballs nearly fall out of my head. Gretchen snatches the check from me and hands it to Mom, who begins to cry like a newborn baby.

"It's not quite everything I owe you, but it's a good start. You'll be getting monthly payments from me until I've repaid you every penny," Gretchen promises.

"But how . . . when . . ." Mom asks in spite of her tears.

"I've been scrimping and saving and stashing everything away for years, investing in the very funds I sell to my clients. Despite ups and downs in the economy and stock market, I've done well. I hope you know how much I regret the actions of my youth and how they've affected you guys since then. I couldn't possibly be sorrier than I am. I've been spinning in a helix of humiliation ever since I left home, knowing how horrible I was to both of you. Please know that I'm clean and sober and making something of my life like you always wanted me to."

"Oh, Gretchen," Mom cries out, and her shaky hand covers her mouth. My sister slips from her chair and goes to my mother. The two of them embrace, arms enfolding each other in a warmth that spreads to all of us.

"Mommy," Gretchen whimpers out into my mom's shoulder.

Dad gets up and joins in the reunion, kissing my sister on the top of her head.

Tears flow as much as the love surrounding us.

The air is lighter and hope lingers high above.

My family is whole again.

We *are* truly blessed.

As we're cleaning the table, putting food away, and loading the dishwasher, my cell phone rings. It's Lora.

"Merry Christmas!" I say cheerfully.

There's a marked silence on her end to the point where I think either the connection failed or she was just butt dialing me by accident.

Then I hear her weeping quietly.

"Lora?"

"Hayley . . . I don't mean to ruin your Christmas or anything," she starts off. "It's my uncle."

"Ross? What about him?"

He was fine when I talked to him on the phone last night. He was excited that he was getting turkey and dressing to eat today and hoped it wouldn't upset his stomach. What could possibly be wrong?

"He's taken a turn for the worse," Lora reports. "The treatment isn't taking. His body isn't accepting the chemo, and the doctors are grim."

"Grim? Like he could . . . ?" I can't finish the sentence.

"He wants to see you. Can you come with Mom and me?"

My heart cracks at the thought of Ross suffering on this beautiful day of days—or of him being miserable at all. Not after what we've been through together and how he's helped my family. Now I have to be there for him.

"I've got to make few phone calls, and then I'll meet you at the hospital."

I hang up and waste no time dialing the next number.

She answers on the third ring.

"Hey, Chloe . . . It's Hayley. I know it's Christmas, but I really need your help . . ."

CHAPTER FORTY-FOUR

'Tis not always in a physician's power to cure the sick; at times the disease is stronger than trained art.

—OVID

I TUCK THE COLLAR OF my long winter coat up under my chin as I walk down the well-lit hallway of the fourth floor of Maxwell Memorial Hospital.

In front of Ross's door, I take a gulp of air into my lungs for strength. The room is dark, silent, and there's a stiffness in the air. Light from the television splashes against the walls dancing over the machines Ross is hooked up to.

Slowly, I approach his bed in my sneakered feet, trying not to wake him up. My new friend has nearly withered away to nothing in a matter of months, about the same amount of time I was hospitalized. Only, my situation seems to have a happy ending. Ross will not be as lucky.

I sit unobtrusively, choking on the lump of disbelief in my throat. It seems like only yesterday that Ross stood at midfield on homecoming night as his niece was crowned. And now . . .

No.

Stop.

I can't cry.

Not here. Not now.

I wave my hand in front of my eyes, fighting off the sting.

I have to be strong for the friend who has supported me through my darkest hours. It's hard to accept the bitter pill that sometimes cancer wins out, no matter how hard we struggle to battle it with all our might.

Damn cancer.

Chemicals, medication, surgery, and even prayers often fall short in the war against this malevolent disease.

I clench my fists tighter, staving off the hurt and anger at my utter inability to change things.

I want to scream until there's no air left in my lungs.

Until I have no voice left in me.

Until my friend is made whole again.

But . . . it won't happen.

I have to make the best of the situation, although I tighten my hands on the arm of the chair as the resentment toward the disease churns inside me.

Hell and damnation to cancer and everything it stands for, the evil and destructive blight.

I lift my hand from the chair and extend it over Ross's on top of the sheet. "It's not fair," I whisper, unaware that I've spoken out loud.

His eyes flutter open, and the corner of his mouth moves into a half smile. "Better to learn early that life's not fair."

"Hi, you," I say. "Merry Christmas."

His hand flips over, and we hold hands. An oxygen hose is attached to his nose, and his voice is very hoarse. "Is it Christmas? I guess I've lost track of the days."

"It snowed, too," I tell him.

"Nice." His eyes close again for a moment or two, and his

breathing becomes a tad labored. I don't know whether to go get the nurse or not. He holds me in place and opens his eyes again. "Seriously, Hayley. Life is nothing but a series of hurdles. We can never give up or give in."

"I've tried to be that way."

He moves his eyes to mine. "You have. And you must stay that way. You have no idea what an inspiration you've been to me."

The creak of the door grabs my attention from the patient, but not in a bad way. It's what I've been waiting for since I made the phone call to Chloe.

It's time.

"I'll be right back, Ross. I've got a huge surprise for you. A Christmas present to end all Christmas presents."

"What have you done, Hayley?" he asks with a chuckle, followed by a racking cough.

"I've brought you some Christmas cheer."

I flick the overhead light on and then remove my long coat. Underneath, I'm wearing one of my PHS cheerleader uniforms. I open the door and in rush the members of the entire varsity squad, all in uniform and cheering—just as we planned. Lora leads the march with a huge balloon bouquet full of vibrant colors and curly ribbons, followed by Madison, Tara, and Hannah with their pompoms raised high as they make their way to the far side of the room. Chloe tumbles through the door, executing a perfect backflip right there in front of Ross's bed. Whoa! Ashlee, Ashleigh, and Melanie enter, bringing a small Christmas tree decorated with garland, lights, and homemade ornaments. Lauren, Brittney, and Samantha pull up the rear, carrying a humongous cheer basket they pulled together from their homes, since stores are closed. Miss Lorraine slips in last, not holding back her tears of appreciation.

"Oh my God!" Ross proclaims. He manages to sit up in bed, and he beams at the display before him. "My own personal cheer squad."

We line up in front of him and start clapping. Our captain starts the cheer, and we follow her lead:

"Ross . . . attack!" Clap.

"A-T-T . . ." Clap. "A-C-K!"

"Ross . . ." Clap. "Attack!"

I cross my hands in the proper motions, fist tight, claps cupped. This is the most important performance of my short cheerleading career. We shift to the next chant:

"Fight, fight tonight! Fight blue, fight red, fight white! Fight, fight tonight!"

It's all worth it just to see the smile on Ross's face. Miss Lorraine sits on the edge of his bed, clapping along with us. A couple of nurses pop their head into the room to tell us to keep it down, but nothing will stop us from our cheer focus.

"Jam! Say what? Say what? Jam! That's what we do . . . We jam!"

Turn, spin, clap.

Point. "We do it for you!"

Quick squat to the floor and back up. "We turn around, we touch the ground, get back up and jam it down."

"Go Ross!"

"We love you, Ross!"

"You rock it!"

"Merry Christmas!"

The cheers ring out from each of us as we surround him with as much liveliness and joy as possible.

Brittney retrieves the cheer basket, which we set on the bed next to him.

"Check it out, Uncle Ross," Lora exclaims. "Everything you love."

"I can see that," he exclaims. There's a stack of magazines on golf, boating, sports, skiing, and biking. A dozen or so Snickers bars are scattered around. A Christmas teddy bear with a stocking cap smiles out. There are protein drinks, bottled water, candy canes, some bedroom slippers, and some pens and crossword puzzle books.

Ross's eyes cloud with tears. "Y'all have no idea how much this means to me. I can't thank you enough . . . leaving your families on Christmas Day to be here"—his voice catches momentarily and then he whispers—"with me."

Chloe steps forward. "It was all Hayley's idea. She called me and we made it happen."

I smile her way and wink. Teamwork—that's what it's all about. "Yes, we did."

"I wouldn't want to be anywhere else," sweet little Madi says.

"Me either," several girls repeat.

Lora places her head on Ross's chest and hugs him. "I love you, Uncle Ross."

"I love you, too, monkey." He glances around. "You're a special group of girls. You may not have taken the best squad trophy at camp, but you're first place in my book. Thank you from the bottom of my heart. This is the best Christmas ever. God bless you all."

Chloe smiles. "I couldn't agree more."

"We should let you get your rest," I say.

The girls line up to hug Ross and wish him well.

When Chloe heads for the door, I stop her with my hand.

We face each other and I smile. Then I hug her to me. "Thank you so much for helping me pull this off, Chloe."

She squeezes me back and says sweetly, "It was the right thing to do."

We grab hands for a sec, and a moment passes between us; then she's gone.

Just Miss Lorraine, Lora, and I are left, and I sense I need to give the small family their space. I pick up my coat and thread my arms through the sleeves.

"Hayley, don't leave yet," Ross says through a struggled breath. "I have something to tell you."

I lean toward him so he doesn't have to sit up. "Yeah, Ross?"

He breathes out. "Thank you."

Slipping into my French II, I smile and say, "*Votre bienvenue.*"

I move again to leave, but he stops me with his hand on my arm. "Wait. Hayley . . . I'm so proud of you." He struggles a bit to get the words out. "I'm . . . I'm proud to have known you."

My chest pings in agony at his use of past tense words. "Ross, don't . . ."

"Shhh . . . let me talk."

I smile. "Yes, sir."

"You have a calling, Hayley. A spokesperson for those . . . those who've overcome cancer. You never let the bastard disease grind you down. You never let it win. Hell, you never let it in the ball game. You fought it and kicked its ass." He stops and licks his dry lips. "I never stood a chance. Never. I wasn't lucky enough to defeat leukemia. But I was fortunate enough to have met you and watched you say the hell with what anyone thought of you . . . standing down there with your bandage, crutches, and bald head. You're an inspiration. You cheer. You laugh. You live."

He tugs my hand up to his lips and gives me a kiss. "Keep being strong, Hayley. For you. For me. For everyone who's had to deal with the shit cancer throws at you. Spread your cheer.

Don't . . . don't let it end. Most of all . . . keep being you. Because, you, Hayley Matthews . . . you, you . . . radiate."

The tears escape from my eyes over his meaningful, yet challenging words. "Th-th-thanks, Ross. I'll keep making you proud."

"I know you will." Our hands shake once more, and then he releases me.

"Get some sleep, Ross. Merry Christmas and Happy New Year!"

"Have a nice life, Hayley."

I shift past the major tear in my heart that Ross is ripping away by succumbing to this nasty disease. I wave to my partner and slip to the door, waving one last time. Ross wearily lifts his hand and I exit.

With the door closed, I lean back into it with my head against the wood.

I'm not psychic or intuitive, but I know in my heart of heart's that this is probably the last time I'll ever see my friend again.

* * *

THE NEXT DAY, DAD and I are watching a preview of the college bowl games coming up when my BlackBerry rings.

It's Lora's number on the caller ID.

I don't even say anything.

I just click the button.

A second or two passes in deathly silence.

I know what's coming next.

"He wasn't as lucky as you, Hayley," she says through her sobs. "He didn't discover it in time. Don't ever, ever forget how blessed and fortunate you are."

"I know, Lora. Believe me, I know."

I'm a lucky one . . .
I beat it.
I click the Off phone button and sigh.
Game On CEO and founder Ross Scott passed away at 11:11
a.m. at the age of thirty-four.

CHAPTER FORTY-FIVE

If you believe in yourself and have dedication and pride—and never quit, you'll be a winner. The price of victory is high but so are the rewards.

—PAUL W. "BEAR" BRYANT

LIFE GOES ON, RENEWING itself from the souls that remain. Ross's funeral is simple, elegant, and respectful.

I return to school after the holiday break, more focused and more determined to make the most of my life. My limp is subsiding, and my hair is growing like a weed. I know it's only a matter of time before I'll be back to my old self—if that person even still exists.

When you've been touched by a physical and mental challenge such as cancer, the rest of life's obstacles seem like a piece of cake. I have plans now for my future; promises to keep; college letters to wait for and an academic curriculum to get me to my professional Alps.

Friday night of the first week of school, I come down the stairs in my black cocktail dress and black high heels.

Gabriel is waiting in the living room with my parents, dressed in a gray suit and a fashionably striped tie. He looks so mature and grown up . . . and I can envision us, advancing together through our lives and careers.

"You look beautiful, Hayley," Mom notes. "Shall we get going?"

Mom and Dad are dressed up, too, in their finest to accompany us to the PHS football banquet at the Hyatt next to the Maxwell State University campus. My parents drive Mom's car, and Gabriel and I follow in my Honda—I let him drive.

The room is perfectly decorated in red, white, and blue streamers, silver stars, and white-draped walls. The state championship trophy sits at the head table, along with the rest of the awards to be given out this evening.

Gabriel and I sit with Lora and Will, Ashlee and Anthony Ricketts, and Hannah and Scoop Dogg, dining on a fancy spinach salad, prime rib, baked potato, and grilled asparagus, followed by a chocolate raspberry cheesecake.

The sportscaster from WFFA in Montgomery is the keynote/motivational speaker. He mostly talks about his own meteoric rise in the local media. Gabriel and I are too busy holding hands and totally flirting the whole time to be listening to this guy blather on. Finally, it's time for the awards.

Coach Gaither stands at the head table with his assistant coaches and our principal, Mr. Parish. Mrs. Ingram gets to sit up front, as well. The rest of the team, cheerleaders, and other important participants, such as the trainers and team doctors, are all seated at round tables on the right with family members on the left. There's a crackle in the atmosphere, and we're all sparked by having worked together as a cohesive unit to win the school's first-ever state championship.

For me, it was so much more of a feat than simply that, but I'm happy to be part of the ceremony.

Mrs. Ingram stands up and presents the letters for cheerleading to all of us. I'm proud to file by with the rest of the girls to accept the thick knit blue *P* outlined in red and white.

I clap like a crazy person when Gabriel receives a special-recognition plaque for training the players. Marquis Richardson wins the trophy for "Play of the Year" for his touchdown in the championship game. Daniel receives "Best Offensive Weapon," and Anthony gets "Best Defensive Player." More awards swap hands as parents cry, clap, snap pictures, and get video of the event over the course of half an hour.

"What's left to give out?" I ask Lora, since I'm a newbie to this banquet.

"MVP is the last one," she says. "I bet Daniel gets it."

"Or Skipper," I add.

Coach Gaither stands at the podium and clears his throat. "As you're all very much aware, we had a dream season, the type we coaches plan for, but never know we can execute until all of the components come together. This year, every person in this room counted toward the undefeated season we enjoyed. You parents, who brought your kids to practice, who sat in the stands and rooted them on, and who support them in all they do. The coaches and staff, who are dedicated to making every play count. The band and cheerleaders with their team spirit and unswerving devotion. All of these workings are what make a winner. But there's one person — one Most Valuable Player — who shined far above the expectations of anyone else by far."

He glances about the room, nodding his head at all of us. "This person, this year's winner, is quite unexpected. At the onset of the season, I never would have thought this person would have even been in the running for MVP. However, the situation sometimes defines the individual. This person overcame all obstacles thrown in their way. Someone who showed up for every game, played their heart out, and never said they were too tired to participate or gave up. They inspired their teammates and the entire PHS community with their tenacity, perseverance, and intestinal fortitude. Bravery in the face of adversity. This person is a role model we should all aspire to be like. This person weathered the storms that life threw their way and came out a victor."

"Holy crap," Lora whispers. "Who is he talking about?"

"Not me," LaShawn notes.

Will shrugs, as do I. He certainly isn't referring to Daniel.

Who then?

The coach says, "Please join me in giving a round of applause to our most deserving MVP for the Polk High Patriots. Miss Hayley Matthews."

Lora launches herself onto me in the tightest hug of all time while I'm still trying to comprehend what just happened.

I must be in shock. Or in a coma or something. I can't move or breathe.

Did he just say I'm *the MVP?*

Gabriel kisses my cheek. "It's you, Hayley! Go up and get your trophy!"

Oh my God.

Oh. My. God.

The world tilts on its axis a bit, and I'm deafened from all sounds around me due to the hammering of my heart. Gabriel lifts me out of my chair and hugs me to him. He must offer to escort me to the front of the room, because the next thing I know, that's where I'm headed. Coach Gaither has also motioned to Mom and Dad to join us.

All around me, my teammates, the football players, and their families are cheering for me. Cheering . . . for me. I look around at the many smiling faces watching me as I make my way to the head table. And then I make eye contact with Daniel Delafield, of all people. The person who probably thought he had this award in the bag, he stands up at his table and claps his hands togeth-er harder than anyone else in the room. The others at his table, including Chloe, join him, and soon the room is one standing ovation.

For me?

Gabriel helps me up onto the riser, and I shakily walk to Coach Gaither, who hands me the biggest trophy I've ever seen in my life.

"Congratulations, Hayley. It was a no-brainer vote for the coaching staff."

I can barely hold the trophy as I cover my mouth with my hand. "I'm speechless," I say. "I don't know what to say. Thank you."

Mom and Dad encompass me, and I've never been more moved in my whole life. This was what I wanted. Attention. Popularity. That *something* more. And boy, did I get it.

Mr. Parish stands and takes the microphone. "Hayley, these past few months have truly been your shining moment. This en-tire school—and the entire community of Maxwell—is blessed for knowing you and seeing you through the cancer that attacked you. You certainly came out as our admirable star.

Okay, I cry for the sixth time.

However, these are tears of pride.

Tears of joy.

Tears of accomplishment.

Tears of humility.

Everyone surrounds me. Parents. Coaches. Football players. Cheerleaders.

Chloe pushes through the crowd and presses her hands into mine. "I'm proud of you, Hayley. I really am. All I wanted my whole life was to be the captain of the cheerleaders and have the best squad ever. I know I pushed you a lot . . . but I had my reasons. I see now that it's not about the awards or camp or what have you. It's about the people on the team. I just wanted what was best for our squad, and I didn't realize at the time that *you* were the best thing for the squad. You made us, Hayley."

I swallow hard, trying to dislodge the emotional lump in my throat.

I finally understand my captain after knowing her my whole life. I appreciate the trials she put me through to make me a better cheerleader. We hug, not awkwardly, like adversaries, but more like the warm embrace of friends who've shared lasting memories.

"Thanks so much, Chloe."

She pulls away, and then the captain snaps into action. She deepens her voice and furrows her brows. "Don't get too cocky, rookie. Basketball season is about to start. A whole new set of cheers and routines to learn. No slacking just 'cause you're football's MVP," she says with a wink.

"Aye-aye, Cap'n," I say, saluting.

Gabriel slides his arm around my waist and squeezes. "You good?"

"Super fantastic," I say. Damn, this has been one hairy roller coaster ride of a senior year.

Well . . .

I got that attention I asked for . . . that *something more.*

Boy howdy . . . did I get it.

I look at the amazing guy standing next to me, holding my hand and beaming down at me. I certainly couldn't have gotten this far without him.

Or without my cheerleading.

The two of them *truly* saved my life.

EPILOGUE

*Go confidently in the direction of your dreams! Live the life
you've imagined.*

—HENRY DAVID THOREAU

Two years later

I ADJUST MY HELMET AND double-check the straps on my body
harness. The guide next to me nods and helps assure I'm properly
connected to the apparatus attached to the platform a hundred
feet above the tree line of Walkes Spring Plantation, Jack-in-the-
Box Gully in St. Thomas, Barbados.

"You ever done this before, little miss?" the Bajan guide asks.

I smile and adjust my sunglasses. "Nope, but there's a first
time for everything."

Just like my first time snow skiing, my first time mountain
biking, and my first time SCUBA diving—all things Ross Scott
wasn't afraid to do. And neither am I. I'm cancer free, limp free,
and I have a healthy, thick, wavy head of hair. Go figure—a
chemo perm. No one's the wiser of what I went through my senior
year in high school unless they notice that I have one leg smaller
than the other.

The point is, I'll never forget.

My dad, now CEO of Game On, sent me on a group adventure excursion on behalf of the company for my spring break vacation. A sophomore at The University of Alabama, I have decent grades, I'm on the spirit committee, and I'm a big part of my sorority. Gabriel's on scholarship at Bama, too, and works as a student trainer for the Crimson Tide football team. I'm premed and he's working on his engineering degree. Okay . . . I'll admit it . . . I went to Bama because of the excitement of college football and one of the most successful programs of all time. On top of it, I'm getting a kick-ass education, and I get to be with Gabriel, too.

As I peer over the treetop canopy spread out before me, I remember how I got here. The little domino tumbles that life throws a person's way may lead to one person influencing and helping another until both are all tangled in each other's lives. That was how it was for me being partners with Lora Russell (a current cheerleader at Maxwell State University, engaged to Will Hopkins, and working toward her teaching certificate) and knowing her uncle who helped me with my rehab and gave my dad a job when times were hard. I learned through reading Kurt Vonnegut's *Cat's Cradle* that these are people who are all in my *karass,* all working together for the same collective greater good. And I'm okay with that.

My experiences in the hospital and dealing with my cancer truly made me want to pay it forward. With my skill in math and science, going into medical research is a no-brainer. I want to study cancer, its cause and effect, and help bring an end to it so that no other kid has to go through what I went through and so that no other person — period — has to suffer at the hands of a horrible cancer like leukemia that claimed Ross's life so quickly and unapologetically. In my lifetime, I hope to see cancer totally obliterated off the map.

Oh, I also have a nonprofit charity that Mom helps me run. Called The Radiate Foundation, it sends cheer baskets—like the one I received—to cancer patients in the hospital undergoing treatment. Each cheer basket is ordered through us and shipped around the country to a local high school cheerleading group who delivers the cheers and good wishes to the patients.

I do this for all the people like me who've existed in a hospital bed wondering if anyone (other than family members) really cares or anyone truly gets what they're dealing with. I do it for the memory of Ross and how we touched each other's lives.

I do it because I didn't know at the time why I got cancer . . . I suppose it was so I could share my story with others and give them hope.

Honestly, I do it because I *have* to.

"You're up next, little miss," the Bajan guide says to me.

He hooks me to the galvanized steel cable and pats me on the helmet.

I push off from the platform and hold my hands above my head as instructed. I squeal as I fly over the gully below and the lush green trees that appear to be mere stepping stones from this height. The Caribbean breeze blows against my cheeks as the brilliant March sun shines down on me. I'm flying through the treetops—like Gabriel who went before me and is now queuing up on the next platform. (Showoff!) I zip along at an incredible speed as the world whooshes by me. I'm living life adventurously with no regrets, no excuses, and no turning back.

Up here, zipping through the sky, I'm completely free.

I've got the rest of my life ahead of me, and I'm going to live it to the fullest.

Dream.

Discover.

Explore.

A MOTHER'S PERSPECTIVE

There are certain words a parent never wants to hear in reference to his or her child.

"Cancer" is right up there at the top of the list.

Imagine my horror when a doctor viewed an X-ray of my daughter's sore leg and proclaimed, "It's cancer, a malignant tumor, and her left leg has to come off."

His harsh and quick diagnosis reverberated in my head, stabbing me to my very core until I could barely breathe. He said he'd never seen an X-ray such as this ever before. Cancer. Plain and simple.

I grabbed his arm and removed him from the examining room into the hallway. I put my finger in his face and said, "You can't talk like that in front of my fifteen-year-old daughter."

Immediately, I shot up a prayer to my Heavenly Father to block her ears and not let her hear the diagnosis. In later years, she'd tell me she didn't remember his saying that.

We spent the summer of 1982 at the University of Alabama Birmingham (UAB) Hospital where my daughter underwent various tests, biopsies, X-rays, consultations, you name it. Whatever was growing inside her was unlike anything these doctors had previously seen. Only a few medical institutions in the United States were even able to treat such a rare cancerous growth. Thank heavens UAB was only three hours from us.

The cancer was a puzzle to the doctors, and the only known

treatment at the time was amputation. My husband and I both insisted this was *not* an option.

During the final surgery, it was discovered that the tumor had wrapped itself around her fibula (small bone) and was dangerously close to her tibia (large bone). The lesion was removed, as well as the small bone and a good portion of her periosteal nerve, leaving her with a substantial scar from knee to ankle. She had follow-up treatments of both radical chemotherapy and ten days of radiation to be sure the doctors got every last one of the invading cells.

Her case was among a handful of firsts of its kind, and the procedure and treatment were eventually written up in the American Medical Association's prestigious *Cancer* magazine.

UAB has tracked her progress since 1982, and today, she remains cancer free. There is no medical reason for her to be walking, but, praise God, thanks to surgery and treatment and our daughter's own determination, attitude, true grit, family support, and physical exercise, she has been able to walk ever since without the aid of a crutch or a cane and without a limp.

This experience, as our daughter has freely admitted, was much tougher on her dad and me than it was on her. I'll admit it was the absolute greatest trial my husband and I have ever experienced in our fifty-seven years of marriage—beyond his heart attacks, both of our bypass surgeries, and many other serious family illnesses. I don't have the words to describe adequately the pain and hurt—beyond belief—when something like this invades and attacks your child and you cannot do *anything* about it except to pray and hope that God leads you to the right people who can bring about a positive outcome.

Years after her hospitalization, my daughter and I were on an airplane returning home to Alabama from her sister's in Baltimore, Maryland. We were sitting together when she turned to me and said, "If I had never had cancer, I would have to have it."

She blurted this out of nowhere, and it startled me because it had nothing to do with our current conversation.

"What did you say?" I asked.

Very succinctly she repeated, "If I had never had cancer, I would have to have it."

"I don't understand, Marley," I replied, intrigued.

She continued. "I don't know *why* I had cancer, but I know that I had it for a reason. It just hasn't been revealed to me yet. I do know that I'm a better person for having had it. Maybe my case will help someone else."

I could not have been more proud of her at that moment.

And I'm just as proud of her now as she shares this story with the world. Because she understands now that this was a story she had to tell.

We have always believed it isn't *what* happens to you in life as much as *how* you handle what happens to you. Realistically, we cannot live life without trials and/or tribulations. But we are to be overcomers. Through our most trying times, we are to push through . . . and radiate.

While mostly a work of fiction, the core of this book is true and based on my daughter's own experiences. It's a showcase of how she never let anything hold her back from what she wanted. She was a varsity cheerleader who cheered every game, some with a bandage on her leg. She cheered with no hair on her head, even though I offered to buy her a wig. At the time, she told me, "They can take me as I am or not at all." She continues to go through life as though nothing ever happened.

It is our desire and prayer that this work of fiction will not only entertain, but that it will be used to encourage others, young and old. To help them have hope when everything seems hopeless. To help them persevere when it would be so easy to give up. To have faith when it seems the world is against you. To overcome anything with a positive mental attitude. To hurdle the obstacles that life throws your way.

And like my daughter, to truly radiate.

—Elizabeth Ann Marley Harbuck
February 2011

ACKNOWLEDGMENTS

This truly is a "book of my heart." It's written from memories of an experience I'd rather not relive, but it's necessary to tell in the hopes of inspiring *just one* person dealing with his or her own battle with cancer or other life-threatening disease. If I were to thank everyone who helped me through that difficult time in my life, the acknowledgments page would be as extensive as the novel. I'll do my best to keep it brief.

To my beloved parents, Joe and Lizanne Harbuck, who endured way more than any parents should ever have to, watching their daughter fight off a deadly disease. Your love, support, faith, and encouragement were the keystone to my recovery—and to every step I've taken since.

To my agent, Deidre Knight, for your wisdom, support, and continued belief in me.

To my wonderful editor, Julia Richardson, for helping me pay it forward and share this story with the world. To the amazing team at Houghton Mifflin Harcourt for their hard work on behalf of my characters and me. I am *the* luckiest author.

To my sister, Jennifer Keller, and my brother, Jeffrey Harbuck—who are nothing like the siblings in this book—thank you for being there for me during the rough patch . . . and beyond.

To Ellen Dunn Davies, who brought me cheer, laughter, and extraordinary baked goods during my hospital stay. Also, thanks for sending the Homewood High School cheerleaders to cheer me up. My thanks to them, as well. I know not your names, but your kindness and overwhelming spirit got me up out of my hospital bed, and I'll remember you always.

To my uncle, Dr. David E. Marley, Jr., for diagnosing my cancer, researching doctors, and getting me to the right team of experts to fix the situation. To the staff at UAB Medical Center, particularly Dr. Dunham and Dr. Meyer. Good work. 'Nuff said.

To my best friend from high school, Lee Outlaw, who never treated me differently and made me laugh every day. You were a key to my positive attitude toward everything. And to my cheer- leading partner, Laura Ross Hixon, for keeping me motivated and cheering me on.

Oddly enough, to Rick Springfield, rock star turned actor who played Dr. Noah Drake on ABC's *General Hospital* when it was at its peak. Although I was going through my own daytime drama, my teenage crush on you and the need not to miss a moment of you on the small screen kept my mind off all the tests, surgeries, and treatments. Your music continues to inspire me even today, and I dare say I'm your biggest fan. Rock on!

To my critique partners, Wendy Toliver and Jenn Echols, for who you are and all you do. To the Buzz girls for friendship, ca- maraderie, and support.

To the real Radiate Foundation, which I hope brings much hope and many cheers to young adults undergoing cancer treat- ment. www.radiatefoundation.org.

A jumbled thanks to Mark and Debby Constantino for letting me write a good chunk of this book while parked in your drive- way; Penny Georgoudis for the bracelet that became the theme to my life; my "interns," Hilary Scales and Vanessa Guttry Noble; and to my texting partner in crime, Rachel Heggaton. And to my little fur baby love muffins, Madison and Boo, who slept soundly next to Mommy as she wrote. It's amazing how much joy and happiness you've brought into my life.

And finally, to my heart, my love, and my true-life hero, Patrick Burns, who listened to my tale of overcoming cancer and proudly said to me, "I love that cheerleading saved your life."

Well, sweetie, *so did you.*

* * *

The Radiate Foundation is a non-profit organization focusing on bringing cheer to young adults (13–25) currently undergoing cancer treatment. The foundation works with local cheerleading teams to bring baskets of cheer, as well as smiles, joy, and hope to those battling cancer. With your help and support, The Radiate Foundation will help spread cheer during times of struggle and provide that shining light pointing to the end of the tunnel. The Radiate Foundation — lifting your spirits.

For more information or to donate, visit www.radiatefoundation.org.

ABOUT THE AUTHOR

Marley Gibson's popular young adult series Ghost Huntress contains the books *The Awakening, The Guidance, The Reason, The Counseling,* and *The Discovery.* She is also the author of nonfiction books such as *The Other Side: A Teen's Guide to Ghost Hunting and the Paranormal,* coauthored with her fiancé, Patrick Burns of TruTV's *Haunting Evidence,* as well as *Christmas Miracles* and *The Spirit of Christmas,* coauthored with the *New York Times* best-selling author of *90 Minutes in Heaven,* Cecil Murphey. As a teenager, Gibson fought her own battle with cancer while a high school cheerleader and approached her treatment and healing with humor, lots of prayer, and a positive attitude. A certified SCUBA diver, a closet gourmet chef, and an avid traveler, Marley lives full-time on the road with her fiancé and two rescue kitties, Madi and Boo, in an RV they lovingly call Midge. Follow their travels at www.haunted-highways.com. She can also be found online at www.marleygibson.com, www.facebook.com/marley.h.gibson, or at her blog www.booksboysbuzz.com.